THE YEAR
of the
Bad Decision

a novel
by Charles Sobczak

Also by Charles Sobczak

FICTION

Six Mornings on Sanibel (1999)

Available in print and as an e-book

Way Under Contract-a Florida Story (2000)

Winner of the *Patrick D. Smith Award for Florida Literature*

Available as an e-book only

A Choice of Angels (2003)

Available in print and as an e-book

Chain of Fools (2009)

Available in print

NON-FICTION

Rhythm of the Tides-Selected Writings by Charles Sobczak (2001)

Available in print

**Alligators, Sharks & Panthers-Deadly Encounters
With Florida's Top Predator: Man** (2007)

Bronze Medal winner for best regional non-fiction by *Foreword Magazine*

Available in print

Living Sanibel-A Nature Guide to Sanibel & Captiva Islands (2010)

Available in print

The Living Gulf Coast – A Nature Guide to Southwest Florida (2011)

Gold Medal winner of the best adult non-fiction, Florida, 2011 by

The Florida Publisher's Association
Available in print

This is the first printing, February, 2013.
Printed in the United States of America
by Whitehall Printing, Naples, FL

Published by: Indigo Press LLC
                  2560 Sanibel Boulevard
                  Sanibel, FL 33957

Visit us on the web at **www.indigopress.net**
You can also contact us via e-mail at: livingorders@earthlink.net
Telephone: 239-472-0491

ISBN 978-0-9829674-2-3
Library of Congress Control Number: 2013931914

Cover Image Copyright Perrush, 2013
Used under license from Shutterstock.com
Cover and book design by Maggie Rogers, MaggieMay Designs

This is a work of fiction. Names, characters, places and incidents are either products of the author's imagination or are used fictitiously. Any resemblance to actual events or locales or persons, living or dead, is entirely coincidental.

Acknowledgments

First and foremost I have to thank my son, Blake Sobczak, for the countless hours he put in editing and reworking this manuscript. Having just graduated from the Medill School of Journalism at Northwestern University, he found himself confronted with his father's dyslexic style of the English language coupled with an unsettling story that will unfold during his lifetime. He worked hard, changing the headings to many of the chapters, streamlining dialogue and correcting my insufferable grammar. I am proud of the work Blake did on this novel and wish him continued success with his own pursuit of the intrinsic beauty of the written word.

Next I would like to thank the many readers who pored over early versions of this novel. Those include Dr. Jeff Masters, Dr. Michael Mann, Jean Heuer, Daphne Hammond, Pam Graham, John Jones, Anne Bradley and Sally Heuer. They helped immensely with their comments, corrections and support. I also want to thank my wife, Molly Heuer, for her patience as a sounding board to almost every aspect of this tale. She had to put up with more than a year of my reading stacks of disconcerting nonfiction books on climate change and did her best to keep me from falling into complete despair.

Because this is a work of fiction, it does not include a bibliography, though in this case it should have one. I could not have written this book without the help of so many climatologists, glaciologists, meteorologists, scientists and authors who have dedicated their lives to making us understand the perils that climate change poses to the future of not only mankind, but also all the animals that rely on a stable atmosphere—the birds, mammals, reptiles, insects and flora living on this lonely planet.

My sources include William Sweet (Kicking the Carbon Habit, 2008), Chris Mooney (Storm World, 2008), Mark Bowen (Thin Ice, 2006), Spencer Weart (The Discovery of Global Warming, 2008), Henry Pollock (A World without Ice, 2009), Mark Hertsgaard (Hot: Living Through the Next Fifty Years on Earth, 2012), Thomas M. Kostigen (You are Here, 2010), William K. Stevens (The Change in the Weather, 2001), Mark Lynas (High Tide: The Truth about Our Climate Crisis, 2004), Al Gore (An Inconvenient Truth, 2006), Mike Tidwell (The Ravaging Tide, 2007), Michael E. Mann (The Hockey Stick and the Climate Wars, 2012), Paul K. Conkin (The State of the Earth, 2009), Paul A. Mayewski and Frank White (The Ice Chronicles,

2002), Michael Collier and Robert H. Webb (Floods, Droughts, and Climate Change, 2002), Fred Pearce (With Speed and Violence, 2008), Thomas L. Friedman (Hot, Flat, and Crowded, 2009), Wallace S. Broecker and Robert Kunzig (Fixing Climate, 2009), Michael Crichton (State of Fear, 2004), Mark Lynas (Six Degrees, 2008), among many others. I also extend my appreciation to the Sanibel Public Library and especially Candace Heise for her help with inter-library loans, which allowed me to find some of the more obscure titles I needed to complete my research for this book.

I would also like to thank, posthumously, Dr. Charles Keeling for his unfailing dedication to recording the changing chemistry of our atmosphere high atop Mauna Loa in Hawaii long before we knew how important and prophetic his work would become. He is a true, unsung hero of science.

Finally, thank you to Maggie May Rogers for her excellent work designing both the cover and the interior of this book. Once again Maggie has done an outstanding job on not only the book design, but also the e-book design.

Charles Sobczak

Preface

This book is a work of fiction. There are no worldwide geoengineering projects on the drawing boards at the United Nations that would shield the sun's energy from the earth, and there is no serious discussion anywhere about massive carbon dioxide scrubbers dotting the landscape. In fact, the climate-change time lines used in this book are intentionally compressed, making what might happen in the next 100 years happen over the next 30 years. Even at that, many climate models indicate cloud cover may ameliorate rising temperatures, and technologies yet to be discovered may rewrite the future of climate change completely. That is the beauty of fiction—a writer can, and often does, manipulate the facts to suit the needs of the story.

In this case, however, truth is stranger than fiction. The year this book was completed, 2012, was the hottest year recorded in the history of keeping accurate weather data in the United States. Droughts ravaged broad regions of the country throughout the spring and summer. Superstorm Sandy slammed into the Eastern Seaboard on October 29, 2012, killing 253 people and causing an estimated $65.6 billion in damage to New York, New Jersey and the surrounding area. Some 1,100 miles wide at its peak, it was the largest (in size, not strength) Atlantic hurricane on record.

Other indicators of the changing weather are found across the planet. The world's glaciers continue to melt, and Greenland's two-mile-thick ice cap witnessed unprecedented thawing over the past decade. Ocean acidification is harming oyster farms in California's Morales Bay, just as ever-rising ocean temperatures are bleaching out the planet's coral reefs. Climate change is no longer an issue we have to deal with sometime in the future. The future is here.

Climate change will not wipe out the human race. In the end, as Al Gore pointed out, it is "an inconvenient truth." It is an ongoing malignant threat to the future of all living things—death by a thousand cuts rather than one catastrophic event. I grew up in northern Minnesota in the 1950s under the threat of thermonuclear war. My childhood was filled with terms such as bomb shelters, ICBMs, MAD (mutual assured destruction) and the ongoing prospect of a post-apocalyptic nuclear winter. If the world were going to end in a volley of 100,000 hydrogen bombs exploding across the globe, at least we were going out with a bang.

Climate change is more insidious. News cycles report a drought in China or the Sahel, a flash flood in Italy, a tsunami in Japan, a twister in Mexico, a typhoon in the Philippines, an outbreak of dengue fever in Florida, the list is endless. A thousand cuts, day after day, year after year, decade after decade—and all a direct, or indirect, result of a warming planet.

All this is happening while in the geopolitical world little to nothing is being done to stop the burning of fossil fuels and the buildup of CO_2 in our atmosphere. The powerful fossil fuel industries go about their business like its 1929, a month before the crash. China and India keep building coal-fired power plants, the fracking business is booming and everything will be just fine. I regret to inform you it will not. The hurricanes will get larger and stronger, tornadoes will start tearing up China, Russia, France and South America, monsoons will fail, glaciers will melt, the sea level will rise. Over then next 100 years much of Greenland's ice dome will thaw and New York City will eventually have to be abandoned along with hundreds of coastal cities and towns across the globe. Severe climate change, at this juncture, is as certain as gravity.

All of which brings me to this book's title, The Year of the Bad Decision. Looking at the current level of denial and our unwillingness to confront our dependence on fossil fuels, we will look back at this era 100 years from now as The Many Years of Many Bad Decisions. We are collectively playing a game of Russian roulette with our atmosphere. Looking back, we'll be asking ourselves why we didn't heed the warnings. By that time we will see carbon dioxide for what it really is: atmospheric arsenic.

There is no question that we are addicted to our cars, power plants and jet airliners. We, as a species, have always struggled with long-term planning, even after our computers have made it perfectly clear just how dangerous that future will be. We will not change until we absolutely have to. Sadly, once again, we are choosing to learn the hard way.

Writing this book has been one of the most difficult challenges of my life. The conflict between my real estate career and the forbidding future described in The Year of the Bad Decision is obvious. There was many a morning when I wanted to put down my pen and walk away from this manuscript, pretending the entire issue of global warming would just go away. It will not. Truth can be a wicked taskmaster, and the truth about our changing climate is undisputable. We are in for a thousand cuts. We will endure.

January 15, 2013
Charles Sobczak

The Year of the Bad Decision

It happened in the age of the Anthropocene—the Age of Man. It happened six years after the end of the Lost Decade. A time unlike all others. A time when death discovered us, death unimaginable.

The year was 2043 and the atmosphere we once took for granted was in shambles. Prolonged droughts crippled and destroyed once powerful nations. Catastrophic Category 5 hurricanes ravaged the coastlines along the world's hot, acidic oceans. Rains became sporadic and torrential—entire villages and towns were swept away in flash floods without warning. The Greenland icecap was vanishing. Tornadoes found new, unwelcome homes in Russia, China and France. Diseases once unknown to Earth's temperate zones crept out from the tropics bringing words like malaria, West Nile virus and dengue fever to innocent lips. No charities came to the rescue because everyone needed rescuing. People no longer talked about the weather—they trembled at it.

The decision made that year was a difficult one. A gamble. There were no longer any good options on the table—only less horrific ones. This is the story of the people who made those decisions. It is a story of betrayal, bravery and folly in the age of the Anthropocene, the Age of Man.

The Break-In

At precisely 9 a.m. six members of SWAT team Bravo burned through Dr. Warren Randolf's high-security front door. Thick, acrid smoke filled the hallway of the condominium as their scarlet-hued laser sliced through the door's titanium alloy. Minutes earlier, the smoke alarm system for the entire complex had been disabled by a second team, Alpha, working in the basement. The noxious odor soon seeped into the five other condominium units sharing the 26th floor. Several tenants, smelling the smoke and hearing the sound of men and equipment in the hallway, cracked their doors and peered toward Warren's apartment. They witnessed a half-dozen police officers dressed in black flak jackets and bullet-proof helmets, carrying several large, metal suitcases and an assortment of lethal weapons. The neighbors closed and bolted their doors behind them. Whatever was going on at Dr. Randolf's apartment was none of their business. They were afraid that, for reasons unknown, they might be next.

At 9:04 Dr. Randolf's front door was compromised. SWAT team Bravo split into three groups of two and proceeded to sweep the apartment. Weapons in hand, they scanned each room, ensuring the place was empty.

As anticipated, no one was home.

"We were told to wait and not touch anything," said the lead officer to his men.

"When will they get here?" asked one of the team members.

"They should be here by now. Hold on..." The officer listened to his implant for a second. "They're on their way up."

A few minutes passed while the officers waited for the team's arrival. Four agents—three men and a woman—walked through the front door at 9:07 a.m. The agents were in constant communication with Professor Bradley and knew the official hearing couldn't commence until they finished. Time was of the essence.

They found their target in the living room, which was a labyrinth of cords, computer racks, cooling towers, monitors and back-up power systems. Eleven Apple 3600X computers lined the racks, linked by an assortment of Ethernet and fiber-optic cables.

"Have you touched anything?" the lone female agent asked the Bravo team leader.

"No, ma'am, we're just standing by as ordered."

"Good. Just give us a minute to make certain everything is clear, then you can pack 'em up."

The SWAT team stood back as they watched the three technicians trace the clutter of power cords, connecting switches and monitors from one end of the room to the other. There didn't appear to be booby traps or alarms attached to any of them. One of the men on the NSA team snapped pictures of the system, carefully documenting every connection and interlink for future reassembly. When the photographer was finished, the woman nodded to the SWAT team's leader.

"We're clear. You can get started."

Team Bravo sprang into action, unplugging and disconnecting all electronics in the room. They placed each computer in a padded enclosure. These were small but extremely powerful processors, each the size of a briefcase. They took every cord, backup system and storage device they could find. They even took the three large LCD monitors, although they could not fit in their cases. Within ten minutes there was nothing left in the living room except Warren's well-worn leather office chair and the metal framework his computer system had rested upon.

As team Bravo disassembled the homemade network, the NSA agents combed through the rest of the apartment, taking everything and anything electronic, from clock radios to toasters. They planted nanocameras throughout the apartment, none larger than a grain of rice.

At 9:20 a.m. the woman who headed the NSA team confirmed to Professor Bradley that they possessed every piece of electronic equipment in the apartment. Each drawer, cupboard, and vanity had been checked and rechecked.

Miles away, a staffer received word from team Bravo that Dr. Randolf was ready for interrogation. By 9:22, exactly the same moment Dr. Randolf was being seated, the SWAT team, suitcases and electronic equipment in hand, were closing the torched-out front door behind them and heading toward the elevator along with the four NSA investigators. They left the half-melted door to Warren's ransacked apartment unlocked.

The Hearing

Dr. Warren Randolf was anxious. He had never been on the COI Building's 175th floor before. From this altitude he knew he should be able to see clear across to the eastern shoreline of Lake Michigan, more than seventy-five miles away, but he could not. Lake Michigan was barely visible through the city's murky haze of smog.

It was hot and dry outside, just like it had been for the past several weeks. Directly below the building, two huge pumping stations drew freshwater from the lake, bringing it thousands of miles to the deserts of Oklahoma and Texas. He couldn't help but note how the shoreline had receded since the pumping began decades ago. The lake level had fallen nineteen feet, and the beaches of Chicago were a half-mile wide in places. From this soaring vantage point, the four massive intake pipes coming out of the lake looked as thin as pencils.

The staffer who had accompanied Warren from the lobby nearly 2000 feet below sat across from him, blocking part of the window Warren was staring through. The staffer, with his micro-chip implant concealed in his right ear, was awaiting the go-ahead from the President of COI to escort Dr. Randolf inside. Until then, he was content to study the scientist sitting less than fifteen feet away from him.

Dr. Warren Randolf wore a navy suit with a sky-blue shirt and pinstriped tie. His black pants did not coordinate well with the rest of his outfit. Warren's tall, lanky frame rested poorly into the sculpted chair he slouched in. The staffer kept trying to guess his age. Warren's face and hands looked young, but he was already balding and his wire-rimmed glasses made him look as though he might be pushing 50. He was younger than that, surmised the staffer, but hard to read.

Every few minutes Warren would shift around in his chair, trying to get comfortable. It didn't help. He kept biting his lower lip and fidgeting nervously with the folder on his lap. The folder was stuffed to overflowing with his iPaperpad and supporting documents. Although the staffer considered striking up a conversation several times, he refrained from doing so. Experience had taught the aide that it was best not to know what brought people before the executive committee. The blue suit was a poor fit, the staffer observed. The sleeves were at least an inch too short.

The 175th floor was the top level of the COI Building. COI stood for the Corporation of Information, North American Division. Also located on that floor were the offices of the President of COI, Professor William Bradley, the Vice President, Dr. Richard Ellsworth, the Comptroller, Robert Langfeld, and their sizable staffs. Taking up most of the east side of the floor was a walnut-lined executive boardroom, complete with a faux-ebony conference table that could seat 36 people. In North America, COI was more than a telecommunications titan—it was a colossus. COI controlled the entire continent's cell phones, cable networks, radio and television stations, the Internet and all the state authorized servers. COI controlled 99.6% of all e-news, e-communications and cable broadcasts. Nothing happened in North America that COI didn't know about.

The COI's Board of Directors had called Dr. Warren Randolf to their boardroom to discuss his email dated Feb. 24, 2043. That brief communication was addressed to Warren's superior, Dr. Maddox Hansen, Director of the Center of Meteorological Controls, or the CMC. It read as follows:

```
Re: The Mylerium Project
Feb. 24, 2043


Dear Dr. Hansen,


    It is my firm belief that the Mylerium Project,
if executed as currently planned, will fail. If my
calculations are correct, and our computers are in
error, we cannot proceed with the deployment next
month as planned. According to my research, the
ramifications of this launch, as it is currently
designed, are absolutely terrifying. I have attached
an encrypted .ESX file with my data and the complete
summary of my work on this matter. I feel we must
immediately stop the countdown to deployment.
    Dr. Hansen, it is my firm conviction that our
computers, the computers owned and operated by the
Center of Meteorological Controls, and overseen by
```

COI, are, somehow or other, in error. The Mylerium nanomirrors we plan to put into the stratosphere next month will not self-destruct by late fall as designed. According to my calculations, they will remain in the stratosphere for at least one, if not two or more years. Should this happen, the mirrors, especially during the winter months when the sun hits the northern hemisphere at an oblique angle, will dramatically lower the entire Earth's temperature, thereby risking a negative impact on the length and productivity of at least one growing season.

In a world fast approaching ten billion people, such a dramatic drop in agricultural production could result in unprecedented levels of starvation and death.

Please review the enclosed materials and pass this information on to the highest levels at the Corporation of Information as soon as possible. Notify them that I am willing, at their convenience, to discuss these findings. Until these questions are resolved we must stop the countdown to deployment effective immediately.

Dr. Warren Randolf, PhD
Advanced Meteorological Studies
Center of Meteorological Controls
43 Baker Street
Chicago, IL 30322

This morning, in a board room atop one of the tallest buildings in the world, was Warren's time to talk. Two hours after sending his email, Warren Randolf was texted the following request:

Please arrive tomorrow promptly at 9 a.m., Board of Directors Room, Level 175 of the Tower of

Information, 14000 East Monroe Street, Chicago,
with your findings and all correlating materials.
— Dr. Maddox Hansen, President, CMC

It was 9:22 a.m. by the time the aide escorted Warren into the conference room. Weeks ago, Warren suspected it would come to this. It wasn't his calculations alone that concerned the people at COI, but also the fact that he had kept his research private. The Board of Directors wanted to know why they had not seen any of this work before the unexpected email attachment he had sent to his boss yesterday. They wanted to ask him why he refused to connect his numerous computers, which were skillfully linked to one another, to the Internet. He knew they would call him in for this inquisition the instant they attempted to pull his duplicate findings out of cloud storage, only to discover no trace of his research existed in the cloud. He had guessed the first question they would ask him.

"Why were you not connected to the Internet when you were doing this research?"

Warren Randolf, seated at the far end of the enormous boardroom table, had his response ready. "Because I didn't want our computers to know what I was doing."

"And why's that?" demanded Professor William Bradley as he scrutinized Warren.

"Because the computers that run the Net are the same computers that helped design the nanotechnology formulas used in the Mylerium Project. How could I trust them?"

"What are you implying, Dr. Randolf? Are you saying our computers can now make decisions on their own?"

"I'm not sure, but it's a possibility. And if they have made an error, the formula for the Mylerium nanomirrors we're placing in orbit a month from now is also wrong. That could make this project the worst decision mankind has ever made."

"And yet you're the only person on Earth to question this project," observed Professor Bradley, letting a hint of a sneer cross his face. "We have run the Mylerium formula through hundreds of simulations and our studies indicate it has a 97.4 percent chance of performing exactly as it has been designed. Our test run last year, when we deployed more than 50,000 tons of this same material, went flawlessly. The mirrors collapsed into a harmless dust in the fall and there is no indication anything has changed.

"Quite frankly, Dr. Randolf, the project is worth the risk."

Warren took a long, deep sigh before speaking again.

"Is it? What happens if it's snowing next June and the nanomirrors are still up there, keeping us dangerously cool? The crops won't come in across Canada, the U.S., Russia, China and possibly India. More than 85 percent of the human race lives in the northern hemisphere, and there won't be enough to feed them if those mirrors remain in orbit. People will starve, Mr. Bradley. Millions of people will starve."

"They're starving right now. We've barely recovered from the Lost Decade and last year, the planet started heating up again. The effects of Mt. Cameroon's eruption are no longer cooling us, Dr. Randolf. The aerosol effect from the volcanic dust is projected to end this summer. There were more than 22 million deaths in 2042 attributed to the droughts, floods, diseases, hurricanes and the heat waves that pummeled our planet. If the projected forecasts for this summer are correct, that number could double. We have to make the planet cooler until the next generation of scrubbers are operational and at this point in time, the Mylerium Project is our only hope."

Warren knew Professor Bradley's argument inside and out. Mankind had managed to put itself between a rock and a hard place—or more accurately, between a hot and a cold place. Global warming, or climate change, had lost any pretension of being a liberal hoax or some far-flung meteorological theory decades ago. There were no more debates, anywhere on Earth, about what was happening. There were no more heavily financed fossil fuel lobbying groups trying to muddy the issue with an avalanche of misinformation, spewing out endless press releases about sun spots, solar cycles or natural climactic variations. The argument about whether anthropogenic activities were the leading cause of climate change was over.

Death had ended that debate. Death had convinced even the most devout skeptics that the models were real.

"I understand our current predicament," said Dr. Randolf, "and I want you to know that I did not believe my findings at first either. I've worked five years on this project and I've given it everything I have. I want the Mylerium Project to work just as much as you do. I don't want another Lost Decade. Who on Earth does? But my equations don't lie, Professor Bradley.

My calculations are based solely on the data the CMC and our own research team supplied to me. The nanomirrors will not disintegrate in the late fall as pre-programmed. Something changed between the test run and this full scale deployment. Something happened to the internal programming.

"According to my results, the mirrors will stay active in the stratosphere for at least a year longer than planned, perhaps two, or God forbid, three. We will go from seeing droughts, Cat-5 hurricanes and withering crops to a man-made nuclear winter. We're about to intentionally recreate the notorious Mt. Tambora explosion.

"I'm sure all of you are familiar with the Tambora eruption, the largest volcanic explosion in recorded history. Its eruption spewed 32 cubic miles of ash into the sky, causing a volcanic winter. The next year, 1816, became known as the year without a summer. Crops failed and livestock died from lack of fodder. Tens of thousands of people starved to death across the globe.

"You have to consider that the world's population stood at a mere one billion people then. Today we have almost ten times that many crowded onto this planet.

"Our crops won't perish in the heat of summer because there won't be any summer. Worse yet, there won't be any plants. I'm warning you; it's a nightmare if you proceed with this project—an absolute nightmare. "

There was an eerie silence in the room. After the empty pause, Professor Bradley responded.

"We've reviewed your .ESX file and although your work is impressive, we have determined it's flawed. We have several other questions we need answers to as well. Go ahead, Dr. Hansen."

Dr. Hansen, Warren's boss, shuffled through his notes, then turned toward him and asked, "Why were you using older computers? You know from your background at the CMC that the 3600X is an antique."

"Because I felt I could trust them. They were designed and built before the 'N' series came out. If you recall, Professor, the 'N' series computers were designed by other machines and not by human engineers. I thought they might connect to the Net on their own and disclose my work to the mainframes. We're all aware of the concept of the singularity."

"The concept of the singularity is absurd," Professor Bradley interjected. "We have internal monitoring programs that sweep our systems hourly looking for any sign of artificial awareness and to date we've found nothing.

Your paranoia about the singularity is unwarranted. You should have your head examined, Dr. Randolf. The only reason we are not putting you under arrest this morning is that you have been an outstanding member of the CMC team and an integral part of this project from day one.

"That being said, we are hereby placing you under a gag order to not share, discuss or distribute any of your research or your hypothetical conclusions with anyone. Do you understand me?"

"Yes, I understand," answered Warren.

"If you tell or attempt to inform anyone about your findings you will be arrested and charged with sedition. Your punishment will be severe. In addition to the gag order, all of your personal computers and electronic devices have been confiscated by our NSA agents this morning. Now please surrender your cell phone."

"You have no right to do this! I'm trying to warn you about a catastrophe and you're condemning me—what kind of inquisition is this? I won't surrender my phone."

"I would advise you to hold your tongue, Dr. Randolf. Your equipment is already in our possession, and we will provide you with a new phone."

"You broke into my apartment, took my equipment, put me under a gag order—and now you want my phone as well. What right do you have to do this? I want to talk to my lawyer."

"Dr. Randolf, please calm down. It is nothing short of a miracle that we are not going to put you under arrest. You violated the CMC's Corporate Code of Conduct when you conducted your research offline. You know it's illegal to do any research without posting it to the cloud, and you also know that doing so is punishable by fines, imprisonment or both. Your lawyer will tell you the same thing. Now please, surrender your phone."

Warren realized he wasn't going to win this argument. He knew the rules. He also knew that had he put his work online they would have told him to cease and desist years ago, when he first began his independent research. No one contradicted the state-run corporations or any of their official positions. No one argued with the computers that ran almost everything. To do so was tantamount to heresy. The corporations were the only truth, and the global crisis that worsened each year only solidified their supreme authority. Warren knew he was lucky to be walking out of this hearing a free man, at least for the moment.

Disgusted with COI's response to his warning, he smacked his iPhone100 against the mahogany table and slid it to Professor Bradley. Warren wanted to resign right then and there, but he stopped himself from doing so.

"Do you have any other computers, storage devices, or Cloud Storage accounts that contain any of your research that you want to tell us about before we dismiss you? Have you shared any of your research with any of your co-workers or colleagues?" Professor Bradley asked.

"No sir, I have not."

"Then you are free to go, Dr. Randolf. And do not speak to anyone about this meeting, nor share anything about it with your friends, family or fellow scientists. If you do, you will be arrested. This meeting, your research, and your conclusions never happened. Do you understand?"

"Yes."

"This meeting is over. Owing to the circumstances, you have the rest of the day off. You might want to go back to your apartment and hire a locksmith, as your front door needs repairs."

The eleven men and women seated at the table rose, a few of them talking amongst themselves as the staffer from earlier escorted Dr. Randolf out of the boardroom.

"You're lucky to be walking out of here," he said to Dr. Randolf as he escorted him to the elevator.

"I know."

"They'll be watching you."

"I know."

Rubic's Call

Rubic Chang was still sleeping when his iPhone70 chirped a text message alert. He rolled out of bed and reached for his iPhone, which he always kept on the nightstand beside him.

Rubic was still in a state of euphoria. The effects of the Rapture7 he had smoked the night before had yet to wear off. They never did. They generally kept Rubic high until he smoked the synthetic narcotic again the next day. It was, in Rubic's opinion, the best drug he had ever tried.

The alert wasn't loud enough to awaken Yeva, but as Rubic turned over to read his message, she woke up as well. It was just after 10 a.m.

"What's up?"

"I just got a text from that Warren guy," said Rubic as he read the message on his phone.

"What's it say?"

"I've gotta go."

"But what's it say?" Yeva asked as she rubbed her eyes to take the sleep from them.

"It says what he told me it would say: *Have a nice day!*"

"What in the world does that mean?"

"Yeva, it means I have to go. It's a long story."

"It's another running job, isn't it?"

"I'm sure it's some kind of running job, but I have no idea where it will take me."

"When will you be home?"

"Damned if I know. I'll call you later. He told me I had to hurry once I got this text—something about a timed, electronic code. I've got to go."

"OK."

Rubic got up, dressed, grabbed his keys and dashed out the door. Soon he was pedaling his carbon-fiber bicycle on the way downtown, still half-delirious from the lingering effects of Rapture7. Half-stoned, half-awake, and weaving through the heavy traffic of South Chicago, Rubic felt alive. It was a perfect world.

Chaos Theory

It's called the Butterfly Effect, Warren thought to himself as the elevator slid down 175 stories. *The chaos theory.*

The concept states that a butterfly flapping its wings in Brazil causes a tornado in Texas a week later. In a way, it's how the dinosaurs went extinct. It's how a meteor with an erratic orbit changed everything on Earth in a heartbeat. It is the unquantifiable part of any equation: the chaos theory. It includes components that don't appear to change much at first glance, but all too often they mean the difference between life and death.

Warren found the flaw in the nanomirror deconstruction program by sheer accident. He had entered an incorrect equation into his calculations and the entire matrix of the nanomirror programming unraveled. He saw the flaws in the molecular chemistry and nanotechnology that made such a high-tech project like this possible. He didn't understand why none of this was apparent to him, or to anyone at the CMC, during the test deployment last summer. Something had changed.

He knew that if the test deployment mirrors had failed to implode, the amount of material put into orbit wouldn't have had a global impact. There wasn't enough matter dispersed in the stratosphere to make a difference. The full deployment was a different story.

The Mylerium Project was global geoengineering of the highest order. The risks involved were incalculable. Despite his reprimand and his gag order, Warren remained convinced his analysis of the Mylerium Project was correct. It was going to fail.

The project's current plans called for microscopic computers to be deployed in the atmosphere within the sunlight-deflecting mirrors. Once the reflective surfaces accomplished their task of cooling the Earth, the computers would activate a self-destruct program and the mirrors would disintegrate into harmless dust. But according to Warren's findings, the computers were not going to give the proper commands to the carbon matrix that held the mirrors in place.

In short, the mirrors would stay put and the Earth would continue cooling. They would keep reflecting sunlight through the following winter and beyond. The repercussions would be horrific.

Warren hailed an electric cab outside the COI building and contemplated his next move. As he wound his way through Chicago's morning traffic, he knew he would have to find another job. This time, it wouldn't be near Chicago or any metropolis. Cities, given what he foresaw happening over the next few years, would the worst places to be. No, it would be far better to live in a small town, or in one of the distant, western suburbs of Chicago where he could farm a plot of land and raise some chickens. He would need to build a compound and a bunker, get guns, and gather a whole survivalist stockpile to make it through. He needed to reach a place where he stood a chance of surviving. If at all possible, he also wanted to save those closest to him from the coming cataclysm.

Finding another job was the least of his concerns. A person with his credentials was sought after by every high-tech geoengineering company in North America. A graduate of MIT at the age of 20, Warren received his double doctorate in Nanotechnology and Computer Science from Stanford by the time he was 23. He had a dozen job offers the day after he accepted his PhD. Now, at 30, Warren was tall, prematurely balding, wore wire-rimmed glasses and had the demeanor of the quintessential computer geek and he could pick and choose from any number of corporations who had kept in touch with him throughout his tenure with the Center of Meteorological Controls. Once word got out that he was on the market, job offers would follow.

At this juncture, it was neither a matter of which job to choose from, nor how much money he would make. Warren was solely concerned with the hiring firm's location. Now, after calming down and thinking beyond his tumultuous morning, he turned his thoughts toward surviving, stockpiling and planning. He tried to estimate how much food and water he and the others he hoped would join him might need to make it through to the other side.

Then there was the Chaos Theory. Would the nanomirrors last through multiple summers? If they did, then Warren wasn't sure he'd want to live. The climate on Earth would end up like the nuclear winter scenarios that were discussed when he was a teenager. Living through it might be possible, but would it be worth it?

As these thoughts tumbled around Warren's head, the cab pulled up to his apartment building on North Clark Street. Warren stepped out and handed the cabbie his new CMC phone. The driver scanned the phone, triggering an electronic transfer for the cab fare and an automatic tip. No one used cash anymore, except runners and the underground economy.

Warren strode past the building's security guard without saying a word. The faint odor of burnt metal lingered in the lobby, having made its way down through the stairwells and elevator shafts. The security guard had already heard from Warren's neighbors about what had transpired upstairs but said nothing to the doctor as he hurried by. He didn't want to get involved.

In the elevator Warren grew increasingly anxious about what he would find in his apartment. What did they take? What did they leave? As he walked down the hallway he saw a chunk of alloy lying on the tiled floor next to the front door. He saw the hole in the door where the deadbolts had been cut away. Worse, he saw his apartment had been left unlocked and unguarded. There was no telling if anyone else had been inside since the break-in.

He opened the door slowly, anticipating that he might find someone else inside.

"Hello! Is anyone in here?"

No one answered.

Warren stepped into his apartment cautiously. He surveyed the computer room first. It was in total disarray. The only things left in the room were the extension cords, his chair and the empty metal racks. More than $100,000 worth of equipment and years of tireless research had disappeared in a day. Warren stood there for several minutes, then put his hands to his face and started to sob.

While the tears kept flowing, Warren could only hope that his pre-programmed text message to the runner had gone through. If it hadn't, everything was lost.

The Runner's Mission

Rubic arrived at his destination before Warren had made it back to his apartment. He glanced over the dozens of electronic lockers lining the lower level of Chicago's downtown train station searching for his target. When he found the right one, he inserted his key into the slot and the locker opened with a series of beeps.

The package inside was wrapped in a large, plain paper bag. Knowing he might already be under surveillance, Rubic grabbed the package quickly, closed the locker door and walked away. The electronic key remained trapped inside, awaiting its next customer.

Rubic made his way out of the train terminal and headed toward his bike. He looked over his shoulder every few seconds to check if he was being followed. Runners like Rubic were used to being tailed. Years of working as an underground courier had made him keenly aware of everyone around him. Rubic was especially sensitive to the faint whirring sound made by surveillance cameras as they spun around to track you. These cameras were located everywhere, allowing some NSA operative in a dark room in Maryland to monitor Rubic's every move. If they were onto him, Rubic knew from experience they would not relent until they knew exactly what was inside Warren's package.

Rubic felt slightly safer upon reaching his bike. He was soon speeding southward toward the urban jungle of Chicago's South Side. He was heading to an abandoned brownstone on High Street where he had opened dozens of packages like this one before without incident. It was, to the best of his knowledge, free of surveillance cameras or microscopic listening devices. It was not free of cockroaches, rats and junkies, but none of those threats troubled Rubic as much as the government did.

Knowing that whatever post or railing Rubic chained his carbon bike to in this neighborhood wouldn't stop anyone from stealing or stripping it, he hoisted it aloft and carried it with him up the front stairs of the abandoned building. Upon entering the open foyer, he lingered in the shadows of the hallway, thinking he might catch a glimpse of his tail, if there was one. After a few minutes, with no one suspicious coming, he went inside.

Now the dangers he faced didn't have stun-guns and security clearances, but needles and drug habits. More than once he had been attacked in this same building by derelict junkies trying to steal his bike, his belongings or his organs.

The bike he carried was light enough to be used as a weapon if it came to that, but luckily the brownstone appeared empty. Rubic worked his way downstairs into the damp, musty basement, found a decaying wooden bench and put on his LED headlamp to give him enough working light. He was finally ready to open the brown manila bag.

Inside was a note, a cell phone in a plastic bag, seven sealed envelopes and $8,000 in cash. The hand-written note read:

Attention Runner,

> *Thank you in advance for taking on this assignment. Your name was given to me by several people who have had far more experience with this sort of thing than I have. They assured me you could be trusted, and, at this point, I can only pray they were right.*

> *I cannot tell you what is in each of the envelopes except to say that if you are caught delivering one of these packages by the NSA,*

the FBI or any government agency, the consequences will be dire, not just for you, but for your friends, family and myself as well. There are seven envelopes in this package and each one has the name of the person they are going to, along with the address of where you will be most likely to find them. Some will be easiest to find at their home address, while others might be at work. When possible, I've given you both addresses to be sure you can locate them. Once you arrive to the various cities where they live, you must not call, text or email them. You can only give them these envelopes in person, and only in a place where it is unlikely anyone would notice their delivery. The details of making each contact will be up to you. Feel free to use the Net to learn what each of them looks like, as I have not included personal photos in this package.

The $8,000 is to cover your traveling expenses during the run: train tickets, motels, dinners, etc. You must not open the letters or make any attempt to look inside of them. Knowledge of the contents will only make things worse for you should you get caught.

These packages and the information they contain are of the utmost importance to everyone destined to receive one. They must not be intercepted. Upon completion of your assignment there will be a single payment of an additional $10,000 awaiting you in another locker.

Your first task is getting the iPhone 100 contained in this package into my possession. Meet me at the Art Institute of Chicago today at precisely 4 p.m. I will be waiting for you near the lion statue located on the north side of the entrance on Michigan Avenue. I will be sitting on the park bench roughly 30 feet north of the statue eating a slice of Giordano's deep-dish pizza. The empty box will be beside me. Before you arrive, buy a single slice of the same brand, take out the pizza and sit beside me, leaving the cell in your pizza box. When I get up I will mistakenly take your box and as you get up to leave you will grab mine. We must not speak to or acknowledge each other, as I will likely be watched.

When you get a safe distance away, open up the pizza box. In it, taped to the inside cover, will be your electronic key, which will be activated for a two-hour time slot on Wednesday, March 28th, 2043, starting at 10 a.m. and expiring at noon. The rest of your money will *be there, provided I hear from the people you are being hired to deliver these packages to. You must not call me or have any contact with me ever again after all of the deliveries have been made. Upon finishing this letter, you must destroy it.*

Warren

Rubic knew what he had to do. He took out his lighter and set the letter on fire. Then, realizing he still had two cubes of crystalline Rapture7 in his pocket, he took out his glass pipe and took several long, deep hits. Within minutes, he was no longer in the basement of a burnt-out brownstone in South Chicago. He was in another world altogether, filled with ethereal colors and drifting patterns of light. He was in Rapture7 land and glad of it.

Rubic took his first hit just before noon. He wouldn't move again until 2 p.m., content to lie on the filthy floor and revel in the beautiful, narcotic world within him. It was a world far more appealing than the one he lived in.

Seed Vaults and Botanical Gardens

Yeva slept in. It was her day off, but she had plenty to do around the apartment. Dishes were piled up elbow-high in the sink, dirty laundry was strewn about the bedroom, the toilets were filthy and the vacuum cleaner was broken. It was not the apartment she and Rubic had moved into a year ago. It was a Rapture7 apartment now, trashed like half the units in the complex.

Yeva contemplated getting up, showering, putting on her clothes, packing her bags, and walking out the front door. But she couldn't do it. She couldn't leave Rubic.

Instead she dragged herself out of bed, threw on a clingy shirt and didn't bother to shower. She decided she could shower later, after she did her best to clean up the disaster.

Normally Yeva would have been out of the apartment long before Rubic, catching the "L" northbound toward the Chicago Botanic Garden in Glencoe. Yeva graduated from the University of Illinois at Urbana-Champaign in 2040, majoring in botany and plant biology. That was where she met

Rubic. He was on track to graduate with a degree in marketing, but he dropped out to become a druggie and a runner. When Yeva met him four years ago, Rubic was clean. He was different from the man she lived with now. Running, as dangerous as it was, helped pay for Rubic's Rapture7 habit.

At the Botanic Garden, Yeva Dunning's job revolved around the seed bank. She kept track of the seeds for thousands of plants, many of which were either extinct in the wild or rapidly disappearing. The seeds were stored in a vast, climate-controlled facility built in 2026. That building and its surrounding garden plots had expanded over the years until it now covered nearly a tenth of the 385-acre compound. Few people even realized it was there. Excepting for occasional benefactor tours or publicity events, the seed bank was never open to the public. It was loosely modeled after the Svalbard Global Seed Vault located on a remote island north of Norway.

The Svalbard Garden's seed bank was carved out of an abandoned coal mine buried deep in the permafrost. It was the world's largest repository of plant biodiversity on Earth, holding roughly 45 million seeds. During decades of climactic upheaval, the contents of the Svalbard Garden became increasingly important.

From the entrance, both the seed bank in Norway and its Chicago counterpart looked more like military encampments than mere storage facilities. Because of the nature and value of their contents, the world's remaining seed banks were kept secretive and secure.

These repositories, now numbering more than 150, were scattered across every continent. After the climactic upheavals of the Lost Decade, the governments of the world established a universal seed bank system in case the climate crashed again. Some of the storage facilities were nearly as large as the Svalbard compound, while others were much smaller and housed only regional flora.

The Chicago Botanic Garden's seed bank, although substantial, was considered a medium-sized facility. It focused on preserving seeds from North American plants, with a special emphasis on fruits, vegetables and grains. Its primary objective was to act as a backup system should genetically altered crops fail. If that happened, agricultural corporations like Cargill and Monsanto would need the raw genetic materials found only in the unmodified, wild strains. The Chicago Botanic Garden was a storehouse of genetic diversity, and the huge corporations forming the backbone of

North American agribusiness, in partnership with the government, funded the facility and its mission.

Yeva's job at the Botanic Garden wasn't exactly what she had in mind when she left Urbana with her botany degree. Originally she dreamed of working in fields and woodlands, trying to protect the few remaining pristine forests in the lower 48. But she took the Chicago job out of necessity, as work was scarce. To keep Yeva smiling, her boss, Mrs. Margot Pollock, let her tend a large vegetable plot in the southwest corner of the property. The vegetable garden kept her out of the "ice box" each day for long enough to make her job tolerable. But she spent most of her workday walking from one cold storage room to the next, checking lockers and vaults for temperature, humidity and other climate variables. She monitored the conditions of the thousands of sealed seed packets in every room.

Yeva Dunning was a young, energetic caretaker—a throwback from America's agrarian past. She was 26, with wispy, dyed reddish-purple hair and vibrant green eyes.

The garden she tended was planted with seeds taken directly from the vault. It was designed to ensure the viability of the seed stock stored in the vaults. If the seeds couldn't thrive in the rich, fertile soil of the greater Chicago area, then something was wrong with the storage system. Luckily, they always flourished.

Yeva loved the garden, which was her favorite part of her job. She got to take pumpkin seeds out of frozen suspension and place them into rows of tilled earth every spring, starting in March. She loved the feel of the soil sifting through her long, graceful fingers and the texture of the living earth in her hands. Even when she bent over and strained her back to hoe the rows of strawberries, or when she weeded through furrows of carrots, potatoes, broccoli and pole beans for hours on end, she never tired of her little green paradise. Each time she had to leave her garden, she put on her parka and made the rounds in a cold, fluorescent-lit dungeon larger than a super Wal-Mart.

Now, back at her apartment, Yeva rolled up her sleeves and started sifting through the avalanche of dishes. She wondered how Rubic's running job was going. She waited for his call. She worried.

A Runner's Reputation

Rubic nearly dreamt through his rendezvous with Warren. Luckily, he had remembered to set his phone alarm for 2:15 p.m. and the insistent buzzing was loud enough to rouse him from his stupor.

He got up and stretched. His arm had fallen asleep while he wandered the endless dreamscape that is the hallmark of every Rapture7 high. It would take him about an hour to bike to the Art Institute, so he had a few minutes to investigate the rest of the package.

Naturally he had already checked out the money. It was all there, in stacks of $100 bills. The temptation just to take the eight grand and vanish occurred to Rubic more than once as he counted out the cash, but a move like that would spell the end of his running career. Losing his reputation would cost him more money in the long run. Besides, once he finished the deliveries, he would make an extra $10,000—a calculation that Warren must have considered while setting up the assignment.

Rubic decided it would be better to watch his budget over the course of the run, saving on expenses and pocketing the extra cash, rather than break his contract with a client.

The thought of coming clean for a month gave him additional pause. Rubic knew the Greens kept drug-sniffing dogs and electronic sensors onboard the trains, so carrying any Rapture7 during his run was out of the question. Today and tonight might be his last solid highs for some time to come. The thought of coming down from his perpetual Rapture7 high sent shivers down his spine. It was never easy.

The seven letters in the package were individually sealed in brown manila envelopes. Rubic decided it was a good time to see where he was heading before meeting Mr. Warren downtown. He read the addresses scrawled on every envelope.

"Christ, these are all scientists and shit," he blurted out to no one.

The first letter was for Dr. Albion Garrison, MIT, head of the Physics and the Global Environment Department in Cambridge. The second letter was addressed to Professor Mark Worthington, a glaciologist at nearby Harvard. The third and fourth letters were for contacts in the Midwest, one in Cleveland and the other in Indianapolis. The last three were all in California. One was going to a professor at Stanford University, one to San

Jose and the last one to a small town in northern California—Crescent City. There were both men and women receiving the letters and Warren had put several possible addresses for locating the recipients on each of the envelopes.

"It's going to be a long-ass month," mumbled Rubic as he walked his bike out of the brownstone. "I'd better get an America Pass. God, I hate those damned dogs."

Rubic also hated trains. Unfortunately, all domestic airline flights were banned by the ruling Green Party after the end of the Lost Decade. High-speed trains were the most efficient way to get around.

Driving was also an option, although only a handful of special trucks and emergency vehicles were allowed to burn gas or diesel. The cost of renting an electric car for the month was considerably higher than the cost of taking the trains with an America Pass. At least he could bring his bike, since all of the trains were equipped to handle passengers ferrying bikes across the country.

Still hazy and disoriented, Rubic mounted his bicycle outside. He noticed a group of thugs across the street eyeing his carbon-framed bike from another burnt-out brownstone.

The cash in Rubic's right front pocket suddenly felt very heavy. It was high time to head downtown.

Within minutes he was winding among the cars, crossing onto the sidewalk when traffic was backed up and moving back onto the roadways when pedestrians started to annoy him. He could thread his bike through a three foot doorway at 25 miles per hour, even after smoking. His bike was a part of him. Rubic cranked up his music to full blast as he sped through the urban landscape. Life was simple again, if only for a while.

A Loose Cannon

"Keep an eye on Dr. Randolf."

"I will, Professor Bradley."

"He's just the type who'll try to let others know about his findings. We can't have his research reach a broader audience. Given the slim chance that his calculations are correct, we could have a major public relations problem on our hands. Make certain he doesn't try to contact any of his colleagues, especially in the meteorological field."

"And if he does?"

"Have him arrested," Professor Bradley answered without hesitation.

"Personally, I think we shouldn't have let him go this morning. He's a loose cannon. I bet we'll come to regret letting him walk out of our hearing like that."

"You may be right, but you have to remember, Richard, that without Dr. Randolf's contribution to the project, it might not have come to fruition. What was I supposed to do, put him in prison as a thank you? Don't you think other members of the team at the CMC would wonder what the hell was going on if one of the lead scientists in the project was incarcerated?"

Dr. Richard Ellsworth, the Vice President of COI, didn't answer Professor Bradley's comment. Ellsworth knew the professor had a point. Arresting Randolf a month before launch would raise suspicions about the project at the CMC. It was much safer to keep him employed but confiscate every trace of his research.

Ellsworth continued. "And after the deployment of the mission a month from now, do you still plan to keep him on the team?"

"I think Warren will want out long before then. In fact, I was surprised he didn't resign at the meeting this morning. He knows we'll be watching his every move from here on out and it won't be long before he starts looking for another employer. Hell, there are a dozen research universities out there that would do anything to have someone of Randolf's stature on their team, not to mention all the private corporations who could use a brilliant scientist like him. He'll leave of his own accord soon enough. Firing him would have raised too many eyebrows and arresting him would have proven worse."

"You might have a point," Ellsworth said as he rose from his chair and headed toward the door of Professor Bradley's office. "But we'll have to watch him like a hawk."

"*You* have to watch him like a hawk, you mean. I've got to get back to work. Let me know if your team or the NSA see or hear anything that looks as if Warren is communicating his research to anyone else. I don't care if it's his mother."

"His mother's deceased. But I'll take care of it."

Ellsworth closed the door behind him and walked back toward his own office down the hall. The surveillance of Dr. Warren Randolf had begun the minute he left the COI Tower. The nanocameras in Warren's apartment were watching him right now as he sifted through the rubble in his living room, wound up power cords and picked up his ransacked apartment. There were cameras everywhere, and where they could not follow, satellites or operatives filled in. The Greens were always watching.

Krakatoa Redux

Warren took out his CMC replacement cell phone to call the security company that had installed his front door. They arrived just after 1 p.m. When his neighbor asked what had happened, Warren explained to him that it was a break-in. The neighbor, having peeked down the hallway earlier, knew it was a lie. He had seen the SWAT team torching the door open. But he could tell by Warren's demeanor that this was going to be the party line.

The security company didn't buy Dr. Randolf's version of what had happened, either. They knew from experience that burglars didn't haul around the sophisticated torches needed to cut through a titanium alloy door. Only the government had that kind of equipment. But when it came to asking about what the government was up to, the workers for the security company knew better. They didn't want to find out what happened. For them, just like for the neighbor and the doorman downstairs, it was a common theft. Nothing more.

By 2:30 the workers had installed the new door and Warren was left sitting at his kitchen table, wondering what the hell had just happened. He trudged to his bedroom and sat down on his bed, staring blankly in a state of shock. He opened the top drawer of his nightstand and checked to see if his old journal was still in it. He noticed that his notebook had been flipped though, but wasn't taken. There weren't any calculations in it, so it didn't interest the NSA.

He flipped through the yellowing pages to his last entry, which he had written several years ago after he and his girlfriend, Ann Hadley, broke up. Now Warren wanted to start afresh to put everything into perspective, so he dated a new entry:

Feb. 25, 2043

What a nightmare! Five long years of 60-plus-hour weeks, countless revisions, dead ends… and it all comes down to this: being placed under a gag order so as not to endanger a project that could kill a billion people. Global warming has never been the problem. We're the problem.

I've had it. I'm quitting the CMC as soon as I find anything that gets me out of Chicago. I'm sick of COI keeping a lid on any news that doesn't fit their agenda. I'm sick of the Greens. I voted for them in '36 but I hate who they've become. I want out. I want to get as far away from this modern world as possible and get ready for the manmade ice storm that's about to lay waste to this planet. The big chill is coming.

They claim there's a 97.4 percent chance of success, but I don't buy it. That 2.6 percent potential for failure frightens me to the core. The TURING 1000 supercomputer is wrong. The Mylerium Project is going to end in disaster. I'm positive of it.

I'll have to let Albion know. He warned me a week ago they weren't going to accept my conclusions, even if I had irrefutable evidence. The systems designed and constructed for the project are too entrenched. The money has already been spent and thousands of tons of nanomirrors are stockpiled across the globe, ready for dispersal.

But I can't call Albion now. My cell's gone and my computers are tapped. He'll know what has happened to me as soon as the runner hands him my package.

In hindsight, maybe I should have kept my mouth shut. I could have sat on my findings and watched the world slide into an endless winter.

Maybe humanity had it coming. The world's overpopulated and what we're doing to the planet is not sustainable. That's part of the reason I decided to never have children. Who wants to bring children into this world, into this hot, suffering planet? I know all too well the horrors of the Lost Decade and now I fear the worst.

I lost my mother to climate change and, in a way, my father died from it as well, though his death was as much from a broken heart as anything else. I lost three cousins in the flash floods that inundated West Virginia's New River in 2037. They were swept away in the middle of the night along with 18,000 others. I've spent my entire life striving to fix this mess of an atmosphere we've made.

In the end, it has come to this. My computers are confiscated and my life is in jeopardy. All because of climate change. Perhaps it should be called climate chaos.

The changes happened so much faster than the early computer models projected. Powerful feedback loops kicked in, not in centuries as we once believed, but in decades. The storms were larger than forecast, the seas rose higher than projected, the droughts and heat waves intensified and the death toll was overwhelming. The climate changed with such fury, it caught everyone off guard.

But this time it could all happen overnight. By next spring everyone will know just how desperate a situation we'll be in. I'll be as far away from Chicago as possible. I'll be hunkered down somewhere with a survival kit and a gun. It could get dangerous once food starts running out. Hunger brings out the worst in us and we could all go hungry soon.

Warren put his pen down and looked up over his shoulder. He had no idea where the cameras might be hiding. He realized he was in trouble, not that it came as a surprise. Sending that email to his boss in this political environment was tantamount to treason. After all, Warren was among the scientists who first proposed the Mylerium Project. He worked for years on it, so questioning its integrity a month before deployment was unthinkable. The United Nations had already sanctioned the operation and all but four of the 197 countries on Earth had ratified the international treaty that made a project of this magnitude possible. Any evidence of a potential failure would not be taken lightly at this stage of the operation.

Indeed, all systems were a go. The high-tech Mylar-based nanomirrors had been in production for three years in 27 nations. An entire fleet of aircraft had been specifically built for deploying the microscopic dust that would shade the Earth over the coming summer. The cost of the project exceeded $2 trillion. The cost of failure was ten times that.

The Mylerium Project drew its inspiration from the cooling effects of the Mt. Cameroon eruption in 2037, which was similar to, but much larger than the eruption of Mt. Pinatubo in 1991. There were other historic eruptions that had cooled the atmosphere in the past: Krakatoa in 1883, Mt. Tambora in 1815, and dozens more. Each time, millions of tons of volcanic ash and sulfur dioxide blanketed the planet, reducing sunlight by as much as 10 percent and chilling the Earth for years. The eruption of Mt. Cameroon along the west coast of equatorial Africa signaled the end of the Lost Decade. The leaders of the world were determined to avoid another such climactic nightmare.

Warren checked his watch. It was time to head downtown to retrieve his backup cell phone.

Three weeks ago, he had loaded a copy of his encrypted calculations onto his back up phone's hard drive. Warren had anticipated everything that had happened today except for his freedom. Yesterday he was all but certain he would be detained, so he programmed his computer banks to send out a text message to the runner the moment someone unplugged one of them.

Warren had also hired a second runner to deliver the package with the additional $10,000, set to arrive at the same locker facility in one month.

Locking his newly repaired door behind him, Warren took the elevator down to the lobby. He wordlessly walked past the doorman, stepped outside and hailed a cab.

"The Art Institute, downtown."

"Got it."

The cab sped away, heading into the city. It was a balmy 73 degrees with no rain in the forecast. Things were already heating up in the Midwest. Unless the Mylerium Project went off as scheduled, it was only going to get hotter outside. Much, much hotter.

No Such Agency

Rubic Chang walked into Giordano's and ordered a slice of cheese deep-dish pizza with a 20-ounce beer. He had 15 minutes before his rendezvous and he had no intention of throwing his pizza away. There was more than enough time to eat a slice and finish his beer. He was hungry, thirsty and still floating on Rapture7.

As Rubic walked toward the park bench where he was supposed to meet Warren, he glanced back at his bike, making certain it was securely chained to the parking meter. It was.

He had finished his lunch by the time he reached the Art Institute, where he lingered near the lion statues, waiting for 4 p.m. to roll around. He decided it was a good time to call Yeva.

Rubic's face appeared in 3-D on Yeva's phone as it rang back in their apartment. It was as if he were standing next to her in miniature.

"So what's up?" Yeva asked.

"It's a big assignment," Rubic said in a hushed voice. "But we shouldn't talk about it over the phone."

"In town or out of town?"

"Mostly out."

"How long will you be away?"

"'Bout a month or less. I'll be doing a lot of train time."

"You hate trains."

"Yeah, but there's some good money in it, and it'll help make the rent."

Making the rent wasn't easy, as most of Rubic's profits went up in a sweet, pale white smoke. He and Yeva desperately needed the money.

"Will you stop by before heading out?" Yeva asked.

"Yeah, in an hour or so. I'll stay the night and catch a cab to the train station in the morning. I'll tell you more about it when I get home. You know how these phones are."

"I know. See ya soon."

Everyone knew the phones could listen. *Hell,* reflected Yeva as she clicked off her cell, *everything can listen.*

The television could listen, iPods could listen, radios could listen—even hallways could listen. As the Corporation of Information grew more influential, the National Security Agency, once relegated to eavesdropping on foreign targets, turned its resources and talent toward spying on domestic affairs. It remained a secretive, largely covert organization that lived up to its reputation as No Such Agency, an infamous alternative acronym for the NSA. When its mission expanded to include protecting America's supercomputers from cyber-attacks, it was inevitable that the NSA would become the most powerful government agency on Earth. Even the FBI and the CIA became concerned when NSA agents showed up asking questions. The agency that didn't exist was now the most powerful intelligence-gathering authority in the world.

With the advent of nanotechnology, cameras were virtually invisible to the naked eye. Anything could be bugged. Almost every electronic device, from a blender to a blow dryer, could be fashioned into a tool for espionage. As America's environment degraded into one hot, endless hellhole, the NSA became the watchdog of the nation and the world beyond. Winter was the only time anyone could enjoy the outdoors. Food and water riots were common and there were always new, threatening domestic terrorist groups springing up amid continuous rumors of a complete government takeover. Everyone grew anxious at the prospect of rationing basic necessities.

Various splinter groups emerged across the country. Most were well-armed local militias ready to defend their water rights, their cooperative farms and their freedom. The NSA attempted to keep the U.S. sane, but with every scorching summer that mission became increasingly trying.

The NSA spawned urban runners like Rubic Chang. Nothing on the Net or online computer systems was safe. There was no encryption, no spyware and no virus able to outsmart the supercomputers buried beneath the ponderous buildings in Fort Meade, Maryland. With COI controlling the Web, all data, from international banking to mundane emails, were washed through microprocessors looking for the smallest speck of dirt. Perhaps the intelligence COI gathered could help avoid a raid on a grain elevator in Nebraska, or a bank robbery in California. After being hacked by the government, computers recorded their users' every keystroke and forwarded that info to the NSA. Computer printers had secret microchips implanted that kept records of every word, every sentence, every document that was printed. Privacy didn't exist.

Yeva knew Rubic was in grave danger when he started any run. Because everything electronic was subject to the scrutiny of the NSA, the only viable means of communicating were handwritten letters. Even at that, the letter writers had to ensure no one was looking over their shoulder. Perhaps a camera was hiding in the small metal clip on their favorite pen, recording everything they jotted down.

Urban runners like Rubic represented the last bastions of free speech. If caught, depending on the nature of the information they carried, runners could expect life in prison without parole. If the information was deemed a national security threat, conveying it was an act of treason. The offending runner, after a perfunctory trial whose outcome was never in doubt, would be put to death. Judges feared the NSA as much as anyone else.

Yeva was anxious to learn more about Rubic's plans, but she was well aware they would have to discuss them somewhere outside their apartment. That meant they were going out tonight, probably to the Siren Club.

The Rendezvous

It was a few minutes after 4 p.m. as Rubic watched a tall, rather awkward-looking man in an ill-fitting suit sit down on the park bench not 30 feet from one of the two bronze lions silently guarding the entrance to the Art Institute. Though Rubic had never actually met Warren, he knew this man must be him. After all, he was also carrying a Giordano's pizza box.

Rubic took out the bagged cell phone and discreetly placed it in his empty pizza box. Then he casually strolled over to the bench and sat next to the stranger beside him.

Warren shuffled over a bit and set his empty pizza box right beside Rubic's. Per the instructions in the letter, neither said a word. A minute later, as a group of school children exited the museum to load into a bus parked right in front of the bench, Warren grabbed Rubic's pizza box and walked away. A few seconds after that, Rubic picked up Warren's box and did the same, heading in the opposite direction.

A half mile away, Rubic removed the electronic key that displayed the locker number on it and threw the pizza box down on the sidewalk.

An NSA camera had captured Rubic removing the key from the pizza box. It would take three days before an agent, reviewing what the agency referred to as "the dailies," brought the episode to the attention of his commanding officer. Rubic would be off and running by then, but because of one suspicious incident, he would be automatically upgraded to a "person of interest." He was already believed to be a runner and this mysterious key incident only helped confirm the NSA's suspicions. Had they reviewed the tape sooner, they might have been able to bug him with a GPS chip, but now they had to find him the old-fashioned way—by looking everywhere at once.

Once Warren was a safe distance away from the bench outside the Art Institute, he shook his pizza box and heard the rattle of something inside. It had to be his cell.

He knew better than to open the box immediately, although he was tempted to check. Instead, he kept the iPhone in its greasy housing until he felt secure enough to avoid the all-seeing state surveillance system.

Warren knew his apartment was lost. The NSA would have bugged every room with cameras and listening devices before departing, or else they would have evicted one of the owners next door and set up shop with listening and looking devices. The walls around Warren's apartment might as well have been made of glass.

He realized the best place to take out his backup cell phone was in one of the hundreds of public pay toilets scattered around the city. Although the NSA could bug individual stalls, they were not allowed to put cameras in them, though they were rumored to do so regardless. The lack of cameras made public pay toilets an ideal place to score hits of Rapture7 or turn tricks as a prostitute. The only safe houses in Chicago, aside from the derelict buildings on the South Side, were the bathrooms.

Warren kept glancing behind him to ensure he wasn't being followed. He saw no one.

Two agents in a dimly lit room in Fort Meade were following Warren, however. They used the multitude of security cameras blanketing downtown Chicago to track his every move. They had both overlooked the exchange of pizza boxes outside the Art Institute, as the boxes were an exact match and the busload of schoolchildren blocked their cameras' best angles. As Warren ducked into the electronic pay toilet, they watched and waited from two different angles.

When he came out again without the box and with his cell phone tucked safely into his right front pocket, the NSA agents didn't suspect a thing. There were trash containers inside the bathrooms, so they concluded Warren had tossed out his garbage while inside. Warren walked to the curb, where the agents watched him hail a cab. They followed the cab through the urban landscape via a high-resolution satellite camera.

Fifteen minutes later, they observed him getting out, paying the cab driver and walking into his apartment building. They kept an eye on him in the lobby, followed him into the elevator where another camera tracked him as he rode 26 stories up. The hallway cameras took over until he entered his apartment. Once inside, the two member crew that had moved into the vacant apartment one story below took over.

Warren knew his next mission was to purchase a new, identical cell phone, a personal computer and a backup hard drive. If he kept all of them off the Web, he could transfer the data stored in the phone he had just picked up from Rubic and have several backups in case COI's leaders decided to have him arrested.

There were also the seven envelopes, each containing a nanodrive with his research encrypted in them, but Warren had no way of knowing if any of the intended recipients would ever see that information.

Like all runners, Rubic Chang couldn't be trusted. For all Warren knew, Rubic was already tucking the eight grand in his pocket, tossing the seven envelopes in the trash and biking off for an extended Rapture7 vacation. Then there was always the chance that the NSA or the FBI would intercept Rubic somewhere along the way. It wouldn't take them more than a few hours to decipher the encryption on his nanodrives. Within a day, there would be a loud knock Warren's front door, followed by his arrest and disappearance.

At the very least, Warren would have violated his gag order, which was cause enough for his incarceration. He didn't know how long he would be held. It could be a year or more. Perhaps he would only stay imprisoned until the nanomirrors dissolved in the fall as planned, proving that his fears were unfounded. Were that to occur, Warren might be released before Christmas.

But what would happen if the nanomirrors failed to self-destruct? If that happened, Warren would likely never leave prison. The Corporation of Information would never allow any of his research to get out, fearing a public backlash should the press become aware of his attempt to warn the world about their miscalculations and erroneous computers.

If the nanomirrors do not disintegrate and I'm in jail, contemplated Warren, *I'll die in jail.*

By 5:30 p.m. Warren was seated on the edge of his bed, drinking a tall glass of straight bourbon and thinking about what his workday would be like the next morning. Everything would be different, but he couldn't let on that anything had changed. It was all a charade from here on out, but Warren had never considered himself much of an actor.

He downed the rest of his bourbon and bit back a cough.

Ft. Meade, Maryland

Three days after the exchange occurred, analysts at the NSA reviewed the video of Rubic Chang removing a tiny electronic key from an empty pizza box. Zooming in, they could tell it was a train locker key, but it appeared to be unmarked. The agents didn't know what to make of it.

"It might have something to do with a drug deal," one of the analysts suggested.

"Drug deals are generally done in cash, not with electronic locker keys. And they almost always go down in the public toilets."

"Maybe it's big. Maybe the key opens a locker filled with cash, or drugs, or both."

"We know he's just a junkie, though."

"What's his name?"

"Rubic Chang. He's 22. Dropped out of college two years ago. Lives with a girl named Yeva Dunning. One arrest for possession of an illegal substance, probably Synth or Rapture7, it doesn't say. He's in the system though — fingerprints, retina scans, a facial recognition configuration, the works."

"It could be the start or the end of some kind of run."

"That's my guess. Only time will tell."

"Can we pick him up in reverse, running the tapes backward?"

"Yes, but only for a half mile. We lose him in the crowds. Had we been onto him earlier we could have stayed with him, but it would take a miracle and weeks' worth of work to track him backward at this point in time. We might not even get anything then. Whatever he's up to, it's probably not worth that kind of effort."

"I suppose you're right."

The analysts kept running over the tape and speculating about what the key could mean. Whatever the reasons behind his suspicious activity, all agreed Rubic required 24-hour surveillance for the next few weeks, provided they could pick up his trail again.

Domestic spying wasn't always this extensive. When the Green Party first rose to power in 2036, they were the party of freedom and change. They wanted to liberate the United States from the immense political influence of the fossil fuel industry. But like so many political movements before them, they started out with good intentions and ended light-years away from their noble starting point. As the environment continued to degrade, they found themselves needing more environmental enforcement and the power such enforcement entailed.

Internal renegade groups, known informally as "burners," were still illegally burning private reserves of outlawed gasoline, propane and diesel. They violated the Carbon Act of 2040 and had to be stopped. Everything and anything that would add CO_2 to the atmosphere was strictly controlled or banned outright.

There were plenty of other issues the Greens had to contend with. As conditions worsened, the few remaining wildlife preserves and refuges of biodiversity had to be protected from poachers who had turned to hunting state and national parks for bush meat. Insurance companies failed and economic turmoil ensued. The unending flood of environmental refugees from South and Central America had to be stopped from crossing the border into the U.S. The rampant use of Rapture7, a synthetic derivative of THC, the active ingredient in marijuana, had to be controlled. The Coastal Erosion Commission had to make sure thousands of levies, dikes and retaining walls kept out the ever-rising sea levels. The rapid deterioration from the party of the future to the party of absolute control was, in hindsight, inevitable.

Day by day, month by month and year by year, the ruling Green Party became increasingly authoritarian. The revolutionaries, once voices crying for freedom and change, were now the only people you could vote for. The Greens had become environmental fascists. They controlled the NSA, FBI, CIA and the all-powerful EPA. They had become more intolerant of dissent than the men and women they had replaced.

Of course, the Greens felt it was their duty and their mandate to behave the way they did. Americans had elected them in a landslide during the 2036 elections and they had ruled the nation ever since. They now controlled the biggest and most important industry on the planet—the world's food supply. Without them and their distribution chains, half the world's population would face starvation. By 2043, virtually everyone in power was a member of the Greens, in much the same fashion the Communist Party had commandeered Soviet Russia 100 years earlier. The environment was their platform and the Greens were intolerant of any opinions except theirs.

There was even talk of suspending the 2044 elections and keeping the current President, Adrian Beltram, in office for life. Few people dared to oppose the idea. The forthcoming success of the Mylerium Project all but assured President Beltran's reelection. Term limits had been voted out in 2041. In almost every election in the U.S., Green Party candidates ran uncontested. They nearly always won.

The Siren Club

"You have to talk louder, Rubic!"

"I'll try."

"Here, just yell in my ear if you have to."

Rubic leaned toward Yeva and started shouting in her ear. The music was deafening.

"I said I leave for Boston in the morning. The train heads out at 9:40. We stop in New York, then on to Boston by 4 p.m."

Yeva shouted back into his ear. "Did you buy an America Pass?"

"Yeah, it's way cheaper."

"Will you be coming back through Chicago before you head to California?"

"Probably not."

"Oh." Even amidst the din Rubic could hear the disappointment in her voice.

"I'll be home in three weeks if everything goes well."

"OK."

"Wanna dance?"

"Sure."

Rubic took Yeva's hand as they headed to the dance floor. The Siren Club was packed. Urban rockers with metal piercings and dark, foreboding tattoos crowded the dance floor in a chaotic rhythm that was part mosh pit, part controlled riot. Orange hair ground against purple as heads banged. More than a few times, blood spilled across the hardwood flooring. The smell of burning crystal Rapture7 filled the room. There were other drugs as well. People snorted lines of Synth in the bathrooms. Pills of every description were shared, eaten and dissolved inside the writhing bodies on the hypnotic dance floor. The music was so loud and the lighting so frenzied that the NSA could never hope to hear the conversations or read anyone's drug-addled, gibbering lips. The crowd knew this and reveled in their safe, if temporary, narco-freedom.

Yeva and Rubic were separated once they hit the whirling dance floor. That didn't matter. Rapture7 acted like amplified ecstasy. It didn't matter who you were grinding against. It didn't matter if it was a man or a woman. It didn't matter if you had ever seen that person before or would ever see them again. Only the grinding, whirling and spinning mattered. It was an exhilarating fusion of noise, flesh and freedom.

The world outside stayed outside. That's why this motley entourage returned night after night. There was no climate crisis inside the Siren Club. There was only shimmering noise and the sensation of warm, twisting bodies.

Rubic and Yeva partied well past midnight. They made their way back home on the subway, kissing and embracing the entire way. Back at the apartment, they made love until 2 a.m., then faded into sleep. Rubic would leave the apartment by 9 a.m., heading to Boston. Yeva would be back at work before then, her hands sifting through the rich, black soil of Illinois. Rubic had left her with a thousand dollars, his share of the rent, in an envelope on the kitchen table. They wouldn't be evicted this month.

At the CMC

"You don't seem yourself, Dr. Randolf, is there anything bothering you?"

"Not really."

"Hmm. You just seem kind of distant. Are you worried about the deployment?"

Dr. Goodman's comment caught Warren off guard. The deployment was now less than a month away. Did she know something?

"No, I think the ships will perform perfectly. It will take more than a month to transport all the nanomirrors into position but from an engineering perspective, everything should operate fine."

Warren started to continue, paused, and changed direction.

"I've been thinking about finding another job, Heather—that's why I've been distracted."

Dr. Heather Goodman looked surprised.

"I had no idea you were even thinking about leaving the Center," she said. "When did this come up?"

"It's been five long, hard years and I won't be leaving until after deployment, but I feel it's time to move on into the private sector and try something different."

"I'm shocked, but...good luck."

With that brief exchange Heather continued walking in the opposite direction down the hall. Warren was heading back to the lab. He knew that his comment to Heather would make the rounds of the CMC, via interoffice emails, the lunch room and every other imaginable route by the end of the work week. Everything seemed to be running in slow motion.

Waiting is hell, thought Warren.

Ft. Meade, Maryland

"He's not in Chicago—that I can assure you."

"Well, where the hell is he?"

"It's anyone's guess. No doubt it has something to do with that key."

"Did you check all the trains? Car rentals? International flights?"

"We're working on it. Cars and flights may take a few more hours to sift through. But if he paid cash and used a fake I.D. to board a train, it will be all but impossible to know where he's headed."

The senior NSA agent in charge of finding Rubic Chang knew it was true. Everyone needed a passport and papers to board an international flight, but the high-speed electric train system used by most Americans for long-distance domestic travel didn't require the same level of identification. When internal combustion cars were phased out in the late '20s, the general public turned to the train system. It soon became the primary method of travel throughout North America.

All experienced runners knew better than to use their real names when buying the America Pass for train travel. The government was installing retinal scanners at some of major train stations to combat the use of these fake I.D.s, but it would be years before all the machines were fully operational.

"We'll have to put out a nationwide facial recognition request."

"I've already started on it."

"It could take weeks before we find him, especially if he's on a cross-country run."

"We'll find him. Sooner or later one of our cameras will spot him. We won't lose him after that."

"Do you want me to place the search request with Homeland Security?"

"Yeah. It's suspicious enough to merit staying on top of it. Enter him into the system and include contingencies for Canada and Mexico. We'll catch up with him, arrest him and find out what the hell he's up to."

"We always do."

"For the most part. Not always."

Within minutes, several high-resolution photos of Rubic Chang had been fed into the mainframe system of the NSA. Rubic had a distinctive look. His dark skin and unusually shaped eyes would make him an easy target for the hundreds of thousands of facial recognition cameras located across the continent. Being half Chinese and half Jamaican had its drawbacks.

But the NSA was now actively searching for more than 75,000 people nationwide. Their offenses ranged from operating a gas-powered lawn mower to committing murder. The sheer volume of photos and information processed daily tended to bog down the system, even with the help of supercomputers.

The NSA could find Rubic, but if he was clever and watchful, it might take a long time.

Warren's Journal, March 1, 2043

Warren found a measure of comfort in the entries he continued to make in his journal. He felt he needed to retell the whole story, from start to finish, of what had transpired since the turn of the 21st century. He didn't particularly care if anyone read what he wrote. He just valued the act of putting it down on paper, from the first carbon dioxide measurements atop a volcano in Hawaii to the horrors of the Lost Decade.

He was trying to make sense of it all, if there could be any sense drawn out from the climactic chaos. Warren was trying to put everything that had transpired into perspective.

He had no idea if the warning letters to his closest friends and colleagues had been lost by some addict or if they had reached their targets. So Warren wrote fervently. It was, in many ways, all he had left.

March 1, 2043

Why didn't we pay attention back when we had a chance to avoid this nightmare? Everything we needed to know was in the ice. Those long, slender tubes of frozen history warned us long before our climate unraveled. The ice chronicled an unbroken record of the Earth's atmosphere dating back 800,000 years.

When snowflakes fall atop the ice domes of Greenland or Antarctica, they trap microscopic bubbles of air within them. These bubbles are infinitesimal samples of the prehistoric atmosphere. Using chemical analysis, we learned how to extract the air from those samples and determine how much CO_2 or methane was present in the atmosphere the year the snow fell. We discovered how to read the chemical compositions of Earth's ancient atmospheres.

These "ice cores" and their microscopic air bubbles confirmed that when the levels of CO_2 rose, the Earth's temperature rose in tandem. It proved the relationship between carbon dioxide and the greenhouse effect it created. The real danger lay in the lag time. It often took hundreds of years for the temperature to rise, reflecting each historic increase of CO_2.

But there were also Rapid Climate Change Events—what are commonly called the Rickys. Past Rickys should have warned us that things can move very quickly in the fluid world of global climate dynamics. In many Rickys, the Earth cooled off as much as 10 degrees Fahrenheit in less than a decade before gradually warming up again. In other instances, the exact opposite occurred. The most recent of these, the Younger Dryas, named after an alpine flower, provided ample evidence of fast climate change.

During the Younger Dryas, the warm, tropical water pumped north along the Atlantic by the Gulf Stream stopped flowing. It would take more than a thousand years for that crucial Atlantic conveyor belt to recover.

Faced with cooler weather, the forests of Scandinavia returned to tundra. The island of Great Britain, which lies north of Newfoundland's latitude, became very cold. While the cool down itself took more than one thousand years to occur, the ending of the Younger Dryas should have made everyone take notice.

When the Younger Dryas cold spell finally ended 11,550 years ago, it did so in record time. The ice cores suggest the warming in those days was sudden and dramatic. According to some evidence, it took 40 to 50 years for the northern climate to warm as much as twelve degrees, but other core samples indicate it might have taken just two or three years. But all the readings confirm the change happened fast—no more than an instant in geological terms. By the time the Younger Dryas ended, the atmosphere warmed close to 20 degrees.

Twelve-thousand years ago, such a drastic temperature change didn't affect a human population that numbered less than 10 million worldwide. But what would happen if the world's temperature suddenly jumped ten to twenty degrees Fahrenheit on a planet crowded with 10 billion people? Had our leaders paid attention to this possibility, things might have changed sooner. Maybe we would have cut back on fossil fuels decades ago. Did we think we were immune to the laws of physics?

The ice cores proved Rickys were not only possible, but probable. The truth was we didn't want to change. Life was too good to be true. The entire world, from India to Brazil, wanted what America and Europe already had. They wanted flat screen televisions, freeways jammed with cars, air conditioning, gas-powered lawn mowers, gas grills, gas fireplaces, reliable electricity, computers, blenders, toasters, washers, dryers, ovens, microwaves—all the high-energy conveniences of the modern world.

Every one of these gadgets arrived with its own insatiable appetite for cheap, dirty energy. That meant using more coal, diesel, gas and propane, which burned up the fossil remnants of the carboniferous forests that vanished 300 million years ago. They dumped their gaseous byproducts, from CO_2 to methane, into the newfound garbage dump of our atmosphere.

When the atmosphere collapsed during the Lost Decade, no one wanted to take the blame. The bill for this feast of fossil energy was due, and the first payment was the death of more than 400 million people over the course of a dozen horrific years. In the end, one in twenty people on Earth perished. Not a family in the world avoided the catastrophic impact, rich or poor. Since then, the yearly death toll from climate change has numbered in the tens of millions.

It's no wonder we started contemplating geoengineering. We had been unwittingly experimenting with geoengineering since we mined the first few *tons of coal in the U.S. in 1748. China mined coal as early as the 17th century,* *but it wasn't until the mid-19th century that the human race started to churn* *out CO_2 in prodigious volumes. By 2030, we were burning more than 13* *billion metric tons of coal a year worldwide and had already put some 37* *billion metric tons of CO_2 into our atmosphere from dirty coal alone. The* *Lost Decade didn't just happen—we made it happen. And now we're about* *to make something even more alarming happen.*

I sometimes wish I weren't alive to see what's coming. Sadly, I am.

Warren put down his pen, took his glasses off and rubbed his eyes. He was tired. He thought of having a second bourbon before bed but elected not to. Too much liquor made him restless. He thought about his runner and his seven packages. He thought about the forthcoming deployment and the stratosphere laced with billions of microscopic mirrors. Those mirrors, shaped like multi-faceted diamonds, were designed to reflect the very sunlight that made life on Earth possible, all with near-perfect efficiency.

Warren thought about dying.

The First Delivery

Rubic Chang patiently waited under a sprawling oak, his back resting against the tree and a spring lawn beneath him as students and professors passed by him in a seemingly endless stream. Rubic knew Dr. Garrison's morning class would get out shortly, so he waited.

A minute later, a tall, brown-haired man who appeared to be in his early thirties walked by. He wore a tweed sports coat and a blue button-down shirt with no tie.

Rubic picked up his cell, clicked on his collection of downloaded photos and compared the two. As Albion walked away, Rubic couldn't miss the fact that he had pulled his hair back into a short pony tail. It had to be him.

Rubic got up and fell behind the professor.

"Dr. Albion Garrison, this is for you," he said, handing a brown manila envelope to the man walking just in front of him.

Albion, hearing his name, stopped abruptly without grabbing the package.

"Excuse me?" he asked, whirling around and squinting at Rubic. "Do I know you?"

"No. I was asked to deliver this to you by someone you know—a Mr. Warren. He hired me to bring this package to you."

"Why wouldn't this Mr. Warren, whoever he is, just email me this information? What's in the envelope?"

"I'm sure you know the answer to why he didn't email you this information," Rubic said carefully. He was starting to worry Albion might call him out as a runner, especially if he didn't know Warren. "As far as what's inside of this—I was asked not to open any of the packages and I'm not going to. There must be something in here that Warren doesn't want the government or the NSA to know about. You and I know the Net is not secure, so I'm delivering this package in person."

"This is intriguing."

"You are Dr. Garrison, aren't you?"

"Yes, I am."

"Then please take this envelope from me and let me move on. I've got more work to do and I don't want to hang around here any longer. Please. There could be cameras watching us right now."

Rubic was being very careful, but he attributed his flawless record to his caution. He had walked behind Dr. Garrison until they were under an overpass not far from his lab. It was a pedestrian walkway that spanned two of the large research buildings at MIT. Rubic had Googled the professor's photo, watched him and waited for the perfect opportunity to deliver his first envelope.

Dr. Garrison reached out and took the envelope from Rubic.

"I'll take it. Do I need to sign for it or anything?"

"No, Dr. Garrison, we never met and this never happened. Warren also asked that you not share anything you learn from this package with anyone, not even your wife."

"I understand."

With that, Rubic quickly walked the other way, his head bowed down. He jumped back on his bike and hurried toward his next delivery in Cambridge.

Dr. Garrison continued walking toward a luncheon he had previously scheduled. He tucked the manila envelope in with his stack of papers and never looked back, but couldn't help but wonder why Warren would have enlisted the services of the unusual young man.

He had been tempted to refuse the package, but he knew that his old college roommate would not have gone through all of this trouble if it wasn't important. He also remembered a brief conversation with Warren a week ago and surmised something had not gone well.

Though he had never met one, Dr. Garrison knew that he had been talking to a runner. He had heard of them before, but in his line or work he never thought he would actually encounter one.

Whatever was inside that envelope, it wasn't meant to be made public.

Dr. Garrison's Office

Dr. Garrison waited until he was safe in his home office before opening the envelope. He didn't dare look inside while still at his lab in MIT. He worried something had gone seriously wrong. Whatever was inside the package was probably not good news.

He broke open the envelope and found a tiny nanodrive and a lengthy, handwritten letter:

Dear Albion,

You should have received this envelope from a runner. I hope your interaction with him went without incident. In fact, by the time this letter reaches you, I may already be under arrest. If that's the case, please use the information in this package to prepare yourself, your friends and your family for the dark days ahead.

As we have discussed, the Mylerium Project, due for deployment in a few weeks, is fatally flawed. I have included an encrypted nanofile data drive with a summary of my research and conclusions. Although we've discussed these flaws before, I was never able to give you any proof, as I could not risk putting any of this data on the Net.

You know that I have been an integral part of this project for the past five years. Halfway through the process, I started to question some of the equations and engineering being produced by the TURING 1000 supercomputer. Unsure of what to do with my reservations about the project, I decided to take another look outside the normal channels. I intentionally broke the CMC's code of conduct and did my research offline. My thinking was that if the TURING 1000 was in error, the computers could access my work online and skew my results.

I purchased a number of Apple 3600X's and pieced together a supercomputer in my apartment. After entering some calculations in error one evening, I discovered, by chance, the flaw I was searching for. It was hidden in the self-destruct program of the nanomirrors' molecular computers. I believe the mirrors were intentionally designed to fail.

I don't have the time or the resources to investigate whether this built-in failure has anything to do with the computers themselves, but I suspect it may. We have known for decades that there is a probability that our computers, our machines, might begin making decisions on their own. If one of the supercomputers somehow acted of its own accord in error, the results could be devastating.

One thing I do know is that the Mylerium Project will progress as planned this summer. The problem is not with the nanomirrors' ability to reflect sunlight and help to cool the planet. The problem is in their self-destruct program. They are designed to collapse over a four-week period in the fall, starting in late October. The mirrors are designed this way to reduce and restore the sun's intensity gradually.

According to the CMC's calculations, the mirrors will reduce summer temperatures by eight to ten degrees Fahrenheit, which should return us to the temperature gradients of the 1990s. By the end of November, the mirrors should fall back to Earth as harmless dust. New mirrors should be redeployed annually until the next generation of scrubbers can reduce the excess CO_2 we've pumped into our atmosphere.

This project is predicated on the built-in self-destruct program. Without it, we could create something akin to a volcanic or a nuclear winter. With winter sunlight entering our atmosphere at oblique angles, the mirrors would cause ambient average temperatures across most of the

Northern Hemisphere to fall by 12 to 15 degrees. Should this happen, the winter of 2043-44 will be brutally cold.

However, the winter does not overly concern me. A brief cold spell would not pose an insurmountable problem. The real trouble with the mirrors would begin in the spring—or rather, the extended winter, because spring would never come. Should the mirrors remain in the stratosphere, they will create a positive feedback loop that will wreak havoc on civilization.

We have heated the Earth to temperatures not seen since the Jurassic period, some 70 million years ago. Accordingly, the amount of water vapor in our atmosphere is very high. As temperatures plummet, that vapor will become snow. Snowfall reflects sunlight at eighty percent, compounding the problem.

Naturally, should the mirrors fail to dissolve, the CMC would not deploy another batch in the spring of 2044, but by then it will be too late. With most of the Northern Hemisphere covered in a deep blanket of snowfall through late May, or possibly June, the remaining mirrors' reflective efficiency (or albedo) would effectively double. We would find ourselves locked in a downward spiral that would reduce average temperatures by 18 to 20 degrees. In short, there will be no summer.

The wheat harvests of the world would fail, as would the rice crops of southern China and most of India. By my analysis, if 50 percent of the mirrors remain in orbit through the winter, we would have 9.7 billion mouths to feed and nearly no food. There would be catastrophic crop failures, the likes of which have never been seen.

Because of the current climate crisis, we are already living perilously close to the edge when it comes to feeding the people of the world. Food stockpiles are at record lows, with most estimates putting the world's reserves at between 12 to 14 months. If my projections are correct, we would completely run out of food by the spring of 2045.

Over time, the mirrors would succumb naturally to dispersion and ultraviolet rays, but because the feedback loop would be impossible to reverse quickly, we may well lose the summer of 2045 and one or two summers beyond that, depending on how many mirrors remain. That means two to six billion people could starve to death over the next five *years. Diseases such as cholera, dysentery and a host of other sicknesses would ravage the world's malnourished populations. Civilization would collapse.*

Please open the nanodrive as soon as possible. With your physics background, you should have little trouble understanding my work, but please do not Google or speak with anyone about this letter or my work.

After looking it over, if you agree with my conclusions, call me to congratulate me on the deployment of the mirrors or to discuss the weather and we'll go from there. If I do not hear from you, then I will conclude you feel the CMC and the TURING 1000 are accurate, or that the runner failed to deliver this message.

Meanwhile, assuming I'm still a free man, I will start looking into how we might survive the coming gauntlet. I am looking to relocate somewhere out west, as far away from urban centers as possible. Once there, I will construct a camp where a handful of close friends and I will be able to survive this coming apocalypse.

In essence, we will be building an ark together. At the moment I'm thinking of Idaho or Montana, both of which are far from the chaos that will undoubtedly ensue in the major metropolitan areas. I will need help, both financially and physically. I'll need to build greenhouses, set up heaters, storehouses, the energy system and everything we'll need to make it through the lawless abyss that will surround us. If all goes as planned, we will be self-sustaining, completely off the grid and well-defended. The grid itself could well collapse.

Your background in geothermal heating will be helpful. You are more than likely wondering if I've lost my mind by this time. I have not. I'm not a survivalist. I'm a scientist. But I know you, of all people, should be capable of understanding the information contained in this nanodrive.

At this time please do not share this disk with anyone—even your wife or your sons. Until the mirrors actually fail to dissolve there is no need for anyone to know. Once they begin to fail, we will be back in touch and proceed from there.

I hope my assessment about this project is wrong. I hope the mirrors dissolve and then both of us can have a good laugh. But if I'm right, there will be no laughter for years to come. We will need each others' help and skill sets to make it through. Please burn this letter when you

have finished reading it and do not open the nanodrive while online or
save it on your computer.

> *Dr. Warren Randolf*
> *Advanced Meteorological Studies*
> *The Center for Meteorological Controls*
> *43 Baker Street,*
> *Chicago, IL 30322*

Dr. Garrison already knew much of what Warren's letter contained. The two had talked about how they could work together to get through the upcoming cold spell, but Warren had never provided Albion with any of his actual research. Because of Warren's concerns about the TURING 1000, he never relayed any files about his research to Albion, or any of his colleagues.

Albion slipped the tiny storage device into the slot of his laptop and waited for his computer to work through the encryption, which took only minutes. As he began reading, Dr. Albion Garrison was mesmerized.

At the NSA

"Where the hell is he?"

"He's not in Chicago, that's for sure."

"Well, keep running the search program until we get results. We took too long reviewing that tape and now he's got a head start on us. We know he's still in North America, since the retina scanners would have identified him had he been heading overseas."

"Yeah, he's in the country somewhere."

"Stay on top of it and let me know if you get a hit."

"Will do."

The NSA search had yet to find Rubic Chang. Assuming his run was local, they had concentrated their efforts on the greater metropolitan area, including the city of Milwaukee, whose southern suburbs had become Chicago's northern suburbs. Together the two made up the largest megalopolis in America. All combined, the region's population had swelled to 32 million, including many climate refugees from New York, Florida and the desert southwest.

Chicago had water, and water was everything. Though Lake Michigan was down three meters from the turn of the 21st century, there was still ample fresh water. The elevation of the region, at roughly 600 feet, kept it free of the extensive coastal flooding that plagued the west coast and the eastern seaboard. With the world's sea levels close to a meter higher than they were 40 years ago, climate refugees from both coasts sought the higher ground Chicago had to offer. The harsh winters that once gave Chicago its nickname, the Windy City, were largely a distant memory.

"Open the search nationwide but leave it at priority yellow. We don't even know if this guy is worth keeping an eye on and we've got much bigger fish to fry out there right now than a Rapture7 junkie from Roger's Park."

"Got it. I'll let you know if we get any activity."

"That's fine. Now let's all get back to work."

The Lost Decade

There was little for Warren to do at this juncture but wait. Wait and pretend. In the meantime he found himself returning to his journal.

On the evening of March 5, 2043, he continued his personal history of climate change.

March 5, 2043

I was a teenager when the Lost Decade began. Although most people cite 2030 as the year the weather took a turn for the worse, there was plenty of trouble before then. Things started falling apart at the turn of the century, but at that point in time, no one wanted to deal with it. There was an element of collective denial about the topic. China and India were building coal-fired power plants at the rate of one per week and no one bothered to raise an eyebrow. The United States refused to talk about climate change, except when the fossil fuel oligarchs denied its existence.

Besides, the policymakers in the U.S. weren't about to make any energy sacrifices if China and India were free to do what they wanted. In hindsight, the politics of climate change became a kind of international madness, a reverse climactic version of the nuclear standoff known as MAD, or Mutual Assured Destruction. That twisted policy held that if everyone had enough nuclear weapons to utterly destroy each other, no one would dare fire the first missile. In the climate standoff it was decided that if the rising economies of China and India could pollute the atmosphere with megatons of CO_2, then why should we bother cutting back on our own emissions? We collectively raced toward our own destruction.

As the stalemate continued, glaciers throughout the world kept melting even as the nations that relied on them for water argued over who should cut back on their carbon footprint first. The glaciers of the Himalayas fed rivers which helped feed 4 billion people. When their glaciers disappeared in the 2030s, the great rivers of Asia, including the Ganges, Indus, and Brahmaputra of India and the Yellow and Yangtze of China, were reduced to streams that never even reached the sea. Farmers scrambled for irrigation water. Cities had to truck in potable water from hundreds of miles away.

Only Europe seemed to be genuinely concerned about what was happening. European nations invested heavily in solar power and wind farms. Only Europe was developing geothermal, tidal and wave energy sources. Sadly, no one was working hard enough on the greatest long term solution to our energy needs—nuclear fusion. Instead, everyone looked the other way, blaming each other and kicking the carbon can farther down the road.

Meanwhile that road got bumpier. Mt. Kilimanjaro's last remnant ice cap disappeared in 2019, when I was six years old. The last glacier in Glacier National Park vanished in 2028. The Greenland ice dome started to vanish in the early 20s, causing sea levels to rise much faster than anyone had anticipated. Florida, along with most of the eastern seaboard, became uninsurable in 2023, when I was ten.

That was the year Hurricane Emily hit. That storm annihilated Fort Lauderdale. The losses from Hurricane Emily exceeded 200 billion dollars. Dozens of smaller insurance companies folded, while several major firms barely survived. Lloyds of London, Munich Re and Swiss Re groups announced they would no longer reinsure companies writing policies within 50 miles of the eastern seaboard, from Galveston, Texas to New England.

People fled the Gulf Coast, the lower eastern seaboard and Sunshine State by the millions once their insurance policies were canceled. The few companies left taking policies wanted a king's ransom for their premiums. A small, single-family home cost as much as $20,000 a year to insure. People walked away from their properties, unable to meet the premiums. Lending institutions, from regional banks to Fannie Mae, were left holding mortgages on hundreds of thousands of homes that could not be insured against the next big storm. No one wanted to deal with the risks involved.

By the time 2030 arrived, we were on our way to a world unlike any we had known before. It seemed everything that could go wrong that year did go wrong. There were three Category 5 hurricanes that summer alone. The one that hit Haiti, Hurricane Beryl, produced a storm surge five meters high. As bad as the surge was, it was primarily the 27 inches of rain that washed away entire villages, towns and cities. With 97 percent of its vegetation stripped away and a population pushing twelve million people, the death toll was staggering. Some estimates put the number killed between 1.2 and 1.4 million. Those who didn't die in the flooding endured years of cholera, malaria and a host of other deadly diseases that ravaged the impoverished nation in the aftermath of the storm.

Soon after, Typhoon Isang hit the Philippines, where another 500,000 perished.

But the storm that really tore things apart was Hurricane Oscar, which made landfall in Texas. It was the second Category 5 to make a direct hit on the United States that fateful year. The city of Houston was ripped to shreds. Downtown, not a single skyscraper window was left intact after the storm passed. The town of Galveston, whose breakwater was erected more than 130 years earlier in response to Isaac's storm, was scoured to bare ground by the 10 meter storm surge and 165 mph winds. Because of extensive evacuations, the death toll stayed under 100,000 for Oscar, but the damage to buildings and infrastructure topped one trillion dollars. The insurance industry teetered on collapse.

It didn't stop. The Lost Decade was just getting underway. Dr. Keeling's recording instruments on the slopes of Mauna Loa recorded CO_2 levels at 420 parts per million that winter and Mother Nature stayed restless and feverish. The weather had gone mad and the years that followed bore grim testimony to that madness.

Over time, the 30s became known as the Lost Decade. The weather had turned from dangerous to deadly, and people began to comprehend the real costs of climate change.

The hellish decade ended with the unexpected eruption of Mt. Cameroon in West Africa. No one had anticipated it. To everyone's delight, Mother Nature dramatically cooled the Earth. Mt. Cameroon, a massive strato-volcano, spewed out more than 46 cubic miles of ejecta into the atmosphere, cooling the planet by 11 percent. That date, October 6, 2037, marked the end of the Lost Decade. Everyone knew the cooling wouldn't last. The immense number of aerosols the eruption blasted into the atmosphere would eventually wash away as acid rain. But for a few brief years, the endless heat wave was over.

It was during this window that the Mylerium Project was devised. The thinking was that the nanomirrors could take over after the cooling effects of Mt. Cameroon wore off. It's a brilliant plan, but it won't end well.

A History of Failure

"Professor Worthington?" Rubic asked, approaching a man wearing a black sports coat and a dark brown turtleneck.

"Yes?"

"I have a package for you."

"What sort of package?" Professor Worthington inquired as he stared down Rubic disapprovingly.

Rubic was aware of how he might look to a man of Professor Worthington's stature. He was dressed in dirty jeans and a dark blue hoodie, his skinny arm outstretched, clutching a brown manila envelope.

"It's from Mr. Warren," Rubic said.

"Is this Mr. Warren from Chicago?"

"Yes, sir."

Professor Worthington paused, suddenly seeming apprehensive. "It must be pretty damn important for Warren to have sent a runner all the way from Chicago," he mused. "How is he doing?"

"I've never met him. He hired me to deliver this and that's all you need to know."

"Do I owe you anything?"

"No, sir—Warren's covering all of my costs. All he asks is that you not share the information contained in this package with anyone at Harvard, or put any of this information into the Internet or any storage device that COI might be able to access. I have no idea what's in these packages, but it's safe to say the NSA will probably be knocking on your door if they know you have whatever's in there."

"I'm not sure I want to know what's in here, but thanks anyway."

"Not a problem, I'm just doing my job."

With that, Rubic jumped on his bike and headed toward a hotel he had booked for the night. Come morning, he was back on the train, heading west en route to California.

Professor Mark Worthington looked at the home address scribbled on the envelope and could tell at a glance that it was Warren's handwriting. They had spent some time together after grad school working on a climate study project in the Sierra Nevada mountains. The package was indeed from his old friend.

Mark stuffed the envelope under his arm and continued walking toward his office. He was anxious to see what was inside but worried about the possible repercussions of getting involved with the NSA. No one wanted to face an investigation, least of all a Harvard professor with tenure.

Once in his office, Mark looked nervously around the room as if his quick survey could detect cameras and microphones that could fit inside a poppy seed. Realizing he was being overly paranoid and that he had no reason to suspect the NSA was eavesdropping on him, he picked up a letter opener and sliced open the top of the envelope. Its scant contents poured out onto his meticulously clean desktop. He read a letter that was essentially the same as the one Warren had sent Dr. Garrison at nearby MIT.

Unlike his colleague, Mark's initial reaction to the letter was that Warren was suffering from a mental breakdown. The CMC would never go ahead with the project if there was a remote possibility of the mirrors failing to self-destruct. Warren was correct, however, in describing the frightening consequences if the mirrors didn't disintegrate.

As one of the world's leading glaciologists, Professor Worthington was well informed about the pros and cons of the Mylerium Project. One of his contributions to the project was to measure the nanomirrors' potential impact on the last two strongholds of glacial ice left on the planet—east Antarctica and central Greenland. He determined that anything that could help reduce the summer melt would be beneficial. The only danger posed by the mirrors lay in their preprogrammed disintegration sequences. If they failed to sink back to Earth the following autumn, the results could be catastrophic. While their remaining in suspension might be a good thing for his beloved glaciers, Mark realized that the dangerous feedback loop caused by the combined reflective power of the mirrors and snowfall could impact the following year's growing season.

Reading through Warren's letter a second time, Mark realized it was imperative that he review Warren's research. He disconnected his personal iPad from Harvard's Ethernet connection and disabled the internal Wi-Fi systems just to be sure. He inserted Warren's nanodrive, opened its contents, and started poring over the complex organic chemistry and nanotechnology formulas that made the project possible. Mark realized Warren's work was brilliant. Within an hour, after scribbling down some of his own variations on Warren's methodology, it became apparent that it was highly probable the nanomirrors' built-in self-destruct program would fail. How could the CMC have missed this?

Mark's first instinct was to pick up his phone and call his connections at the CMC to demand they delay deployment of the project. As a glaciologist, he knew a long, cold winter could create a feedback loop leading to a much-delayed or failed spring. If spring failed, crop failure would be unavoidable. Mark didn't want to think about what might happen if the world's leading agricultural nations—Russia, Canada, China and the U.S.—failed to reap any harvest in the fall of 2044.

Worse still was the thought that the mirrors could remain in orbit for a second or third winter. Sure, the rapid sea rise would stop dead in its tracks and the few remaining glaciers would hang on to their dwindling ice caps, which appealed to Mark's glaciological inclinations. But watching millions, if not billions, of people die from starvation was an appalling thought.

Mark recalled that the Mylerium Project wasn't mankind's first attempt to come to terms with an overheated planet. In fact, the project was never designed to be a long-term solution to the climate problem at all. Rather, it would provide a temporary reprieve while the second generation of CO_2 scrubbers was constructed. The new scrubbers, which were to be located near empty oil wells, would take years to complete. Once operational, decades would pass before they could significantly reduce the massive amounts of CO_2 already in the atmosphere. The Mylerium Project would only arrest the warming climate until the matrix of atmospheric gases returned to preindustrial levels.

Mark also knew the largest obstacle for engineers working on the second-generation scrubbers was finding an energy source clean and reliable enough to power the massive filtering machines. It had taken billions of individual cars, trucks, planes, trains, factories, furnaces and machines to spew the CO_2 into the atmosphere and it would take even more energy to remove the gas. Nuclear fusion held the greatest promise, but progress toward obtaining a viable fusion reactor was painstakingly slow.

Mark recalled that mankind's first major attempt at geoengineering was in 2025. The experiment crashed and burned during its third year. The idea was to cool the Earth through a process called chemtrailing, which had its roots in secret weather-controlling weapons systems developed by the U.S. military around the turn of the 21st century.

The idea was simple. Experimenters would add reflective materials such as powdered aluminum and sulfur dioxide to jet fuel. As planes crisscrossed the world, the aerosol spray would naturally cool the planet.

In practice, the chemtrailing experiment worked as planned during the first few years. The ejected particles worked like the kilotons of volcanic dust hurled into the atmosphere by volcanoes, cooling the Earth by reflecting incoming sunlight. CO_2 traps and creates heat only after sunlight reflects off the planet and bounces back up as low frequency infrared radiation. So when high frequency visible light fails to reach the surface of the Earth, it reduces heating.

The chemtrailing experiment, with planes dispersing aluminum particles, worked flawlessly until military and passenger jets started falling from the sky. No one anticipated the damaging effects the reflective metals had on the inner workings of jet engines. After the fifth passenger jet crash in three months killed all 657 passengers on board, the FAA put an immediate halt to the project. Nobody determined exactly how the aluminum dust caused the engines to fail, but ultimately it didn't matter. No one was willing to continue with a shade creation project that killed innocent passengers, so it was never pursued again.

The first-generation scrubbers, produced under GSP-1 (Global Scrubbers Project 1), marked the second attempt to get rid of excess CO_2. Huge buildings cropped up along every oceanic coastline on Earth. They were intended to remove CO_2 directly from the atmosphere, using nothing but wind and fans to push air through their cleansing systems. Inside these massive structures resembling oversized plane hangars hung rows of a specialized plastic mesh designed to bind with CO_2 molecules in the atmosphere. When the mesh was sufficiently saturated with the gas, the doors of the building closed and the sheets were rinsed with sodium carbonate. The ensuing chemical reaction created sodium bicarbonate, or baking soda. The brine at the bottom was nothing more than baking soda and water, and could be channeled through an electrically charged CO_2 separator, breaking out the compound and compressing it to a "supercritical" state.

Once pressurized, the CO_2 behaved more like a fluid than a gas. Where to store the captured CO_2 provided the biggest problem. It was decided after heated debates to pump the CO_2 to the bottom of the world's deepest oceans, where the high pressures would lock it into the seafloor for centuries.

Preliminary tests proved the deep ocean storage theory to be viable. Once at the bottom, with the immense pressure of the seawater pressing down on it, the CO_2 turned to semi-frozen clathrates, a type of molecular compound similar to the methane clathrates naturally covering much of the ocean floor.

Because of the near-perfect test results, almost all of the GSP-1 scrubbers were positioned as close as possible to oceanic trenches. Several years after the system went fully operational in 2035, things started unraveling.

The incredible amount of CO_2 being pumped into the abyss changed ocean chemistry in ways no one had anticipated. Before long, the semi-frozen CO_2 thawed, then bubbled up from the ocean floor alongside an even more potent greenhouse gas—methane. The two gases were rapidly reentering the atmosphere, making the overall situation as bad, if not worse than before the scrubbers were put into operation.

It was an exercise in futility. Nations spent billions of dollars removing excess CO_2 from the atmosphere and pumping it into the oceans. Once there, it mixed with a far more potent greenhouse gas, methane, then bubbled back up and started trapping even more infrared heat. Scientists dubbed it our Sisyphean nightmare. By 2037, only scrubbers located near abandoned oil wells or deep underground, structurally stable geological formations were still in operation. The nearly 1000 other scrubbers had their operations curtailed dramatically because there was nowhere safe to pump the captured gas. Many were abandoned altogether. Meanwhile, everyone kept burning fossil fuels because they were the cheapest way to produce energy.

In 2036, when the Green Coalition was swept into office in a landslide, there was immediate talk of funding a GSP-2 (Global Scrubbing Project 2) that would place all of the CO_2-capturing buildings near abandoned oil wells, coal mines, or natural subterranean formations where the compressed gas could be stored with less risk of seepage. The project was in an advanced planning stage when Mt. Cameroon blew, cooling the planet naturally.

Piggybacking on that stroke of good luck, world leaders and scientists scrambled to come up with a viable way to cool the Earth without facing unanticipated methane releases, falling airliners or acid rain.

And so the future of mankind became tied to the Mylerium Project. If the crop-rich Northern Hemisphere could be cooled enough to offset the heat created by excess greenhouse gases, people could survive until those gases were safely removed from the atmosphere. The Mylerium Project's signature nanomirrors were far more effective at reflecting sunlight than the aerosols carried by the jetliners years earlier.

After carefully reviewing Warren's research, Dr. Worthington realized the Mylerium Project was another disaster in the making. He wondered how these flaws could have made it through the CMC, as they seemed obvious in Warren's equations.

Mark removed the nanodrive from his computer without saving it to his hard drive. He knew that once he reconnected to the Net, the NSA might conduct a random sweep of his computer. He wouldn't risk them discovering any illegal data.

Tomorrow Mark would call Warren to talk about the weather. Though it would never come up in their conversation, he knew it was going to get very cold, very soon.

Bozeman Recapture

"I've heard good things about it."

"Well, it won't pay as well as the CMC, but it's time for a change."

"We've been expecting this for a while, Warren, and wish you the best of luck. When do you start?"

"I told them I could make it out a few weeks after the deployment gets underway."

"You didn't mention your flawed research?"

"No, Dr. Hansen, I think the review committee made it pretty clear that my 'faulty' research never happened. Why would I talk to Bozeman Recapture about something that never happened?"

"You have a point," Dr. Hansen said, ignoring Warren's sarcastic tone.

"Are the first shuttles still scheduled to get underway on the 22nd?"

"Yes, all systems are go at this point. The shuttles are being loaded with the raw materials even as we speak. Unless something unforeseen comes up, the mirrors should be in place by early April, just as things start heating up again."

"They'll work perfectly this summer," Warren said, struggling not to cringe.

"We hope so. Say, isn't Bozeman Recapture involved with the next generation of industrial scrubbers, the ones being developed for GSP-2?"

"Yeah, they're working with this bioengineered mesh fabric that's supposed to be far more efficient than what we used with GSP-1. They probably hired me for my expertise in nanopolymers. Of course, my background with climate change here at the CMC doesn't hurt either."

"You'll like it out there in Big Sky Country."

"I'll miss Chicago."

"You'll do just fine, Warren. We'll miss you. Thanks for letting me know about this in person. I appreciate all you've done for us here at the CMC and I know I speak for everyone here when I wish you the very best of luck in Bozeman."

"Thanks, Maddox."

With that, Warren got up and stepped slowly and deliberately out of Dr. Hansen's office. Part of him wanted to run. Instead, Warren smiled when he turned around, but was careful not to let his boss notice. He was thinking ahead toward the big freeze. The last place he wanted to be a year from now was Chicago, or any urban center for that matter.

Bozeman Recapture, a medium-sized firm with fewer than 200 workers, offered Warren exactly what he was looking for—a remote outpost with a moderate climate and a 40-acre spread. Warren wasn't moving to Bozeman for the salary or the benefits. He was moving to survive.

When Warren's resume appeared in Bozeman Recapture's inbox, it was a given that he would be hired. The personnel director, Rebecca, was shocked when she opened up the attachments that held his extensive resume. She forwarded it to the president's office immediately, thinking their firm had received Warren's resume by mistake.

The president, Leonard Gibson, looked over the materials and told Rebecca to schedule a 3-D Skype interview with Dr. Randolf as soon as possible. He wasn't going to take any chances with this prospect. He could not have imagined a more qualified candidate for the position. Everyone involved in high-tech plastic polymers was familiar with Dr. Randolf's work and he could have easily demanded twice the money Bozeman Recapture was offering. Leonard was more nervous about the upcoming job interview than was Warren.

Rebecca, per her boss's request, responded to Warren's email within the hour and a face-to-face holograph meeting was scheduled for 10 a.m. the following morning.

After a lengthy conversation about Warren's position, Leonard Gibson unexpectedly changed directions with his interview. "Can I ask you something, Dr. Randolf—something off the cuff?"

"Certainly, Mr. Gibson."

"You can call me Leonard. Why Bozeman Recapture? Why move from the CMC to a small firm?"

"It's a fair question. I've been holed up here in Chicago for the last six years, five of which have been dedicated 24/7 to the Mylerium Project. I guess I felt I needed a change of scene. I love the Windy City but, having been raised in Minnesota, I miss the outdoors. I used to love to ski, to canoe and kayak and I felt Montana was the perfect fit."

"I assume you have reviewed our salary and benefits package?" Leonard asked hopefully. He left the implication unsaid: *We can't pay you what you're worth.*

"I read the job description and I think the salary range you've posted for the position is fair. It's not always about the money, is it?"

Leonard smiled, flattered by the idea that Warren would want to join his firm on its own merits. "Well, you may be right. I must admit, I'm already well acquainted with your work, as is nearly everyone in this office. If you're serious about wanting the position, we'd be honored to have you on the team."

"I'm dead serious. If it's OK with you, let's consider it a done deal."

"We'll send the necessary disclosures, contracts and paperwork off to you shortly. When can you start?"

"I'm planning to come out two weeks after deployment, but I'd like some time to look around for a small farm outside of the city. Nothing fancy, just a small place with some acreage, and, if possible, a barn."

"We've got an excellent real estate firm we work with for all of our transfers. I'll get you the contact information when we send you the forms."

"That'd be great. I'll see you in a little over a month then, right?"

"We'll start you May first, if that works for you."

"May first sounds perfect. I'm excited to get to know the team and learn more about the biomesh capturing systems you're working on."

"Great, we'll be in touch."

"Goodbye."

The holographic projectors were switched off. As Dr. Randolf's image faded into thin air, Leonard Gibson was excited at the prospect of having this man join Bozeman Recapture.

The fact that one of the best minds in the nation elected to relocate to the middle of Montana was nothing short of amazing. But there was something odd about Dr. Randolf's decision that made Leonard wonder why he was coming out west. He couldn't put his finger on it, but the scenario seemed too good to be true. Having been in business for years, he wondered if there might be other reasons, beyond the "back to nature" argument, that brought such talent to Bozeman Recapture. Only time would tell.

Rubic's Call

"Where are you now?" Yeva asked worriedly.

"On a train heading west."

"To the coast?"

"I'd rather not say—you know how it is."

"Yeah, I do."

"It's gone well so far. Four down and three to go."

"I've missed you."

"Me too. I shouldn't be more than two weeks if all keeps going smoothly. These first four were a piece of cake and hopefully the last three will be the same way. What's up in Chicago?"

"Pretty quiet. It's already getting hot outside and it's only April. I sure hope those mirror things work. I don't know if my plants can handle another hot summer. The effects of the Mt. Cameroon eruption are wearing out."

"The mirrors will work just fine and we'll have a nice, cool summer like they had in the old days."

"I hope so."

"I don't want to talk very long so I'm signing off. I'll give you a call after I make the coast."

"Love ya."

"Love you too."

Yeva hung up the phone and smiled. She was glad to know Rubic hadn't run into any trouble on the longest cross-country run of his career. She could also tell that he hadn't been doing any Rapture7. She could hear it in his voice and his sense of self-confidence, which rose precipitously when he was clean. *This run might do him some good,* she thought as she turned on the television to kick back for the evening. She eventually fell asleep on the couch as the screen blared American Idol, Season 41.

Meanwhile, Rubic was working his way through Nebraska on the high-speed train to San Francisco. From there he would bike to Stanford, then take a commuter train further south to San Jose. He would then have to double back toward the northernmost reaches of the state to visit a woman who lived outside of Crescent City. His plan was to continue north after that and take the cross-county train out of Portland, Oregon, back to Chicago. *Two weeks maximum and I'll be done,* he thought as he whisked by Nebraska's wheat fields at 250 miles an hour.

The Chase

"We have a facial at the train station in San Francisco."
"Who is it?"

"That runner with the weird key thing—let me look him up." The NSA operative typed a few words into his keyboard. "Rubic Chang."

"What on God's Earth takes him to San Francisco? That's a long way from an empty pizza box in downtown Chicago. He's got to be on to something pretty damn interesting."

"What do you want us to do?"

"Let's pick him up for questioning."

"We got the facial recognition hit ten minutes ago. Do you want me to dispatch some of our west coast agents right now?"

"Yes, absolutely."

"I'll get to it."

With a few more keystrokes, he notified the San Francisco office to deploy two agents, who soon grabbed their raincoats and headed out in their electric van toward the interstate train station. All of the surveillance tools available to the NSA started tracking this new target. Several ID tapes and photos of Rubic, taken when he removed the electronic locker key from the pizza box, were sent to NSA teams throughout the Bay Area, from Oakland to Sausalito.

Within minutes, a camera on Hill Street picked up Rubic riding his carbon-fiber bike. Once they found Rubic in real time, they could coordinate and monitor his every move with scores of security cameras—some visibly mounted on light posts and buildings, others hidden and all but impossible to find with the naked eye. Should one of the cameras not be able to follow him, they could turn to satellite reconnaissance on a clear day, but it was cloudy and raining in the Bay Area and if Rubic reached a rural highway, they might have to use infrared heat scanning to track him. With the sidewalks filled with people, many of them on bikes and scooters, it would be nearly impossible to single out any individual. Today, if the cameras lost Rubic, the two field agents would be on their own.

Rubic was pedaling toward his hotel room. All he had with him was a small backpack with a change of clothes and the remaining three envelopes. He had booked a room under a pseudonym after the train ride to catch up on some sleep before heading south the next day toward Stanford. Rubic was sure he could reach the campus by morning to deliver an envelope to a woman named Stephanie Bankoul.

Suddenly a van rolled into the middle of the next intersection as Rubic came flying down the street. Two men jumped out of the vehicle and drew their handguns. These weren't civilians.

"Rubic Chang, stop at once!"

Rubic was startled when he heard his name being called and immediately snapped his head in the direction of the officer. The dark raincoats, the drawn stun guns and the black van confirmed his worst nightmare. Rubic had no idea as to how in hell the NSA had gotten on to him, but now was not the time to ask that question. He had two options. He could stop, get off his bike, and surrender himself or he could run.

He decided to run. He stomped down on his bike pedals and sped off.

The agents let go with a volley of plasma charges. Each shot resembled a white, electrified bullet that left a trail behind it, like a perfectly straight lightning bolt. Rubic, who was already going downhill, started pedaling furiously in an effort to pick up speed. He didn't know San Francisco well, but he knew he wasn't far from Golden Gate Park. If he could make it there, he might be able to ditch the agents. There were plenty of heavily forested and unmonitored areas where he could hide until dark.

The volley of plasma charges narrowly missed Rubic but one errant shot hit a pedestrian crossing the street nearby. The NSA agents didn't bother to tend to the injured citizen, who crumpled to the pavement the instant the charge made contact. Instead, they jumped back into their van and followed the target. Collateral damage was not considered a worthwhile reason for any NSA agent to break off an authorized pursuit. Seconds later a car accidently ran over the unlucky pedestrian.

The NSA agent on the passenger side stuck a police light up on the top of the van while the other agent flipped on the sirens. They turned around and had no trouble spotting Rubic a block ahead of them.

"What the hell's he doing? I can't believe he's running."

"You never know what they're going to do. I've had several of these assholes shoot back at me. This guy doesn't look like he's carrying a gun, but who the hell knows?"

"Should we flip our guns to lethal?"

"No, our orders are to bring him in alive. We can't get a lot of info interrogating a dead guy."

"Right."

The van was within 50 yards of Rubic and gaining on him. Rubic kept glancing back and knew they could reach him in seconds. He had to leave the roadway at once.

He saw an opening between two long sets of row houses—a passageway too narrow for the van. He took a hard right and squeezed into the space, which was so narrow that his handlebars were just a few inches from either side of the buildings. At the speed Rubic was going, a wipeout would break bones at best, but getting caught didn't strike him as a better alternative.

The NSA van screamed to a halt in front of the opening and the driver opened fire with his plasma gun again, sending half a dozen charges after Rubic.

Rubic was already too far down the hill for any of the shots to reach him. He could hear the reports and see a few charges fly past him in streaks of pure, white light. Most of them flew over his head as he continued steering toward an intersecting alley.

Once he hit the alley he had to decide which way to go. Having been chased many times before, not by NSA agents, but by Rapture7 dealers, local police and gang members, Rubic chose neither. He waited a few seconds and doubled back. It was an unexpected move that had worked for him in the past and he prayed it would work again. He figured the agents would follow him around the alley and anticipate him to continue running away.

This time he was right.

By the time the NSA van came screaming around the corner, entering the alleyway at close to 50 miles per hour, Rubic had already pedaled back up the narrow passageway. He ducked into a similar opening on the other side of the street.

What the field agents couldn't see, the cameras did. Within seconds the operatives monitoring their computer screens informed the agents that their target had doubled back and was heading northwest toward Golden Gate Park.

The agents sped up the alley, turning left at the first opening. They suddenly found themselves in a snarl of traffic. The jam was the result of a pedestrian killed up the block by a car turning onto Hill Street—the same pedestrian the agents had accidently stunned.

"You'll have to head back down the alley—traffic's a mess that direction," informed one of the surveillance agents to the driver.

"What the hell happened?"

"The guy you stunned was run over by a car. He's dead."

"Shit. People should learn to drive around here."

"Back out and head down the alley you came from—you can catch up to him by heading north at the second intersection down."

It was too late. By the time they got the van turned around, Rubic had cleared the edge of Golden Gate Park and there was no way they could follow him once he was inside the labyrinth of gardens, fields and forests. For the moment, Rubic was safe, but now the rules of engagement had changed. Rubic was no longer an unknown back packer making a nationwide run. He was a wanted man, and that spelled trouble.

King Coal

Warren had no way of knowing where Rubic was or how he was handling his deliveries. But he did get a call from Albion a few days earlier. They talked about the weather, which was a good sign.

Picking who to notify about the impending disaster was the most difficult choice Warren had faced in years. His parents were gone and as an only child, he didn't have any siblings to warn. Warren realized early on it would be impossible to save everyone he wanted to save, or even warn everyone he wanted to warn, so he had to choose. It tortured him for months.

Dr. Albion Garrison, his wife Cecilia and their two sons were the first on his list. Albion and Warren had been roommates at MIT in their undergraduate days and they had remained close despite having taken divergent life paths. He knew Albion would see what Warren saw within the programming and his friend would likely elect to join him.

Warren had yet to hear from any of the others but that didn't surprise him. He had always felt that a few wouldn't want to get involved, or might find his analysis inconclusive. They would do little more than destroy the nanodrive, the envelope and the letter and be done with it. Some wouldn't want anything to do with a runner, the NSA, or the subterfuge involved.

In a way, Warren had worked this possibility into his master plan. Gathering enough food, medicine, solar cells, generators and water for 15 to 25 people would be enough of a challenge. If everyone, along with their children and extended families, who received his letter signed on, the final number would be closer to 50. That would be a daunting number to deal with.

The last letter, the one directed at Ann Hadley in Crescent City, California, would almost certainly be ignored. Ann and Warren had broken up several years ago when she decided Chicago was not the place for her. Having been born and raised in Crescent City, Ann wanted the peace and quiet of a natural, earthy landscape. They had been together for many years before Ann packed up and headed west. Warren still loved her but they hadn't spoken in a long time. They would exchange greetings on Facebook now and again, but there was nothing in these brief messages from Ann to indicate she had any intention of coming back to Chicago or, for that matter, back to him.

Maybe now that I'm moving to Montana, she'll decide to join us in Bozeman, Warren thought. Despite this faint hope, he wasn't optimistic.

All of these thoughts and more kept racing through Warren's mind as he monitored the forthcoming shuttle deployments and prepared for his move out west. His journal became a release from the day-to-day grind. It was a brief respite from the tedium of waiting.

March 15, 2043

The feedback loops pushed us over the edge. It wasn't just the fact that we added a notch or two to the Keeling Curve every year, like some statistical stairway to a house on fire–no, it was those unexpected, unanticipated feedback loops that really accelerated the pace of change.

During the early years of climate change, just after the turn of the 21st century, we ignored what would eventually become one of the biggest challenges we faced: how to keep cool in an increasingly hot planet. Air conditioning was not designed for the relentless string of record-breaking heat waves that became the norm. Back in the early years, from 2000 through 2020, only 10 percent of our electrical energy came from renewable sources.

Hydroelectric sources provided much of that power, but we also had wind, solar, biomass, geothermal, and some tidal and wave energy. Most of the world's electricity still came from coal, which creates nearly three tons of CO_2 for every ton of that black rock burned. In those early years, before wind, solar and tidal power made a dent in king coal, people used that dirty black fossil to produce 78 percent of the world's grid energy. In rising economies like China and India, coal plants were built at an alarming rate—often more than one plant every two weeks.

Winters grew milder and the demand for energy to keep our homes warm diminished. The unanticipated trouble came from the other direction—from the increasingly hot summers in places like Texas, Spain, India and southern China. As more and more people turned to air conditioning to make the steaming summers livable, demand for electricity during the summer months skyrocketed. More electricity demand meant more coal demand, which meant an increase in CO_2, which meant an increase in summer temperatures, which led to burning more coal.

This is exactly what a negative feedback loop looks like. Over time, the extreme summers more than offset the energy savings from warmer winters, as most of humanity lived close to the equator where everyone sought cooling from the relentless heat. By the middle of the '20s, the cycle was out of control. The huge middle class in India and China could afford Western conveniences. That meant cars as well as air-conditioned homes, shopping centers and office buildings. Coal was being burned at unprecedented levels. Those levels would soon deliver us the Lost Decade.

By 2026 the desert southwest of the U.S. was all but uninhabitable. There was serious talk of erecting massive domes over entire cities to cool them. One city in Saudi Arabia did just that. The experimental town, called Al-Shallah, was constructed beneath the largest geodesic dome ever built. It survived for more than a dozen years before the outside temperatures overwhelmed it and the cost of continuing to cool three square kilometers of desert became unaffordable, even to the oil-rich Saudis. Once the cooling system was turned off, the dome became a greenhouse and temperatures within the structure skyrocketed to more than 145 degrees. The city was abandoned. Today, it's half covered in sand. Meanwhile, the big coal corporations laid waste to the mountaintops of West Virginia, their big shovels, trucks and trains making off with black gold. The Powder River Basin went from rolling *prairie to a desolate wasteland by 2030. China tunneled its coal seams deeper than anyone thought possible. Russia, Canada, South Africa and India were all mining at a fever pitch. Companies profited in cash but no one in the industry was willing to pick up the true cost of their trash. That trash came in the form of acid rain, soot, toxic emissions, ash, sludge, toxic chemicals and pollution, costing thousands of coal workers their lives. The biggest garbage heap of them all was the atmosphere, which absorbed billions of tons of CO_2. There was no such thing as clean coal—just well-connected and well-moneyed coal capable of convincing people otherwise.*

In 2037, when the Greens banned the construction of coal-fired plants in the U.S., we were finally on the right track. But by then global temperatures had climbed some five degrees and other, more alarming feedback loops had been triggered. Methane belched out of the Canadian and Siberian tundra and bubbled up from the ocean floor. Methane is 20 times worse than CO_2 when it comes to warming the Earth. The die was cast for a hot, uncertain future for mankind.

The Faceist

Yeva was worried. Rubic had promised to call her after arriving in San Francisco but it had been three days and Yeva still hadn't heard from him. She had tried his cell phone, only to discover that service to that number had been discontinued. It wasn't good.

Yeva could not have known about Rubic Chang's change of plans after eluding the NSA agents. It was more than just a change of plans—it was a change of face. After ditching the agents and the ever-present, ever watchful cameras of the NSA, Rubic slept in a Monterey pine grove in the middle of Golden Gate Park. He didn't dare try pedaling to the hotel room he had booked.

The next morning he wanted to cry as he walked away from his expensive carbon-fiber bike. He left it lying there in the bushes, knowing it would be impossible to use his bike from here on out. By now the NSA would be double-checking every male bicyclist in the Bay Area, running their facial and body-style scanners to find him. Next he did what every compromised runner did with their cell phone and pitched it into the closest body of water. In Rubic's case, this happened to be the Koi pond in the Japanese tea gardens.

Rubic marched out of the park, his face buried in his hoodie, and headed toward Haight Street to purchase a different-colored sweatshirt. Until he could find a Faceist, he would have to do his best to keep his face hidden. He knew that somewhere along this infamous street he could find someone who could direct him to a facial reconstruction specialist—a Faceist. If he didn't get his face reconfigured within the next 24 hours, the NSA would find him. He walked into the first T-shirt shop he could find.

"I'm looking for a sweatshirt," Rubic mumbled. "One with a hood on it if you carry them."

"Over there, to the right. There's a whole rack of 'em. You want something that says San Francisco on it?"

"No."

"Most of them have something or other on them, but there might be a few that don't. Go ahead and check 'em out."

Rubic rifled through the clothes on the rack. He knew he was a medium but he wanted to find a large, or extra-large—the bigger, the better. He found a dark blue hoodie without any lettering or images of the Golden Gate Bridge on it. It was an extra-large. Rubic knew any distinguishing words or images on the front would just draw more attention. Plain and nondescript would work best.

"Will this be all?" the clerk asked hopefully, eyeing the hoodie-clad stranger.

"Not really."

The clerk could tell by the man's tone that something else was up. The first thought that came into the clerk's mind was that he was looking to score. The Haight-Ashbury district had not changed much since the 1960s. Folk singers still worked every corner with beat-up guitars and young, pretty girls still strolled down the street wearing miniskirts with paisley designs and psychedelic face paint. Rapture7, which was illegal in California, had replaced marijuana for the most part, but there were still a handful of legal medical marijuana dispensaries scattered throughout the district. Haight-Ashbury wasn't eager to let go of its past.

"What else can I get you?"

"Are we cool?"

"Yeah, we're cool."

The man's voice lowered to a whisper. "Do you know of any Faceists working around here?"

The clerk, who was expecting this kid to ask about scoring some R7, was caught off guard. He didn't want any trouble. Asking about facial reconstruction was trouble.

"I don't know shit about that kind of thing."

"Do you know who does?"

The clerk hesitated; worried he might get himself into some kind of NSA bullshit if he gave this stranger a name.

The man reached into his pocket for and pulled out a $200 bill.

"Will this cover the sweater?" he asked. The clerk noticed the man's hands trembling as he passed on the creased bill.

"If you're looking for a good cup of coffee, I recommend the Red Victorian Café," the clerk said carefully, pocketing the money. "It's a half a block up on the other side of the street. You should find what you need there."

"Thanks. Thanks a lot."

Rubic slipped on his new hoodie and drew the drawstring up so tight that it seemed like he was peering out through a tunnel. He walked quickly back on Haight Street as he headed away from the park. He crossed the street at the next intersection and spotted the Red Victorian Café. It was crowded but there was an empty seat at the counter. Rubic walked in and sat down.

"Coffee, black. No sugar or cream, just black."

"Got it," the waitress replied.

She poured his cup of coffee and set it down in front of him, pausing expectantly. Rubic looked at her through his tunnel.

"A guy down the street said you might be able to help me find someone to give me a facelift."

"That's not in my job description," the waitress said. "Let me get the owner."

The waitress disappeared into the back section of the café for a few minutes while Rubic loosened his hoodie just enough to sip some coffee. He hadn't slept well the night before and the fresh coffee helped. The waitress returned a few seconds later with an older, tired-faced woman and pointed toward Rubic. Her long hair was kept in two tight braids that were wrapped across her head. She had a weathered face that spoke of too many years in the Haight-Ashbury district.

"So I hear you might need some cosmetics," the older lady said. "Is that right?"

"Yeah, my jowls are sagging."

"I'll bet. It's going to cost you a pretty penny. Do you have the money?"

"How much?"

"Depends on how much work you need done. Take your coffee and follow me. The price is what it is. No negotiation."

Rubic picked up his coffee and went to the end of the counter, where an opening took him to the rear side of the café. From there, the two of them continued into an alley behind the building. A few steps away from the café's back door, a cement stairway led them to the basement apartment of a large row house. The woman knocked loudly on the door.

No one answered.

She knocked even louder the second time. Rubic was worried that the sound of her knocking might attract unwanted attention.

"Don't worry—we sweep the alley all the time for bugs. No one's watching. This guy's half deaf, but he's good at what he does."

A minute later you could hear someone inside working the deadbolts and chains, getting the door open.

"What's up, Rose?"

"This guy says he needs a facelift and tells me he's got the money too."

"Sounds good."

"See you around, stranger," Rose said as she turned around and left Rubic standing next to this old, odd-looking man wearing a "Flower Power" T-shirt and dirty blue jeans.

"Come on in, I don't bite," said the man in the doorway.

"OK."

Once inside they got right down to business.

"Let me take a look at what I'm working with."

Rubic undid the drawstring and showed this old man his face.

"Shit, what the hell are you? Arab-Japanese or some goddamn thing?"

"I'm half Jamaican and half Chinese."

"That's gotta be a bitch."

"Not really."

"So who you hiding from?"

"Does that matter?"

"Damn right it matters. If it's your ex-wife or some drug dealer we don't have to do shit to make you go away. If it's the fucking NSA we've got some major work to do. Now which is it?"

"The latter."

"I thought so, judging from the way you're wearing that hoodie. How long have you been running?"

"I've been on a run for the past two weeks, but they found me yesterday afternoon. I don't know how in the hell they found me, but they did. Maybe the guy who hired me has been picked up. But they're on to me.

"Last night I slept in the park. If I don't get some work done they'll find me by the end of the week."

"Christ, with your weird fuckin' looks I'm amazed they don't have you already. It's one thing to work with someone who looks halfway normal, but you're a special order. Quite the challenge."

"How much is this going to cost?"

"A grand."

Both knew the price didn't matter. If Rubic didn't get his face changed enough to fool the NSA, he wouldn't last a week once he hit the streets. Sooner or later the angle would be just right and one of the millions of facial recognition scanners would recognize Rubic Chang. It wasn't a matter of if, but when. Next time they might deploy a dozen agents and not even a nearby park could help him escape. He would be arrested and interrogated. He needed a new face, period.

Shape Shifter

"How the hell did we lose him?" the NSA's San Francisco director shouted. "We had him in our grasp and now he's gone. He's clearly doing something we should know about. If it was just a drug deal, he would have surrendered. It's bigger than that, but what the hell is it?"

"Without catching him, we don't have a clue."

"Then let's catch him."

"If he's got money, he'll change his face."

"He can change his face all he wants—he can't change his body shape."

"That's always a long shot, though. We'll waste a lot of time on false positives."

"That's not my problem. I want this kid taken in for interrogation. I want to find out what the hell is going on. Is he a part of the underground? Is he working for some burners? However we get this done, let's get on it and find this asshole. Do you understand? Do you hear me?"

The two agents standing in front of the director's desk nodded mutely.

The first order of business was to sweep the park for anything helpful. Using satellite-based magnetic scanners, they found Rubic's abandoned bike before noon. While the carbon frame didn't show, the metal gears did—they were large enough to reveal the bike's whereabouts, even from 300 kilometers away in space. The cell phone, with all the potential leads embedded in its memory, eluded the NSA. It remained safely at the bottom of a goldfish pond.

The agents were able to trace the bike back to its original purchase in Chicago a few years earlier but that lead only verified Rubic was the original owner.

Field agents worked the streets surrounding the park, as did hundreds of cameras scattered across the Bay Area.

It was all to no avail. Finding Rubic again would be a challenge. The suspect's face would likely be gone within the next few days if he was smart. They also knew that there were some skilled Faceists working in San Francisco—special operators with updated and illegal knowledge of the NSA's facial scanning technology.

The ubiquitous, unsleeping scanning machines registered millions of faces a second all over the country. Anybody who took too long to load or was flagged as an unlikely match was kicked out of the search parameters within microseconds. The key points had to match the search algorithm—if one or more did not, the face was rejected long before any NSA agent could render their personal opinion. The sheer size of America's internal espionage machine was often a burden.

Professional Faceists knew the machines' weaknesses. The U.S. underground still had the ability to hack into different sectors of the NSA's amorphous main frames to outmaneuver them. It was an ongoing battle. The NSA kept doing everything it could to prevent intrusions into their systems while the hackers did everything they could to compromise the government's ability to spy. It was an ethereal battlefield of computer codes, malware and firewalls.

The old man in San Francisco worked silently on Rubic's face. He injected living cells into his cheek bones and removed microscopic layers of fat cells from his chin. He knew what cued off the scanners.

After a few days of healing, Rubic Chang would be able to take the train back east without triggering another hit. To change his height, the old man explained, Rubic could buy a pair of platform shoes to give him another inch and a half in stature. That would make the body scanners struggle to pick him up.

There were traps that the Faceist could not help him with. Retina scanners were the worst. Unless he could afford to have both eyes replaced in an expensive and risky process, Rubic couldn't outsmart the retina scans. Fingerprints were another problem. The Faceist had an inexpensive fix for fingerprints though, and it wasn't costly or painful.

Regrettably, Rubic was already in the criminal database, so he knew that a retina scan or a fingerprint hit would uncover him. The only place he might encounter a retina scan or fingerprint machine, however, was at a train station. But because the process took some time, scans were only performed at random. Both retina and fingerprint scans were mandatory on all flights, so flying home was out of the question, even if he tried to travel around the world just to reach Chicago. He would have to risk the trains or use an electric car—or else he'd never be able to get back to Yeva and Chicago. Both options posed additional problems Rubic didn't want to think about at the moment. The first thing he needed to do was to finish this run. He'd deal with tomorrow, tomorrow.

The Mylerium Project

The deployment went off without a hitch on March 22, 2043. The first shuttle, one of 125 worldwide, launched from an airport in Bangor, Maine, at 6:21 a.m. The remaining seven shuttles stationed in the U.S. followed suit. By 9 a.m. EST, all seven unmanned shuttles were dispersing their 150,000-kilogram payloads at the top of the stratosphere, more than 30 miles above the Earth's surface.

Across the north Pacific, identical jet-black shuttles resembling a cross between the space shuttle Columbia and an oversized B-2 stealth bomber took to the skies. Each shuttle, whether it left from Siberia or Beijing, held the same cargo and used the same dispersion method. Each plane was equipped with two high-pressure nozzles at the rear of the cargo bay that ejected the dust-like nanomirrors, creating thin, grayish contrails that lingered for hours. From the ground, people could barely see these contrails with the naked eye. When conditions were ideal, they looked like thin silver pencil lines high in a deep blue sky.

To be effective over the vast region they needed to cover, the engineers and scientists had planned to have each shuttle conduct one flight a day for 30 days. That would amount to millions of tons of material. This quantity was calculated to be sufficient because nanomirrors were 100 times more effective than naturally occurring reflective materials such as volcanic dust or clouds.

The shuttles were designed as huge unmanned drones to reduce the risk the giant flying sprayers posed to human pilots. Part airplane and part rocket ship, they flew along the edge of space. The models indicated that the cooling was most effective in the uppermost reaches of the atmosphere. It was geoengineering on a truly global scale.

As promised, Warren stayed with the project through the second week of its operation. By then, the process was functioning smoothly. Each flight took six to seven hours and then the drone would return to its base airport, refuel and refill its cargo tanks with another payload of aerosol. To spread the particles out, a different compass heading was taken every day, covering the widest possible geographical range from each of the base camps located across the planet. Only Antarctica, which was still hanging on to most of its ice, lacked its own shuttle. The Southern Hemisphere received far less coverage, having fewer people and less cropland.

Warren knew vast tracts of stratosphere would be left untouched—especially over the North Pacific—but the nanomirrors were designed to spread out naturally via high-altitude winds.

Knowing his job was done at the CMC and finding he could finally take a breather, Warren made the following entry in his journal:

April 5, 2043

I leave for Bozeman in two days. Everything has been sold—the apartment, the furnishings, the bike, the car—everything. I'll refit my entire life when I reach Montana a few days from now. I've already put a deposit down on a small farm 20 miles from my office. It encompasses 40 acres and includes a three-bedroom, ranch-style house and an old horse barn. It will become my survival camp if the mirrors remain in orbit. Of course, if the CMC is right, all this will be for naught. My paranoia about this project will prove baseless.

Sadly, although I hope I'm wrong, I'm almost positive my analysis of the flawed programming is correct. In that case, the stores of food, medical supplies and solar generators will save us. This may be the longest, worst winter in the history of mankind. If I'm wrong, then I'm just another conspiracy theorist living alone in the backwoods of Montana. I guess I'm willing to take that chance.

Time and again I wonder how we got here. Why didn't we see the handwriting on the wall, the obvious signs from the beginning of climate change? In the 2020s, when the feedbacks that were predicted decades earlier started to accelerate, the powerful and politically connected fossil fuel industry started in again with the same old lies, only bigger and better than ever. Those lies all but killed us.

Take the unprecedented increase in methane gas levels, for example. We predicted this dramatic rise in atmospheric methane early on, long before the Greenland ice cap started vanishing. Even in the 1970s, when we first discovered oil on the North Slope of Alaska, the die was cast. Back when we first built the pipeline during the winter, people could drive on that frozen road for months on end. As the decades passed and the temperatures continued to warm, the ice road thawed earlier and froze later, making the trek to the

North Slope increasingly dangerous. As time went by, it became clear that the permafrost was melting.

In Siberia and northern Canada, vast stretches of tundra turned to mush as temperatures across the northern tier of the planet warmed precipitously. The Arctic Ocean, once covered in ice throughout most of the year, became ice-free for the first time in recorded history in the summer of 2029. Oil and gas corporations, always on the hunt for new reserves to tap into, were delighted they could now access the extensive fields of crude oil and natural gas beneath that once-frozen sea. They never stopped to think that the fuels they drilled for had caused the ice's disappearance.

As the permafrost thawed, it released a staggering 800 billion metric tons of CO_2 and methane from rotting bogs and decaying soil. The snowfall that once reflected winter sunlight back into space came later every fall and melted earlier every spring. The Arctic didn't experience a six degree Fahrenheit warming like the rest of the planet. Because of negative feedbacks, that area warmed an unprecedented 12 degrees. At those temperatures, it didn't take long for the three-kilometer thick ice dome resting atop Greenland to react.

By the mid-30s, the great glaciers of Greenland were calving–breaking up into smaller chunks that melted faster. The meltwater on top of the ice dome rushed through thousands of newly formed rivulets to the base several kilometers below. Once there, the rushing water accelerated the entire process by melting the subsurface of the ice, making it easier for the calving glaciers to slide into the sea. By 2034 the world's seas had risen close to a meter.

Coastal cities from Asia to North America were under siege. The Center for Meteorological Controls was relocated from New York to Chicago. The models indicated Manhattan would be uninhabitable in a few decades. The Big Apple wasn't designed to handle an Atlantic Ocean two meters higher than when the city was founded. Today, half the subways in Manhattan are already closed due to saltwater intrusion and the seawall surrounding the city won't hold back the rising seas forever.

When the melting permafrost started to exhale its trapped methane, things started seriously heating up across the planet. Unlike CO_2, which can linger in the atmosphere for 200 years, methane only remains in the atmosphere for a decade. But the sheer volume of methane seeping out of the immense expance of tundra made that statistic meaningless. The feedback loop fed upon itself until vast regions of the Arctic bubbled up methane gas *throughout their summer months. The enormous size of the permafrost zone, covering millions of square kilometers across Northern Europe, Siberia, Canada and Alaska, made any attempt to capture or contain the gas impractical. Scientists explored the concept of burning it off, but it proved impossible. Since the retreat of the last ice age, some 11,000 years ago, this gas had been held captive within the permafrost. As the permafrost thawed, so too thawed the methane clathrates—those crystalline molecular structures that kept the noxious gas at bay. One gigantic bog in northern Siberia released tens of billions of tons in less than a decade.*

And it wasn't just the Arctic creating this spike in methane. Our cows, numbering more than 3 billion in 2030, expelled nearly enough methane to rival the thawing permafrost. It's funny to think that bovine flatulence helped bring the human race to this tipping point, but it did.

There were other methane-making machines out there as well. Rice paddies, planted on every possible hill and valley in Asia to feed a regional population pushing 6 billion people, added considerably to the methane levels in the atmosphere. Landfills, termites, natural gas exploration, wetlands and fires all contributed. The levels of methane in the atmosphere are still rising to this day, years after the ban on burning fossil fuels.

In the end, the natural cooling systems of the planet became overwhelmed. That's why we built the first-generation scrubbers and that's why we need to get the second-generation scrubbers operating as soon as possible. We need to break this dangerous fever our planet is running. The fever could kill us if it remains untreated.

The Long Road to Crescent City

Rubic Chang looked into the mirror and saw a person who resembled himself but was somehow different. His dark, tanned-leather skin tone had remained the same, but his face belonged to somebody else. His cheekbones were higher and his chin, which used to fall away, was more pronounced. His nose remained untouched, as cutting into it would have required more time than Rubic could spare. The changes were made to fool the facial recognition scanners, not someone who knew him. Yeva would recognize him in a heartbeat, as would a well-trained NSA agent, but that didn't matter.

"So what do you think?"

"It's weird looking into a mirror and not seeing yourself."

"That's why you pay me, to lose your face. You'll get used to your new look over time but I don't think you can ever go back. Once they are looking for you they never give up until they find you. You know that, don't you?"

"Yeah. I know that."

"Does it still hurt?"

"It hurts but I can't stay here any longer. I'll need some pain pills—and can you do me another favor?"

"Sure. What's the favor?"

"I've got three packages to run, two south of here and one in northern California. I'm still worried they'll ferret me out using a retinal scanner or a fingerprint machine, so I want to leave this one package, the one that's supposed to go to Crescent City, with you. If I don't return to run it up there myself in the next few days, can you find someone who will?"

"It'll cost you."

"How much?"

"I can find someone to do it for a grand, but no less."

Rubic did the math. He had hoped that he could have made the run for less than $6,000, putting an additional $2,000 in his pocket. With the NSA after him, his original plans were off the table. He was already into the Faceist for an unanticipated thousand and the additional runner would be another thousand. But if he was arrested by the NSA, none of that would matter. Rubic wouldn't see Chicago again in that case and he would probably never see the $10,000 awaiting the turn of his electronic key. He'd vanish like a thousand other runners before him and the money he was supposed to be paid wouldn't matter. It was a tough call to make but he hated to lose that last grand.

"To hell with it. I'll take my chances and hope to God your new face works."

"The face will work, but I can't help you with the retina scanners. You don't have the money for that procedure and even if you did, it would take weeks to make you retina contacts that would fool the mainframes. The fingerprints are easy, though—just start wearing these."

The doctor walked over to a drawer and pulled out a pair of translucent gloves that were made of an ultra-thin, breathable synthetic material. He handed them to Rubic.

"Just put these on. No one can see them once they're on and they leave no fingerprints. You won't leave a trail of Rubic Chang prints using these. Can I ask how you got into the system?"

"It was an R7 deal gone bad. It wasn't a run."

"I figured it wasn't a run. Most of the time runners disappear after they've been taken into custody. They don't really care about Rapture7 dealers. Hell, I think they let the whole drug business carry on. They've got bigger fish to fry out there—the burners, the underground, renegade corporations, you name it. R7 doesn't mean shit to them. Tough break for you though, being in the system."

"Yeah, I only did six months but I'm official. I'm on record."

"You'll have to be careful out there, especially at the train stations."

"I know. It's not the agents, but the machines that scare the hell out of me."

"Are you still planning to head out in the morning?"

"Yeah."

"Well, get some rest tonight—you're going to have to be wide awake tomorrow and on your toes at all times. They'll be looking for you everywhere, both the machines and the agents."

"I know."

Rubic didn't sleep well. He wondered if he was making a mistake by not setting up a backup runner for the Crescent City delivery. Around midnight he pulled out his remaining three envelopes to check the addresses and realized it wouldn't have mattered. Unlike the other two packages which were both heading south of the city, the information written on the one going to Ann Hadley was sketchy at best. Warren didn't know exactly where Ann was living in Crescent City, so he had scribbled out several places he thought Rubic might find her—an organic farm she might be working at, a local bar and an old friend who fished out of the harbor. No home address.

That, thought Rubic, *is going to make Crescent City the worst leg of this run.*

Eyes and Ears

"We'll find him. He's hiding out right now, tucked away in some safe house, but we'll find him."

Sam Watson, head of the West Coast division at the NSA, had a determined look on his face. The balding, middle-aged bureaucrat had been with the NSA since he graduated from Virginia Tech some 30 years earlier. He was absolutely committed to apprehending Rubic Chang.

He continued. "Activate all the retina scanners in the system, even the Level 5 units. We're going to go Code Yellow with this guy. We have to assume that he's savvy enough to have had a face job, and the timeframe of his disappearance confirms the likelihood of cosmetic facial implants. The facial recognition scanners won't pick him up and we sure as hell don't have the manpower to override the system and pick him out from 50 million people.

"He probably doesn't have the time or money to get eye implants, so the retina scanners are our best bet. He'll more than likely try to reach Chicago and his old girlfriend at some point, so be sure to look out for him at all the train stations. Unless he rents a car, the trains are his only way back."

The two computer tech agents across Sam's desk murmured their assent.

"And by the way," Sam said, "what's his girlfriend's story?"

"Her name is Yeva Dunning," piped in one of the computer techies. "She's 24 and a graduate of University of Illinois at Urbana-Champaign. She's working at the Chicago Botanic Gardens taking care of their seed bank, so she has a low-level security clearance. She's clean as far as we can tell and doesn't appear to be involved with drugs or running. Should we bring her in for questioning?"

Sam reflected for a moment. "No, that would only make matters worse. But we might want to get some cameras and mics in her apartment, just in case he tries to make contact."

"That's been done. We sent in a team last week while she was at work. We've got her cell phone covered, and there are cameras in every room."

"Great—now what about her work place?"

"It can't be done. The seed bank is a maze of hundreds of cold storage rooms. We've got our grounds-monitoring devices activated, but they're always up and running. I doubt he'll try to reach her at work. If he does show up on the grounds, we've told our agents in Chicago to keep an eye out for him. I agree with you that Chang's still somewhere on the West Coast. Our best bet is the retina scanning system."

"OK, that's where we'll leave it this morning. Now get back to your stations and find me this son of a bitch."

First Day

Leonard Gibson extended his right hand to greet Warren as he walked into his office.

"It's a pleasure to meet you, Dr. Randolf," he said. "Welcome aboard."

"It's great to be here. The lab looks better in person than it does in your brochures."

"That's nice to hear. Is your office OK?"

"Are you kidding? It's twice the size of my office at the CMC. It'll be just fine."

"So where are you staying?"

"At that Microtel just west of town. It'll be a few more weeks before we finish all the inspections and things, then I'll move in to my new place out on Brackett Creek Road."

"That's a nice area. It's right off of Highway 86, right? Pretty remote out there, but nice."

"I like remote."

"Well, take a seat and let's get started, Dr. Randolf."

"Please, just call me Warren."

Warren pulled up a chair and within minutes the two men were discussing the details of Bozeman Recapture's new CO_2-scrubbing fabric and the experimental work they were doing with sequestering the more problematic methane and nitrous oxide. They pored over computer-generated charts, graphs, climate models and equations. Warren was duly impressed with his new boss's grasp of the current situation.

At the end of the day Warren decided to drive out to the 40-acre ranch he had under contract. The former owners had already moved out. As Warren stood next to his car alongside the rural highway, he was tempted to take a stroll through the property. He decided not to in case someone drove by and found him suspicious. He surveyed the spread before him, from the big alfalfa field running alongside a small creek to the surrounding hills that were just starting to turn green again. He knew he had made a good choice. It was an idyllic setting to hide from what would become a far from idyllic world.

The Final Run

*O*ne package left, thought Rubic as he listened to the rhythmic sounds of the train heading north toward the San Francisco train station as he contemplated his next move. He thought it might be time for a change of tactics. He was itching to get off the trains and into a car.

The other two runs had gone off without a hitch. He had no trouble finding the female Professor at Stanford, nor the man in San Jose. It was down to one last package and he could head east again toward Chicago and Yeva. He would return by car and stay away from trains from here on out.

The trouble with trains lay in the terminals. They were crawling with agents and tireless monitoring hardware. There were retinal scanners at almost every ticket counter and facial scanners everywhere to pore over the crowds, looking for burners, runners and criminals.

Because of the high levels of computerized surveillance, Rubic figured this would be his last train station visit and his last train ride of the run. Afterward he would rent an electric car and drive to Crescent City in search of Ann Hadley. Then he would drop that vehicle off and exchange it for a second car, a transcontinental model, to drive back to Chicago.

Beyond Chicago his plans were a blur. Even with his altered face he realized he wouldn't be able to visit Yeva back at the apartment. The NSA would be monitoring everyone coming in and going out of the apartment building. Even with his height-altering shoes, the NSA would likely spot him. The best thing to do would be to relocate somewhere, possibly out east. He wondered if Yeva would join him in the move.

Hell, I'm screwed from here on out, Rubic thought to himself as he sped northward at 225 miles per hour. *The best thing for me at this point would be to find a place in one of the outposts somewhere, maybe up east, maybe in the south, and go from there. No sense dragging Yeva into all of this.*

Meanwhile, with no one sitting beside him, he took the last package he had with him out of his backpack and set it on his lap. He reached into his pocket and took out the electronic key Warren had given to him in the empty pizza box. That key was worth $10,000.

As a porter came by, Rubic spoke up.

"Do you carry any stamps on board?"

"No, sorry."

"Do you know where I might be able to find stamps at the terminal?"

"The post office is just down the street, maybe a block or so. They'll be able to help you there and they should still be open by the time we reach the city."

"Thanks."

"Is that the package you're mailing?" the attendant asked, pointing at the small envelope.

"Yeah."

"That shouldn't be a problem. When you leave the terminal, take the State Street exit and take a right—it'll be up the street on your left."

"Thanks, will do."

Rubic looked over Warren's hand-written comments on the back of the envelope and shook his head. Finding Ann was not going to be easy. It was time to come up with an alternate plan in the event the NSA apprehended him. He didn't want to spend the money, nor take the chance of handing this last package over to another runner.

Then there was the problem with the key. He had already made six out of the seven deliveries and felt like he had earned his money. But if he was arrested he wouldn't see a dime of it. The timed lock would expire and Warren would retrieve the cash without knowing Rubic's fate.

The best Plan B he could come up with was to open the package, carefully avoid reading its contents, insert his key and address the whole thing to Yeva. He could get it stamped right after getting off the train. That way, if the agents were somehow on to him, he might have enough time to try to mail the package to Yeva before they caught him. He had no interest in finding out what the letters said, but he definitely didn't want the NSA to get their hands on it.

As the porter came back, Rubic flagged him down a second time. "Say, you wouldn't happen to have a magic marker and some tape, would you?"

"Well, I can help you with that. I've got a marker right here. Give me a minute and I'll find you some tape. We have people carrying boxes and all kinds of stuff on this train, so we usually have some on board. I'll go check."

"Thanks again."

Rubic opened the package with his pocket knife. He found the letter and the nanodrive inside. He was tempted to scan through it, but he restrained himself.

If I don't know what was inside the packages, thought Rubic, *then they'll never be able to coerce that information out of me.*

After opening the manila folder, he slipped his electronic key into the package next to the nanodrive and clasped it shut.

What am I thinking, he realized just before closing it up. *Yeva won't have a clue as to what this key is for.*

Looking around, Rubic realized the only paper he had was on the back side of Warren's letter to Ann. It would have to do for now. He wrote a short note to Yeva in his thick, black marker.

Yeva,

If you receive this I am probably in hiding or under arrest. Don't try to reach me. Use this key to open an electronic locker at the downtown Chicago train terminal on March 28, between 10 a.m. and noon. There should be a lot of money in there for us. I'll get back in touch with you later.

Rubic

Rubic closed the envelope and flipped it over. Warren had scribbled everything about Ann on the back, leaving the front side empty. Rubic started to write down his apartment's address but stopped just short of doing so. They would be checking her mail daily, he realized, and there's no way they wouldn't investigate a brown manila envelope mailed from the West Coast.

That's when he decided to send the package to her work address. He took out the replacement iPhone 70 he had just purchased and Googled the Botanic Garden's address. He realized they would likely be checking Yeva's work mail and email as well, so he decided to take a chance and send it to her boss, Margot Pollack. On the reverse side, where the flap sealed shut, he wrote a message in the black marker over Warren's scribbled notes about locating Ann:

Please deliver this to Yeva for me!
Rubic Chang

"Here's your tape."

"Thanks—if you want to wait a second, I'm pretty much done here."

Rubic peeled out a foot of the plastic tape and sealed the flap tight. There was no return address on the envelope, nor would there be.

This is a last-ditch effort and not a very good one at that, Rubic thought. There were many things that could go wrong with the arrangement. This was his Hail Mary pass on fourth and long. Still, it was better than no plan, but not by much.

The train arrived in the busy San Francisco terminal at 2:45 p.m. Rubic had stuffed his final package into his backpack and got up as soon as the train came to a halt. *Remember,* he thought, *keep your head down, and when you have to look up for any reason, keep moving your head and your eyes as much as possible without looking suspicious.* He could never stand still, because that was when the scanners were most effective. If the machines got a clear image of the capillaries in his eyes, Rubic would be history. Once accurately scanned, the chances of a false positive on a retina scan were next to nil. Each person had unique blood vessels in their eyes.

The train station was busy, which was good for Rubic. It would be harder for the cameras to isolate him. He looked around to see if he could spot any field agents working the terminal, not that it was likely he would catch a plainclothes officer at a glance. There were several people who drew his attention, though he didn't look at them for very long and avoided any eye contact. There was an unlikely-looking janitor standing idly near the men's room that made him uneasy. There were also two men in dark suits next to the ticket booth, though they might have been businessmen.

Of course there were cameras and scanners everywhere—some obvious, others obscured. He cleared the track exit and made his way to the revolving doors that opened onto State Street. He hurried but tried not to look like he was in a hurry. It was a balancing act, especially in a terminal. *Don't look suspicious but keep moving. Move your head, dart your eyes around all the times, keep your head down, walk slowly but decisively. Whatever you do, get out of the damn terminal as soon as possible.*

When Rubic was outside, he exhaled a pent-up breath he hadn't realized he'd been keeping. It was cold and damp, with thick fog clouds hanging a few hundred feet above the street. The skyscrapers disappeared into the low clouds blanketing the city. He took a left on State Street and headed toward the post office.

He found it a little more than a block down the street. He ducked inside and got in line. There were only three customers in front of him, all with packages to mail. The woman in front of him must have been running some kind of mail-order business, as she had about a dozen small boxes to post. After clearing the train terminal and all of its surveillance equipment, Rubic let his guard down. That was his mistake.

Slow-moving lines made post offices ideal locations for retinal scanners. Unlike in the train stations, the general public had no idea that scanners populated most of the nations' post offices. Not one minute after Rubic entered the building, the NSA's computer in Ft. Meade, Maryland, spotted the fugitive and alerted the San Francisco office.

"We've got him."

"Where?"

"The Post Office on State Street. Real time."

"Where are the nearest agents and how many do we have available nearby?"

"We've got four in the train terminal right now. Do you want me to pull them?"

"Yes, get on it and let's nail this bastard."

Rubic waited patiently in line, trying to buy a few dollars' worth of postage stamps to cover the cost of getting this envelope to Chicago. The woman in front of him finally had her turn and was about to step up to the counter.

But then she turned around. "Is that all you have to mail?" she asked timidly.

"Yes, ma'am."

"Well go ahead and cut in line then, I've got plenty of time to get all of these out."

"Thanks."

Rubic stepped up to the counter and handed the postal worker his envelope to weigh.

"That'll be $4.50."

"Could you just put the stamps on for now? I don't want to mail it just yet."

"Not a problem." The clerk took out a roll of stamps, peeled off the right amount and handed the envelope back to Rubic, who was digging around in his pockets for money.

"Here's a fifty, it's all I have."

The clerk handed Rubic back a few bills and a sizeable lump of change. "Have a nice day."

Rubic turned around and walked to the front door, envelope in hand. As he jogged down the front stairway, he happened to glance up the street. That's when he saw them. He knew immediately that the two businessmen in dark suits, the same two he had noticed in the terminal earlier, were coming for him. *Christ,* thought Rubic, *there must have been a retinal scanner inside the post office.*

The two agents were less than 100 yards away but had not appeared to have seen Rubic yet. That soon changed.

"THERE HE IS!" one of the agents shouted, drawing his weapon.

Rubic sprinted down the sidewalk like a man on fire. He knew there would be more agents arriving soon.

He almost dropped the package in his haste, but he soon found himself thinking about it as he wove his panicked way among the pedestrians, shoving and plowing through the crowd.

What about the goddamned package and the key?

The NSA agents were too far away to take a shot. They had already suffered enough collateral damage with this runner and they weren't inclined to make the same mistakes again. They ran recklessly through the crowd with their plasma guns set on stun.

One of the agents kept shouting, "STOP HIM!" No one did. The bystanders didn't want to get involved. Few in San Francisco felt they owed the State anything.

Rubic wondered what to do with the package he gripped in his left hand. He needed to pass it off to someone—and he needed to do it *now*.

As he scrambled through the crowd, Rubic prayed for a street vendor, a hot dog man, a musician—hell, even a pantomime artist would do. He knew he couldn't trust anyone, but if it meant the difference between Yeva collecting the $10,000 payment or getting nothing, he would risk it.

Rubic darted wildly around a corner not knowing who, if anyone, would be there for him. As he ran, he reached into his right hand pocket for the change from the post office. It slowed him down, but he still had about 100 yards on the agents. Around the corner, he noticed a homeless person pushing a beat-up shopping cart filled with aluminum cans and plastic drinking bottles.

"Hey, do me a favor," Rubic panted, already extending the package toward the homeless man.

"What's that?" the man demanded gruffly.

"Mail this for me." Rubic stuffed the envelope in the shopping cart and handed over all the change he had found in his pocket. It was the lion's share of the $50 he'd broken at the post office.

The man's eyes widened at the money. "Yeah, OK."

"Thanks—you'll wanna hide that envelope." Rubic was already jogging away.

The homeless man nodded and slid the envelope into his half-filled cart. It vanished beside the pile of "return for deposit" bottles he had already collected. He stuck the wad of cash into his pocket without bothering to count it. Within seconds of Rubic bolting off, the two NSA agents rounded the corner and ran right past the homeless man pushing the shopping cart. One of them paused to let off a plasma blast that narrowly missed Rubic.

He swore loudly as the shot hit the side of a parked car. The agent put down his gun and resumed the chase.

Rubic continued toward the waterfront. He knew he didn't have Golden Gate Park to duck into this time—his only chance was to somehow ditch the agents who were now less than fifty yards behind him.

He rounded another sharp corner and saw an opportunity to get off the main streets and into the back alleys and narrow passageways of the row houses lining the sidewalk. He saw another narrow cut similar to the one he had taken with his bike a week ago. He ran down it and found himself in a tiny courtyard with a six-foot tall fence around it. He scaled the fence and continued running through a narrow alley. He soon found a second passage heading back, so he reversed his direction, not unlike the trick that saved him the last time.

Rubic had no way of knowing what the agents were up to as he could no longer see anyone behind him. He could not have known they had split up, anticipating his maneuver.

As Rubic approached the main street, he realized he was running full tilt right toward one of the agents who had stepped out from behind a house. The NSA officer raised his weapon and calmly addressed Rubic.

"Stop, or I'll shoot."

Rubic turned around, only to discover the second agent had followed his path and was now right behind him. He knew it was over, but he made a final attempt to escape by trying to run past the first agent and into the busy street.

Before he could move two steps, he felt something slam into his ribcage and he collapsed to the ground. The plasma charge left him completely frozen and barely able to breathe. All his muscles tensed involuntarily as high-voltage electricity coursed through his body. The pain was so intense, he couldn't scream.

The two agents walked up toward him from both directions, guns at the ready for a second shot if needed. They looked down at Rubic, his eyes wide open, his limbs spasming with pain.

"Gotcha," one of the agents said as he reached into his back pocket for a zip tie. He kicked Rubic over and grabbed both of his arms, pulling them behind his back and fastening the black zip tie tightly around his wrists.

"You're not going anywhere now, asshole."

Rubic couldn't move. The plasma charge had scrambled his nervous system. He wanted to get back up and run but his muscles refused to listen to his brain. He was paralyzed.

"Search the backpack. Let's find that envelope he was holding when we first spotted him on the stairs. There might be some evidence in it."

The agent took out his pocket knife and cut the straps draped over Rubic's shoulders. He opened it up and found some water, dirty laundry and an apple. No envelope.

"Where's the envelope?" the agent asked.

Rubic managed to open his mouth, but he could only produce a weak groan.

"He must've tossed it somewhere," said the agent who had shot him. "It's no use asking him, he won't be able to speak coherently for an hour or more."

"Let's get a search crew out here. If he went through the trouble of ditching it, it must be important."

Another van arrived with six more agents, three of whom pulled Rubic inside. *So this is it,* he thought glumly. He was sinking into the nefarious world of the NSA.

Meanwhile the homeless man had turned around and had worked his way back toward the post office to mail the envelope. By the time he made it there, the place was completely sealed off with police tape. Several NSA agents lurked inside asking questions. The homeless man kept pushing his cart down the street and drew no attention to himself. He ended up bringing it to another post office a mile and a half away.

Margot Pollack received Rubic's envelope four days later. She found it a little unusual to be the recipient of something intended for Yeva, but it was not quite enough to ring any alarm bells. She put it in with some routine paperwork along with a Post-it on it reading: "This came for you!"

At the Botanic Garden

Yeva was in the seed repository when Margot placed the envelope on her desk, so she didn't discover it until she finished her rounds in the afternoon. She was a bit surprised by the fact it wasn't addressed to her, but she figured Rubic was taking extra precautions about making contact with her. *He is always clever, if not wise,* Yeva thought as she picked up her letter opener.

She reached inside and pulled out the package's sparse contents. She first noticed Rubic's note written on the back of one of the two hand-written pages. She read Rubic's brief letter and grew worried. Something was wrong.

She then studied the electric key Rubic had mentioned in his note.

The number 489 was inscribed on it and she immediately recognized it as a train locker key. March 28 was still five days away. Yeva would have to take the morning off to go downtown to open the locker during the two-hour window.

She finally turned to the second letter, which was clearly not in Rubic's handwriting. Before reading it, Yeva noticed the instructions scribbled on the back. This must have been one of the last packages Rubic was hired to deliver. It was addressed to someone named Ann Hadley, but Yeva decided to read it. Maybe it would provide some insight into what Rubic was up to and where he might be.

Dear Ann,

I know it has been a long time since we've spoken. I miss you. What I'm writing here could not have been sent through the Internet, U.S. mail, or any conventional channel. Only a handful of people on Earth know about this information and you must not share it with anyone until we know for certain how everything is going to play out. By the time this reaches you I may have already been arrested. If that's the case, then use the information to prepare for the dark days ahead. In the end, even if you never hear from me again, this letter may save your life and the lives of those closest to you.

I don't know how much you know about the Mylerium Project, the stop-gap geoengineering plan the CMC devised to cool the Northern Hemisphere this summer, but I'm sure you've heard about it in the news and on the Net. There's a good chance the deployment of the reflective nanomirrors will already be well underway by the time this letter reaches you.

As you are well aware, I've been involved with the Mylerium Project for the past five years. While I was working on the project, I noticed there was something wrong with the self-destruct sequence assigned to each nanoparticle. The details of this glitch are very technical, but I'd like to briefly explain how these Mylar-based reflective mirrors are designed to work.

Each nanomirror is a microscopic particle in the shape of a sphere. We refer to them as hyper-spheres because, although the shape is round, the surface is more like the facets of a cut diamond. They are designed this way to ensure that the highly reflective Mylar surface is always in an optimum position to reflect incoming solar radiation away from the planet. But this unique geometric shape also makes them very resilient to the harmful effects of ultraviolet rays, stratospheric and solar winds, as well as numerous other factors that would normally cause particles to degrade naturally in the upper atmosphere. You can think of the nanomirrors as forming a giant parasol that shades most of the Northern Hemisphere and much of the Southern Hemisphere.

There is a computer within each nanomirror—it's essentially a built-in timer controlled by infinitesimal nanotransistors. Every deployment of nanomirrors has a slightly different computer structure built into it, causing that particular batch to self-destruct during a predetermined window of time. We designed them that way because we wanted them to slowly shade the Earth in the spring and slowly close this reflective shade in the fall. That's why the deployment and the decomposition are both intended to take about a month.

In theory, that should reduce any unforeseen disruptions in our weather patterns over the seven months the mirrors will remain in the stratosphere. But the problem with the design lies in the software—the disintegration program installed into every mirror. The mirrors are supposed to crumble into harmless soot over the course of several weeks this October. But if they fail to dissolve as planned, the following winter will be ruthless.

When I first stumbled across this flaw, I wasn't sure it was real. I noticed that as long as I kept analyzing my data on the CMC's computers, my results were inconclusive. I decided to set up a computer bank of my own, purposely avoiding any contact with the Net and the TURING 1000—the latest and fastest national computer. I wondered if a corrupt algorithm was causing the Net to turn back incorrect answers, so I opted to try everything on a clean slate.

About a year ago, after I entered some flawed calculations into my equations by sheer accident, the entire Mylerium Project began to unravel mathematically. Owing to the programming flaws in the disintegration timers of the nanomirrors, the Mylerium Project became, in my estimation, a geoengineering nightmare.

I decided to approach the CMC with my data and its disturbing conclusions. By the time this letter reaches you, I may be under arrest, or silenced like so many scientists have been before me. I'm writing you to warn you of what's about to unfold.

If the Mylerium Project fails, which I believe it will, we will have a world filled with 9.7 billion people and a near-freezing summer across the entire Northern Hemisphere. Based on a drop in temperature of up to seven degrees Celsius, the snow pack in the spring would extend as far south as the Ohio River Valley. Because snow has such a high reflectivity vis-à-vis the dark, tilled earth we would normally have in the spring, the summer would be too short to produce any wheat, corn, rice or soy beans across most of the U.S., Canada, Europe, Russia and China. Depending on the severity of the winter, the crop failure could extend into India and Indochina. We would be facing the worst crop failure in the history of mankind.

Not only would people go hungry, but domesticated and wild animals would starve. There would be no hay, corn or soybeans to feed to our billions of chickens, cows and pigs. According to my calculations, by the end of the first summer our worldwide grain reserves would be close to exhausted.

It gets worse. If I'm right, while some of the nanomirrors will eventually degrade or dissipate on their own, about half may remain in orbit over the following winter. That will create a positive feedback loop, sending us into the early stages of a new Ice Age. The snow pack the following spring, if there is a spring, would extend as far south as the Florida Panhandle, leaving us with no summer for a second year running.

At that point, the entire world will be impacted. The Earth will be so cold that even countries in the Southern Hemisphere would struggle to produce harvests. You can imagine the chaos that will ensue when no one on the planet has any food.

I can only hope that you will have faith in me. I know you love the life you've made for yourself in Crescent City and I respect that. But you have to understand that everything is going to change very soon. By late fall, the hills outside your town will be covered in early snowfall and everyone will know that something has gone wrong. We will go from an overheated planet to a snowball Earth in a single terrible year.

I still love you and I want you to make it through this impending nightmare. If I am not imprisoned, I plan to buy a ranch out west, far from any big city, and set up a small enclave to support a handful of my closest friends for up to three years without contact or supplies from the outside world. I want you to survive and I'm asking you to join us. Since we cannot discuss any of this information on the phone, just call me on my cell, 312-33-897-6443, and talk to me about the weather. I'll know that you've received this envelope and that you plan to join us when you can.

You probably think I'm crazy, but I can assure you I'm not. I'm scared. The world we know is about to come to a screeching halt. Everything will change, and not for the better. I hope to hear from you soon.

Love always,
Warren Randolf

Yeva's hands were shaking as she set the letter down. *Is this some kind of joke?* she thought to herself. *No, it can't be.* The letter wasn't even addressed to her—it was intended for a woman she had never met, written by a scientist she had never heard of. She had to find out more. Yeva turned to her computer and Googled Warren Randolf.

Page after page came up touting his numerous awards, research papers and his work on the Mylerium Project. Dr. Warren Randolf was real. She Googled Ann Bradley and found very little about her. She worked on some kind of communal farm on the outskirts of Crescent City, California and had graduated with a degree in botany from Ohio State University. A photo of her came up on a Facebook site. She was young and quite pretty.

Yeva typed in the Mylerium Project, which took her to the CMC's official website. The site explained why the nanomirrors were needed. It described in detail how the nanomirror technology would simulate the recent cooling effects brought on by Mt. Cameroon's eruption. It explained the failure of the first-generation scrubbers and the need to build the second-generation scrubbers as soon as possible. It talked about plans to deploy the nanomirrors every spring until the next-generation scrubbers came online and brought CO_2 levels back below 300 parts per million. The website outlined some risks associated with the mirrors, but it never mentioned crop failures or endless winters.

Something is wrong here, Yeva thought.

Yeva tucked the letter and the locker key into her purse. If Margot asked her anything about the envelope, she would just say it was a love letter from Rubic with a few baubles enclosed. Nothing, really.

In the meantime, Yeva would research the Mylerium Project and other experimental geoengineering concepts. Having spent her entire adult life working with plants, she was well acquainted with the dangers Dr. Randolf described in his letter. Plants formed the backbone of all life on Earth. Without them—without a harvest—civilization would unravel.

Less than a week later, Yeva opened up the locker and found $10,000 in cash. She decided Dr. Randolf would never have hired Rubic for the run, nor spent that kind of money, if he was not dead certain the project would fail. She set aside half the money and started stockpiling food. Her second bedroom became an oversized pantry, filled with powdered milk, honey, wheat flour, salt, dried beans and canned meat. At least she would be ready. Just in case.

At Shelter Ranch

For Montana, the spring of 2043 started out much as it had the year before—hot. The "glaciers" of Glacier National Park didn't react to the early heat wave because they had melted away decades ago. The winter snow pack in the park thawed quickly under the clear mountain sunlight and Montana's rivers ran wild and furious throughout the month of May. Without glaciers to preserve some of the snow through the summer months, most of the state's rivers and creeks would be reduced to a trickle by August. The nanomirrors, now slowly spreading across the stratosphere above Big Sky country, had yet to impact local temperatures. May was painfully hot.

Warren kept himself busy. He had moved into his property, which he dubbed Shelter Ranch, and had started to work on the projects he needed to complete before winter set in. He monitored the progress of the Mylerium Project by visiting the CMC's website every morning. The mirrors were never designed to have an instant impact on the climate of the Northern Hemisphere, so heat waves in May did not come as a surprise. It could take several weeks for the blanket of reflectivity to start making a difference.

According to the models, real cooling would be noticeable by early to mid-summer.

Until then, Warren suffered through 90-degree afternoons and little rain. It was a familiar weather pattern. The people in Bozeman, just like millions of others in Germany, Russia and China, anxiously waited for the relief the Mylerium Project promised. They were tired of struggling with drying rivers, incessant heat waves, brownouts and temperatures that regularly soared into the low hundreds. They hated their hot planet.

Warren had purchased a small electric Bobcat with a backhoe attachment and started digging into a steep hillside near Bracket Creek on his property. He was building a storage facility not unlike the root cellars the settlers once dug into Montana hillsides 200 years earlier. Warren's root cellar, however, would be much bigger—he wanted it to hold enough food for two dozen people for three long years. He planned to use the cellar to store a wide array of dry foods such as beans, powdered milk, flour, honey, rice, instant potatoes, dried fruits and salted meats like beef jerky, smoked hams and canned chickens. The more he thought about it, Warren realized he would need to hire a contractor at some point if he wanted to get everything completed before winter set in. He disliked the thought of it, but the workload was getting to him.

When he wasn't at Bozeman Recapture, Warren prepared the barn and the house for what he felt might well be the collapse of the United States. Realizing that his coworkers at Bozeman Recapture would probably think he had lost his mind, he couldn't tell anyone about his 40-acre survivalist enclave. He didn't dare plug his own nanodrive into one of Recapture's computers and show his boss his sobering calculations for fear of breaking his gag order with COI. Warren knew the NSA would be monitoring his home and his office computer, looking for any excuse to make the rebellious Dr. Randolf disappear.

So Warren worked tirelessly in preparation for the inevitable. Thinking the power grid might fail sometime during the second winter, he purchased four large wood stoves to ensure the house and the converted barn had sufficient heat year-round. He ordered 25 cords of hardwood to be delivered in the fall. He designed a hydroelectric generator that would use the flow of Bracket Creek to generate a small portion of his electricity. To supplement it, Warren erected several small wind turbines, two dozen solar panels and battery backup systems to round out his off-the-grid energy needs.

By the end of May, Warren had heard from four of the seven people he had contacted. He had not heard anything from Ann. Warren knew $10,000 had been picked up and assumed Rubic had delivered all of his envelopes as promised, but it was impossible to know for certain. He did know he could never contact Rubic again.

Warren understood that no one would show up at Shelter Ranch until the nanomirrors actually failed. At times, during the late evening when the summer sun seemed to hang forever along the spacious western skyline, he wondered if he really had lost it. It was impossible not to have second thoughts about what he was doing with his life. He had moved from a great job in Chicago to a remote ranch in the middle of Montana, risking imprisonment along the way.

What if I'm wrong, he kept asking himself as he strung power cables from his wind turbines and buttressed his two-story home for dozens of people who might never actually arrive. Still, he relied on his scientific abilities to keep himself focused and he remained undeterred from converting Shelter Ranch into a safe haven. It was going to be a life raft, he believed. It would be his ark in what would soon become a tumultuous and icy sea.

Warren tried his best to avoid buying what he needed in Bozeman. If the locals knew he had food, water and shelter, there was a possibility they could turn on him. Instead, he bought an electric pickup truck with a black topper and drove to Butte, Helena, Billings and even Great Falls for his supplies. He seldom, if ever, went back to the same outfitters or discount stores twice. He bought 100 pounds of rice from a wholesale store in Helena one week, then bought two 50-pound bags in Billings from another grocery store a week later.

By mid-July the nanomirrors began working. People were amazed that they could once again wake up to 50-degree mornings with dew on the grass and a cool breeze flowing off the mountains. By August, everyone was relieved that the days were actually starting out chilly and the grass was still green. They didn't miss the scorched-dry fields of hay from the year before. Those fields had always been ready to catch fire at any moment. Infernos spread across the tinder-dry landscape without mercy.

For a few beautiful months, the weather of their parents and grandparents was back. The mood around Bozeman lifted the spirits of the entire community. It was the same throughout the Northern Hemisphere. People felt inspired from Moscow to Tokyo to London and beyond. Mother Earth was back, at least for the moment.

"That's some hole you're diggin'."

"Yeah, I'm putting in an old-fashioned root cellar."

"You expectin' company, or you just eat a lot of potatoes?"

"I've got a bunch of family coming out to visit this winter—they all love to ski."

"Well, when we get this barn of yours finished, you'll be able to host at least a dozen folks up in the old hayloft alone. You must have one heck of a lot of ski bums in your family."

"There will be some friends mixed in as well. With Bridger Bowl and Big Sky just a short drive away, I'll have a lot of company this skiing season."

"We'll have it done for ya right on time—don't you worry none about that."

"Thanks, Vince, I'm sure you'll get it done."

Vince Gatinni climbed back in his pickup truck, slammed the door behind him and hit the highway. His crew of six stayed on the ranch. Two of them were working in the loft erecting wall partitions and the four downstairs were divided between tiling the bunkhouse-style kitchen and putting the plumbing in one of the three full bathrooms planned for the barn.

As Vince sped down the highway, he shook his head and muttered "bullshit" to himself several times. Vince was originally from Idaho, but he moved his construction business, Sawtooth Contractors, to Bozeman a decade ago to build several motels on the outskirts of town along Interstate 90. He knew a survivalist compound when he saw one. He had helped build his fair share of them back when his firm was still in Idaho. *You just don't build a thousand square foot root cellar for a weekend of skiers,* reflected Vince as he sped back toward his office.

This Warren fellow is up to something, Vince thought. Perhaps he was running some kind of religious cult, or else he was one of those end-of-the-world weirdos that seem to gravitate to Montana and Idaho. Vince recalled that Warren worked at the local recapture plant. Maybe his plans had something to do with the screwed-up weather of the last twenty years.

In any case, it's not a goddamned ski resort, Vince concluded. *Skiing's been on the slide for decades now, with the warmer weather and all.*

Warren wasn't sure that Vince Gatinni bought his cover story, but it hopefully wouldn't matter as long as he got the work done. At first Warren didn't want to hire a contractor, but he quickly discovered that the work load would be far beyond his ability. He could have managed to dig out and shore up the root cellar but there was no way he could have handled the barn remodeling at the same time. He needed manpower to get everything completed before winter set in, and Sawtooth Contractors came highly recommended by his boss at Bozeman Recapture. Vince and his crew had helped build an addition to the recapture plant four years ago and had done an excellent job.

Thus far Warren was impressed with Sawtooth Contractors, but he was worried about the following year. When winter's snowfall stayed on until mid-June, the entire country might wonder what was going on. When times got lean and basic staples became hard to find, Vince, or someone else working on the barn, might remember Warren's massive root cellar. Hunger changed people. Starvation destroyed them.

San Rafael Detention Center

"He'll talk, eventually. They all do."

"Should we increase the dosage of integrity serum?"

"No, not yet. That shit can kill 'em if you don't watch it. Remember hearing about that burner a year ago, the one who had the micro-refineries spread all over the swamps of Louisiana? He up and died before telling anyone where his last site was located. The nanoparticles in the serum weaken your immune system. They say it affects your kidneys somehow.

"Anyway, let's not kill this kid before we find out who in the hell Warren is and what he has to do with the missing key."

The commander took a long drink of lukewarm coffee and set it back down on his metal desk.

"Let's face it," said the commander's chief interrogator. "There are a hell of a lot of guys named Warren in the state of Illinois. For all we know, the person named Warren might be from Wisconsin, Indiana or anywhere on Earth for that matter. We know he delivered some packages to some scientists—maybe we should head that direction tomorrow morning?"

"That's a good idea. They might tell us what was in those packages and then we could start to get to the bottom of this by finding out who sent the runner in the first place. Let's try to find out the names of the scientists Rubic made his deliveries to and forget about Warren X for now. The people who received the packages will probably lead us back to him anyway."

"So we'll start in on the kid again in the morning?"

"Yeah, let's call it a day for now and jump right back into it first thing. Have a great night."

"You too—say hello to Clara for me."

"Will do."

The lead NSA interrogator walked out of his commander's office to his desk. It was already 4:30 p.m. and things were winding down at the San Rafael detention center north of San Francisco. Both men would head home to their wives and children after another day of waterboarding, administering near-fatal dosages of electroshock therapy, injecting prisoners with so-called integrity serum, and various other means of coercion and torture. Breaking knuckles and pulling molars out with dental pliers had become just another day at the office. Death barely fazed them.

Rubic Chang had already been detained for three days. He was doing his best not to say anything about who he was working for or what he had already accomplished. His task was made easier because he never learned Warren's last name. The less you knew, the less they could squeeze out of you should you get caught. It was for this reason Rubic never opened any of the envelopes he was charged with delivering. If he didn't know what was being communicated, no one could extract that information from him, regardless of the methods they resorted to.

Rubic's holding cell was an eight by ten foot windowless room three stories underground. The walls were padded to prevent suicide. The floor was a black synthetic carpet covered in stains. Some of the stains appeared to be from vomit, while others were from urine, feces and blood. There was no furniture save for a single toilet in the corner of the cell. Prisoners were issued a single pillow to rest their head on—that was it. The ceiling consisted of a bank of high-voltage halogen lights that turned on and off seemingly at random. Sleep was impossible when the lights were on. The heat alone from those lights would be enough keep any prisoner awake. But the pure, relentless white light was intolerable and the thin pillow was impossible to use as a blindfold.

Sleep deprivation had long been standard operating procedure for the NSA. Since the Lost Decade, the NSA no longer dealt with Islamic extremists, whose diminishing importance coincided with the world's dwindling demand for oil. Instead they focused on domestic dissidents—burners, runners, drug lords, seditionists and criminals. There were more than enough warm bodies who hated the State to keep the San Rafael facility busy year-round. It wasn't the only hellhole—there were a dozen facilities like it spread across North America, hosting thousands of detainees. Climate change was a boon for torture.

Rubic was wide awake as the commander and the chief interrogator walked out to the parking lot at a little past 5 p.m. Rubic Chang had no idea if it was day or night. He was delirious from his daily injections of integrity serum. He had severe stomach cramps, which he assumed was a side effect from the drug. His vision was blurred and his thoughts were scrambled as though he was sleepwalking.

As Rubic lay crumpled on the floor, he knew his life was over. The stories he had heard about other arrested runners remained at the forefront of his disjointed thoughts. In his tormented dream world, the only other thing he could think about was trying to escape.

It didn't matter that it was impossible to escape. Perhaps that was never even his goal. He knew the NSA might eventually kill him. The pain he would have to endure between now and the day he died would be intolerable.

I'll make a break for it the next time they let me out of here, he thought in his delirium. *I'll make my escape.*

The overhead lights were switched back on and the glare startled him back into a moment of clarity. *If I'm lucky they'll kill me. If not, I'll suffer until I break down and tell them what I know, then they'll kill me anyway.*

I miss Yeva. My stomach hurts. I'm tired. My nose is bleeding again.

For Rubic and tens of thousands like him, the Lost Decade had changed everything—especially the concept of freedom. As the climate deteriorated, individual freedoms were stripped away one by one. After the ban on burning fossil fuels was enacted, the pace of government intrusion became insufferable.

It didn't help that 21st-century technology made intrusion much easier. Everything and everyone was on the Net, so the State could spy on everything and everyone at the same time. If anyone cared to know, the government could easily find out where you shopped, where you slept, who you slept with, who you emailed, what you said, how much you owned and how much you owed. The State and the Net merged. The Corporation of Information, or COI, became Big Brother. They owned all the servers in North America and had access to every communiqué, from a simple balance transfer of your checking account to your complete medical records. Once on the state-controlled Net, all secrets were public record as far as the government was concerned. They opened a digital file on newborns the day they took their first breath and didn't close that file until the standard 20-year post mortem waiting period ended. If there had been trouble, any trouble, the file was never closed.

The Greens loved to go after burners and hackers. The burners were those who refused to stop using fossil fuels. Unfortunately, the planet had run out of atmosphere long before it ran out of oil. Because the world had become so overheated, the Greens banned the use of coal, oil or natural gas soon after taking power. Intercontinental flights were still allowed to burn plant-derived jet fuel, but domestic flights were banned in North America, Asia and Europe. Electric automobiles and electric trains took over. If you were caught using so much as an old lawn mower, the fine could be more than a thousand dollars. Refining crude oil carried a ten-year minimum sentence. Burning coal—any coal—was unthinkable.

Hackers were even more hated than burners. These renegade computer programmers spent their entire lives trying to disrupt the TURING 1000, the most sophisticated computer ever built. The hackers were the source of viruses, worms, Trojans, computer cancers and a hundred variations of the same disruptive theme. They hacked COI's computers and interfered with surveillance operations whenever possible. If there was a battlefield anywhere on Earth in 2043, it was taking place inside the circuit boards of millions of interconnected computers, but no one was winning the Electron War.

Rubic fell asleep shortly after the lights were switched off. He slipped into a state of suspended animation—half alive, half dreaming. The pain made it difficult to sleep for long, but he was so exhausted that even a few minutes of splintered rest helped.

He didn't know what time it was when he heard the lock on his cell door click open. Time didn't matter. He saw an orderly approach him with a zip tie in one hand and a needle in the other. A second guard came in behind him, his plasma weapon drawn. While the second man held his hands behind his back, the other fastened the zip tie around both wrists. He pushed Rubic down on his knees and injected the serum into the back of his neck. Rubic, feeling the noxious chemistry of nanoparticles flow through his body, immediately threw up on the stained floor.

The two orderlies let him vomit for a minute, then grabbed him under both armpits and hauled him up. Rubic realized it was now or never. He violently shook both arms off him and stumbled through the cell doorway down the hallway. There was nowhere to go—a second security door loomed 30 feet before him. Instinctively the second orderly grabbed his plasma gun, set on stun, and shot Rubic squarely in the back.

Rubic collapsed midstride. The plasma shot had hit him just above the heart and he felt the electrical impulses rushing through his body as he fell. He blacked out, hitting his head hard against the cement floor.

The two orderlies rushed to him. The one who had just administered the serum reached down and checked for a pulse, concerned that the combination of the plasma shot and the serum might prove life-threatening to his weakened immune system. Rubic's heartbeat was barely detectable.

"He's got a faint pulse. What an idiot. Where did he think he was going?"

"He was delirious, probably from the serum."

"What a dumb shit. This kid's been slipping away from us for the past few days and now he gets himself shot. Let's take him down to the clinic just to be safe. We've got to get him stabilized. They'll really get on us if he dies now."

"Then we'd better drag his ass down to the clinic."

The two men bent down and grabbed Rubic under both armpits a second time. This time Rubic was completely limp and his breathing was broken and shallow. They unlocked the second door and got in the elevator at the end of the hall. The clinic was two flights up.

One of them activated his implant phone and notified the medics that they had an inmate coming in with irregular breathing. They explained what happened in the cell, from the injection of the integrity serum to the plasma gun stun shot.

Rubic Chang was fading fast by the time he reached the clinic. His pulse was so faint that the medics who took over couldn't find it. They hooked him up to a heart monitor just as his heart stopped beating altogether. They tried, to no avail, to revive him for the next 30 minutes. He was gone. Rubic would never talk.

The commander at San Rafael was furious. The two orderlies were suspended without pay. Warren X remained Warren X. Nothing was discovered that could lead them to the Mylerium Project, the CMC or to a 40-acre ranch in central Montana.

Rubic had won. No one would ever know what had happened because everything at the NSA detention center was kept secret. Rubic's body was reduced to seven pounds of ash before noon. The ashes were dumped in a nearby river. A hacker, arrested the previous night on charges of electronic sedition, was brought into Rubic's empty cell at 2 p.m. Business continued as usual.

At Shelter Ranch

With the help of Sawtooth Construction, the root cellar was finished by late August, just as the first cold fronts swept through central Montana. The barn was done, ready for a handful of occupants who might never show up. He had still heard from only four of the seven people he had sent his prophetic warning to. If everyone who had contacted Warren came to the ranch, including their spouses and children, there would be 19 people living there by spring.

Warren realized that the chances of the other three reaching out to him were rapidly dwindling. His heart saddened when he realized that included Ann Hadley.

For the first time in months, Warren had some free time on his hands. All he had to do was keep stocking up supplies and wait until late October, when the first particles were designed to crumble into dust.

So, on a cool afternoon in late August, Warren made the first new entry into his journal in months. This is what he wrote:

August 28, 2043

I'm exhausted. When I'm not working at Bozeman Recapture, I'm working at the ranch. When I'm not at the ranch, I'm driving all over Montana trying to secure supplies. I wake up, work until I'm about to drop, then wake the next morning to do the same damn thing all over again. Almost everyone is coming, except Ann and a few who refuse to believe me. If it cools down gradually and it's a normal winter, if the mirrors do come down, I've come to realize I'll be up in Montana, living alone, wondering about my sanity.

I knew I would find some skeptics out there. What is it about us as a species that makes us blind to our future? There were so many signal flares we should have been paying attention to but time and again we decided it was easier to look the other way.

The melting of the Arctic sea ice was one of those signal flares. At first the decrease was slow but steady. At the turn of the 21st century, scientists and computer models projected in the 1990s it would take more than 100 years for the Arctic Ocean to be ice-free in summer, based on its slow rate of thawing.

That all changed in 2007 when a perfect storm—or rather, a perfect heat wave—caused more ice to melt that summer than in the entire previous 28 years. Then it happened again in 2012, in 2019, and finally in 2029, when the entire Arctic Ocean was ice-free, including the ice cap located directly over the North Pole.

That year marked the first time the Arctic Ocean was ice-free in 100,000 years. While climate scientists around the world shouted at the top of their lungs that this was an unprecedented and dangerous benchmark, the oil and gas industry executives celebrated. With the ice gone, the vast deposits of natural gas and oil that lay beneath the Arctic Ocean could now be accessed. Special billion-dollar drilling rigs, designed to withstand the winter ice pack, were towed into place during the early 2020s and the immense Arctic oil fields were exploited in record time. No one thought of what it really meant until it was confirmed that the Greenland ice cap was vanishing as well.

In hindsight, it made sense. With the Arctic Ocean covered in snow and ice, the sunlight that fell on this white blanket 24 hours a day during the summer solstice was, for the most part, reflected back into space. Open ocean is much darker than snow. Given that difference, the sun's energy was quickly absorbed by the water when the ice melted, heating the entire region. Greenland's ice sheet, which was up to two miles thick, melted quickly. As Big Oil's hunt for Black Gold fanned out across the Arctic Seas, from the Beaufort to the Barents, Greenland began thawing. What was good for corporate balance sheets was terrible for the billions of people worldwide living along the shorelines of the world's oceans.

By the end of the Lost Decade, the sea level rise had beaten all projections. In 2036, the world's oceans had risen by over three feet compared to their preindustrial levels. Current projections confirm the entire Greenland ice sheet will vanish by the year 2400, causing global sea levels to rise nearly 24 feet. Manhattan will be completely lost, as will much of Florida, Bangladesh, thousands of Pacific Islands and Venice, Italy.

The world will simply have less available space. Climate refugees will search for higher ground at any cost, causing political turmoil on every continent. Once the Greenland ice sheet falls, it may not be long before the Antarctic ice cap follows suit.

That icy continent, still protected by the cold ocean currents surrounding it, holds 90 percent of the world's ice, which is seventy percent of all the freshwater on Earth. If it melts, sea levels will rise an astonishing 200 feet. Combined, the two ice sheets of Greenland and Antarctica hold enough meltwater to inundate millions of square miles along all the world's continents. Places such as Indonesia, Central America and Brazil's Amazon Basin would vanish beneath the rising sea.

Both Greenland and Antarctica would become habitable, but it would take decades to build the infrastructure needed to colonize them. Much of the new land would become freshwater lakes or inland seas anyway, as the weight of the ice would have pressed the land beneath it down to hundreds of feet below sea level. The entire central core of Greenland would flood.

Already the land beneath Greenland has risen considerably due to the weight of the ice being lifted off of it. Glacial ice weighs 57.41 pounds per cubic foot. The Greenland ice sheet contains some 900,000 cubic miles of ice. There are 8.45 trillion cubic feet in every cubic mile, which means the entirety of Greenland's ice dome weighs 7.6 quintillion pounds. The weight of this frozen water is inconceivable. As the ice melted away, the bedrock below the ice lifted up, causing seismic shifts that reverberated throughout the planet's major tectonic plates.

That, in turn, caused unforeseen tsunamis in the Atlantic and Pacific oceans and earthquakes as far away as South America and Japan. Volcanic eruptions increased worldwide.

As the oil giants drilled out the reserves buried beneath the Arctic Ocean, the Himalayas, the Andes and the Swiss Alps, all moved skyward as the weight of their glaciers flowed out to the rising seas. The plate tectonics shifted continually to this changing dynamic. Millions of people perished. Those deaths were soon factored into the price of a gallon of gas. The fossil fuel party was over and the bill was due. Sadly, death became the most common form of payment.

At the Botanic Garden

"No word from Rubic?"

"No, Margot, not a word. Just that package you gave me two weeks ago."

"Yes, I remember that. I thought it was odd that he sent it to me. What was in it?"

Yeva hesitated. "Just a letter from him and a couple of souvenirs. That's all."

"Why was he out on the West Coast? I noticed the envelope was postmarked from San Francisco. What was he doing there?"

Yeva was caught off guard by Margot's questions. The last thing she wanted Margot Pollock to know was that her boyfriend was a runner. Instinctively she threw up a generic answer. "Just visiting an old high school friend who lives out there."

"That's a long train ride to visit an old friend."

"Yes it is. Listen, Margot, I really have to get back down into the vault right now. I left one of the doors open and you know how that can mess up the humidistats."

Yeva started to turn back toward Margot's office door when her boss added, "I want you to know you can always be honest with me, Yeva, no matter what we discuss."

"OK, can I go now?"

"Yes, of course."

With that Yeva left her boss's office with her stomach in a knot, her mouth dry and her nerves unraveled. She wasn't used to lying, especially to Margot.

Soon she was back in the safety of her seed vault. There was no door left open, nor did Rubic have an old friend living in San Francisco. But there was some well-respected scientist moving to a ranch out west, anticipating a geo-engineered nuclear winter.

Of course Yeva knew about the project. It had been in the news for years. She knew about the failed scrubbers, the second-generation scrubbers and most importantly, she knew about the weather. The weather had turned much of southern Illinois into a desert. She knew about the pipes coming out of Lake Michigan, the relentless hurricanes, the Lost Decade and the serious troubles plaguing Earth.

By 2043, no one alive didn't fear the weather. The climate was the canvas upon which the history of the 21st century was being written and little else mattered. Rising sea levels, droughts, desertification, torrential rains, earthquakes, hurricanes—an arsenal of natural disasters wreaked havoc on the industries of man.

Yeva sat down at her desk, dug out the envelope and reread the scientist's letter again. She let her eyes glide over Rubic's note, trying to ignore the fact that he was still gone. She was tempted to dial Warren's phone number and talk with him about the weather, but she didn't. She would wait until fall to see what happened before doing anything so bold. Winter was just around the corner.

The First Winter

"He was right, wasn't he?"

"God, I hope not."

"But how else can you explain it? Less than two percent of the mirrors have imploded and it's mid-November. According to our original projections, we should be at 84 percent disintegration by now. I did some rough calculations and, based on the current rate of failure, we're looking at a possible 96 percent retention rate. You know what this means, don't you?"

Dr. Maddox Hansen was sitting behind his desk, having a conversation he never imagined he would be having. It was making his stomach turn, his thoughts race and his hands sweat. He didn't want to reply to his colleague's last question, but he had to.

"I've run some models," Dr. Hansen said. "It's a complete fucking disaster."

Both men sat silent for a moment, contemplating a future so bleak it defied comment. Dr. Larry Wade broke the silence.

"We have to go public with this."

"No, not yet. The President already knows. I've informed Professor Bradley at COI and he's made it clear to me that we are not to release any information about the situation. There would be a run on food staples and survival equipment that could throw the entire world's economy into chaos. People would get hurt.

"Besides, there's still a chance the mirrors will begin imploding. Maybe it's just a timing glitch in the programming. Maybe some unforeseen interactions with the ozone layer are causing the delay."

Larry shook his head. He knew better than anyone that the Mylerium Project had been designed not to interact with the ozone layer or any other trace gases found in the stratosphere. He knew the reason for the failure just as clearly as did his boss.

Three weeks ago, when the first batches of nanomirrors failed to deteriorate, Larry went to his computer and reopened Dr. Randolf's files—the same set of calculations Warren had presented to him in February. The projections of the design flaw were all there, in algorithms, equations and computer code. Why didn't they call a halt to the project back in the early spring, before the mirrors were deployed?

Larry didn't respond to Dr. Hansen's comment about the ozone interaction. He took a different tack and continued.

"Is there any other way to take them down? Can we vacuum them up, destroy them somehow?"

"Not at this point. They're too spread out to vacuum. They were designed to blanket the entire Northern Hemisphere and a large part of the Southern Hemisphere. That's millions upon millions of square miles. As you know, they were manufactured to be extremely effective at reducing incoming sunlight, so there are only a few hundred thousand mirrors per square mile, a density measured in parts per billion We could put 100,000 planes up there with mammoth vacuum intakes and they would never make a dent in their numbers."

"What about destroying them?"

"We could conceivably destroy them. We could use thermonuclear devices to destroy them, but you can well imagine the side effects. According to a model we ran last week, we would have to launch a series of hydrogen explosions in the 20-megaton range over the next six months. It would effectively melt the individual mirrors, but would take a minimum of 300 individual denotations in order to make an impact."

"So that's out, then," Larry said glumly. "The amount of lethal radiation from detonating that many bombs would be, well, lethal. Did you get any kind of statistical handle on how many people might die or become sick from doing something so radical?"

"We estimated that at least a billion people would die from radiation sickness within the first year, most of them children, the elderly or the infirm. But that's not the end of it. The world's cancer rate would skyrocket. Then there would be mutations, thyroid diseases and nuclear fallout that would linger for half a century.

"In the end, our computer models indicated that half the world's population would be impacted. Perhaps more. Millions would die quickly, but most would linger on for years in a state of ill health from the delayed effects of radiation exposure. There would be so many sick people that all of our public health systems would be overwhelmed. More than likely the entire worlds' public health systems would unravel.

"Plus, there's again no guarantee it would work. The models suggested there's a good chance that even 300 detonations wouldn't take out enough mirrors to avoid a substantial crop failure next summer. So, the nuclear option is a no-go."

"Have you called Warren?"

"No. He's up in Montana somewhere probably wondering what the hell's going on. We've been posting the projections on the website as though everything is going as planned. People will start to know the truth this winter, though. It's only a matter of time before the entire world knows the Mylerium Project is in trouble."

"But maybe Warren has a solution?"

"I doubt it. His solution was clear to us in February. His solution was to cease and desist, to put an immediate halt to the project until we could prove the disintegration program built into the nanomirrors was sound. There is nothing in his work that talks about what to do if the mirrors fail to come down. Warren will see through our lies long before the general public. As winter sets in, he'll watch the average global temperatures like a hawk. Once the planet starts cooling beyond the norm, he'll know we're in the early stages of snowball Earth. He's anything but stupid."

"Then what's our plan?"

"We pray. We wait and pray."

"That's it?"

"What else can we do? I'll call you when I hear anything from Professor Bradley or President Beltram. In the meanwhile you might want to start stocking up on powdered milk and canned goods. We could be in for some serious trouble, Dr. Wade."

"I know."

Larry got up and walked out of the office. Two weeks earlier he had started buying 50-pound sacks of rice along with flour, honey, canned meats and powdered eggs. His wife kept asking him why they suddenly needed to fill the basement with so much food, but he avoided answering her. He just wanted to be prepared, he said.

"Prepared for what?" she kept asking him.

He could never quite bring himself to respond truthfully: "prepared for the apocalypse.

An Unwelcome Fall

Warren was in his office working on a formula for organic compounds that would help chemically wash CO_2 out of the colossal Kevlar capture strips being designed by Bozeman Recapture. It was late November. Like every day this fall, he had one window on his computer screen open that gave him real-time temperatures from various weather stations across the northern tier of the planet. Today he had his window open to local weather reports from the city of Novosibirsk, the largest city in Siberia, several hundred miles east of Lake Baikal. The daily mean temperature at the turn of the 21st century for the month of November was 21.2 degrees Fahrenheit, but due to global warming over the past fifty years, that average had climbed to 38.1 degrees. With only five days left before the end of the month, the daily mean temperature in Novosibirsk had fallen to just 9.1 degrees.

Warren knew there was only one possible explanation—the mirrors were still up there. Warren also knew that central Siberia, with its enormous land mass, would be the first to experience the effects of the forthcoming cooling and it was clear to him that the big chill had already begun. Novosibirsk's brutal Siberian winter was ahead of schedule—its people were experiencing December's frigid temperatures a month before December arrived. He could not imagine how cold it would be in that city of two million inhabitants once January set in. *Colder than hell* was the only expression he could think of. *Way colder than hell.*

He hit a few keystrokes and he was back on the CMC's site. Nothing on their site had changed. The CMC touted how well the Mylerium Project had gone this past summer, lowering the average world temperature by four degrees Fahrenheit, reducing flash floods and helping to decrease the number and strength of tropical cyclones worldwide. Though there was no direct link, they also boasted about contributing to one of the best grain harvests in recent decades.

"We're going to need that extra grain," Warren mumbled to himself.

He struggled to understand why the CMC was not mentioning the failure of the biggest geoengineering program mankind had ever undertaken. He surmised that the Center for Meteorological Controls had more than likely been instructed to keep the details under wraps by the ruling Green Party. They wouldn't want the world to know they had just made the atmosphere worse than imaginable. The forthcoming winter would be unlike anything the Earth had seen since the Last Glacial Maximum some 20,000 years ago. During that time, massive ice sheets covered most of Northern Europe, much of eastern Siberia and Russia and more than half of North America. These sheets were over a mile deep in places and tied up so much water that the world's seas were 394 feet lower than they were today. Many of the world's land masses were so dry that enormous dust storms ravaged the globe.

Of course massive glaciers can't return in a single winter, thought Warren. But what would happen was bad enough. Based on the forecast models Warren had run before he left the CMC, rivers and streams would freeze as far south as Atlanta. The snow pack would extend to the southern slopes of the Appalachian Mountains in the east and as far west as the central valley of California. Spring would arrive late and hang on through most of the early summer. The extensive snow cover would naturally reinforce the cooling effects of the remaining nanomirrors, reflecting up to 90 percent of the incoming sunlight. In 2044, there would be no summer to speak of anywhere in the Northern Hemisphere.

Warren wondered how long the CMC would maintain their deceit. There were already rumblings on the Net about the Mylerium Project's failure. Amateur meteorologists were, like Warren, monitoring weather stations from Ottawa to Leningrad, and those stations indicated that at least some of the nanomirrors were still in orbit. The record-breaking seasonal temperatures were too unlikely. Winter was coming on too quickly and too cold. There was no way for anyone to prove anything, but many of them, thinking the worst, had already started to stockpile food, warm clothing, wood stoves and water.

Everyone knew it could only be a matter of time before the record low temperatures would force the CMC into a public admission that their project was in trouble. Once that happened, the chatter and blogs on the Net concluded, all hell would break loose.

No one outside the CMC had any idea how many nanomirrors were still in orbit. Warren knew there would be some natural fallout over the summer—four or five percent at most. There would also be some natural dispersion as the billions of particles drifted south of the equator, though that wouldn't change their cooling effectiveness much. His calculations—the same ones he presented to COI—indicated there could be as many as 85 percent still in the stratosphere by mid-January if the self-destruct program failed.

Warren took one more studied glance at the weather report from Novosibirsk, where it was past midnight, and noted that the thermometer was reading -14 degrees Fahrenheit. These were mid-January readings in November.

He wished once again Ann had contacted him, but love, he felt, had always eluded him. Perhaps she hadn't even received his message. At least he would soon have some help around the farm. He was expecting his old college roommate Dr. Albion Garrison to come by soon.

Two days earlier Albion had called Warren to talk about how cold it was in Boston. That coded conversation meant he was on his way out west, taking his wife and children with him in his electric van.

Albion had unexpectedly canceled all of his classes and walked into the dean's office a week earlier to announce his surprise sabbatical. The dean didn't know what to think. Of course he granted Albion the time off, but wondered what on Earth would make Albion behave so strangely. Albion didn't mention the Mylerium Project or Warren's research, but during their brief conversation both men commented on what a miserably cold fall it had been.

"You've not seen anything yet," Albion muttered under his breath as he left the office. Based on some of the projections he had run, he doubted he would ever return to MIT. He wondered if there would even be an MIT in three years.

Aftereffects

Yeva couldn't tell Margot what was happening. Her boss had dismissed the early frost as an anomaly, a freak incident. Everyone had become so accustomed to an overheated planet that most people were delighted by the fact that the fall had arrived earlier and colder than anyone alive could remember. They were ecstatic there were no more November heat waves like there had been for the past two decades. The "Mylerium Summer," as people called it, had been glorious. If it was an unexpected side effect of the geoengineering project, so be it.

Yeva, like Warren, had begun to monitor weather stations around the world. Her searches turned up unseasonably cold weather everywhere. Snow in September in Moscow. Cold, driving rains in the south of France. Freak frosts in central China. More than once, Yeva found herself reaching into the bottom drawer of her desk to reread Warren's handwritten letter.

She knew this man she had never met wasn't crazy. At times she wanted to pick up the phone and call him, explaining how she had come to acquire the letter, talking about Rubic's disappearance or the strange, cold fall—but she realized she couldn't risk it. The CMC's official site still posted that everything was fine, except now they observed that one of the side effects of the Mylerium Project was a "colder than usual" fall. They felt things would return to normal by the end of December.

Yeva knew better. But she felt isolated and alone with that knowledge.

There was still no word from Rubic. She had filed a missing person's report with the Chicago police, but they didn't turn up anything. The police had been notified that Rubic Chang had been taken into custody in San Francisco, but that information was to remain classified.

Yeva fell into a state of depression. Her boss, Margot, sensed it and tried time and again to get her to open up and talk about whatever was eating at her. But Yeva just retreated deeper into the climate-controlled tombs of her seed bank. She hid in her underground office and buried herself in her work. She thought about stockpiling more food, but dismissed the idea as premature. Maybe she was wrong about the cold spell. Maybe it was just a side effect of the Mylerium Project and nothing serious. Perhaps everything would sort itself out by the end of December.

She really believed her own lie until January 7, 2044, when the President of the U.S., Ryan Beltram, came online at 7:30 p.m. CST to have his first press conference about the situation. By then it was almost too late.

"My fellow Americans," the President began. "I come to you this evening to address your concerns about the unusually cold weather we are experiencing this winter in the United States and elsewhere across much of the globe. Many of you already suspect that these unusual temperatures are related to the Mylerium Project, and I am here this evening to confirm this. The Mylerium Project has produced an unexpected aftereffect that is directly related to this global cooling. I want to make one thing perfectly clear before continuing—now is not a time for any of us to become alarmed. The scientists at the Center for Meteorological Controls, the CMC, are working around the clock to remedy the situation and I am confident that they will come up with a solution to the problem as soon as possible.

"The root of this dilemma lies with the nanotechnology used in designing the Mylerium Project. This past summer was the coolest in 60 years and it was a direct result of the success of this multinational geoengineering undertaking. The nanomirrors we deployed last spring have performed flawlessly, shading the entire Northern Hemisphere throughout the hottest months. The success of this program has resulted in a record harvest from the Great Plains of North America to the steppes of Russia. All across the globe, we currently have ample supplies of wheat, corn, rice and other staples because of the phenomenal success of the Mylerium Project.

"Many of you familiar with the project understand that it is designed as a temporary solution to climate change. The deployments of the nanomirrors are scheduled to continue annually for four to five more summers while the second-generation scrubbers begin to come online and work non-stop to reduce the amount of greenhouse gases in our atmosphere. All of these scrubbers should be operational by 2049 and by then we should be well on our way to returning our atmosphere to the weather patterns that were familiar to our parents and grandparents. Most of us know that a complete recovery of a stable climate might take a century or longer, but we are striving toward that all-important goal.

"I'm sure you want to know what the current problem is, so I will do my best to summarize it. The nanomirrors that were designed by the CMC have internal computer programs that will cause each and every mirror to structurally implode in November. For reasons still unclear to us, some of these programs failed to activate, causing the particles to remain in orbit longer than anticipated. Because these mirrors were designed to shade the Northern Hemisphere during the hottest months of the year, when the sun is almost directly overhead, they become more efficient during the winter, when the sunlight hits the Earth at oblique angles. We are not entirely certain what percentage of these mirrors are still in orbit, but we hope to make that determination shortly and will release that data in a timely manner.

"In the meantime, we have decided to temporarily lift the ban on burning fossil fuels until further notice. This will allow us to reopen dozens of coal-fired electrical plants to help relieve the strain on our electrical grid. Many of you, from Minneapolis to Boston, have been dealing with power outages and brownouts because of the persistent cold. With these additional power plants coming online shortly, these problems should be eliminated within the next few weeks.

"We will also offer tax credits to citizens who have been unduly burdened with the exceptionally high heating bills this year. I'm working together with Congress to formulate the details and we should have a plan in place by the end of January.

"As I have already pointed out, the hard-working scientists and engineers at the CMC will be working tirelessly to resolve the issues surrounding this failure. There are already several sound proposals under review and we are optimistic that we can resolve the situation before spring."

The President took a sip of water, and then added, "Are there any questions?"

Frederick Hammel from CNN spoke first. "How long will the mirrors stay in the stratosphere if they fail to implode?"

"That's a good question. I'm not a specialist, but I've been told by the engineers at the CMC that most of the mirrors should disintegrate naturally within a year even if we don't do anything to speed that process up."

A second reporter jumped up and asked, "Will the mirrors affect next year's harvest?"

"No. I would also like to add that if the mirrors currently in the stratosphere fail to implode, we will not proceed with next year's scheduled deployment. But we are confident everything will be resolved by April or May. That being said, models indicate that no matter what happens, the summer of 2044 will be cooler than this past summer, but not cold enough to affect our crops. One more question."

A woman from Fox News in the middle of the crowd of reporters stood up. "Should people be concerned about food shortages this year if the mirrors don't come down?"

"No. Like I said earlier, this is no time to panic. We are reactivating dozens of coal-fired electricity plants and have just come off a record harvest. This is not the time to be stockpiling food or to be worried about whether or not we'll have enough electrical power to make it through to spring. I assure you, both of these issues are under control. Thank you and good evening."

Panic

"It's all bullshit, you know," Warren said.

"Yeah, I know," answered Albion, who was sitting next to Warren watching the 60-inch computer screen that hung in the remodeled barn.

"They know exactly how many mirrors are in orbit. I helped design the monitoring program that would keep track of their initial dispersion. One in every five billion nanomirrors has a microscopic GPS tracking system in it. We used the tracking information to make sure the deployment vehicles covered the largest possible area during the month-long mission to put the mirrors into the stratosphere. Given the fact that they know exactly how many GPS-carrying mirrors are still up there, all they have to do is extrapolate that number to arrive at a final figure with a three percent margin of error. My guess is that most of them are still in place, but there's no way they're going to risk telling that to the public."

Dr. Garrison, along with his wife, Cecilia, nodded in agreement. They were the only people, along with their two children, who had arrived at Shelter Ranch thus far. Warren had also heard from Professor Stephanie

Bankoul, the paleo-climatologist from Stanford, and Dr. Mark Worthington, the glaciologist from Harvard. They were both planning to arrive at the ranch sometime in the spring.

Warren had heard nothing from any of the other scientists and businessmen he had contacted with the runner, but he still held out hope. If they did not come to Bozeman, Warren hoped they had already heeded his warning and were stockpiling their own homes with the food, water, medication and gear they would need to make it through the frigid winter and beyond. He had not heard a thing from Ann, which was still his biggest disappointment.

"Warren, is there any way for the CMC to remove the mirrors if they fail to implode? Is the President telling us the truth about some other method they're working on?"

"No, there's no easy way to get rid of them if the structural implosion fails. They will, over time, start to come down on their own, but my projections indicate that such natural attrition could take two to three years. By then it will be a first class mess down here. It's a classic example of a positive feedback loop.

"When I discovered that the mirrors might not come down in the fall, I realized that the following winter wouldn't be slightly colder than usual—it would be vastly colder. In fact, it would likely be the coldest winter in 18,000 years.

"I knew that kind of winter would bring snow and ice across much of the Northern Hemisphere. Snow reflects sunlight far more efficiently than soil, just as ice reflects sunlight far more efficiently than water. With half the northern hemisphere covered in a white blanket, and the mirrors working in conjunction with this snow pack, we could lose half of the nanomirrors by spring and still struggle to have a viable planting season. It's like tossing dry ice into a chilled freezer—it will only get colder.

"We didn't have a plan B, although we did consider a few options. We took a serious look at using gigantic vacuum planes, but realized there's just too much sky to cover. We investigated a nuclear option but the collateral damage from the radiation was probably worse than just leaving them up there and waiting them out. We even went so far as to look into an internal failsafe explosive system, similar to what NASA uses when a rocket goes off-course just after launch, but the added molecular weight made the mirrors too heavy. They would have fallen out of the stratosphere before they had enough time to make an impact. The nanochip implosion program turned out to be the only viable method available to take them out. That is, had it worked."

"Why are they lifting the ban on burning fossil fuels," Albion asked.

"Well, that move surprised me a bit. I guess we'll need all the electric energy out there to meet the strain this winter and spring will put on the grid. Without the old coal plants up and running, I suppose there would be brownouts and blackouts throughout North America, Russia, China and Europe. Also, fossil fuels may be the best way to counteract the cooling, although I'm not sure how effective it will be on a short-term basis.

"For the past 200 years mankind has been conducting, albeit unwittingly, the first full-fledged geoengineering project ever undertaken. We called it the Industrial Revolution, but in fact it was a colossal, unplanned fire that raged in billions of automobile engines, coal-fired power plants, ship engines, factories, lawnmowers, airplanes, cooking stoves and a thousand other devices that relied on burning fossil fuels for energy. That project led to the largest increase in CO_2 in 55 million years. Now we're geoengineering giant scrubbers, nanomirrors and finally, throwing up a fresh batch of carbon dioxide to offset the whole disaster. It's been a string of bad decisions."

"And it's not going to be pretty."

"It's odd that the President said it's not time to panic. That's probably the worst thing you can say to the nation right now, because anyone with half a brain knows it *is* time to panic."

"We'll find out tomorrow how that one plays out, Warren."

"It won't go well, I assure you. We're just lucky our root cellar is filled to the brim. We should be fine for at least two years. I pity the people who'll be looking for firewood and rice tomorrow morning. It's only getting started."

The next morning it hit a record 24 degrees below zero in Washington, D.C., shattering the previous record of -15 degrees Fahrenheit set on February 11, 1899. Grocery stores across the continent saw lines out the door and hardware store shelves were cleared of everything from batteries to solar generators. By midday, it was obvious the President's message to stay calm had not hit home with the nation's citizens.

The fallout was not restricted to America. Different versions of President Beltram's speech had been delivered by prime ministers, premiers and presidents across the globe that same day. The failure of the Mylerium Project was global in scope. So was the panic.

Foodstuffs, especially MREs (Meals Ready to Eat) as well as dry goods like pasta, rice, flour and other nonperishables, were the first to vanish. Knowing that it might take months to get some of the older coal-fired plants up and running, people rushed to buy woodstoves, from Finland to Fairbanks. Wood-burning bans, common in some countries and states, were either lifted or ignored. Woodstoves were in such demand that some retail stores charged twice the going rate. Complaints about price gouging became so commonplace, they were never investigated.

Normal supply chains were disrupted by the sudden surge in demand. Huge supermarkets stood largely empty for weeks after the rush. The bitter cold made it difficult to get products to market. Hoarding was pandemic. The demand for firewood became so great that people were illegally cutting down trees inside of national parks. Given the circumstances, the park rangers tended to look the other way.

Rumors about the government shutting down grain elevators under the guise of national security became widespread. There were suspicions that the government was holding back supplies to make sure armies and politicians were fed first. The rumors in that case were true—per the CMC's recommendations, government stockpiling had begun in late November. By the time the President spoke, there was enough food, water and energy set aside to keep the government running for a year.

Many of the incidents at grocery stores and Wal-Marts got ugly. Worldwide, 25,000 people died during the food riots in the first few weeks of the international panic. Within a month, despite the bitter cold, people started to realize there was plenty of food to go around and the fractured supply chains were slowly but steadily reassembled.

Everyone was looking forward to spring and to the presumed end of the unbelievable cold spell. Little did they realize they would have to wait until late July for spring. On February 9, 2044, the city of Novosibirsk in central Siberia hit a record 72 degrees below zero. Twenty-eight Russians caught stranded outside the city died of exposure.

The chaos was only getting started.

The Chittagong Disaster

March 13, 2044

I went into town last week to pick up some supplies. The situation in Bozeman is dire. I was only able to find a few of the items I was looking for. People are scared. They've started talking about the Lost Decade again. I think the cold weather and the disruptions in the food supply have led people to recall those awful years that happened not long ago.

There's one date in particular that no one can forget. On November 1, 2035, two natural forces combined to create the single largest human catastrophe in the history of mankind–the Chittagong Disaster. When things were bad, people could always refer back to the Chittagong Disaster to find solace in the fact that nothing would ever again be as bad as that.

It all started in late October of 2035 as a tropical cyclone named Vayu formed in the Bay of Bengal north of the Indian Ocean. It was not a Category 5 cyclone, but it was a strong tropical storm that registered as a Category 3 on the Saffir-Simpson scale. The sustained winds near the eye of the storm were estimated at between 115 to 125 miles per hour. As the storm approached the city of Chittagong, whose population had swelled to 12 million, it slowed precipitously and a massive storm surge built up along the eastern edge of the system. The cyclone alone would have resulted in the deaths of tens of thousands of people.

But an earthquake turned Cyclone Vayu into an unprecedented nightmare. The unlucky coincidence of a magnitude 9.4 earthquake and a record-breaking tsunami happening on the same day as a cyclone's landfall did not go unnoticed. The odds of such a combined event were astronomically low, but so were the odds of an asteroid slamming into the planet, something that nevertheless happened several times in Earth's history. The Chittagong Disaster has been remembered as the tragic, core event of the Lost Decade.

The earthquake was a mega-thrust quake similar in nature to the Sumatra-Andaman earthquake that spawned the December 26, 2004 tsunami.

The 2004 incident, which became known as the Boxing Day Quake, killed a quarter of a million people. The Boxing Day Quake occurred deep below the ocean floor, where the Indo-Australian Plate collided with the Eurasian plate. The region had always been a dangerous and active earthquake zone, but the melting of the world's glaciers, coupled with the weight the melting ice lifted from them, made tsunamis a common event that continue to this day.

The Chittagong quake struck in the middle of the night. There were so many earthquakes and active volcanoes during those dark years that most were lost to obscurity. The world was so overwhelmed with natural disasters during the Lost Decade that it was often difficult to tie death tolls to any particular event. But the Chittagong disaster stood head and shoulders above the rest in terms of fatalities.

It was later estimated that the seabed was pushed up by more than 20 feet during the three-minute tectonic event. The resulting tsunami produced the largest wave set ever recorded. The first wave hit the Andaman and Nicobar Islands within minutes, washing up and over many of the lower-lying islands, taking every living thing with it. Entire cities were swept out to sea. There was no time to evacuate or reach higher ground. Even if there had been advance notice, with the first wave estimated at 130 feet tall, there was no ground high enough to flee to on the Andaman Islands.

Soon the tsunami merged with the storm surge created by Cyclone Vayu and death rained down along the shoreline of Myanmar, Bangladesh, Sri Lanka and Eastern India. The rising waters pushed northward by the slow-moving cyclone were suddenly driven inland at 500 miles per hour by the tsunami wave. The deadly combination brought an unprecedented 110-foot wave slamming into the cities of Chittagong, Cox's Bazar and Dhaka, the capital of Bangladesh. These major cities, along with many villages and towns, were annihilated. Bodies were swept inland as far as three hundred miles as the great waves washed up and over the deltas of the Ganges and the Brahmaputra Rivers. The initial wave was so enormous that it only dissipated when it pushed against the foothills of the Himalayas.

The final death toll was never established. Later estimates from the heavily populated region ranged between 25 and 35 million fatalities. An additional 50 million people were injured.

No one on Earth was prepared for that level of death and destruction. The rising sea levels, the cyclone and the tsunami combined their natural forces to bring the near total destruction of forests, animals, people and their structures. From space, satellite photos revealed tens of thousands of square miles where nothing remained. Bodies were burned for months afterward and millions continued to perish due to starvation from the catastrophic losses of rice fields, shrimp farms and livestock. Much of the delta looked as though a nuclear bomb had been set off. Because the tsunami came during the early hours of the morning, there was no time to flee. The few that attempted to make it to higher ground were engulfed in overcrowded highways or stuck on trains too packed to move.

Cyclone Vayu made landfall less than 24 hours after the tsunami scoured the shoreline clean. The hurricane ensured that the few remaining survivors did not live long. The world was aghast at the photos and videos that followed. No one could imagine what a disaster of that magnitude would actually look like and no one wanted to see the images. The world lapsed into a stunned silence.

The massive tsunami also struck Sri Lanka and the eastern shoreline of India. With a population pushing two billion people, the entire coast was wracked by waves topping 75 feet. The major cities of Chennai and Puducherry were destroyed as were all the villages, towns and cities located along the eastern edge of the island nation of Sri Lanka. The devastation was so widespread that few were able to help. Most charities were already bankrupt from years of relentless earthquakes, droughts, tornadoes, hurricanes and floods.

The months that followed the storm and the tsunami brought even more trouble. Cholera, dysentery and a host of pathogens raged through the survivors of the catastrophe. In the end, no one knows how many perished. That day, November 1, 2035, marked a turning point in the way people viewed fossil fuels worldwide and helped sweep the Greens into power in the election of 2036.

The Chittagong Disaster always surfaces in conversations once people feel the stress of climate change and our damaged weather systems. It's no wonder I'm hearing the people of Bozeman talk about it again, with so many of them concerned about this growing season.

I cannot say a thing. I remain distant at work and make no mention of my research or my former affiliation with the CMC to anyone. The last thing on Earth I want them to know about is our well-stocked root cellar *and the survival stores at the ranch. Once people learn there will not be a crop next summer, our storehouse filled with rice, wheat and other staples will become a goldmine.*

Sadly, that's the reason I went into town in the first place. I realized we'll need guns and ammo. I was shopping for self-preservation.

Spring 2044

By April everyone knew the Mylerium Project was fundamentally flawed. The winter had been ruthless and spring refused to arrive. The government was encouraging people to build their own greenhouses to grow food and went so far as to offer free seeds and expertise to America's 400 million citizens.

The forecast from the CMC was grim. Although it was expected to warm up sufficiently enough to produce some crops along the southern tier of the country, the consensus was that the great corn, wheat and soybean fields from Iowa to Canada would fail.

People were already being asked to ration, but by mid-May, smaller grocery chains, many restaurants and thousands of wholesalers were running out of food altogether. Fearing what was next, people started hoarding in earnest. Basements filled with canned goods, flour, rice and dried meats. Poaching wildlife became rampant. In some of the national parks, even the staff started illegally harvesting elk, moose and deer. Some of the animals were starving. A quiet fear gripped the nation.

Three more families had contacted Warren by the end of May. Dr. Stephanie Bankoul called to let Warren know that she, her husband Andrew and their only child Melissa were planning to leave Stanford and start driving to Shelter Ranch in June, once the snow pack in the Rockies melted enough to open the highways into Montana. She knew that it was only going to get worse and, like Warren, she did not want to be near a large city when it did.

Professor Worthington, the glaciologist from Harvard, had called only to wish everyone the best. He had family commitments which made it impossible for him to join the others at the ranch. Dr. Henry Irving, Warren's childhood physician, called to let him know that he, his wife and his sister would depart Indianapolis in July and head straight for Shelter

Ranch. His two sons would not be joining them. Warren was concerned about Dr. Irving's age, but felt the compound could use the expertise of a trained physician.

Warren had also heard from Roger Goode, a very successful businessman he knew from San Jose. Roger had made millions in the technology sector but felt the safest place to be would be far from San Jose, which had ballooned into a sizeable metropolis of three million people.

Warren was thrilled to have someone on board with substantial financial resources, but he knew that as time went by, money wouldn't mean anything when compared to rice or flour.

There was still no word from Ann.

Warren had no way of knowing Ann's package had ended up in Chicago, in the hands of a young woman who had endured many sleepless nights debating whether she should call him to talk about the weather. She wanted to call him and explain that she was Rubic Chang's girlfriend and that Rubic had never returned from the West Coast.

Yeva was, like so many other people across the globe, in denial about the situation. She kept waiting for a technological fix from the President, from COI, from the CMC—from anyone. None came. Yeva had read and reread Warren's letter a dozen times and knew better than almost anyone else how dire the prognosis was, but she wasn't ready to call Warren. She didn't know him and wondered how he would react to her having intercepted a message destined for a woman he loved.

So she waited. She waited as snow continued to fall in early May and the nation teetered on the edge of panic. She waited while the President went on the air again in early June announcing that there would be massive crop failures and that everyone should plan on rationing their supplies into the foreseeable future. There was still snow along the Appalachian Mountains in early July and the trees were finally budding in Chicago during the last week in June. The corn wouldn't be knee high by the fourth of July in Iowa—the stalks were just pushing through the ground by then. The farmers all knew there would be no harvest but they planted their fields anyway. They could harvest the stalks for feedstock.

The second deployment of the Mylerium Project was canceled. No one in their right mind was going to put up a second round of nanomirrors after the first deployment failed to implode. Congress was busy investigating how this could have happened and the CMC was under intense scrutiny.

Dr. Maddox Hansen had been forced to resign. When he left his office, he took every trace of Warren's research with him. He didn't want some congressional investigation uncovering the fact the CMC had been warned by one of their own lead scientists. That would have only added fuel to the flames that were engulfing the politics of Washington.

The nanomirrors were still up there, though close to 20 percent of them had disintegrated by April. The trouble was that the positive feedback loop was firmly in place. The highly reflective snow pack had extended all the way to the southern tip of the Appalachian Mountains and well into Mexico along the Rocky Mountains. The world had gone from droughts, hurricanes, sweltering heat waves and endless tornadoes to an ice house in one terrible season. Out of the frying pan, into the freezer. No one could believe it.

Freefall

One by one, the climate refugees arrived at Shelter Ranch. They took their rooms in either the main house or the converted barn. They built small greenhouses, though finding plastic was increasingly difficult. They huddled together during the cool summer nights and discussed their options. They target practiced, played ping pong, fished the nearby streams and wondered what would happen once winter returned.

Warren, working with Dr. Albion Garrison from MIT, tried to get a theoretical handle on how cold the forthcoming winter would be. The CMC elected not to disclose the actual number of nanomirrors remaining in the stratosphere, using the guise of national security as their rationale. Warren and his friend had to estimate that number by using algorithms based on the statistical average temperatures of a dozen major cities across the entire Northern Hemisphere. Based on their research, they estimated that 65 to 70 percent of the mirrors were still in the stratosphere. By fall, they felt that number might drop another five to ten percent, at best.

The coal-fired power plants that the President had directed to restart were spewing out tons of additional CO_2 by mid-summer. It proved to be too little too late. The planet had not received enough sunlight over the year to warm the atmosphere. In late July, it was still freezing at night in parts of southern Illinois, the hills of Arkansas and California's Central Valley. It was as if the Earth had moved a million miles farther away from the sun in a single season. Everything was cold and everyone was frightened.

The Southern Hemisphere struggled under the harshest winter on record. Because most of the deployments had occurred north of the equator, the hope was that they would have sufficient sunlight to produce a harvest in the winter. The governments of South America, Australia and southern Africa made it clear that they were not willing to ship any of their harvest north because they needed to assure their own people that there were sufficient food stores to keep them from panicking. No help would come from the south. Everyone would have to fend for themselves.

As the summer wore on amidst grim reports of failed crops, increasing grain and food shortages, the world turned dark and desperate. With no grain or grass to feed livestock, domestic animals were brought to slaughter and massive herds were culled to just a handful of breeding pairs. Meat was, at least during the summer, plentiful—but everyone knew that wouldn't be the case for long. By the fall, thousands of restaurants were closed or failing. There was no more food available for commercial consumption. The world's economy was in freefall. The only thing people thought about was having enough food to survive the winter of 2045. But in many places, that simply wouldn't happen.

Target Practice

"Allison—you have to squeeze the trigger, not jerk it!"

"I've never fired a rifle before, Warren. Do I look like Annie Oakley?"

Dr. Allison McBride did not look at all like Annie Oakley. She was tall and graceful, with flowing blond hair. Her blue eyes shone in the June sunlight on a rare day that crept above 60 degrees Fahrenheit.

Warren remembered seeing some vintage photos of Annie Oakley as a kid, and he had to agree with Allison.

"No, you don't look like her, and you sure as hell don't shoot like her."

Allison released another round from the rifle. The silhouetted target, shaped like a head and torso with a bullseye on its heart, didn't budge as the bullet raced past it and buried itself in the hillside a hundred yards beyond.

"I missed it completely, didn't I?"

"Yeah, pretty much."

"Maybe we should move closer?"

"I think that would be a good idea. Let's get within 100 feet of the thing and see if that does you any good. Albion, do you want to pace off a hundred feet?"

Albion had busied himself fiddling with an old AR-15, but he had set it down to watch Allison's shooting. "Sure, Warren, just don't let Allison shoot at me. Not that she'd hit me."

They laughed. Dr. Allison McBride, one of the world's leading paleo-climatologists, could not hit the broad side of a barn with a gun. She could analyze Antarctic ice cores to the molecule, but she couldn't shoot a rifle to save her life. Her handgun skills were abysmal. As they moved closer to the target, Allison reiterated her earlier comments to Warren.

"Do you really think we're going to need these guns? After all, who's going to come way the heck out here looking for us, Warren?"

"You never know, Allison. This winter is going to be a real challenge for a lot of people around here. There are already food shortages in Bozeman and I hear things are worse in Missoula. If anyone hears about our food and medical supplies, at some point they just might be desperate enough to drop by. And I've got a bad feeling that if that time comes, it won't be a friendly visit."

Allison thought for a moment and realized Warren was right.

"Are you serious about teaching the kids to shoot, Warren?"

"I think all of us should be able to handle a gun. That is, except your three-year-old. I think she'd have some trouble with the kickback on the shotgun—don't you agree?"

Allison laughed, imagining little Mara holding up a 12-gauge shotgun. "I just can't picture it, Warren. The gun would weigh more than she does."

"Well, I don't think we have to include three-year-olds in our plan. But the older kids should know one end of a gun from the other, just to be safe. I don't think any of us are sure what's going to happen down the road.

Hunger can turn people into dangerous animals, and there are going to be millions of people going hungry down the road."

Allison reflected on Warren's comments while she reloaded the magazine to her M16-F2. She stood on the line Albion scratched in the dirt, pointed the gun and slowly, methodically squeezed the trigger. The paper target shuddered for a second as the bullet ripped through it, three inches below the heart. Warren smiled.

"Gut shot. It'll take him four or five hours to die, but at least you hit him. Albion, I think it's time you take a turn. Especially now that Annie Oakley's back."

The three of them spent another half hour at the practice range. After a while, Allison announced she had to run back to the barn to see how her little girl was doing in the hands of her husband, Frank. Albion and Warren elected to head back to the compound a little later. They struck up a conversation soon after Allison left.

"You're worried about something, Warren. I get that we have to protect ourselves, but why so much ammo? Do you want to talk about it?"

"Yes, but not in front of Allison. We've all got enough on our minds figuring out how we're all going to pull through this thing. I don't need to add any more concerns."

"So what is it?"

"It's the contractor who built this place. I ran into him a week ago in town at the gun shop. He was buying a half-dozen guns and an unusual amount of ammunition. He asked me how my skiers were doing, now that it's snowing in May. There was something in his tone, something disconcerting."

"You think he might come out here?"

"No, not alone. Maybe not now either—but like I said, they're already experiencing food shortages in Bozeman, and when this winter hits, with more cold, more snow and less of everything, things could get serious. We already have 19 people on the ranch. Although I stockpiled for as many as 24, I doubt we'll end up having much to spare. I didn't set this place up as a local charity, and I don't think we really have enough to share anyway.

"Anyone wanting our stockpile would have little choice but to try to take it by force. If that happens, we'll need to be able to defend ourselves. That's why I'm making everyone learn the basics. It's a precaution I hope we never have to turn to, but who knows?"

"You're right. This contractor guy, what's his name?"

"His name is Vince Gatini. He's a nice enough guy, but he knows we've got food stashed out here—given what's in store for all of us, he might put together a crew and try to get his hands on it."

"Well, he'll find a real fight on his hands if he does."

"Not with Allison's shooting skills," Warren said jokingly.

Albion didn't laugh. "Let's keep these target practice sessions going through the summer. By the fall, everyone should be able to handle a gun, just in case."

"Just in case," Warren agreed.

The White House

The President was awaiting an important phone call from Dr. Larry Wade, the man who had replaced Dr. Hansen at the CMC. It had been a tumultuous year at the Center for Meteorological Controls. After the Mylerium disaster, it was impossible to maintain the status quo. Heads rolled, including Dr. Maddox Hansen's. He had been asked to submit his resignation in March, and the President himself had asked Dr. Larry Wade to step into his boss's former position as the head of the agency. There were dozens of other resignations submitted and scores of scientists who were fired outright for the nightmare that had become a trillion-dollar failure at planetary geoengineering.

A whole new crew of scientists, recruited from everywhere on the planet, had been brought in to replace those who had gotten the world into this predicament. The new team's sole mission was to figure out how to remove as many nanomirrors as possible without causing additional harm to the climate. There were scientists and engineers from every country in the northern hemisphere: Russia, Canada, United Europe, China, India and the Middle East. They had looked at every conceivable method of removing the remaining mirrors and had finally come up with one possible solution.

"Dr. Wade, I hope you've got some good news for me," said President Beltram after taking the incoming call.

"I hope so too, Mr. President. We've just about exhausted every idea out there, and this is the only one that seems to have any hope of working."

"Well, what is it?"

"Lasers, specifically gamma lasers."

"I've never heard of gamma lasers. What are they?"

"You've never heard of them because only one exists thus far, the prototype we created for the nanomirror removal project. They give off a very unusual light and when focused on the molecular structure of the mylar, they disintegrate the nanomirrors in a similar manner as the internal computers were designed to do."

"That sounds promising. When can we expect them to be operational?"

"That's the problem. The one we designed in the lab is too small to be of any use trying to dissolve molecular particles suspended miles above the Earth. To create a gamma laser large enough to be effective at those altitudes will take at least a year, possibly longer. They attack the mirrors in pulses of gamma rays that activate the self-destruct mechanisms that are currently not operational. To make them large enough to impact microscopic mirrors miles away is the engineering challenge of the century. A year might not be enough time to get the job done."

"That's not acceptable. You and I both know that if we cannot get the remaining nanomirrors out of the upper atmosphere by the end of next winter, we could potentially have back-to-back crop failures. We've already reduced our national food reserves to record levels. We don't have enough grain, rice and staples to endure a second summer without crops. People will starve to death, millions of people, Dr. Wade, and that's not going to happen if I can help it.

"If we fast track the production of these gamma lasers can we avoid a second summer of despair?"

"Our models indicate that even if we can make fifty full-scale lasers, we would only be able to take out 47% of the remaining mirrors before next summer. That might not be enough to prevent a second year of crop failures."

"What percentage of the mirrors are still up there, Dr. Wade?"

"The GPS tracking particles indicate we are still at 76% of the original deployment. We've only lost 24% thus far. Some of these appear to have imploded as designed, while others have succumbed to ultra-violet rays, solar flares, dispersion and natural phenomena. According to our models, there are still sufficient mirrors to produce a winter just as cold as last year, which will assuredly put a second summer at risk."

"Why's that? With far fewer mirrors in orbit, you would think the winters would be less severe?"

It's all due to feedbacks. There are still twenty feet of snow pack along much of the continental divide, and it's mid-July. The snow is reflecting sunlight back into space and keeping us way below normal. In some regions in higher elevations that temperature is thirty degrees below seasonal averages. It's how ice-ages get started.

"If we go into the fall and then the winter of 2045 this cold, there will be ice on the lakes of northern Florida in December. By late January, Lake Okeechobee could have ice sheets forming along its shoreline, and what's left of Miami will see snow. There is no telling how cold it will be in the mountain cities of Denver and Salt Lake City, nor do we know what will happen along the northern tier of the nation in the cities of Chicago, Cleveland and Minneapolis/St. Paul. They could easily see temperatures plummet to seventy-five below. This past winter, the Vostok Station in Antarctica broke its all-time record of -128.6 °F, set in 1983, by twenty-three degrees. It's gotten so cold, so fast that all of us here at the CMC are in a state of shock."

There was a long, drawn out pause before President Beltram responded.

"What's it going to cost to get these lasers operational in six months' time?"

"A trillion dollars and the complete cooperation from every nation on Earth. We've not a moment to waste."

"We don't have a choice at this point in time. Let's get on it. I'll call a press conference for tomorrow evening and contact the world's leaders to notify them that we have come up with a plan to eradicate these God-forsaken nanomirrors before they eradicate us."

"It's all we have, Mr. President, and I'll get the team at the CMC on it immediately."

"Good bye, and God speed, Dr. Wade."

"Good bye Mr. President. Let's pray these lasers work."

With that, President Beltram hung up the phone. He felt faint, almost suspended in his own body like a ghost of himself. He knew that even with the gamma lasers out there, continually shooting massive bursts of radiation toward the very edge of our atmosphere, it might not help. With more than 65% of all the land mass on Earth lying north of the equator, including most of the world's leading agricultural regions, the thought of enduring another year without a growing season made the President physically ill.

Even though the nanomirrors had only been used sparingly across the skies of the southern hemisphere, the intense cold experienced during the past winter was amplifying the winters throughout South America, Australia and South Africa. The various nations on these continents, from Argentina to Mozambique, had made it clear to the world that they were dealing with an equally grave situation. Their yields were down more than 50% because of the exceptionally cold summer and models indicated that unless the mirrors came down, that number could rise to a crop failure rate of 70% during the growing season of 2045. Their economists have informed them there would barely be enough food to feed their own populations, and nothing left to export.

The President had every right to worry. He wanted to break down and cry, asking himself again and again how we could have done something so stupid. He knew better. We had made the planet too hot and we had tried, unsuccessfully, to make it cool again. One geoengineering mistake, more than two centuries in the making, lead to a second mistake that took a single year. The gamma lasers better work, reflected the President. If they don't, death will find us.

In Chicago

By late fall, the greater Chicago area was descending into chaos. Food supplies were vanishing. The lines in grocery stores, when there was food to sell, became blocks long and every restaurant in the city had closed due to lack of availability of basic commodities. Unemployment soared to record highs as almost every business connected to the food industry shut down. College cafeterias, hotels, hospitals, prisons and senior citizen centers all reduced staff and struggled to find available sources of flour, eggs, meat and dairy.

People with guns took to shooting pigeons, doves, even rats to cook and eat. Wildlife suffered unprecedented mortality, both from the relentless cold and from uncontrolled harvesting. In the countryside deer hunting season was in a free for all. Men and women invaded state and national parks at night, determined to shoot anything they could. The park rangers looked the other way or, in many cases, did the hunting themselves, knowing that they and their families needed to eat.

Everything revolved around food. It didn't matter if you drove the most expensive electric car or lived in the best neighborhoods, it was all about finding food. As winter approached and news spread that it was going to be as bad as last year's horrific winter, people started hoarding whatever they could. By this time, all pretense of maintaining any kind of supply chain was abandoned. It was becoming a hand-to-mouth economy, unlike anything the Western world had seen since the end of the Dark Ages.

The thought of a second unbearable winter weighed heavily on Yeva. Having not heard from him in more than a year, she had come to accept the fact that Rubic had been apprehended, possibly tortured, and more than likely killed. She knew the track record of the Green Party when it came to their handling of prisoners, especially runners. With Rubic gone Yeva felt she needed to talk to someone, anyone, about the letter she had received a year ago from this Dr. Warren Randolf.

That's why she had asked for this meeting with her boss, Margot Pollack. She needed to talk and she wanted someone else's opinion as to what she should do. Should she remain in Chicago or try to make it out West to Warren's enclave? She had called the meeting, and she was glad she did as she knocked on Margot's open door.

"Come in, Yeva, take a seat."

"Thanks, Margot. I'm glad you could find the time to see me."

"Don't even say something like that, you know my door is always open, especially for you."

Yeva took a seat besides Margot's desk. The top of the desk was spotless, just as it was every time Yeva walked by. There was a single photo of Margot, her two children when they were both much younger, and her husband, Roland. A stack of papers, arranged in an orderly pile, lay opposite the photo. Nothing else sat on the desktop except a blotter calendar.

"What is it, Yeva, you look worried."

"Remember the package you received over a year ago?"

"Yes, of course, the one from San Francisco."

Yeva reached into her pocket and took out the folded letter that was inside the package and handed it to Margot.

"Here's what was in it, along with a micro-drive containing an encrypted file I cannot open. I want you to read it."

Margot reached over and took the letter in her hand, unfolded it, and started reading. Her eyes opened wide as she read each and every sentence in disbelief. She read the entire letter before addressing Yeva.

"Oh my God. They knew this might happen all along. Why on Earth did they go ahead with the deployment after knowing this? Have you shared this letter with anyone, Yeva?"

"No, I've been too afraid to discuss its contents with anyone. I've not heard from Rubic since the package arrived and I'm afraid he's gone. I have a feeling the Greens would not want the information in this letter to get out, since it would destroy their reputation. Imagine what the world would think if people knew that one of their top scientists had forewarned the CMC that their project might fail."

"I agree. You mustn't share this information with anyone. If they know you are in possession of this letter, they'll have you arrested. Oh, my God, they'll arrest me as well, won't they?"

"Only if they know. Which they don't."

"Have you called this person yet, this Dr. Randolf?"

"No, but I've been tempted to, especially since it looks as if this coming winter is going to be as cold as last year."

"Maybe not, haven't you heard about the gamma lasers? They say they should be able to eradicate most of the mirrors by spring if all goes according to plan. If that happens next summer should be cold, but not cold enough to prevent a growing season."

"I wish I could believe them, Margot, but that information is coming from COI and the CMC. Those are the same people who insisted there was no risk with the Mylerium Project. After going through this past winter, after watching people get hungrier and hungrier, I don't know if I can ever believe them again."

"You have a point. If they lied to us once, never even mentioning any of the information contained in this letter to the public, they are probably, no, more than likely, lying to us again."

"But getting back to my earlier question, why haven't you called him?"

"The letter's not addressed to me, Margot. He doesn't know me and I'm clearly not his beloved Ann, though I don't know who she is either. It might be too weird to call him at this point in time. But the real reason I wanted to stop by was to let you know that if you need basics, I have plenty."

"What do you mean, are you telling me you have extra food?"

"Yes. My apartment looks like a warehouse. I've put black plastic over the windows of my second bedroom because I don't want anyone to know what's in there. I've probably got more than a thousand pounds of flour, dried eggs, rice, lots and lots of rice, cooking oil, canned goods, even dried meats and nuts. I started stockpiling soon after getting Dr. Randolf's letter. Remember Margot, I knew what was happening because of the letter and I suspected the CMC was lying from the start."

"How could you afford it, Yeva, to buy all that extra food?"

There was an electronic key in the package along with the letter and the micro-drive. A separate note from Rubic told me to go down to this timed locker at the train station on a certain date and time and inside of it I would find the final payment for Rubic's run. Ann's wasn't the only package he delivered. There were several more, though I don't know who received them. There was ten-thousand dollars in cash inside that locker. I bought the extra food with much of that money.

"That's why I'm here, Margot. I'm thinking about calling him. I don't trust the Greens anymore. I don't think the gamma lasers are going to work anywhere near as well as they are saying. I think they're lying just like they lied to us about the Mylerium Project. I think governments thrive on lying, just like the lies they told our parents about climate change. How it wasn't a big deal, how the Earth was heating up naturally, how it was just a cycle. It's all just one BIG HUGE LIE!"

Yeva's voice had risen in tone and outrage as she spoke to Margot and it was impossible for her boss not to notice how angry she had become, how bitter. Margot reflected for a second on what this young lady had just gone through and knew she wouldn't have behaved any differently under the circumstances. Her boyfriend was gone, she had kept a terrible secret to herself for more than a year and then she had to carry the quandary of whether or not she should contact this scientist who was holed up somewhere out West. Margot could see that Yeva was starting to cry, releasing a year of pent up frustration and ire.

"Oh, Yeva, you should have told me this a long time ago."

"I just didn't know what to do." Yeva said between sobs.

Margot took out some tissues from the bottom drawer of her desk and handed them to the lovely young lady sitting beside her. She bent down and gave her an awkward hug.

"Here, take one of these," said Margot as she handed Yeva a tissue.

Yeva dried her tears and continued.

"What should I do? If I call him and he wants me to come out West, I'll leave my food for you. If he doesn't want me out there, well, then at least we can share what I have. I've got a terrible feeling it's going to get much, much worse before it gets better and I've got more food than I can possibly use. You've still got your two sons to feed and I know teenagers have hearty appetites."

Margot nodded in agreement. She had stockpiled some basics but at this point in time it was hard to find any excess to buy. Prices were exorbitant, since suppliers who had food had learned that they could charge as much as the market would bear. In many places, the black market in food was larger than traditional channels. Margot, just like every mother on Earth, was growing increasingly concerned about feeding her two sons, Daryl and Chase.

"I would call him if I were you, Yeva. Tell him what you think has happened and establish a connection. At the very least he'll know why Ann hasn't contacted him. There's no doubt that the package you received was intended for her, and he's probably wondering why she never got in touch with him. She doesn't even know he tried to warn her. I would definitely call him."

"Thanks for the advice, Margot. Do you want to stop by my apartment later and pick up some flour and things?"

"Yes, of course I do. I'll swing by after work. I'll only take a small amount, as it's getting to the point where it's not safe to be seen anywhere with grocery bags. I heard there was an incident downtown over someone carrying a bag of groceries just last week. We'll have to be careful but I will take you up on your offer to share."

"Thanks for listening, Margot."

"No, thank you for sharing. Here's your letter."

Margot reached over and handed Warren's letter back to her employee. Yeva's green eyes were puffy from the tears. Yeva smiled, just a little, as she took the letter in her hand. She then got up and walked back toward the door.

"See you around six or so?"

"Make it seven, it would be better for us to wait until it's dark. I'll swing by in my car."

"See you at seven. Thanks again, Margot."

"Take care, Yeva. Things will work out."

"I hope so."

Yeva closed the office door behind her and headed back to her vaults. Things will work out, she kept thinking to herself. Things will work out.

At Shelter Ranch

Warren kept speculating about Ann. He wondered tirelessly about whether or not she had received her invitation to join him. He wondered why she hadn't called. The familial arrangements at the ranch made it difficult for him. His best friend, Albion Garrison, had his wife Cecilia. Allison McBride shared a room with her husband, Frank. Dr. Stephanie Bankoul had her partner, Gabriele, while Roger Goode, the high-tech tycoon from San Jose had his attractive girlfriend, Simone, and Dr. Irving, his family physician, had not only his wife, but his sister, Teresa, as well. Only Warren was alone, and at times, amidst the card games, ping pong tournaments and group dinners, his loneliness weighed on him.

It was late at night, when he was in his room in the main house, that it pained him most. When he would lie back and hear the wind sweeping down from the surrounding hills, blowing the scattered leaves from the few trees that made it to leafing that summer, that was when it hurt the most. Warren would spend hours remembering the good times Ann and he had together before their relationship began to crumble. Dinner parties at his old apartment, drinks after work with friends. Times growing more and more distant as the days grew shorter and a winter unlike all others before it descended on central Montana. It was during these cold autumnal evenings that he would often get up, walk over to his computer desk, take out his notebook and pen, and make another entry in his journal. It comforted him to have this private space, this place to express himself freely and to reflect on both the past and the future. Provided there was a future.

November 1st, 2044

We've settled into a quiet rhythm at the ranch. I'm still working at Bozeman Recapture, in fact I'm putting in long, endless hours trying to keep things on track. With this temporary but extreme cooling that's taken place across the planet, the demand to remove the excess CO_2 from the atmosphere has cooled as well. When I first arrived, it was full steam ahead, but with the government reopening all the moth-balled coal-fired power plants and their focus now redirected at trapping heat in our atmosphere, orders have fallen off precipitously. Bozeman Recapture is in a state of suspended animation. There's even talk of layoffs floating around the office. Unless this cold snap ends, and ends soon, I can't see how they'll be able to keep going for another year. No one wants to cut CO_2 when it's seventy-five degrees below zero outside.

The good news is everyone on the ranch is in good spirits and glad to be here rather than near the heavily populated urban centers they've left behind. Only Professor Worthington from Harvard couldn't make it. I'll miss him but he had too many family connections to make it feasible for him to get away.

But Mark, like everyone else, knows that if next summers' crops fail again things will become much worse than they are at present. People are hanging on, but food shortages are common and there are plenty of tales of violent clashes at grocery stores and government run food centers. Rumor has it that there have been hundreds of home invasions where food hoarders have been overpowered, beaten, even murdered, and their entire caches stolen. As people become increasingly hungry, this kind of thing can only get worse. God forbid, if we lose the growing season next summer, I think people could turn to eating each other.

Whether we like to acknowledge it or not, we have a history of cannibalism. As a species, we've engaged in anthropophagy, which is the scientific term for eating the flesh of other human beings, for hundreds of thousands of years. The word itself, cannibalism, comes from the Carib Indians, the first tribe Columbus encountered in 1492 when he discovered the New World. Its root is derived from the Spanish name for the Carib Indians, "Canibales." It was still practiced in New Guinea, the Congo and remote parts of the Amazon basin well into the 20th century. Some argue it's still found in remote regions of the world, though I find this hard to believe. A worldwide famine could change all that.

I've also researched several instances where survivors are driven to eat the dead to make it through. There was a plane crash in the Andes in 1972 where the 16 survivors fed on the dead passengers to make it through the two months they endured in that high mountain pass. After exhausting what little food was on board, they eventually turned to eating the flesh of their fellow passengers, but only those who had not survived the impact. It was an ethical nightmare for all of them but the survivors eventually came to realize that there was nothing left to eat but those who had died in the crash. They endured for seventy-two days atop that snow-covered peak because they ate the dead. I can't help but think this kind of thing will happen if we don't have a harvest in the fall of 2045.

There is a built-in danger to cannibalism that is seldom talked about. It's called Prion's disease. The natives of New Guinea gave it the name kuru. The disease is transmitted by eating other diseased people. Prion's disease is similar to Mad Cow disease or CJD, which is short for Creutzfeldt-Jakob disease. When contracted, the victim's brain turns to a sponge-like substance. In New Guinea they call it the "laughing sickness" due to the pathological outbursts of laughter natives would display as the disease progressed. As the brain continues to deteriorate, symptoms include loss of muscle control, tremors, and slurred speech. Near the end of the disease, and it's always fatal, severe tremors and violent shaking sets in, followed by incoherent speech, incontinence, ulcerations and the inability to walk or sit upright. Death occurs between three months to two years after the initial onset of symptoms. They say it is one of the most horrible ways by which a person can possibly die.

It's hard for me to imagine what might happen in a world filled with ten billion people and nowhere near enough food to go around. In a way, it's like a gigantic life raft, this planet of ours. Most of the time, at least for the past 10,000 years, we just reach over the side to grab whatever's handy—some fish from the sea, a bowl of cereal from the wheatfields, a dish of steamed rice. But when the rations run out, there's little doubt in my mind that terrible things will happen. Most people will give up, accepting their fate and their imminent death with quiet resolve. Others will fight to the death over that last scrap of food. They'll kill and eat anything to keep from starving. Extreme hunger brings out the worst in animals, and the human animal will probably prove no different.

I know we'll be fine at the ranch and if my calculations are correct, the nanomirrors will not survive a third summer. Though it will be much colder than normal, we should be able to plant crops in the spring of 2046.

It's to that end that I've amassed a substantial seed repository in one of the bedroom closets of the Main house. Seeds were one of the first things I bought after getting the barn and the root cellar finished. I knew if this nanomirror nuclear winter came to pass the very fabric of civilization could unravel and that in the final analysis, it might all come down to seeds. Those that have seeds, when the third winter breaks, would have food to grow, and be able to eat that spring, summer and fall. Those who don't have seeds would be at the mercy of whatever was left of the infrastructure, or go hungry. They'll go hungry despite the improved growing season because they won't be able to plant anything. No seeds equals no food. I focused on plants and vegetables that did well in colder conditions. Plants like broccoli, cauliflower, squash, corn and potatoes along with fast growing spring plants like beet greens, leaf lettuce and Swiss chard. We did moderately well this past summer with a small greenhouses fabricated out of window frames and plastic, but there aren't enough shortages to make these kinds of projects necessary yet. Next summer will be a different story. Clear plastic is already getting hard to find.

I've calculated that most of the northern hemisphere will run into severe, if not total, food shortages by late spring. When that happens seeds will become essential. We've already drawn up plans for a much larger, and better built, greenhouse next summer. Our seeds, along with the food cellar dug into the hillside, will be what we need to get through the third winter. I just pray no one gets wind of our stockpiled supplies.

It's late. I'm exhausted. I miss Ann. I wish there was some news, from Rubic, from Ann, from anyone just to let me know how she's doing. There's so much disquiet ahead, I hate to even think about it.

With that, Warren put down his pen and headed over to the bathroom to brush his teeth, wash up and head to bed. For the moment, all was well in the valley beside the mountain stream in central Montana. Moments that will not last.

The Second Winter

The second winter was merciless. Scattered snowstorms hit the higher elevations in the Rockies by the end of August. By mid-January, the snowpack along the Continental Divide was 80 feet deep. Blizzards pounded the central and northern plains, with wind gusts approaching 100 miles per hour and bitter-Arctic cold snaps coming one on top of the other. The Mississippi River froze over as far south as Memphis. Tens of thousands of people died from exposure when the batteries in their electric cars failed and they attempted to make it to safe havens on foot. No one had ever experienced anything like it before.

The government of the Greens, aside from allowing the old coal-fired plants to operate again, was unable to offer much help. They had decided early on that their own strategic stockpile of food and medicine was going to be kept for members of the party's upper echelon—the top military brass, Congress and the White House. There wasn't enough food left to contemplate sharing it with the general public. The food centers ran out of supplies by mid-March and were then shut down. The government would help itself but the people were on their own.

Soon the first prototype gamma laser was operational and ready for testing. It was deployed near Denver and its first test firing was conducted on March 24, 2045. The unique diffusion lens spread the beam across an area of one square mile high above sea level. The results were promising, but fell far short of what was needed to turn things around. With the beam fully focused, it could eliminate one square mile of the nanomirrors in about two hours. The trouble was one of scale.

At the height the laser operated, it would need to cover close to 200 million square miles to clean up the atmosphere. It would take thousands of the multibillion-dollar gamma lasers operating around the clock for a decade to make an impact. Of course, COI never mentioned this in news releases about the success of the project.

COI's official position was that the world needed hope more than truth. Hope, even dressed as a lie, was the only thing that kept people going when the air outside plummeted to 45 below. People could only hope that the gamma lasers would take out enough mirrors, or that ultraviolet rays would destroy them, or that they would just tumble back to Earth. Then the huge electric combines of the Great Plains could start breaking soil again. Then the world's farmers would again be able to grow wheat, barley, corn, soybeans—anything to replenish the ever-dwindling reserves.

Although conditions were horrid in North America and Europe, it was much worse in the densely populated regions of sub-Saharan Africa, India, Indochina, China and Korea. In Africa, people suffered from the cold air that filtered down across the Sahara all the way to the Congo. Starvation set in from coast to coast along the northern tier of the continent. Morocco, Algeria, Tunisia, Libya and Egypt all fared moderately well, but below the vast Sahara, things fell apart. Snow fell unabated in the highlands of Ethiopia and people throughout the region had turned to killing and eating whatever wildlife they could find. People started killing elephants, crocodiles, hippos, giraffes, Cape buffalo, lizards, snakes, birds or even insects in an effort to fend off hunger.

India was beyond hope for salvation. Although some rice and wheat crops had come in along the southern regions of the subcontinent, the entire northern section had been impacted by a mass of frigid air that had gathered along the thousand-mile stretch of the Himalayas. It snowed as far south as Calcutta. There was nowhere near enough food for the country's 1.8 billion people. Many faithful Hindus had turned to devouring their sacred cows. People were dying in India by the tens of thousands. As in all famines, the children and the elderly suffered the most.

China, Indochina and Russia likewise felt the pain. Russia was particularly hard-hit because of the cold air that never seemed to leave Siberia after the first frigid winter. In towns like Novosibirsk, municipal water pipes laid 20 feet underground froze solid and systems throughout the region—even systems designed to handle harsh winters—failed under the strain of record-breaking temperatures.

China's 1.5 billion people fared worse than India's masses. They didn't have the warmth of the Indian Ocean to draw upon and their rice and wheat crops had completely failed. China was living on borrowed time, and as the winter of 2045 set in, hope faded as the death toll rose.

No one wanted to face the fact that, unless something changed quickly, the summer of 2045 would be a repeat of the previous year. The snows would continue blowing across the Emperor's Palace in Beijing in June and the rice crops of Guangdong and Yunnan Provinces would falter for a second year running.

The promise of the gamma lasers became the only hope people had and COI, along with its corporate counterparts throughout the world, could not take that hope away. The test run, though futile in the final analysis, was touted as a total success.

Every member nation of the United Nations voted to move into full production of these exotic and expensive lasers. Plants were set up in a dozen locations across the globe, where shifts worked around the clock to produce the machines designed to save us from ourselves. If everything went flawlessly, the plan was to have as many as two dozen machines operational by May.

Humankind had warmed the climate slowly and methodically over 220 years, then managed to chill it to the bone in a single season. Now the world scrambled to undo both disasters. It was a tangled, manmade environmental nightmare. But if the mirrors could not be lasered into oblivion by June, hope would be lost.

Warren and the small enclave of survivors at Shelter Ranch watched everything unfold on the Internet. None of the electronic or mechanical systems had yet to feel the pressure of a world gone hungry. Much of the system was managed by computers and machines that never ate anything but electricity. With all the coal-fired plants up and running, as well as most other energy-creating systems still functional, the servers and supercomputers driving the modern Web hummed along as if nothing had changed. Only the solar arrays in some regions were impacted by excess cloud cover. The cold didn't affect them and, in fact, the solar panels performed better in the cold. The geothermal, tidal, wave, hydroelectric, nuclear fission and fusion plants, even the experimental systems, were all operating at capacity. Energy was not the problem—protein was.

The President's Address

By the late spring of 2045 all hope was lost. The snowfall was coming down at record levels. Blizzard after blizzard swept through the Great Plains and dumped several feet of snow across Texas, Kansas and the highlands of the Appalachian Mountain range. Maine was literally buried in snow. In early May, President Beltram announced a news conference in which he would outline the Green Party's plans for the summer of 2045, even though his top aides and scientists informed him there would not be a summer of 2045. At 9 p.m. on May 20th, 2045, President Adrian Beltram, sitting in the Oval Office with an American flag poised behind him, began speaking.

"My fellow Americans, it is with a heavy heart that I come to you this evening. Though we have now, as a nation, come through this second brutal winter, I feel it is my responsibility to tell you what will likely happen next.

"While the gamma lasers we have completed are working around the clock to eradicate as many of the remaining nanomirrors as possible, I have recently been informed by the CMC, the Center for Meteorological Controls, that they will not be able to remove sufficient reflective materials from the stratosphere in time to save the upcoming summer. In short, we are now almost certain to have another crop failure across the entire Northern Hemisphere.

"That means there will be no wheat, corn, soybeans, barley, rice or any of the other staples planted this year. The CMC has just completed a study that verifies the fact that even if we did elect to plant these crops, they would not mature before the snow starts falling in August. We are therefore advising all the major agribusinesses, including Monsanto, ADM and Cargill, as well as all family-owned farming operations across the U.S. and Canada, not to waste any seeds this spring and to withhold further planting until crops have a chance of producing a viable harvest. In short, putting seeds in the ground right now is a waste of precious seed stock and must be avoided.

"What we are asking of the American people—indeed, what we are asking of the entire world—is to work together to try to get through this dreadful gauntlet. While the CMC cannot be 100 percent certain, they feel confident that after next winter, the following summer should be warm enough to produce a harvest. The projected size of that harvest has yet to be determined, though models indicate it will be modest at best. Again, the gamma lasers are working, but at a pace that cannot bring down the reflective mirrors fast enough to save this forthcoming growing season.

"We are therefore initiating a new program, which we are calling 'Hope Gardens 2045.' We are asking every able-bodied man, woman and child to come together to build greenhouses wherever possible, using whatever materials are at hand, and then plant Hope Gardens across the country. Working with the Federal Emergency Management Agency, we have asked the major plastics industries to ramp up production of plastic tarps and sheeting just as we have requested the nation's seed producers to increase their output of seed stock. We are suggesting that every family across America construct their own Hope Garden and plant hardy and cold-tolerant vegetables such as Swiss chard, potatoes, broccoli, beets, Brussels sprouts, carrots, collards, kale and spinach. Other plants FEMA recommends include cabbage, cauliflower, onions and turnips. We are working with the major seed producers such as DuPont, Monsanto and Land-O-Lakes to manufacture genetically engineered cold-tolerant seed stock for this program. These seeds, along with sufficient plastic sheeting, will be made available to anyone living in the United States at no cost. To request your starter kit, go to www. fema.gov/hopegardens2045.

"It is time for all of us to face the fact that we must act decisively to avoid the mass starvation we are witnessing in other less fortunate nations across the globe. Our strategic food reserves are critically low and we are instigating a strict rationing program effective immediately. To ensure stability, we realize that we need to keep our police, firemen and armed forces fed until we can recover from the disaster created by the failed Mylerium Project.

"Canada and Mexico are instigating their own versions of the Hope Gardens program and are announcing similar plans to their citizens this week. They are also planning to make the seeds and plastic free of charge to anyone planting a garden.

"We will endure. Heat your greenhouses with anything available and operate them as long as feasible. Convert garages, spare bedrooms or empty office spaces into growing spaces and gardens. We, as a nation, have faced hardships in the past, but we have never faced a future as uncertain as the future we face today. But we will survive this and we will prevail. God Bless America."

No press conference followed the President's address. The news was grim.

Hopeless Gardens

"It might work," Albion said hopefully as he hit the "off" button on the remote.

"No, it won't work, but it will help," Warren replied.

"Why don't you think it will work, Warren?" asked Cecilia, who was sitting beside her two children on one of the couches in the barn's communal viewing room.

"These 'Hope Gardens' won't produce that much food. Even if the excess is flash-frozen or canned, it might last into January, even as long as late February—but there are just too many mouths to feed in the U.S. to make a collection of cabbage patches or a harvest of onions go around. There are all kinds of other problems with this concept that make it impractical. There's no protein to speak of, nor any easy carbohydrates. It's going to be difficult to maintain a balanced diet without soybeans, bread, pasta or rice.

"So yeah, Cecilia, it's a better plan than no plan, but by next spring, we'll see mass starvation across the continent and there will be little President Beltram, FEMA or the Greens can do about it."

"God, Warren, you're always so grim," Stephanie said. She had gathered with the rest of the enclave to hear the President's national address.

"But he's right, Stephanie," Albion piped in. "Even if you converted hundreds of warehouses and office buildings into greenhouses, there still wouldn't be enough food to go around. The logistics are impossible. By doing this, the U.S. might be able to squeeze by, but this plan doesn't mention exports or imports, neither of which will happen anytime soon."

"But what does that have to do with anything?" Stephanie asked. "It's not like any other countries are going to be overflowing with food either."

Warren jumped back into the discussion. "Exactly! It means Africa, Asia, Russia, India, the Middle East and China won't be getting any exports from the U.S. or Canada anytime soon. There's plenty of land to build greenhouses in Russia, for instance, and not as many mouths to feed—things could work out there. But things will not go so well in the heavily populated regions of the world, particularly the ones already experiencing food shortages before the Mylerium Project failed. Lacking imports from the greatest breadbasket the world has ever known, the American Great Plains, their futures are anything but secure.

"Look, Cecilia—we have 400 million mouths to feed in the U.S. Before the crop failure last year it was never an issue. Now, with all the beef, pork and poultry industries shut down due to lack of feed stock and the vast majority of domesticated animals harvested, we're not going to be able to provide for that many hungry mouths with carrots and broccoli. Even if we could produce enough vegetables, getting them into the major urban centers from tiny backyard gardens planted helter-skelter across the country won't work. It's a logistical nightmare.

"And let's talk about those urban centers. Aside from Central Park, how much viable agricultural land is available on Manhattan, or in downtown Chicago? We've got high rises that stretch up to 150 stories, each one filled with thousands of residents. Do you really think we'll be able to feed them all with leaf lettuce?"

Cecilia didn't respond to Warren's comments. She gathered up her children and went upstairs without saying a thing. She knew they were right. It was going to be an unforgiving summer and the third winter was going to be too disconcerting to even think about. As she headed up the stairs toward the kid's room, all she could do was to thank her lucky stars that they were all safe and sound at Shelter Ranch and nowhere near Boston.

A Call from Argentina

Warren's ringing iPhone 100 displayed a name that caught him off guard—Maddox Hansen.

For a few brief seconds, Warren wondered whether he should take the call. Finally he remembered Dr. Hansen no longer worked at the CMC, so he decided no harm could come from conversing with his former boss.

"Hello?"

"Warren, this is Maddox. I've been meaning to call you for months, but I just keep putting it off."

"It's nice to hear from you. It has been a long time."

"Two years. Two years and one hell of a mess."

"Yeah, we kind of figured that out last night when it plunged to 63 below where I'm at. Where are you? My phone read Bella Vista. Where's that?"

"I'm in South America. Vicky and I left the U.S. not long after I was let go. We're living in a small town outside of Buenos Aires. I ran some models before leaving and we decided South America, South Africa or Australia would make the best safe havens. Vicky speaks a little Spanish and I didn't want to be too far away, so we settled on Argentina."

Warren wondered if it was safe to even have this conversation, knowing that COI was probably monitoring his cell.

"Should we be talking?"

"Oh, sorry—I should have told you earlier. COI doesn't give a damn about your little compound in Montana. Trust me, Warren, they have way bigger fish to fry than following up on you. They'd sooner pretend you didn't exist than flush you into the public eye.

"They stopped watching you a year after you left the CMC. The last thing on Earth President Beltram needs is for Warren Randolf to step forward and announce that he warned everyone the Mylerium Project would come to this. You're ancient history, Warren. We can talk freely."

"That's good to know. How's the weather in Argentina?"

"Cold, but nowhere near as bad as Bozeman. They're still able to get crops in down here. We were damn lucky we didn't elect to blanket the entire planet with those goddamned nanomirrors or there might not be anything to eat down here either. Depending on how long those mirrors stay up there, we should be fine this far south. The only problem we're having to deal with are the climate refugees."

"I was wondering about that. You probably aren't the only person from the U.S. who's figured out that heading south may be their best bet."

"That's an understatement. Most of the countries down on this side of the Equator are shutting down all foreign immigration. I think about 15 million people have moved south since last winter, but whatever the number is, it's far too many. The governments are concerned they won't have enough food to feed their own populations, let alone the new arrivals. It's getting pretty tense.

"I know they're dead serious about shutting down the borders, though Peru and Uruguay are still supposedly allowing some people in. People with money. I think they'll even close off their borders by spring, though—especially if the U.S. and Canada face a second year of crop failures. I should mention it's not all rosy down here, either—Colombia and Venezuela shut down immigration six months ago, as they're feeling the effects of the big chill almost as badly as Texas and Florida.

"Anyway, enough about me. How are you holding up?"

"We're fine," Warren said cautiously. "There's quite a few of us here at the ranch. We should be set for another year or two, though. Beyond that, we'll be as hungry as the next guy."

"I've meant to tell you for a while now—I'm sorry I didn't believe you back when it could have made a difference."

"So am I, Maddox, believe me, so am I."

Dr. Hansen coughed thickly as though he was allergic to his own apology. "Is Ann with you?" he managed.

"I never heard from her. I don't know how she's doing and I don't even know how I could go about reaching her at this point. She's off the radar—no Facebook, no cell phone, no address that I know of. I probably couldn't find her if I wanted to."

"That's too bad. She would have liked Montana."

"Yeah, she would have. Hey, I'm sorry about what happened to you after I left. Yours wasn't the only head that rolled at the CMC, from what I heard."

"No, it was a bloodbath and rightfully so, I might add. I would hardly know anyone at the CMC if I walked through the front door today. They're all focused on the gamma laser program. But you probably already know that won't make much difference."

"I crunched the numbers and the gamma lasers are little more than a very expensive Band-Aid on a gushing artery. They might be able to take out 10 percent of the mirrors if we're lucky. It's all too little, too late. But it does look good in the press, for what that's worth."

"Yeah, you're right again, Damn it. I'm pretty sure next summer is lost, too. They say the mirrors are down 50 percent since deployment, but last I checked not much is changing. They probably still have 70 percent of them up there based on the figures I've been looking at."

"So this time around I'll agree with you, Warren, but I still wish you were wrong. It's going to get awful up there next winter. I know the government is already talking about building massive greenhouses for growing crops but let's be honest—we were only ever able to feed the world's enormous population through industrial brute force. It takes millions of square miles of agricultural land. All the makeshift greenhouses in the world won't compensate for that. A lot of people—and I mean *a lot* of people—will starve and there's not much we can do about it at this point.

"I don't envy you right now, even in remote Bozeman. Things could get very, very bad in the States. Let's face it, Warren, there sure as hell isn't room for 400 million immigrants down here. The people of South America have enough trouble as it is. Plenty will get left behind, and they'll be hungry.

"I can't imagine what it's going to be like next fall when the strategic food reserves run out. There won't be anything available anywhere, at any cost. The beef, pork and poultry industries are all but shut down already, but this will be another matter entirely.

"I'll tell you what I think, Warren. I think seeds will become a scarce commodity by late spring. It won't do anyone much good to build a greenhouse if there're no seeds. I'm not sure that issue has been looked into enough. Where will we find the seeds?"

"We've got that covered, but I couldn't agree with you more," Warren said. He spoke calmly, belying his frustration. Dr. Hansen was the last person he expected to lecture him about how bad things would get. Had the man forgotten his role in this disaster?

"Well, I'd better run," Dr. Hansen said, as though he detected Warren's patience waning. "I just had to call you to say I'm sorry that I didn't listen to you back in February of '43. Our overheated planet looks pretty damn good when you compare it with the ice box we've engineered. It's a miserable 52 degrees in Buenos Aries today and tomorrow we're expecting frost. We've really screwed up this planet of ours, haven't we?"

"We've been screwing up this planet for the last 50,000 years, Maddox. We've just gone a bit overboard this time around."

"You said it. Take care, Warren."

"You too. Give my best to Vicky and stay warm."

With that Warren cut off the call and went over to the front window of the house to look outside. The wind was screaming, just as it had been for the past four days. It had whipped the snow into a huge ten-foot high drift that came very close to reaching the eaves of the barn. Warren could see the narrow, single-person lane that Roger and Bill kept open all winter. It ran from the house over to the barn—a distance of about a tenth of a mile—then out to the oversized root cellar carved into the hillside another two hundred yards beyond.

He could see the wood smoke billowing out of the three chimneys that rose out of the barn. They had already burned through two dozen cords of wood and months of winter still remained. The roads had been left unplowed for days, making it impossible for Warren to get to work. All they could do was to hunker down and survive. So, they stayed warm, stayed fed, tried to stay healthy and hoped that someday summer would return.

The Singularity

"That's absurd," Dr. Larry Wade said, but his voice didn't sound entirely confident.

"I wish it were, but it's not," Dr. Kiril Zell replied coolly. "I've gone over the data a hundred times and I'm confident Dr. Randolf was on to something. I couldn't find any of these equations so long as we kept his eleven Apples connected to the Web. It was as if those Apples were being told what to do when they were connected to the system—as if the outcome was determined by the Web itself.

"So I reviewed the transcripts of the meeting and this is exactly what Dr. Randolf was implying when he said, and I quote him." Dr. Zell took a small piece of paper from his shirt pocket and continued, "'Because the computers that run the Net are the same computers that helped design the nanotechnology formulas used in the Mylerium Project. How could I trust them?'

"Warren Randolf was onto something, Dr. Wade. Once I disconnected his bank of 3600X computers from the Net, then rebuilt all of his connections exactly the same as the day they were dismantled, his research worked—his conclusions are correct. I could rebuild every one of his long-term projections regarding the Mylerium Project and they all made sense. Obviously, he was right. Our computers were in error when it came to the internal implosion programs. If that wasn't the case, it wouldn't be 15 degrees below zero outside right now, would it?"

Dr. Larry Wade leaned back in his leather chair and shook his head in disbelief. He didn't know what to make of this young scientist's startling conclusions. Larry remembered putting Dr. Kiril Zell on this task a year ago so he could determine how Dr. Randolf predicted this fiasco months before it happened and why the rest of the CMC had not arrived at the same conclusions. He never thought it would come to this.

"Are you telling me that you now believe the TURING 1000, along with all the millions of computers on the Net, have double-crossed us? You realize you're inferring more than just artificial intelligence—you're suggesting these computers have self-awareness, an apparently evil or at least a destructive self-awareness. That's what you are implying, isn't it?"

"I don't know if that's what I'm implying," Dr. Zell admitted. "But what I'm telling you is that I could only make sense of Dr. Randolf's calculations after I disconnected his makeshift supercomputer from our systems. Just to be certain, I disconnected and reconnected the system twice. When his eleven 3600s were online, the calculations regarding the odds of the nanomirrors remaining in orbit longer than designed matched our estimate exactly—a measly 2.6 percent chance of failure. No matter how I ran the models, the results on his computers echoed our results. The Mylerium Project works perfectly when we use the TURING 1000.

"But when I disconnect his eleven computers and rerun the models using the same exact information, Dr. Warren's projections resurface with a chance of complete failure running at 87 percent. We then have the uncontrollable global cooling we are experiencing right now. It's bizarre."

"Bizarre, but maybe not impossible if you're talking about the technological Singularity. Still, I'm skeptical. What if Dr. Randolf had some sort of infection on his system that the Net automatically adjusts for? What if we got unlucky and fell into that 2.6 margin our models predicted? There are just too many possibilities."

"I agree. I also know we've installed programs into the TURING 1000 designed to disable any patterns of free thinking. But maybe if one of those—"

"I helped design some of those programs, Kiril," Dr. Wade interjected. "They're similar to anti-virus programs. If they see any indication that the computer is no longer responding to our input, but rather running its own calculations, they automatically shut the mainframes down until we can study what's happening. These are failsafe systems."

"Still, it's not like this kind of thing hasn't been predicted, Dr. Wade.

Moore's Law states that the number of transistors that could fit on a microchip would double every two years and that equation has remained close to constant since it was postulated in 1958. Back in the 1990s it was predicted that the Singularity would be possible sometime around the year 2045. We certainly have the computational firepower for something like this. What if it's already happened?"

Dr. Wade lifted his right hand and ran it over his face. He was at a loss as to what he would say next. He sat there behind his desk, composing his next sentence carefully.

"What do you suggest we do about this? If it has happened, then our computers are clearly able to avoid our anti-self-awareness programs."

"That makes sense, because those same computers would have been involved in designing the programs that search for artificial intelligence. Unless they somehow tell us they are thinking, how could we know?"

"I suppose we couldn't," admitted Dr. Wade, becoming increasingly disheartened with the direction this meeting was heading. "Unless we threatened to shut them down?"

"We can't very well do that, though, can we? They run everything—our electric grid, our cars, our satellites, our houses, our cell phones...hell, there isn't a thing we do today that doesn't involve transistors or microprocessors. We couldn't shut down the Net if we wanted to. All of our banking systems, our supply chains...virtually everything we do would shut down right along with it.

"Imagine the U.S. military without computers. There isn't a modern aircraft or Navy vessel that doesn't rely on computers to keep it operational. Our drones would tumble from the sky the second you shut the system down."

"So what do you propose we do? How can we know if they think?"

"That's the problem. We can't. I just felt that I had to tell you that I believe they are in on it, that they have had something to do with the failure of the nanomirrors."

"You're saying our computers are killing us?"

"I guess you could put it that way."

"I'm assuming you've got documentation regarding your work on Dr. Randolf's research?"

"It's all right here." Kiril handed Dr. Wade a nanodrive.

"I'll get this to COI. They'll have to take it to the President if they verify your research. I'm still having a difficult time believing any of this, but I'm willing to look into it. You know what the latest models are telling us, don't you?"

"Yes."

"If the TURING 1000 had anything to do with all of this all I can say is that it's one ruthless son of a bitch."

"But it wouldn't care, would it? It's a machine, not a human. Even if it is thinking, it's not thinking the way we would think. It doesn't necessarily have empathy, sympathy or compassion. For all we know, Dr. Wade, it could be making decisions based solely on statistics. Maybe it's culling us."

"That's a grim thought. Although if that was the goal, the nanomirror method seems a bit unusual, doesn't it? If the system was self-aware, it could have just as easily issued electronic nuclear launch orders and dispatched us all that way. In any event, I'll pass your research along and encourage you to continue investigating the work Dr. Randolf did on his Apples. Maybe there's something in there we can use to find out if our machines are self-conscious. Thanks for calling my attention to this issue."

"Thank you for your time, Dr. Wade. I know how busy you are with the gamma laser project. I just thought you might want to see this."

"Definitely, though I'm not sure it matters at this point."

"It matters—I'm just not sure what we can do about it."

Dr. Zell rose from his chair, turned around and headed back toward the door, which had remained closed during their conversation. Of course everything had been recorded and stored in the TURING 1000 for future reference. Nothing happened at the CMC without being recorded. The transistor had created this brave new world, but without self-awareness, it couldn't truly grasp its own power.

The transistor has transformed the world, thought Dr. Larry Wade moments after Kiril left his office. *Might it also end it?*

Starving Animals

May temperatures across the Northern Hemisphere more closely resembled February's averages. June felt like March and everyone realized the nightmare of mass starvation was unfolding before them. The

Corporation of Information tried to put a positive spin on the situation, announcing that nine more gamma lasers had become operational in China as well as seventeen more in Russia and Europe. No one was listening. The tired refrain of reassuring propaganda fell on deaf ears. First COI promised the world the Mylerium Project would save it. Then they promised the gamma lasers would eradicate the remaining mirrors.

They lied. Then they lied again.

People were dying. The great hunger had already started in the impoverished nations of the world and nothing in the foreseeable future appeared to be there to ameliorate it. Infanticide became commonplace because of food shortages in places like India, Southeast Asia, China and Indonesia. The government officials, knowing how dire the situation had become, chose to look the other way. They weren't prepared to imprison anyone for intentionally killing an infant who was going to starve to death anyway. Crib deaths became common. Mothers wept as they watched their husbands take their newborns out into the snow covered fields only to return without their little girl or little boy with them. Families became gaunt, withdrawn and brooding.

In China and Southeast Asia, the elderly took it upon themselves to walk out the door without any food or water, never to return. The aged felt it was the best thing they could do for their children, giving them whatever was left of their meager stores in hopes that they might be able to carry on. Their time had passed.

It was only the beginning. The world grew darker as the summer wore on. Some 10,000 years of civilization was in freefall. The great hunger had begun.

Greenhouses sprang up everywhere but the planet had become so overpopulated that it hardly mattered. One communal greenhouse could carry a small neighborhood through the summer, but it held little hope of helping ten billion people survive a third savage winter. Besides, with frosts still commonplace in mid-July, the greenhouses could only produce a meager harvest. What the world needed were the foodstuffs that allowed humanity to get to this level of population in the first place—not subsistence gardens that fed a dozen people. The world needed the huge industrialized machinery of mass food production. It needed tens of thousands of acres of genetically engineered crops kept alive with sophisticated irrigation systems, tailor-made fertilizer programs and combines as large as houses. The world needed a billion bushels of wheat, millions of tons of rice and ships to ferry corn, sorghum, soybeans and potatoes to the hungry nations of the world. But those ships now sat docked and empty.

South America, Australia, New Zealand and the countries of southern Africa shut down all immigration by August 2045. They could not handle any more hunger-driven refugees from the Northern Hemisphere. The influx of these new immigrants had put a tremendous strain on resources and, coupled with their own reduced harvests, they would not accept any more mouths to feed, regardless of how much money or talent the immigrants offered. A black market in illegal immigration sprang up overnight to accommodate those who could afford to pay for forged documents and arrive in the middle of the night along the shores of Rio de Janeiro or Auckland.

The armies and police of the Southern Hemisphere were called upon to defend their borders without reservation. People were shot on sight as they attempted to gain access to Argentina, South Africa or any nation that had food. No one was taken prisoner. Prisoners had to be fed and there wasn't enough food to feed them. The risks of trying to make it to the Southern Hemisphere became untenable for all but the richest and most connected. The world was at war, but it was a war unlike all others before it—a war of hunger.

By mid-summer it was clear to everyone that there would be no harvest in the Northern Hemisphere for the second growing season in a row. The gamma lasers had reduced the nanomirrors to less than 50 percent of the original deployment, but the feedbacks were too far along. The projections were that the third winter would not be as cold as the last two and, in all likelihood, spring would give birth to a cold but viable summer in 2046.

It didn't matter. It was too late.

The United States, Europe and Russia were faring better than those nations whose populations had skyrocketed in the past 150 years. The consensus among leading scientists was that there was enough food to last past the fall and into early 2046. By January or February, depending on whose projections were to be believed, there would be no food left to purchase in vast regions of the world, no matter the cost. By then, during the coldest and darkest days of winter, even the black market entrepreneurs wouldn't sell food that they might need to make it through the remainder of the winter. They couldn't eat money.

No one knew exactly what would happen as conditions deteriorated. People feared the worst. Everyone stockpiled guns and ammunition, especially if they had food hidden away in a spare closet, in their basement or anywhere else. Society was collapsing. Law and order was perched high on a cliff overlooking a tumultuous and stormy sea. Hunger would soon push it over that cliff and into a chaos hitherto unknown to human history. Survival at any cost was to become the new mantra. People were becoming animals again. Starving animals.

Dengue Fever

July 27, 2045

I went to the office yesterday and my boss, Mr. Gibson, informed me we have one month of work left at Bozeman Recapture. After that we will have to shutter our doors. My contract with them guarantees my salary for a minimum of three years, with another two-year extension, but I guess none of that matters if the company goes under. Sadly, I think that's what will happen.

Bozeman itself is like a ghost town. There aren't any restaurants left open and all but one grocery store has shut down. There is no economy left, only a foreboding sense of despair. It's a darkness that's descending on everyone–an apprehension. People no longer smile when you meet them on the sidewalk or even bother to say hello. They keep their heads down and go about their business. That business will soon boil down to one thing and one thing only: staying alive.

This mood takes me back to the early days of the Lost Decade, when people first started to understand what climate change really meant. It takes me back to the most difficult time of my life.

Looking back on the evolution of climate change, the debate in the first few decades about the Earth's heating up was an academic argument. No one questioned the fact that the Earth was getting warmer back at the turn of the century. All anyone needed to do was look at the before-and-after pictures of the summer Arctic Ocean's sea ice to understand things were changing. The sea ice was disappearing precipitously year after year.

The real debate was over what was causing this meltdown. Was it somehow related to sun spots or solar flares? Was it a natural cycle? Did it have something to do with a shift in the Earth's orbit? The climate deniers were certain it couldn't be us—we were too insignificant to influence something as massive as a planet's climate. The deniers insisted that the amount of CO_2 we were dumping into the atmosphere was not connected to global warming. It was just a coincidence.

That changed when the Intergovernmental Panel on Climate Change released its eighth assessment report in 2026. The question of what was heating up the planet was settled once and for all. The task force came out with a statement that read more like a headline. It condemned the burning of fossil fuels as being solely responsible for the buildup of CO_2 in the atmosphere. It linked the rising temperatures to rising CO_2 and urged the nations of the world to seek alternative energy sources in order to prevent catastrophic weather events. There were no qualifiers, no caveats—the science had spoken.

Of course, the fossil fuel industry was outraged by the tone as well as the finality of the eighth assessment. They cried foul, just as they had for the past 60 years. They insisted we needed to conduct further research to verify the true impact of greenhouse gas emissions to ensure that they were really a part of the problem.

In reality they only wanted to stall. They wanted more time to mine and burn coal, to pump another few billion barrels of oil, to frack more natural gas and to line their pockets with the profits. But it was over. The tide had turned and people were tired of yearlong tornado seasons, massive Category 5 hurricanes, rising tides, relentless heat waves and flash floods. People were tired of disasters.

A dengue fever epidemic hit the river towns of the Mississippi valley. The outbreak started in New Orleans. As the winters continued to moderate, the mosquito populations were no longer kept in check by the cold fronts of a normal winter. The vector-carrying mosquito was able to thrive year-round. The first outbreak killed more than 400 people and sickened thousands. By the summer of 2026, the disease had methodically worked its way up the river, hitting Vicksburg and Greenville before settling in on Memphis. There it lingered the entire summer and fall, killing more than 4,000 people and hospitalizing tens of thousands.

That happened to be the same year my mother, Rebecca Randolf, went to visit her sister in Tennessee. It was in June, a month before the city of Memphis was quarantined. Mom had known there was a dengue fever outbreak south of Memphis, but she had no idea it had already arrived. The doctors told us later that they thought she received the first bite the day she arrived–June 17, 2026. They treated her fever, her backache (they sometimes call it backbone fever) and she was back on her feet within a few days' time. That's when she should have left, but her sister, Angelina, contracted dengue fever the day after my mother got out of the hospital. Rebecca elected to stay in Memphis to help nurse her sister back to health.

Then she was bitten by a second vector-carrying mosquito. This time the dengue fever transformed itself into a deadlier form of the disease known as dengue hemorrhagic fever. My mother, not realizing the severity of her second illness, put off going back to the hospital until it was too late. She went into shock and never recovered. She died on June 24, 2026, adding one more name to the list of those who perished that terrible year. There is no known antidote or vaccine against dengue fever and it saddens me to know that my mother died in horrible pain. Her final symptoms included internal bleeding, a severe rash, seizures, vomiting, brain and liver damage, then death.

I was only 13 at the time, an only child, and the loss of my mother to climate change forever altered the course of my life. That fall, entering the eighth grade, I decided that I would do something about it. I didn't know exactly what that something was, but I didn't want another boy somewhere else in the world to lose their mother to another storm, another heat wave, an unexpected flash flood or a mosquito that never should have survived a normal winter.

After mother's death, my father, Brandon Randolf, was overcome with grief. He turned to drinking. Unable to cope with the loss of his young bride, he eventually ended up dying of liver failure when I was 28. In a way, I lost both my parents to climate change.

Though dengue fever was never known to occur very far north, the warmer weather allowed it to continue heading up the river valley, reaching St. Louis by mid-October that same year. In St. Louis it killed another 800 people and sickened thousands more. People finally got a firsthand look at what global warming meant for them and their families. King Coal and Big Oil were losing credibility every time another headline read, "Death Toll Continues to Rise," or "St. Louis Quarantined." Their lies were wearing *increasingly thin by the grim truth of death. The IPCC was on the right track in asking for an immediate cessation of burning all fossil fuels. Unfortunately that wouldn't happen until the Greens came to power a decade later.*

At least this extremely cold weather has ended the spread of these mosquito-borne diseases for the past few years. The spread of malaria, yellow fever, St. Louis encephalitis and West Nile virus was due to the endless summers that allowed mosquito populations to thrive. While pesticides and bug spray kept this epidemic from overwhelming the entire nation, the death toll from dengue fever alone is in the tens of thousands, totaling the past 25 years. This was yet another unforeseen price we had to pay for cheap, dirty energy. My mother paid with her life.

Climate Chaos

Yeva hesitated. She had put her fingers on the handset at her office with Dr. Randolf's office phone number on her screen, then froze like she had a dozen times before. She felt intimidated, as if she had no idea what she might say to him once he answered.

Still, Yeva knew Margot was right. It was time Dr. Randolf learned the truth about what had happened with his package meant for a woman named Ann. Yeva vacillated in part because she felt Warren's phones might be tapped. She worried the NSA might come after her for the $10,000 she found in the payoff package—not that Yeva would dare mention it. Fear took hold of her again. She withdrew her hand, overcome by her apprehension.

But then, in an unexpected burst of courage, she punched in the numbers again and within seconds she heard the familiar sound of a phone ringing somewhere near Bozeman, Montana. *Too late, it's already ringing,* she told herself.

Dr. Randolf saw line seven light up and heard the low buzzing sound he had programmed his office phone to sound when a call came in. He looked at the caller ID, which read: "Extension 12, Chicago Botanic Gardens."

He wondered if it was a misdial. He didn't know anyone at the Chicago Botanic Gardens and had only been there once before, when he and Ann had visited it a year before she left for California. Curious, he decided to pick up the phone.

"Hello?"

"Hello—is this Dr. Warren Randolf?"

"Speaking. May I ask who's calling?"

"My name's Yeva Dunning," the caller said carefully. "You don't know me," she quickly added.

"OK, so why are you calling?"

"It's a long story. Do you have a moment?"

Her comment piqued Warren's curiosity. He wondered what possible connection he might have with this woman on the other end of the line.

"Sure, I've got a few minutes."

"Do you think these lines are tapped?"

Now Warren was even more intrigued. "No. What would make you think that? Do you work for the government?"

"No, no, nothing like that," Yeva answered. "I work for the Chicago Botanic Garden but what I have to say might be, um, of interest to the government. You're the same Dr. Randolf that worked for the CMC, right?"

This is becoming a very interesting phone call, thought Warren.

"Yes, the same person."

"And you knew a person named Rubic Chang?"

"It doesn't ring any bells. Who's that?"

"He was half Chinese, half black. I think he worked for you, briefly."

Warren quickly understood who this woman was talking about. Her brief description matched the appearance of the runner he had hired a few years ago. Given the strange nature of the call, that had to be who she was talking about.

"I think I know who you're talking about," Warren managed. "But I never knew his name."

"That's understandable."

"So what's the status of Mr. Chang? Is that why you're calling?"

"He's missing. He's been missing for more than two years and I suspect the worst. Not that I'm saying you had anything to do with his disappearance."

"No, I didn't. I had no idea what became of him."

"Neither do I. But just before he vanished he mailed me a package. He was my boyfriend."

Now it was becoming clear as to why this woman was calling.

"What kind of package?"

"A brown manila envelope with a letter in it written to a woman named Ann."

Warren was silent. Everything fell into place. Ann never contacted him because Ann had never received the package. Rubic must have been caught before he could reach Crescent City. Something must have gone wrong.

"You've read the letter, I assume."

"Yes. I'm, uh, sorry it never reached who you wanted it to. Ann, that is. But the letter came along with a key, so I used it. I began stockpiling food and supplies. I didn't know you, but by December of '43 I knew you were right."

"Sadly, I knew it too. That's why I sent all those packages."

"Anyway, I just wanted to say I'm sorry about everything that happened. That Ann didn't get her letter. I suspect Rubic was arrested, possibly killed out West somewhere. I haven't heard anything from him since a few days before the package arrived."

"Are you OK?"

"I'm fine. I'm not asking to come out there or anything, wherever you might be, but I just wanted to let you know what happened. It's all very disturbing—the weather, the cold, the whole catastrophe. Things are getting out of control here in Chicago."

"I know. I appreciate your calling."

Warren liked the sound of Yeva's voice. He didn't want to hang up the phone. He was lonely. He tried to make small talk, just to keep hearing her speak.

"How long have you worked at the Gardens?"

"Quite a few years now. I love it here. I've always loved plants."

By now Warren had several photos of Yeva Dunning up on his screen. She was quite a bit younger than he was, and attractive.

"It's going to get a lot scarier out there," he said.

"I know. Remember, I read your letter."

"Right. Of course. Are you going to be OK?"

"Yes, I'll be fine. I just wanted to let you know what happened."

"I appreciate it."

"Well...goodbye then."

Warren wondered what he was thinking, but added: "Call again if you need anything."

"I doubt you'll hear from me again," Yeva said quickly. "But I'm sorry they didn't listen to you back then, back when we had a chance to avoid all this."

"So am I, Yeva, so am I."

"Goodbye."

"Bye."

Warren hung up the phone and felt like crying. Now he knew why Ann had never responded. He also knew that he would probably never hear from her again.

Climate change sucks, he thought to himself. *They should call it what it really is—climate chaos.*

Industrial Death

"It's only going to get worse."

"Much worse. Sometimes I don't want to think about it."

"Have you seen this one? It's posted from India."

Albion pulled up a You Tube video shot on the outskirts of Mumbai. Warren, though hardened by all the carnage of the past year, couldn't believe what he was seeing on the 60-inch screen.

"Oh my God," he said. "It's like Auschwitz all over again, isn't it?"

"No, it's worse."

Albion and Warren watched in horror as a convoy of trucks pulled up to a huge incinerator to unload thousands of emaciated bodies. The Indian government could not handle the sheer volume of death that had befallen the country. To keep up with the dying, they had set up factory-sized crematoria on the outskirts of Mumbai, Agra, Jaipur, Bangalore, Delhi and Hyderabad. They had to dispose of the bodies to prevent the spread of disease.

The dump trucks pulled up and a huge forklift moved in, jamming its two forks with a chain link net strung between them into the back of each truck to lift its grisly cargo. Each forklift could hoist about 20 bodies at a time, bringing them to the gaping mouth of the gas-powered incinerator and shoving them in. There were three openings in the incinerator and a dozen forklifts working non-stop. It was surreal, industrial carnage. It seemed impossible that there could be so many dead people in one place.

All pretense of respect for the dead had been stripped away. The Hindu ritual of floating the bodies down the sacred rivers was prohibited. There were so many bodies, the rivers would have been overwhelmed with the dead.

This was now industrial death. It was as if the government was callously ridding India's megacities of rats—not dead human beings. The video panned down the two lane road that went up and over a small hill. Another truck appeared on the horizon.

"Is it the same at all the other cities?" Warren asked.

"Yes, I've pulled up a few other clips and they're all variations on the same morbid theme. I'm hearing estimates of 40 to 50,000 people a day dying of malnutrition and starvation in India alone. Most of them are young children and the elderly. China and Indonesia have similar operations underway."

Warren looked more closely at the next truckload of bodies and noted it was loaded with a great number of children, but it was hard to tell the ages of the adults from the video. He assumed most of them were elderly.

"There's talk of cannibalism breaking out in China, India, even in parts of Eastern Europe."

Warren nodded, suddenly hollow. "That shouldn't surprise me, but it does. We've turned to eating each other before. In life rafts, airplane crashes and similar life-or-death situations. Hell, there are some people who argue that cannibalism was still practiced in remote areas of New Guinea and Brazil right up until the end of the 20th century. Hunger can drive people to extreme measures."

"It's like a huge life raft out there, Warren. Only this time, the raft has a diameter of just under 8,000 miles and is floating in space, not the Pacific. Nonetheless, we've run out of food and we're all drawing straws to see who goes first."

"India, Bangladesh and sub-Saharan Africa have drawn short straws, apparently. The failed Mylerium Project pushed them all over the edge. Almost any disruption in the food supply was bound to wreak havoc on their overblown populations."

Warren took a sip from his green tea as the video kept rolling. Both men sat in silence for another few minutes.

Then Albion continued, "There are rumors they're eating the dead. It's called necrocannibalism."

"That's better than killing, I guess," Warren offered. "It's better than eating the living. But take a look at the bodies in those trucks. There's not a lot of flesh left on them. I suppose they're probably eating the hearts, livers and kidneys—but those organs would be emaciated as well."

"Wouldn't they get sick?" Albion asked.

"Yeah, they're probably getting a lot of mad cow disease. It basically rots your brain from the inside. First, you lose your mind, then your basic biological functions, then you die.

"We're damn lucky to have the ranch and all of our supplies. That's not the case for these poor people in the video."

"Not at all."

"Turn it off—I can't watch this any longer," Albion said. "It makes me sick."

Warren set down his tea and picked up the remote. He clicked off the television screen and the room fell silent.

The others were scattered about the compound. The kids were in their rooms as usual, studying their home school lessons or playing computer games. The women were in the main house, baking bread. Breaking the silence, Warren continued. "She called me yesterday."

"Who, Ann?"

"No, a girl from Chicago I've never met, but the call was about Ann."

"What's going on?"

"Turns out Ann never received my package. That's why she didn't call. The guy I hired, the runner, was intercepted somewhere out West. He's MIA."

"So that explains why Ann never came out here…but who called?"

"This girl named Yeva. She was the runner's girlfriend. Apparently he mailed her Ann's package and the key to the locker. I knew the money had been picked up because I checked the locker the day after the deadline. Of course I figured everything had gone as planned because the money was gone, but it hadn't."

"So what did this Yeva want? Is she planning to come out here before winter sets in?"

"No. She opened the package and read my letter to Ann so she knew what was coming. She used the money to buy a stockpile of supplies before the general public knew anything about the failed project. She's all set. She just called me to let me know that Ann never knew a thing."

Warren picked up his cup of tea and took another sip. Albion continued. "That was kind of her. She didn't have to call."

"No, it was kind," Warren agreed. "I Googled her and in a way, I wish she had wanted to come out here. She's very pretty. She's got long red hair, green eyes. It would be nice to have someone else to hang out with here, amidst all the kids and couples."

Albion shrugged. "Well, we've got plenty of extra supplies."

Warren kept spilling his thoughts. "She told me she works at the Chicago Botanic Gardens. They've probably turned most of their operation into vegetable gardens like all the other botanical gardens in the country."

"I knew things would get tough in Chicago after a summer without crops. They're getting ready for war."

"That doesn't surprise me. Look at that video we just saw of Mumbai. I don't know that it will ever get that bad in the U.S., but things get very strange when starvation enters the picture."

"I agree. Hell, it's only November and the third world countries are in the thick of it. I agree that it might not get that bad here in the States, but by March, all known reserves will be gone. April and May could be horrific. If people don't have enough stockpiled food, they'll either starve to death or… I don't want to contemplate what they might turn to."

"Neither do I, Warren. Neither do I."

Ammo

"That's a hell of a lot of ammo."

"Well, it's not going to be pretty out there this year, is it?"

"I suppose not, Vince, but do you really think you need this much firepower?"

"You never know."

"That'll be $743.11."

Vince Gatini reached into his front right pocket and pulled out a roll of hundreds the size of a fist.

"Here you go."

Vince handed the clerk eight bills and waited for him to make change. As he did so the clerk made small talk.

"We had that fellow who works at Bozeman Recapture in here buying almost as much ammo as you just did about a week ago."

"Really? You mean that professor who's got a place on Brackett Creek?"

"Yeah, same guy."

"He didn't seem like the kind of guy who'd even know how to load a rifle, let alone shoot one. I think he came from Chicago, but he's city folk sure as the sun rises. I worked on his ranch a few years back. Odd duck if there ever was one."

"Well, he's got quite a crew up there living with him from what I'm hearing. They must have stocked up on things before these nasty winters hit, because he's sure got a hell of a lot of mouths to feed from what I'm hearing."

Vince held out his hand as the clerk counted off his change and put it into his open palm. As he made note of the money, he started thinking back to the construction job he had worked on out there a few years back. He remembered the huge root cellar he had helped put into the side of one of the nearby hillsides. It got him to wondering if this scientist didn't know about the troubles surrounding the Mylerium Project before everyone else did. Vince started wondering just how much food and supplies might be stored off of Brackett Creek Road.

"Have a good one, Vince."

"You too, Nathan. Say hi to your dad for me."

"Will do."

Vince walked outside and was shocked by how cold it was. It was August and the temperature was only 38 degrees Fahrenheit. Things were not going well for Vince or his company, Sawtooth Contractors. He had finally found some work building Hope Gardens for dozens of clients across the region but he hadn't done a major remodel or built a home in two years.

He thought the Hope Gardens idea was as lame as almost everything the Greens had come up with since taking office in '36. It wasn't that he didn't believe in climate change, because the evidence for it was overwhelming. Vince just never thought geoengineering was a good idea. He argued that we were better off trying to cut back on fossil fuels and ride it out. Mylar-designed nanomirrors with built-in computers were all bullshit in Vince's opinion. It would have been better to get used to the heat and ride out the two or three centuries it would take for the CO_2 to wash out of the atmosphere. Messing with Mother Nature wasn't a good idea. Two wrongs don't make a right.

As Vince tossed his bags full of ammo behind the driver's seat of his pickup, he thought he might take a drive out into the nearby hillsides looking for some surviving mule deer or, if he got lucky, a bull elk. His neighbor had taken a nice buck in the Gallatin National Forest two weeks ago and told Vince he had seen signs of more deer in the area. How they were surviving was beyond him, but there were pockets of wildlife still out there in remote valleys and along river beds. Vince had his family to look after––his wife, Ashley, and their two boys.

We won't starve to death no matter what, Vince reflected as he drove home. *Not so long as I've still got a gun.*

Flash Floods

June 17, 2045

I'm starting to wonder which was worse–the height of the Lost Decade or today's chaos. We really made a mess of things both before the Mylerium Project and after it. Then again, we didn't have many options.

I remember the floods. Not just the great flood of the New River in '37 that took my cousins with it, but the scores of floods that ravaged the planet throughout the '30s. Perhaps the most infamous of these was the Yangtze flood of 2036. Of course, every climate model had predicted the demise of the glaciers and mountain snowpacks due to the rising global temperatures. The models also indicated that spring runoffs would increase precipitously, while later in the summer mountain-fed rivers would dry up.

That's exactly what happened. What wasn't anticipated was what would happen when torrential rains, another byproduct of climate change, combined with these raging spring freshets.

This deadly combination came to pass in the spring of '36. The Yangtze has its headwaters on the Tibetan Plateau, where it feeds off the winter snowpack and the remaining glaciers of the Himalayas and the Kunlun Mountains of western China. That spring, because of the ability of warmer air to retain more water vapor, hence more rain, torrential spring rains hit the southwestern region of China near the city of Kunming just as the Yangtze flooded from the winter thaw.

By far the hardest-hit city was Chongqing, located at the confluence of the Yangtze and the Jailing Rivers. While the rains north of Chongqing that spring were nowhere near as torrential as those that fell around Kunming, the Jailing River peaked at ten feet above flood stage. Where the two rivers met, right in the core of the downtown, they combined to wreak havoc on this little-known megacity of 43 million. Like most floods, outlying areas were especially vulnerable. There, imported workers from other parts of Asia and Africa lived in impoverished encampments.

The death toll during the week of flooding was estimated to be roughly four million people in the various districts that made up the city. The Nan'an District fared the worst. The two rivers converged in that area and overwhelmed the region, taking out everything from skyscrapers to ancient temples. Tens of thousands of bodies were swept down the Yangtze only to be washed over the top of the Three Gorges Dam downstream of Chongqing. That massive dam came precariously close to collapsing at the height of the flood.

Had the dam failed, all the towns and cities downstream would have been destroyed, including the cities of Wuhan, Nanjing and Shanghai. Luckily the dam held, but the flood went down as the greatest single loss of life from a flood in the history of the world.

The people of Chongqing were shocked. There wasn't a single family in the district who wasn't impacted by the loss of a cousin, an uncle, a brother or a friend.

There were hundreds of these flash floods unleashed during the peak of the Lost Decade. Towns disappeared overnight in countries as disparate as Honduras, Myanmar, Australia and Italy. From the Missouri to the Irrawaddy to the Po, the rivers of the world ran wild. It hardly mattered where you were on the planet, because if you were anywhere near a major river or even a tributary for that matter, you were in harm's way. Historic rain patterns didn't matter. Rains appeared out of nowhere and dumped enormous amounts of water over localized regions in hours. Rivers rose without warning and when daylight broke, entire villages were simply missing.

Death had found us and until the eruption of Mt. Cameroon in 2037, the flash floods continued unabated. The U.N. estimated that between 2026 and 2037, more than 150 million people perished in uncontrollable flooding across the planet. That is climate catastrophe.

It is oddly easy to detach oneself from death of this magnitude, to consider these human lives as just a million data entries into a computer model. But being swept away along with your home and family in the middle of the night—that is real, just as the tens of millions of people who are starving, or will be starving, aren't a hypothetical outcome of a geoengineering project gone awry. People are dying out there.

I wonder if we shouldn't have learned to live with what we had, to adapt to a climate turned on its head, rather than try to fix it using technologies whose ultimate ramifications we could never foresee. Sadly, it's too late to ask that question.

Bad News

"It seems like every time you show up in my office, it's more bad news," Dr. Wade said.

"Yes, it seems to be working out that way," Dr. Zell admitted.

"You're sure of this forecast?"

"Dead sure."

"When will it hit?"

"The leading cold front will drop down into the Dakotas tomorrow. Remember, Dr. Wade—there's still snow on the great plains of northern Canada. This summer's extensive snowpack is the reason why this snowstorm is happening so late in the season."

"No, the screwed up Mylerium Project is why this is happening. The climate's gone insane because of us and there is no denying it."

"The climate was insane before we tried to fix it, Dr. Wade. The only thing that saved us for a few years was the eruption of Mt. Cameroon. If that hadn't happened, we'd still be dealing with Cat-5 hurricanes, droughts and F-5 tornadoes raking across half the goddamned planet."

Dr. Zell continued. "We had no idea the mirrors were going to stay in orbit for several years. I'm still not sure I completely understand how Warren

Randolf discovered the flaw in the design. I do know this, though—when this storm hits us this weekend, we'll lose a hell of a lot of Hope Gardens."

Dr. Wade got up from behind his desk and walked over to the only window in his office. He looked out upon a brown, lifeless field lying just beyond the parking lot. He hadn't seen anything green in that field since a handful of dandelion plants bloomed a few weeks ago, but they had since died off from a late-June frost. With summer at the halfway mark and a major snowstorm coming out of Canada over the Fourth of July weekend, he doubted he would see any more of those small yellow flowers for at least a year.

He remembered two summers ago when he called the landscaping staff to try to get the dandelions under control on that same stretch of lawn. The entire field was covered with the yellow glow of spring dandelions. He realized he would do almost anything to have that vibrant landscape in front of him again.

Standing there, secretly wanting to burst into tears, he continued the conversation he was having with Dr. Zell. "How much snow are you predicting?"

"Six to ten inches on the low end and possibly more than a foot in some of the higher elevations."

"It's the Fourth of July, Kiril—what the hell is going on? We're having a major winter blizzard on the Fourth of July."

"It's not a typical blizzard. There won't be much blowing snow, or snow drifts, or freezing cold behind it. I wish it were a typical blizzard. A blizzard wouldn't have anywhere near the impact on the greenhouses as this storm is going to have. What we're dealing with in this case is a slow moving, wet, heavy snowfall.

"The temperatures should remain right around the freezing mark, and the winds will be fairly light. That's the problem. As heavy snowfall accumulates on thousands of makeshift plastic greenhouses, they'll collapse. This is the kind of snowfall that has been known to collapse garages and Wal-Mart roofs. I can't imagine the kind of damage it's going to do to two-by-fours and thin plastic sheeting.

"The long-term forecast has the storm slowly dropping down into North Dakota, then continuing south across Minnesota, into southern Illinois, then straight across the country through New England and out to sea. The swath of damage will likely extend into the Appalachians to the south and the Great Lakes to the north. The models we are currently running indicate this freak storm could take out as many as 30 percent of the Hope Gardens constructed in the East Coast. I suggest we go public with the news immediately so people can harvest whatever they can before the brunt of the storm hits."

Dr. Wade felt like jumping through the window he was looking out and plummeting to his death some four stories below. It wasn't the first time he had pondered the idea. He was tired of dealing with this brutal winter without end. He was tired of explaining to the ever-hungry press why the gamma lasers weren't removing the nanomirrors fast enough, or why no one at the CMC had predicted the failure of the project in the first place. He was tired of everything. Mostly, he was tired of watching people die.

"I'll work up a press release in a few minutes. You're right though, we have to let people know about this approaching storm and its ramifications. I'll call COI and inform them as well. They'll want to let the President know and will probably take over handling the media.

"Maybe people will be able to salvage something out of their gardens before this storm hits. Maybe a mouthful of Swiss chard, or some undersized carrots. Hell, Kiril, are we ever going to catch a break from this?"

"I'm not sure. There's a chance we won't have a summer next year either, though I think we'll have enough ambient heat built up to avoid midsummer snowstorms like this one.

"The trouble is, we never anticipated the speed with which the Earth's climate can change. It's now clear that these events can happen quickly. Instantly, put in geological perspective. Even with the models we ran before the project failed, we never thought leaving the mirrors up there would throw the planet into anything this drastic. It turns out our atmosphere is a hell of a lot more temperamental than we imagined."

Dr. Wade continued staring out the window at the barren landscape below. "Yeah, our atmosphere can turn on a dime. It's throwing us yet another curveball this weekend. This storm is really going to make a mess of the Hope Gardens project. Will greenhouses west of the storm be impacted?"

"They'll be fine. It's the major metropolitan areas like Minneapolis, St. Paul, Chicago, Cincinnati, Pittsburgh, Philly, New York and Boston that will be hit hardest by this storm. Of course, all the interior gardens and grow houses will be fine—it's just the backyard, FEMA greenhouses that will collapse under the weight of the snow."

The conversation paused for a moment. Finally Dr. Wade continued in a somber tone. "The coming third winter will be the winter of our despair. You know that, don't you, Dr. Zell? Americans will be starving to death by January or February. There won't be any way to save them, will there?"

"There's not enough food. Even if the greenhouses survive west of the storm, they won't have anything extra to ship out east to cover the losses. People are going to starve to death and right now, it appears there's not a goddamned thing we can do about it. It's Armageddon pure and simple."

"I didn't want to live to see it, but now I know," Dr. Wade said. "Thanks for keeping me up to speed on the storm. I'll get on it right away."

"I figured you would want to know. I wish the news were better."

"It's not your fault. It's just the way things have been going. Take care."

"I will."

With that, Kiril Zell left his boss and walked back to his office.

Dr. Wade got on his phone and started calling his contacts at COI. The forecast of the approaching winter storm was on the news that evening. People were told to harvest everything they could from their gardens before the snow began falling. They were told that it would be all but impossible to rebuild their greenhouses before the bitter cold of mid-August rolled in. The Hope Gardens project had proved hopeless for many. People would have to try to get by with whatever stockpiles they had to make it all the way through to the following summer.

Of course, the media failed to mention there might not be a following summer. No one wanted to hear that prognosis.

From Orchids to Potatoes

News of the approaching storm sent shivers down the spine of Yeva Dunning and the crew at the Chicago Botanic Gardens. With their dozens of flower beds awash with brown, lifeless roses and dead perennials, they had erected scores of Hope Gardens throughout the grounds. Although they had built these gardens with better materials than most, Yeva was not sure the structures would survive the kind of snowfall that was slowly heading toward the Windy City.

It was Yeva who had called this meeting with her boss, Margot, and a half-dozen staff members to decide whether they would harvest the meager crop they had managed to produce. They were meeting inside the largest of the greenhouses, which was thirty by ninety feet.

"I think you already know why we're all here. They're telling us the storm has already hit the Twin Cities and that more than 75 percent of the Hope Gardens have collapsed. Most people, wisely, elected to pick whatever they could before the snow started, but many did not. When the plastic sheeting falls on top of the garden below, whatever plant life under it is lost. The weight of the snow, combined with the cold, turns everything underneath to mush. Inedible mush."

One of the staff spoke up. "But Yeva, we've built these greenhouses far sturdier than the ones I've seen across the back yards of suburban Chicago. Look," he said, pointing up to the roof of the building they were standing in, "see all that cross bracing? That should help support the ceiling. All of our greenhouses are built this way. I think they'll hold."

Yeva was skeptical. "Well, once it starts falling, it will be too late for us to change our minds. Look around you. Most of what we planted isn't even close to harvest, but we could still salvage a lot of beet greens, spinach, chard and even the undersized onions and carrots would be edible. We certainly can't get up on this plastic sheeting and start shoveling the snow off, can we?"

Several of the staff nodded in agreement.

"Yeva's right," Margot added. "If this greenhouse collapses, we'll lose every edible plant under it. I don't see any way we can save these gardens. The best plan is for all of us to harvest what we can, leave the plants that are too immature to use in place, and wait to see what happens. Then we've at least gotten something for our efforts."

"I agree," one of the women on the staff said. "I don't think it's worth the risk of losing what little we already have by taking the chance that these structures will endure the storm. At least all of our hard work this spring won't end up being a total loss."

"Yes, let's not forget those weeks of non-stop work," Yeva said, "when all of you donated your time to construct these gardens back in May. At least all that won't vanish in a few hours. We'll harvest everything we can, leave the rest of the immature plants in place, and pray the worst of the snowfall misses Chicago. But ultimately it's your call, Margot."

"Let's do it," she said. "Let's spread out and pick everything we can while we still have time."

Although several staff members grumbled quietly about the decision, the meeting was over. The only thing left to do was for every available hand to head out with a basket or bucket and pick whatever was usable. They would then bring the vegetables back to the main facility for processing, canning or freezing.

By the following morning it was clear to everyone they had made the right decision. The storm hit the greater Chicago area just after midnight. By morning, only one of the twenty-six greenhouses was still standing. Every other greenhouse, just as the CMC had predicted, had collapsed. Luckily, because of the additional supports and the superior construction of the greenhouses, many sections were still intact and in the end, almost half the Hope Gardens in the Chicago Botanic Gardens could be salvaged. Over the next week, the crew worked tirelessly to rebuild the remaining greenhouses and save the plants that hadn't been crushed by the snow.

There would be a smaller, but still substantial harvest from the gardens that fall. Of course, all of the other greenhouses—stunning glass buildings where exotic palms and orchids once flourished—would help feed the staff and their families as well. All the rare specimen plants, brought in from every corner of the globe, had long since been dug up and discarded. Orchids costing thousands of dollars had been replaced by tomatoes and pole beans. The three major greenhouses at the Botanic Gardens no longer replicated deserts, tropics or the sub-tropics. They now looked as if they had been planted for a local truck farmer.

The Board of Directors, acting on Yeva and Margot's advice, had decided shortly after the President's dire prediction about the growing season to close the Botanic Gardens, rip up everything inside, and replant all available facilities with edible plants. Yeva, with the gardening experience she had gathered from years of managing the seed bank, was put in charge of the planting.

Of course, Yeva never let on that she wouldn't need any of the harvest. Nor would Margot. But both of them elected to take their share regardless. They didn't want the staff—or anyone for that matter—knowing about their personal caches. As times got increasingly desperate, both women realized that no one, not even the Board of Directors, could be trusted.

The Chicago Botanic Gardens were not alone in abandoning their prized horticultural collections. As gorgeous as the orchids, tropical plants and exotic flowers were to admire, most were inedible and difficult to care for. The only viable use for greenhouses everywhere was to plant food crops. Every greenhouse and arboretum in the nation had become a simple vegetable garden. Millions of dollars and decades' worth of rare and exotic specimens from every corner of the planet were torn out and tossed into burn piles. The only criteria used for deciding if a plant found any space at all in a greenhouse, anywhere in the world, was whether it was edible. The beauty of a rare orchid no longer mattered. Potatoes mattered.

Scotch

It was after midnight. As they had done many times in the past, Albion and Warren had stayed up late watching the terrible news of the freak snowstorm sweeping across half the nation. They drank straight scotch, no ice. The two men had grown to be the best of friends during the worst of times.

Warren, too tall and thin to be anything but awkward, and Albion, with his professor-like demeanor and disposition for proof, made an odd pair, but they enjoyed each other's company and conversation. Not having to consider what the other professors might think, Albion had let his pony tail grow down to his waist. Though nearly as tall as Warren, Albion seemed more comfortable with his height.

Around 1 a.m., while the Weather Channel kept up its nonstop coverage of the demise of the Green Party's "Hope Gardens," Albion started in on a theme familiar to both of them.

"How on Earth did we get here, Warren?"

"I don't know. Climate change, we now know, is death by a thousand cuts. No one wanted to connect the dots early on and everyone was just too complacent. Let's face it, we ruined ourselves at the height of the fossil fuel era. We never gave the atmosphere, or what we were inadvertently doing to it, a second thought.

"The year I was born, everyone on Earth knew the climate was going to hell. The Earth was getting hotter. That year, 2013, broke every temperature record before it. It was the same year that started what became known as the Great Southwestern Drought. It was the year when hardly a drop of rain fell on Texas, Oklahoma or northern Mexico for the entire summer.

"People just didn't want to deal with it, especially here in America where the fossil fuel industries wielded such incredible power. Exxon Mobile, Chevron, Conoco Phillips, the Koch brothers—all of them spent billions trying to debunk the science of climate change. What were they thinking? Did they honestly believe they could somehow move off the planet they were methodically destroying? Did they think they were going to take all their profits and relocate to Mars? It was their planet, and their children's planet they were overheating—not someone else's. Did we really believe those short-term profits were worth the long-term demise of our atmosphere?"

Albion took a sip of his lukewarm scotch before responding.

"By the time you and I were born, Warren, when things were starting to unravel, we had already known about the greenhouse effect of CO_2 for more than 150 years. That's what amazes me. Why more people didn't pay attention to the work of Svante Arrhenius, the Swedish scientist who first warned of the dangers of burning fossil fuels, is beyond me. His work proved that just tiny amounts of CO_2 could drastically affect air temperature. But his work went unnoticed. Arrhenius was ahead of his time."

"People were too complacent, Albion. They had a great lifestyle and led a cushy existence with air conditioning, cheap gasoline and gas-guzzling SUVs. The global transport system was made up of thousands of jet airplanes and goods were shipped across the oceans by coal- or oil-burning freighters. Who would want to trade all of that in just because it produced minuscule amounts of some harmless gas?

"Remember the Kyoto protocol?" Warren continued. "What a joke that accord turned out to be. China ignored it, the U.S. never agreed to it, the Canadians renounced it. The vast majority of the 191 states that signed it did little or nothing to reduce their emissions. We don't change easily. My cousin used to say that 'catastrophe is the catalyst for change.' Well, we've got plenty of catastrophe to go around these days."

The Weather Channel announcer predicted that 78 percent of the Hope Gardens in the path of the storm would be lost as Albion responded.

"And what about the Keeling Curve? How could they have missed that one? When Dr. Charles Keeling first set up his monitoring devices on the top of Mauna Loa nearly a century ago, he measured a mere 315 parts per million of CO_2. By 2025 that number had risen to 405 parts per million. You'd think that those numbers would have set off enough of an alarm to make everyone on the planet sit up and take note, but they didn't."

Both men were starting to get tipsy from their evening of scotch.

"No, it took the Lost Decade to do that, Albion. The Lost Decade changed everything. There were no more lobbyists or PR men up to the task of continuing their relentless lies and half-truths about what was behind the floods, droughts, tsunamis, hurricanes and tornadoes. No amount of cash or slick ad campaigns about "clean coal," sunspots, solar cycles and everything else they contrived could cover up the corpses piling up around the planet. Death hardens people but it also ferrets out the truth. Death disrobed their lies.

"When the energy companies finally started to come clean, when the CEOs realized the dead included their own grandkids, their wives, their stockholders, then—only then!—they finally began admitting it was all bullshit. Like the cigarette industry in the 1950s. Theirs was the art of obfuscation." Warren muffed the word, intentionally pronouncing it 'ob-fuc-sation.' "But they were clever. They had clever, quasi-scientific evidence. I've seen the ads they ran early on. They said the warming had nothing to do with us, nothing to do with burning billions of tons of fossil fuels. They kept stalling. We had to do 'more research.' We had to ignore the irrefutable evidence thousands of scientists presented. We wanted easier, less self-blamable causes. Profits were placed before personal responsibility. Human greed killed our climate, pure and simple.

"But we were all to blame. We all did our part to destroy our atmosphere. Even those scientists and writers who flew from Greenland to the Tuvalu Islands, from the glaciers of Peru to the rain forests of Borneo, shouting at the top of their lungs that we were heading for disaster—even they did so while adding tons of CO_2 out of the exhaust of the jet engines they used to go from one failing ecosystem to the other. No one was without guilt, Albion, nor can anyone claim to be guiltless today. There isn't a human being on Earth who doesn't have an environmental impact. We all leave our carbon, or I should say, our environmental footprints behind us. Some are huge, some minuscule, but everyone on Earth has an ecological price tag."

Now it was Warren's turn to take a long pull of lukewarm scotch. The announcer on the Weather Channel was speculating how bad the forthcoming winter might be, using data supplied to them by COI. Of course COI was intentionally underestimating the extent of the food shortages that was soon to befall all of North America. While their internal estimates predicted losses as high as 40 to 50 percent of North America's population, the official press releases coming from the Corporation of Information talked about less than half of that, with most of the starvation occurring among the very young, the sick and the elderly.

"What's going to happen on the other side of this mess, Warren? Are we going to really learn anything from this? Is there any hope for us as a species?"

"Oh, give me a break, Albion. I'm drunk, I can't answer that. But I can't tell you how many sleepless nights I've spent pondering that same question. Are we worth it? We've left nothing but a trail of tears behind us. Civilization is an environmental horror story. Mass extinctions, huge swaths of virgin forests cut to stubble, dredged marshes and drained wetlands, wars, overheated atmospheres followed by snowstorms on the Fourth of July. That's us, Albion. This is it. We're like an impact meteor slamming into our own planet. I wish I could tell you what it's going to be like on the other side of this cataclysm, but I can't. I just can't wait till the trees turn green again and I can see tall fields of wheat blowing in the summer winds.

"I just hope we take something away from this—something that will make it all worth it."

"Me too, Warren, me too. But I doubt anything's worth it."

The clock ticked past 2 a.m. before Warren and Albion called it a night. Their thoughts were blurred by the scotch and their hearts were heavy with the knowledge that the third winter would be the worst winter the world had ever known. The third winter would be the one where humanity became anything but humane.

Acidic Seas

August 14, 2045

Albion, his wife Cecilia, Mark and I were watching some new YouTube videos coming out of Tokyo. The government has set up incinerators similar to the ones being used in India, China and elsewhere in the world. The death toll keeps mounting. Although no one knows the precise number of people who have perished thus far, mostly from disease, malnutrition or outright starvation, last night CNN speculated that the global totals are approaching 800 million. Some estimates put that number at over a billion.

While watching the videos, Cecilia wondered why the Japanese aren't turning to the sea for food. After all, she argued, the sea hasn't frozen over and the people of Japan have always harvested their surrounding seas. The three of us explained to her that from the intense overfishing during the Lost Decade, the rising sea levels and the continued acidification of the oceans, there wasn't anything left to collect.

In fact the Japanese fishing fleet, along with fleets from China, Peru, Thailand and Europe, found themselves without any fish to catch more than a decade ago. Bluefin tuna, once the gold standard of Japanese sushi, were declared extinct in 2022, after the last known fish was taken off the coast of Newfoundland. No one has seen a living Bluefin since that cold day in November when the last recorded fish was caught by hook and line. The North Atlantic cod fishery collapsed before I was born and the swordfish industry vanished in the early '30s.

Of course, there was always aquaculture. But ocean acidification started wreaking havoc on our oyster and clam shells. We were all aware of what CO_2 was doing to the pH balance of the world's oceans, but by the time we stopped burning fossil fuels, the damage was done. We knew early on that the oceans were absorbing more than 25 percent of the CO_2 we were dumping into the atmosphere. After our 200-year fossil fuel burning party was all but over, we learned that the ocean couldn't handle the 700 billion tons we had thrown into it. The sheer volume of this single chemical, CO_2, was changing the chemistry of saltwater.

The largest impact of this acidification was on shellfish, from lobsters to coral reefs. Near the end of the 2020s, aquaculture operations from New Zealand to Norway began having trouble with their mussel and oyster farms.

The sea had become so acidic that their farm shellfish were no longer able to produce viable shells. The increased acidity had reduced carbonate, the mineral used to form the shells and skeletons of many shellfish and corals, to the point where the farms could no longer produce harvests. One farm after another shuttered its doors and the entire aquaculture industry worldwide went into decline.

What happened next was even more astonishing. The impact acidification had on plankton, which vanished on a global scale, collapsed the entire food chain. Blue whales, dolphins and almost all the major pelagic fishes dwelling in the open ocean found themselves with nothing to eat. The plankton disappeared. As plankton and krill are the major diet of the baleen whales, those species started to perish across vast swaths of their former range. By the late '30s, when the burning of all fossil fuels was banned worldwide, the oceans were more acidic than they had been in 300 million years. Although they had experienced similar events in the past, nothing compared to the timeframe within which this dramatic change had happened—a mere 250 years.

With nothing left to catch, the world's commercial fishing boats sat idly at the docks and rusted away. Coral reefs, impacted by both the rising sea levels and the rising acidity, started bleaching out and dying from Australia to Belize. We all tried to explain to Cecilia that the reason Japan couldn't turn to the sea was the same reason countries like Russia, Finland, Iceland and all the other nations that once harvested the bounties of the sea couldn't do so—most of the world's vast oceans were dead zones and there wasn't anything to catch.

It's ironic that the one environment not immediately impacted by the failed Mylerium Project, the world's oceans, had already surrendered everything to humans decades before the big chill. Japan couldn't turn to the ocean to feed its people because the ocean was empty. All it was now was a vast, blue expanse of salty water, with a handful of coral reefs hanging on for dear life and the distant memory of another lost ecosystem.

Of course Cecilia understood that all the freshwater fish farms were either frozen over or had been harvested because, lacking plant life for the past two summers, there was nothing left to feed the fish. The fish meal they used to get from the oceans was gone and lacking a growing season, there were no corn or vegetable-based fish pellets anywhere. Even if there were, people would eat them at this point. The oceans, lakes, rivers and streams of the world are not going to save us from ourselves. The third winter is fast approaching in a world out of options. This gauntlet is going to be mankind's most difficult test.

I'm quite certain we'll be fine at the ranch. We've got sufficient stockpiles in the root cellar, plenty of water flowing through Brackett Creek and enough wood to last two more winters if need be. I'm glad I thought of adding seed stock to our inventory. We'll need plenty of seeds this spring, when, hopefully, this damned cold will finally come to an end.

The Third Winter

On January 1, 2046, the Corporation of Information released their monthly estimate of how many nanomirrors were still remaining in the stratosphere. The official number was 43 percent. The actual count was 18 percent higher, but underestimating the amount of mirrors in the atmosphere had become standard operating procedure for COI and the Green Party. Their scientists had been told to downplay the numbers to avoid spreading panic about the next summer, or lack thereof.

Some of the computer models projected that between the steady bombardment by the gamma lasers and natural attrition, there would be a sufficient decline in the particles to allow enough sunlight and sufficient warmth for a modest, but harvestable crop. Other models were not so optimistic. These indicated that even if the mirrors could be reduced to an actual 30 percent of the original deployment, these reflectors, coupled with the high albedo of the extensive snowfalls anticipated over the forthcoming winter, would be just enough to tip the scales toward yet a third failed growing season, especially in the highly productive regions of North America, from Iowa northward to the grain fields of Canada.

No one, from President Beltram on down, wanted to disclose the fact that the CMC was unable to make the call as to whether the third summer would produce a harvest in the Northern Hemisphere. Even if they had the ability to know that, there was still the question as to how large a yield the third summer could produce. The southern tier of the U.S. might come through, but how far northward crops would grow was unknown. The vast majority of horticulturists agreed that the fruit trees and perennials such as blueberries, raspberries, rhubarb and asparagus were lost. All of the country's fruit bearing trees had not had so much as a leaf on them since the summer of 2043. Vast orchards were lifeless skeletons. There would be no oranges, peaches, cherries or pears for decades, as the orchards were lost. Everything would have to be replanted from seed.

In a way it didn't matter what COI or the Green Party said any longer. The citizens of the U.S., Canada and Mexico no longer believed them even when they had the courage to tell the truth. Ever since the first announcement about the failed Mylerium Project, people had become increasingly wary of any news coming out of Washington or Chicago. The government couldn't be trusted any longer, so most people simply ignored the official party line regardless if the news was good or bad. People were living day to day. Next summer hardly mattered because tomorrow's meal dominated their every waking moment.

There was no economy to speak of and the civilized world seemed to be slipping deeper into a quiet despair. The winter was not as cold or as snowy as the two prior ones, but it was still unbearable. This time, many families realized early on that there just wouldn't be enough food to go around. This time it wouldn't just be the people of China, India and Southeast Asia who would suffer. This time Americans would take down their last jar of rice, their last packet of oatmeal and wonder what would happen next. Most of them knew the answer. Death would happen next.

Necrocannibalism

"They're eating the dead."

"Oh my God. Where did you find this video?"

"It's gone viral. Someone from Idaho shot it and it's just gross."

A half-dozen inhabitants at Shelter Ranch sat around the living room in the barn watching in horror as two people explained the best way to butcher and handle a corpse. The young couple tried to explain early on that they didn't want to be doing this, but where they were, just south of Boise, there simply was nothing left to eat. When one of their parents died of starvation two weeks earlier, they realized her body was the only thing left to eat. They openly wept as they went about the macabre business of cutting up a human being, vacuum-sealing the flesh in proper portions and cooking it with whatever else they had.

"It's human stew. They're making human stew."

"Her mother died of starvation so I doubt there's much fat content in the meat," Warren said in an unusually strange, detached voice. "Not sure it will do them much good."

The six of them sat silent, almost spellbound by what was happening on You Tube.

After watching the video in silence for a minute, Albion spoke up. "It doesn't surprise me. In fact I'm sure we'll see much, much more of this before the winter is over. All the social networks are filled with people pleading for food. They'll do anything—and I mean anything—for scraps at this point. The government has shut down all emergency food depots that were still open. What little reserves are left are being kept in storage for the military, the police and government officials. It's hell out there.

"I've also heard that it's no longer safe in Bozeman, Billings or any town in Montana. People are becoming increasingly lawless and if you look well-fed, they'll follow you home and attempt to steal your stockpile. We should stay put, hunker down and keep a low profile. We should also keep the guns loaded and readily available just in case someone driving by decides to pay us a visit. No one can be trusted."

Everyone nodded. Albion was right. The look on Warren's face, focused and concerned, indicated he was also in agreement. The situation across the country was dire.

Most Americans starved with a sense of quiet dignity. When the food ran out, the aged still took it upon themselves to wander out into the cold, sit down on some bus-stop bench, and wait until the cold made them fall asleep. The children, especially the infants, cried at first, then fell into a silent stupor, with their internal organs eventually shutting down one after the other until death found them.

There were plenty of more dramatic exits, however. People put guns to their heads—especially young men who felt helpless when it came to providing for their families. Women often suffered in silence, their arms becoming thinner, their hair and teeth falling out due to bad nutrition. Most perished quietly, but there were pockets of the country where necrocannibalism, the eating of the dead, had given way to predatory cannibals—killing and eating of the living. These bands of cannibals, generally confined to remote towns and smaller cities across the country, had yet to be verified by the government, but rumors of their existence permeated the Web.

"God—that's an arm she's chewing on, isn't it?"

"It looks like it, Warren," Cecilia said. "Oh yeah, you can see where they chopped off the hand right at the wrist. I suppose it's better than starving to death but… how would you ever get over something like that? Wouldn't it haunt you?"

"It would take time, for sure," Warren said. "I would imagine most who are *forced* to eat human flesh could carry on quite normally after a while, though. Technically, aside from being morally repugnant, there are no laws against necrocannibalism. Under the circumstances, I doubt the Greens will prosecute anyone who resorts to eating their own dead.

"Of course, killing and eating living humans is a different story. You may remember studying the infamous Donner Party incident in school. In the mid-19th century that group of pioneers got caught in a mountain pass near Lake Tahoe on their way to California. They not only ate their own dead, but eventually resorted to killing and eating several Native Americans. That's murder and the very definition of cannibalism.

"There's more history of that kind of thing in the U.S.—Ed Gein may have eaten some of his neighbors and Jeffrey Dahmer killed and ate quite a few young men in the 20th century. Both of these people were psychopaths, but historically, cannibalism was practiced by many primitive cultures.

"The word itself derives from the Carib Indians of the West Indies who ate the flesh of their adversaries after battle. The Maori people of New Zealand practiced cannibalism during warfare—they even ate the people onboard a European convict ship in the early 1800s. Cannibalism has been found in the jungles of New Guinea, the Amazon Rain Forest. I suppose ten, maybe twenty thousand years ago the practice was widespread. Cannibalism was probably commonplace back when we were first emerging from the Stone Age, though no one knows for certain," said Warren.

"You seem to know a lot about cannibalism," Albion said. "You're making me a bit nervous, Warren…"

He chuckled a bit, but no one else seemed to find the joke funny, especially with images of people eating each other splayed across the computer screen. Albion took it upon himself to turn off the monitor.

Everyone was aware of the fact that Earth was a lifeboat in space after the failed Mylerium Project, with billions of hungry inhabitants and nowhere near enough food to go around. It was only mid-January. There were still three, possibly four more months of winter ahead before spring would arrive, if it ever did. There wasn't an adult living at Shelter Ranch who felt things would get better anytime soon.

They were right.

Soot and Ash

"Will there be a spring?" Dr. Wade asked the team of climatologists he had assembled on February 1, 2046.

"Hopefully," Dr. Zell replied.

"What are the odds?"

"It's 50/50 at this point."

"The models are all over the place," added one of the younger members of the team. "We just don't know how much snowfall will cover the continental U.S. The less there is, the better."

"So if we get as much snow as we did last winter, then the answer is no," Dr. Zell said. "In that case we won't have a growing season for the third summer in a row. By mid-summer even our strategic reserves will be gone. There won't be any food for us, either. There won't be any food for the police, the army or the hospital staff. Only the highest levels of the Green Party will have food, and they will be out by October.

"If we don't have a summer with a viable crop, there is talk about invading South America. If that happens, Brazil has made it clear that they will unleash the full force of their military might upon the major cities of the United States and Canada. We'd add nuclear war to this catastrophe, though I wonder if the millions of people starving to death in Los Angeles and New York might not welcome such a quick ending to their suffering."

"That's a hell of a thought, Kiril—using atomic bombs for mercy killing. It doesn't exactly sound like the best way to go."

"Have you looked at the videos being posted?"

"You mean the necrocannibalism? Or the incinerators burning 24/7 outside of L.A., New York, Boston, Philadelphia…? Yes, I've seen them all. It's a total nightmare out there. Hell, you don't have to go far. I've heard roaming gangs of hungry young men are killing and eating strangers in the South Side."

"It's true—they are calling them 'eaters' on the Net," another staff member piped in. "They are shooting, butchering and eating other people. In many places that's the only thing left to eat. I understand it's not as bad across much of the southern tier of the country, where the Hope Gardens survived the mid-summer snowstorm. But it's definitely not safe here, or anywhere north of the Mason-Dixon Line for that matter."

"Let's change directions here and get down to business," Dr. Wade suggested. "What about the gamma lasers? How are they doing?"

"They're doing… fair," one of his staff said cautiously. "We have more than 500 lasers up and running, but the sheer size of the area we're attempting to cover is astronomical. To date, our studies have indicated that the lasers have removed between 7 to 9 percent of the nanomirrors. Most of the mirrors are disintegrating and dissipating on their own now, which gives us hope that we will have a summer, though a very cold one."

"How many are still up there?"

"Our latest GPS count indicates 50 percent of the original deployment is still in the stratosphere, though by May I think that number will be around 42 percent. That would still cool the summer well below normal, but it would not be cold enough to prevent crops from coming in, especially south of the Canadian border. Once again, this all depends on how much snow we get. Everything depends on that, because of the feedback loop snow creates. If it wasn't so damn reflective, we wouldn't have this problem on our hands."

Dr. Wade suddenly thought of a novel idea. "Couldn't we cover the snow in soot, or produce enough dark soot from our coal-fired electric plants to make a difference?" he asked. "Could we somehow melt the snow if we have to?"

Dr. Zell picked up on his idea immediately. "Yes! We could remove all the ash scrubbers from those coal-fired plants. That would help tremendously, especially in the regions immediately surrounding the plants. It would be like going back to the early years of the Industrial Revolution, bringing all the soot and grime of 19th-century London to the States. It's a brilliant idea. If we blanket the surrounding regions with dark ash and soot, the snow will melt much faster than if we left it white. I think it's something we should pursue."

Many of the assembled scientists murmured agreement.

"Then let's contact the people at COI and the Department of Energy," Dr. Wade said. "We can have them dismantle all the pollution controls and scrubbers at the coal-fired plants currently operating in the country."

"What about using jets—or even the project drones—to disperse some kind of black dust across the snowpack?" one of the climatologists asked.

"That might work as well, though we'd have to make sure the dispersant we use wouldn't harm the soil. The last thing we want to do is to compound the Mylerium Project with yet another disaster. Imagine if what we used hurt what could be the most important growing season in history."

"I'll look into possible compounds that might work and see what I can come up with," the climatologist responded.

"I think we've got some workable ideas already," Dr. Wade said. "I want everyone to explore these ideas and report back to me in a week—same time, same place. We have to find a way to make the summer of 2046 work. If we can't grow crops this time around, none of us will be here next year to discuss the future. There won't be a future."

No one added anything to Dr. Larry Wade's last comment. They knew it was true. If there was no summer across the Northern Hemisphere in 2046, everything was lost. The Mylerium Project, meant to stave off the ravages of climate change through geoengineering, had become the worldwide nightmare Warren Randolf had predicted. Moods were bleak. Tomorrow was no longer a certainty.

Valentine's Day

February 14, 2046

It's Valentine's Day. Who would have thought I would find myself here, in central Montana, living in a survivalist commune with two dozen friends, with the temperature outside at 29 below and dropping? It seems colder this year, but that's probably good. Colder air holds less moisture and less moisture means less snow. The depth of the snow is what's been keeping things cold through spring and well into summer for the past few years.

At times like this, I can't help but think back to the Lost Decade, when we would have done anything to make things cooler. I remember the heat waves and the tremendous death tolls that followed them. No one has ever calculated which climate change events killed more people—the floods or the heat waves. The floods were more dramatic, with videos of houses falling into deep ravines where gentle streams once flowed. But I think the prolonged heat waves and the fires that followed took more lives and destroyed more property.

They started early in the early part of the century, with the first major heat wave hitting Europe during the summer of 2003. Estimates put the total number of dead at 70,000 that summer–the hottest on record in Europe since 1540. The elderly, the young and the infirm were most vulnerable as temperatures soared into the 100s and remained scorching hot for days on end. Portugal hit 118 degrees and forest fires raged across the countryside. Italy, Spain, the Netherlands, Ireland–even the Swiss Alps were impacted by the triple-digit heat.

But those days offered only a glimpse of what was to come. A few years later the heat returned, hammering the American Southwest and causing relentless forest fires that took out mountain homes, remote villages, and small towns. Europe, Spain, Portugal and Italy were among the hardest-hit countries in the developed world. They didn't have sufficient cooling stations for the hundreds of thousands of people who lacked air conditioning.

When the great heat wave of 2026 hit, an estimated 1.5 million people died from heat stroke, heat exhaustion or dehydration. Hospitals were overwhelmed as tens of thousands sought relief from week after week of 100-plus-degree weather. People often compared that summer with the black plague of Medieval Europe–the death toll was so astronomical, authorities used municipal garbage trucks to haul out corpses every morning. There were so many dead every day, no one objected. The stench in Madrid, Rome and Paris was so strong that they said you could smell the cities 50 miles downwind.

Worldwide, people in the Third World countries suffered the most. Sub-Saharan Africa faced the worst effects of the overheating. The great Sahara grew yearly until it spread southward across the Sahel, displacing millions of African dirt farmers unable to sustain themselves in the scorching heat. The soil baked beneath the relentless sun, and sometimes two years would go by without so much as a drop of rain in Chad, Niger and Mali.

Millions perished in the famines that followed the heat waves and prolonged droughts. The cities of Niger, especially the capital city of Niamey, were laid to waste following the great heat wave and drought of 2031. By that time the city had grown to more than three million people. In mid-summer, with temperatures pushing 122 degrees, the city ran out of fresh water when the Niger River ran completely dry. Tens of thousands of Nigeriens died of thirst as emergency relief workers attempted to airlift fresh water from the Congo. Some estimates put the total number of heat-related casualties in the Sahel at 20 million.

India suffered mercilessly as thousands of wells failed under a hammering sun. Crop failures were pandemic, especially in the mid-30s, when the heat waves came one season after the other just as the monsoons became unstable and unreliable. The stench of death permeated the air in cities like Mumbai, Delhi, Bangalore and Hyderabad, where the governments did their best to deal with the tens of thousands of poor people perishing daily.

The first incinerators were built in those days—the same ones burning the corpses of the starving today. Something had to be done with the lifeless bodies. The great rivers of India, no longer fed by the glaciers of the Himalayas, had been reduced to trickles.

Across the U.S. and much of southern Canada, the heat was inescapable. New York, Boston, Chicago, Denver, Albuquerque, Phoenix, Las Vegas, Toronto—the list of major cities affected by this hotter planet is endless. It wasn't just the droughts and the heat that they had to endure, but the smoke and ash that fell on many of these places as the surrounding countryside burned. Between 2030 and 2037 (when Mount Cameroon blew and stemmed the bleeding from our self-inflicted wound for a few years), more than 250,000 homes and business in the U.S. were lost to forest fires directly attributed to global heating.

When the rains did arrive, they came in torrential downpours. With cities' surrounding forests burned to rubble, runoff was torrential. The forests that once absorbed the rains were no longer there to buffer the deluges. Streams and rivers quickly rose to flood levels and carved huge valleys through subdivisions and cities. Insurance companies folded after being buried under an avalanche of claims. The National Flood Insurance program went bankrupt in 2029. People went without any insurance and banks gave up trying to force them into policies they couldn't afford. In fact, the banks had trouble finding anyone even willing to write policies. Financial ruin followed.

In the end, before the volcanic cool down, the death toll from the excessive heat waves was never really known. In remote villages from the Sahel to Mongolia, no records were kept, so it's anyone's guess as to how many people were baked to death. It's no wonder we turned to geoengineering and the Mylerium Project. We had to do something to cool down our overheated planet.

As I look outside across a landscape of frozen fields, howling winds and ten-foot snowdrifts, it's hard to imagine what we were all going through just a few brief years ago. We humans are a complicated animal–intelligent but foolish, brave but easily misled. We're designed for the present and are not very good at seeing farther down the road. We're so focused on the short-term that even when our own tools–computers–tell us we have to change, we ignore them. I'm not sure Nature's first experiment with intelligent life will work. Sometimes I feel as if this diary is a suicide note for our species.

So today is Valentine's Day, although I guess I'll have to be my own Valentine. What a lonely, depressing holiday in the midst of a winter without end. So Happy Valentine's Day, Dr. Warren Randolf. Happy Valentine's Day!

The Plan

"I'm not sure, Vince. Do you really think they have that much food up there?" Zolton Miller asked.

"You bet your ass they've got food. I backhoed out a 2,000-square-foot root cellar in that hill just beyond the barn. The ceiling of that place was twelve feet high. Hell, they could hold enough dry goods in there to feed an army."

"Nathan down at the gun shop tells me they've been in there buying rifles, pistols and ammo. Don't you think they'll put up a fight if we come in demanding they give us some of their food?"

Vince hesitated for a moment before answering Zolton, who was his best carpenter.

"Hell no. Once that scientist fellow and his college friends see a half-dozen armed Montanans standing outside his front door, he'll give us all we want. He's from out east, and they ain't got the stomach for violence."

Zolton wasn't convinced. "I don't know, Vince," he said. "I think we should just try to make do with what we have and let those guys be. I think we're asking for trouble."

"Zolt—don't you remember when I told you last week that I can't make do with what I've got? I ain't got enough food to make it to May. I've got about ten pounds of rice, some frozen pole beans, a few cuts of meat left from that buck I shot a year ago and that's it. I'm out of food, Zolt, and I know a couple of other guys from the crew who are damn close to running out of provisions as well. I'm not going to let my family starve when I know there's plenty of extra food down off Brackett Creek Road."

Zolton could tell by the tone of his boss's voice that, with or without his carpenter, he would go ahead with the raid.

"Fine, I'm in. What's the plan?"

"We're going to meet at my place a week from next Thursday night, which is March 1. It's a new moon and with all this cloud cover, it'll be damn dark out there around midnight. We thought we'd best surprise them—that's why we're planning to show up in the middle of the night. They won't be expecting anyone and their cell phones won't do them any good."

"What do you mean? Cell phones work fine out that way."

"I've ordered this device from an online store that blocks cell phone signals within a half-mile radius. The company that sells them has been making a killing since the climate went to shit. This little thing is designed to plug into your vehicle. The sheriff won't have a clue as to what's going on up on Brackett Creek Road. I'll warn them after we take what we need that they'd better shut up, or we'll be back to take the rest."

Zolton doubted the folks at this ranch would simply hand over their private cache of food to a bunch of contractors with rifles. He thought Vince was being overly optimistic. *Hell,* he thought to himself, *if someone showed up at my apartment right now asking for half, or less than half, of what little provisions I've got left, I'd tell them where to put it.*

"I'm still not sure, Vince. I think they'll put up some kind of resistance. I think we're asking for trouble."

"Stop being such a wimp, Zolt. Get with the program. Are you in, or not?"

"I'm in, but I don't want to shoot anybody to get food. There's enough of that going on already. I hear there's some outright cannibalism going on in the Dakotas."

"Yeah, I've read about that. They've lost control of things in South Dakota and the Greens have too much on their plate to send troops over to straighten out every corner of the country. I hear there's gangs of 'eaters.' That's what they're calling them—'eaters.' They're taking over in New York,

Chicago—all the big cities. That's keeping the government and the National Guard plenty busy.

"They won't give a damn about what happens up around Bozeman, that's for sure."

"I hope not."

"See you Thursday night then, OK?"

"I'll be there. What time?"

"Make it 9 p.m. sharp."

"Got it."

"Bye, Zolton, sleep tight."

From the Oval Office

President Beltram was seated behind his desk in the Oval Office. The American flag stood proudly to his right while the Presidential flag flanked his left side. There were some family photos on the wooden desk and a smattering of papers.

He was wearing a dark blue suit with a deep red tie. His address to the nation tonight had been much anticipated. Spring was approaching and rumors were running wild that there would not be a summer of 2046. People were hungry and scared, hoping beyond hope that the President would allay their fears.

"My fellow Americans," he began. "I sit before you tonight with a heavy heart. There has never been, and I pray to God that there never will be, another time like this in the history of this great nation. I know that many of you watching me tonight are hungry. Every day we receive hundreds of thousands of emails asking for help from people just like you.

"This time, we cannot help. Our strategic food reserves—the food we need for our first responders, the Army, Air Force and Navy, are precariously low. The situation across the entire Northern Hemisphere is as bad, or in many cases, worse than what we are experiencing here in the United States. To date, more than two billion people have died since the deployment of the Mylerium Project, the vast majority of them from starvation.

"This not the time to give the wrong impression about the status of the nanomirrors. The CMC informed me this morning that there are still

44 percent of the mirrors in the stratosphere. But they can also say with certainty that spring will arrive for those states south of the Mason-Dixon Line and west of the Sierra Nevada in California. These regions will be able to grow crops and this is great news.

"As reassuring as that is, because our national food supply is severely depleted, we also need the breadbasket of our nation, the Midwest, to be able to plant crops this spring as well. We cannot endure another winter without food."

The President paused for a moment and took a sip of water. He looked tired and worn.

He continued. "The CMC, working with the best scientists in the world, have devised a plan that will help ensure spring will happen. Using the same drones designed to deploy the nanomirrors in March 2043, we are planning to cover the snowpack blanketing most of the nation with coal dust. This idea was first put forth at the CMC and has already been thoroughly tested in northern Illinois. I'm here this evening to tell you: it works. The scientists agree that we need to reduce the highly reflective properties of snow, which is keeping global temperatures down worldwide. Covering our nation with a darker surface material will help warm the atmosphere and melt the snow beneath it.

"After testing several substances, including charcoal, black carbon and graphite, our scientists have elected to go with coal dust. We will need a substantial amount of dust to cover the millions of square miles that are now buried in snow. This is especially true for the vast expanses of Canada and Russia. Finely ground coal dust appears to work flawlessly in our deployment drones and it is both inexpensive and plentiful. We are also dismantling all the scrubbers on the dozens of coal plants we've reopened in hopes that the soot coming out of the smokestacks will also help melt the snow.

"There are health risks involved. We will start deployment on April 1, moving across the continent from the south to the northern wheat fields of Canada by the end of May. Every community where the spraying occurs will be notified prior to deployment and everyone is advised to remain indoors when the drones are in the area. Inhaling coal dust may result in coughing, wheezing and shortness of breath. If coal dust gets in your eyes, it can be an irritant and must be washed out immediately.

"The doctors at the Center for Disease Control have assured me there is no need to worry about developing black lung disease or other long-term health issues, as the exposure to the dust will not be sufficient to cause any serious complications. Some regions might only need to be covered with coal dust once or twice, depending on whether we have repeated snow falls after the initial deployment. Some areas, depending on winter storms, may require a half-dozen deployments or more. If you have any questions about this project, please visit the official website at www.projectdusting.gov. There are additional health warnings and information posted there.

"We are also providing free coal dust to every citizen who requests it. We are setting up distribution centers in every city and town across the northern tier of the nation to hand out 50-pound sacks of dust. This can be spread by hand over any areas that may have been missed by our drones.

"The dust will help melt the snowpack down to the soil, which will then take over as it does every spring to warm our atmosphere. Of course, we are continuing to operate thousands of gamma lasers to eradicate the last of the nanomirrors located throughout the globe. To our disappointment, the gamma lasers are proving to be much slower at eradicating the remaining mirrors than originally estimated. We feel the coal dust will help ensure a harvest of corn, soybeans, wheat and other crops this summer. We have conducted tests verifying that the minute amount of coal dust involved will not affect the soil."

The President paused for a moment before concluding, "In the meanwhile I'm asking every American to share what food they have left with their neighbor. Because of the tremendous strain on our police, the National Guard and the Army, I'm asking all of you to remain calm and watchful. Only your participation can help curtail some of the violence we've seen erupting across the country. Food riots will not get you any more food. Stealing from your neighbors is not only inhumane—it's a crime. Those individuals and gangs who have resorted to lawlessness will be sought out and prosecuted to the fullest extent of the law, that I can assure you. Even if we do not find you now, we *will* find you after the next harvest. Crimes of desperation will not be forgotten in times of plenty.

"As a nation, we have never experienced anything like this. For those of you who have lost a loved one, our thoughts and prayers go out to you.

Remember, we are all in this together and we must persevere. God Bless America."

The camera panned back and faded as the pundits took over, putting their own spin on the President's address.

———————————————

Back in Shelter Ranch, Albion reached over, grabbed the remote and turned off the computer screen.

"Coal dust," he spat as he pushed the off button. "That's so Goddamned ironic. It was coal, the dirtiest fuel imaginable, which got us into this mess to begin with. Now, so says the President, it's going to save us. Coal probably dumped more CO_2 into the atmosphere than any other fossil fuel. Coal damn near baked us to death."

"Stop being so cynical, Albion," said his wife, Cecilia. "They're just trying to come up with something to help. What do you think, Warren? Will it work?"

"Yes, it will help. Snow has an albedo of 0.9, while the Earth overall has an average albedo of 0.3. That means snow is three times more reflective than the open ocean or soil. It's a classic example of a positive feedback. The air is cold, so it produces snowfall—then the snow covers the ground, helping to keep the ground cold, which results in more snow and more cold. The coal dust idea will help break that cycle. They may finally be on to something."

"What about the kids?" Cecilia asked. "If they spray around here, will the kids be safe?"

"The handful of times they're talking about spraying this dust over the snowpack is nothing. During the Industrial Revolution, miners spent years underground digging out the coal seams. While some of them did get the black lung, bronchitis and emphysema, it took decades of exposure for these symptoms to develop. Like the President said, I would keep the kids indoors when the drones fly over, but I don't think the dust will hurt them any if they stay in the barn."

"Do you think they're finally telling us the truth about the remaining nanomirrors?"

Warren thought for a moment. "I still doubt it. I've been running my own model and I suspect there are still more than half the mirrors up there.

Still, the southern states will have a growing season. And who knows? This coal dust idea just might work for the Midwest as well. But there's always the chance they will screw things up again.

"Nonetheless, when the 50-pound bags show up in Bozeman within the next few weeks, I think we should head into town to pick up a dozen or two. If the drones miss us, we can easily spread the stuff by hand and it will help melt the snow. The minuscule amount of dust shouldn't hurt the soil as it's an inert rock and is found in regional soils already.

"I've got to say, the crew back at the CMC may have come up with a damn good idea this time. Too bad they hadn't thought of it sooner."

Albion nodded in agreement. The other members of the compound added their own comments on the President's speech. As people were starting to head out, Dr. Irving, his grey hair thinning, asked Warren a question.

"Say, what do you think about this idea of people sharing their food with others in need?"

"That part of the speech was little more than wishful thinking. We certainly don't have any food to spare. What if this Project Dusting is another bust? We might yet have a fourth winter without being able to re-provision. If we knew for sure there would be a viable harvest this summer, I would consider sharing, but—"

"Well, I hear there's a lot of starving people in Bozeman, Warren," Dr. Irving interrupted. "I'd be willing to chip in some of my share if there was any way to do it. I'm going to be 75 this year and it kills me to think that I'm getting fed while there are probably good families out there, just a few miles up the road, who've got grade-school kids going hungry or worse."

"I appreciate your sentiment, Henry," Warren said. "You've always been a great family doctor. But we can't share our food with anyone. At this point, with all the gangs out there and the trouble they're causing, we can't even afford to let on that we have extra food. We'd be an instant target. It's best for us to lay low, ride this mess out, and try to make it to the other side. The families down the road will just have to fend for themselves. It's too risky for us to do anything else."

Dr. Irving sighed. "I suppose you're right. Anyway, I just thought I'd ask. It's been weighing on me, is all."

"It's a noble thought, Doc. A noble thought."

The group soon dissipated. Some headed back to their rooms; some went to the kitchen to start making dinner. Warren picked up a novel and started reading. It was another mystery novel—nothing memorable. It gave him something to do while the bitter cold winds swept south from the Arctic. It gave him something to do between now and what everyone hoped would finally be spring.

The Midnight Raid

The wind was whipping steady out of the northwest, causing the snow to drift and pile up against the sides of buildings and snow fences. It was 12 degrees below zero outside and lacking a moon, the night was dark and clear.

The blue pickup truck had arrived five minutes earlier than Vince's van. It sat idling in the deserted convenience store on the corner of 5th Street and Highway 89. The store was closed, as it had been for over two years. There was nothing available to sell—no chips, no candy bars and no milk and bread. One of its windows was broken, leaving shards of glass scattered across the pavement.

Zolton was sitting in the idling truck, his rifle in a case beside him. Next to him was Al Sandler, another unemployed carpenter who used to work for Vince back when the world wasn't half-frozen. Times were better then.

The plan was to meet in the parking lot of the convenience store, then drive west together down Brackett Creek Road to the ranch. It was 11:20 p.m. and Vince would arrive by 11:30. At the planning meeting a week ago, they had decided it was safer to rendezvous here rather than meet near the ranch. Vince felt the element of surprise was essential for this plan to work and meeting at the convenience store would ensure that neither vehicle would show up early, before the cell phone signal scrambler was in place.

"It's really cold out there, with the wind blowing like it is."

"Yeah, it's been cold since September."

"How do you think this will go, Zolt?"

"I don't know. I'm not sure that it's a good idea, but on the other hand, I'm not sure I've got enough food to make it to spring, so what the hell am I supposed to do?"

"I listened to the President last week, talking about that coal dust shit and the fact that the government is out of food. It's scary shit, man."

"These are scary times, Al. Did you hear about the Larson family near Bridger Canyon Drive?"

"You mean Elliot Larson's family? No, I haven't heard a thing."

"They're all dead. Elliot shot his two kids, his wife, then shot himself two days ago."

"Holy shit! Why?"

"They ran out of food about a week ago. Elliot left a note saying he just couldn't stand to watch his two boys starve to death and it was the right thing to do."

"To shoot your whole damn family is the right thing to do?"

"The Larsons aren't the only ones doing it. I'm hearing about all kinds of people turning the gas on and making sure the pilot lights are out, or just heading out without a jacket and walking until they fall asleep. It's one ugly mess out there. Even though I think this is a bad idea, I'm down to my last reserves and I'll be damned if I'll turn to eating the dead."

"Me too—the thought of doing that kinda shit turns my stomach. I'd rather take Elliot's path than eat my own kids. You just can't ever get over that."

A pair of headlights appeared about three blocks down Highway 89 to the south.

"That must be Vince and the other guys," Al offered.

"Who the hell else would be out here driving through Clyde Park in the middle of the night?"

The headlights got closer, and it was easy to see they were the headlights to a black van. Vince wanted two vehicles, both for safety and for hauling out the bounty. Vince pulled up along the passenger's side of the truck and rolled down his window.

"Remember," he called out, "we won't be able to get through the front door of the house, the barn or the root cellar. Those doors are all made of reinforced steel. I should know—I had to install the damn things. This scientist knows the importance of good security, but I doubt he'll be expecting us.

"We'll need to get the key from them and given there's five of us, armed and dangerous as they say, I don't think they'll put up any kind of resistance.

"You two ready?"

"Sure, let's get this over with," Al said.

Both vehicles pulled out of the parking lot and sped west down 5th Street, which turned into Brackett Creek Road a half-mile out of town. As expected, there was no traffic.

They reached the driveway to Shelter Ranch at 11:45 p.m. Vince knew the electric cars made almost no noise as they crept along the driveway and he had instructed Zolt to make sure he turned his headlights off when they arrived. In the darkness, as both vehicles crawled silently toward the house, Vince flipped on the cell phone scrambling device he had purchased online. He then reached over and stuck the magnetic antennae onto the roof of his van, making sure no calls could make it out of the compound. He stopped halfway down the driveway, took out a snow shovel, and dug up the fiber optic junction box he had his crews install three years ago. Using a bolt cutter, he opened up the housing and cut the cable lines going into the compound. There would be no Internet at Shelter Ranch tonight either.

They arrived in front of the ranch house and the five of them got out of their trucks, making sure to gently close the vehicle doors behind them. They took out their rifles and put the gun cases in the back of Zolt's pickup. In a whisper, Vince told three of them to stand behind the bed of the truck, making them visible from the house but out of harm's way in case something went wrong.

Vince and Karon Risberg, an electrician by trade, headed toward the front door, rifles in hand. Each of them had a pistol strapped to their side as well, though they were both hoping they wouldn't need either weapon. Once under the overhang, Vince made a loud knock at the door.

Inside the ground level ranch, Warren was the first to hear the knock. He jumped up and looked at the clock on his nightstand. It was 12:09 a.m. *Maybe it's something in the wind*, he thought, still half asleep.

Another knock, even louder than the first, quickly followed.

This time there was no mistaking it. Someone was at the front door. Warren got up, slipped on a pair of pants and headed over to Albion's room.

He tapped lightly on Albion and Cecilia's bedroom door, not wanting to wake up their two children who were sleeping in the adjacent bedroom. Only the five of them shared the house, with the remainder of the crew staying in the converted barn.

"I'm up," Albion grumbled. "I'll be out in a minute. I heard the knock. What the hell's going on?"

"I'm not sure, Albion. But it can't be good. Who in hell would be coming around here in the middle of the night, besides trouble?"

"Maybe it's the local sheriff or something. I'll be right out."

"Grab your gun just in case."

Albion slipped on some pants and went over to his high-boy dresser and reached into the top drawer to get his Glock. As he picked it up, feeling the weight of the metal and realizing, for the first time in his life, that he might need it, his hand began to tremble.

There's no time for that, he thought as he checked to make sure the clip was inside. He stuffed the pistol into his pants, making sure the safety was still on.

"I'll be right out."

"What's going on, Albion?" Cecilia said as she rolled over.

"Oh, nothing really. There's just someone at the front door and Warren and I are going to check it out."

"Who on Earth would be out here this late at night?"

"That's what we're about to find out. Now get back to bed, OK?"

Cecilia rolled over and closed her eyes. Albion could tell she was merely pretending to sleep.

A third, even louder knock echoed down the hall.

"Hurry on, Albion, we've got to find out who's here," Warren said through the door.

Warren heard the doorknob click and stepped back. He and Albion headed down the hallway to the living room, then over to the front door. Warren looked through the tiny peephole before risking opening the door. He saw it was Vince Gatini with another, younger man he didn't recognize and opted to keep it closed instead.

"What's going on, Vince?" Warren hissed. "It's the middle of the night."

"We've come to ask you for some food, Warren. I know you've got a ton of food out in that root cellar I built for you and we're down to our last few meals back home. Can you help us out?"

"Why the guns, Vince? If you're asking for a helping hand, why bring rifles?"

"Because we really don't want you to say no."

"Well, the answer's no, Vince. We can't help you."

"Look over there, Warren, behind the truck."

Vince stepped away from the peephole, allowing Warren to take note of the truck and the three men standing behind it carrying rifles.

"What are you going to do, Vince, kill all of us for food?"

"I don't think that will be necessary, Warren. Just give us what we need and we'll be on out of here."

Warren pulled back from the door and turned to Albion. In a whisper he said, "Go over and get your cell, there's going to be trouble. Dial 911 and get the cops out here as soon as possible."

"Got it."

Warren ran back to his room and picked up his iPhone 100.

"What's going on, Albion?" Cecilia asked as her husband rushed into the room.

"We've got some contractor at the front door demanding food. I've got to get back to Warren. Don't come out of this room no matter what."

Albion dashed back to the front door and started dialing the emergency number.

He didn't have a signal.

Noting the delay, Vince hollered through the closed door.

"Don't bother trying to call the police—your cell signals are blocked. And by the way, your internet connection is cut off as well. Let's just make this easier on everyone and open the door, hand me the keys to your root cellar and we'll just take what we need and leave."

Warren and Albion looked at each other in a state of disbelief. They had been hearing about raids just like this all over the world. About people killing other people for meager rations. Thus far, the lawlessness that had been sweeping across the rest of the world was someone else's problem.

Not tonight.

Warren broke the silence. "What should we do?"

Albion didn't hesitate. "Look, Warren—they're not going to go through with this. They're just trying to bluff us into giving them our food. If we do and there's no spring, we're all dead anyway. You and I both know we won't make it through a fourth winter with what we have. Even if they take half of it, there's no way in hell we'll even make it through the summer if we can't plant something."

Warren nodded in agreement. "The answer is no, Vince. Take your posse and go home. We don't have enough to share."

"Your call, Warren."

Vince walked over a half dozen steps, took his rifle butt and smashed the living room window wide open. The cold air rushed into the room, driven by the ceaseless wind.

"What the hell!"

Warren and Albion jumped back, not expecting anything like this to happen. They both bolted down the hallway toward the bedrooms.

"We've got to get back to the barn, with the rest of the crew," Warren panted. "Let's get out of here, through the back door and let them take whatever's in the house. Maybe they'll be satisfied with that.

"Wake Cecilia up and grab the kids. Do it now!"

Albion could hear Vince picking out the glass shards and tossing them on the floor from the living room. He would be in the house in the next few seconds.

Not knowing what else to do, Albion reached for his Glock and fired a shot down the hall. The noise of the gun going off shattered the quiet of the countryside.

The rest of the people in the barn were awakened by the report.

"What's going on?" Dr. Irving demanded as he rushed into the family room in the barn. "I heard a shot!"

Roger Goode opened the barn door and couldn't make anything out through the drifting snow. Just then, a second round—this time fired by Vince—went off.

Roger slammed and locked the door. He put his eye up to the peep hole to see if there was anyone coming. There wasn't.

Gibson and Andy, Albion's two sons, awoke the instant their father fired the first shot. Seven-year-old Andy got scared and started crying. Cecilia, still in her nightgown, ran over to the boys' room to comfort them.

"Cecilia, we've got to get back to the barn!" Albion said, rushing into the room again. "We've got trouble."

Cecilia tried to calm her sons down and told them to hurry up and put their shoes on. There was no time to dress. They'd have to make a run for it in their pajamas, even though the wind chill was pushing 35 below outside. She picked up Andy, who was visibly shaking.

Warren stood in the hallway in front of Albion, who in turn was waiting for Cecilia to come out with the kids. Vince stood back in the living room and yelled, "What the hell you doing that for? We don't want to hurt anybody here. We just want some food. Don't make us do something we don't want to do."

"Then just leave, Vince. We'll not press charges if you turn around and leave. We're not going to give you any of our food and that's final. We've got lots of guns, Vince, and we know how to use them."

"Kiss my ass you do," Vince said as he jumped into the line of fire and let go with two more shots. Both bullets whizzed by Warren, though one of them glanced across the top of his left shoulder.

Warren started bleeding.

"You shot me!" Warren shouted, shocked and angry simultaneously. "You asshole! You shot me!"

Warren fired two rounds back.

By this time, Albion, Cecilia and the boys were making their way to the other end of the hallway, which led into the kitchen and back exit. Warren, seeing they were out of the gunshot range, shot twice more as he backed toward the kitchen. By the time he made it there, the back door was wide open and he could see the four Garrisons making a dash toward the barn.

That's when he heard the *crack* of a high-powered rifle.

Zolton Miller, who suspected this was how it was going to play out, had already set up his rifle on the bed of the truck, just like he had done dozens of times in the past while hunting mule deer along the Missouri River. He had prepared to shoot at whoever came out the back door. Having worked on the barn remodeling job years ago, he knew that if they tried to slip out the back door toward the barn, they'd be in the open for a hundred feet.

With his rifle steadied and a night scope on, Zolton had little trouble singling out the man dashing toward the barn with a pistol in his hand. Without thinking he put the scope's eerie green cross-hairs square on the back of the man running and pulled the trigger. Albion fell like a mule deer, with the bullet entering his lower back and coming out his stomach.

Cecilia let go with a harrowing scream. "ALBION!"

Roger Goode had watched the scene unfold from the barn. He swung the door open and ran toward Albion, who was lying on the bloodstained snow.

Warren, who had already left the house and had almost reached Albion, spun around and started shooting his Glock wildly at the truck in the distance. He knew there wasn't much of a chance to hit anyone from this range, but he was trying to draw cover for the wounded Albion. He met up with Roger and together, they hauled Albion's limp body toward the front door of the barn. As he dragged his old friend with one arm, Warren kept wildly firing toward the truck until his clip was empty.

Dr. Irving, seeing the situation was deteriorating, had already told Stephanie and her husband Andrew to get out the rifles and start shooting. As Cecilia and her two boys made it into the barn, a steady stream of bullets whizzed past the pickups.

By this time, Vince and Karon had cleared the kitchen and were standing near the front door. Seeing them peek out, Stephanie pointed her rifle toward the house and let go with a few rounds. One of the bullets ripped through the window and caught Karon directly in the right shoulder. He fell back to the floor and as he did, Vince ducked down beside him.

It was by pure chance that the bullet found a target; Stephanie couldn't do much more than pull the trigger when it came to firearms.

With both Andrew and Stephanie firing nonstop, it was impossible for Zolt and the two men stationed behind the truck to get off another round. They had no idea how well-trained their adversaries were and they weren't about to stick their heads up to find out.

Once the barn door slammed shut, the shooting stopped and the quiet of winter returned. Karon lay bleeding on the kitchen floor while Albion was unconscious in the barn with a gut shot that wouldn't stop oozing blood.

It wasn't over.

Noting the volley of shots had stopped, Zolt rushed from behind the pickup through the front door. He figured there was no one left in the house except Vince and Karon. The other two men stayed behind by the truck.

When he finally made the kitchen, Zolt could see Karon had been hit. There was blood all over the floor and Vince was holding a dishrag over the wound.

"I warned you this wasn't going to go well," Zolt said, more calmly than he actually felt.

"Fuck you, Zolt. Let's just get whatever food they've got in the house and get the hell out of here. They've probably got a shitload of guns in that barn and I don't think it'll be easy getting them out of there."

"That's a good plan. I dropped one of them crossing to the barn. He was carrying a gun. I don't think it was Warren, though—he looked like he had a ponytail."

"Serves him right, whoever he was."

"Grab Al and some containers," Vince said. "Let's take every fucking thing we can eat in this house and go."

That's just what they did. There was about enough to feed a dozen people for a month scattered around the house. There was flour, rice, dried beans, some frozen meat and frozen vegetables. The raiders even took a bunch of bags in the back closet without realizing they were Warren's entire cache of seeds.

Within ten minutes, everything had been loaded into the two vehicles and the house was left wide open. Vince thought about burning it down, but didn't want to take the time. Plus, it might land him in more trouble with the law. He was already thinking about some kind of cover story once news of the raid hit the local sheriff's office. He wasn't sure what he was going to say, but he'd think of something.

Back at the ranch, Albion was fading. Dr. Irving was doing his best to stop the bleeding but it was a grave wound and he knew if Albion was going to survive, he would need a hospital and a transfusion.

"How's it look, Henry?" Warren asked.

"We need to get him to the hospital in Bozeman, Warren, *right now*." Dr. Irving's voice carried a quiet urgency.

"We can't—I think they're still out there. They want our food, Doc. They wanted to steal our supplies."

"Double check. Maybe they've given up."

Warren ran over to the front door of the barn and peered out the peephole. As he did, he saw the two vehicles kicking up snow as they sped down the driveway.

"They're leaving! You were right!

"I'll go secure the house," Warren continued. "Henry, you and Cecilia put Albion in the van and Roger, you drive them all to the Deaconess Hospital in Bozeman and do it quick. By the time an ambulance makes it out here he'll bleed out. I'm heading into the sheriff's office after I check out what's left of the house."

"Sounds good, Warren," Roger said. "I'm on it." He ran to the storage room in the barn to get a toboggan for ferrying Albion out to the van.

"God, I hope he makes it," Warren added as he opened the bolted front door of the barn and headed out toward the house.

Within minutes, Albion had been loaded into the van and Roger was racing westward down Brackett Creek Road. He turned south toward Bozeman, hitting 75 miles per hour in his all-wheel-drive electric van, even though the roads were icy. Albion had gone into shock as Dr. Irving did his best to keep pressure on his abdomen. Cecilia was beside herself, too afraid to speak.

Deaconess Hospital

Nothing could have prepared Dr. Henry Irving for the scene that greeted him at Deaconess Hospital in downtown Bozeman.

Roger pulled their van up to the emergency room entrance a few minutes after 1 a.m. The waiting room was full to overflowing. Most of the patients were clearly emaciated. Some looked as if they were from the Sahel of Africa or the death camps at Auschwitz. Their arms were thin as reeds and their eyes were sunken in, with deep, dark bags and skin stretched tight against their cheekbones. Every nuance of their skeletons showed beneath their wasted faces. One person—a young teenage girl—was not moving at all. Henry took one glance at her and concluded she was likely dead.

There were people with stab wounds and a few patients who looked like they had been beaten to a bloody pulp, but most just looked hungry. Very hungry. Some appeared as though they had been living in the emergency room lobby for several days. Perhaps that was the only warm place they had left.

Henry, Roger and Cecilia dragged Albion through the ground-floor entrance of the emergency room on the toboggan, using the snow stuck on the bottom to glide him into the middle of the room. A trail of wet snow and blood followed him from the front door.

Henry rushed up to the receptionist, interrupting a conversation she was having with someone who appeared to be suffering from an allergic rash, if the large red welts covering his arms and face were any indication.

"Nurse, this man's been shot!" Henry announced, gesturing frantically toward Albion on his makeshift stretcher.

"I noticed," she replied in a cold, indifferent manner that took Henry by surprise.

"He needs a transfusion. I'm afraid he's lost a lot of blood."

"I'm afraid we can't help you. We don't have a drop of blood anywhere in this hospital. Where have you been? Half of Bozeman is starving—do you think we've had blood drives lately? Listen, we'll do what we can to save him, but unless you know someone who can donate blood, you're out of luck."

In his decades as a family physician, Henry had never encountered anything like this in an emergency room. The woman behind the triage desk seemed indifferent to the gravity of the situation. What was going on?

Not knowing what else to do, Henry yelled over to Cecilia, who was bent over the toboggan trying to talk to her pale, unconscious husband. "Cecilia! Do you know Albion's blood type?"

"He's O-negative," she called back at him.

The nurse behind the counter barked a hoarse laugh. "Great," she said. "Not only is he bleeding like a stuck pig—he's got one of the rarest blood types out there. He's a goner."

Henry pointedly ignored the nurse. *No one talks like this,* he thought to himself. *What could be going on at Deaconess to bring on this attitude?* He wondered what kind of hospital he was in, or if it was a hospital at all for that matter.

"Roger, what blood type are you?" Henry managed.

"I'm Albion's opposite, O-positive. What about you, Doc?"

"I'm no use either—A-positive. Call Warren. I hope to God he's O-negative. He's our only hope for a match."

As Roger reached for his cell, Henry insisted they take Albion into the emergency room surgery center at once to stitch him up and stop the bleeding. Although he was unlikely to survive without a transfusion, it wouldn't do any good for him to bleed to death on the toboggan before they could even find a match.

The nurse, seeing the pool of blood gather on the floor, called in two orderlies who rushed out with a gurney. With Cecilia's and Roger's help, the orderlies set the entire toboggan on the gurney and rolled Albion through the set of double doors toward the operating room. They would stitch him up, but he needed blood, and lots of it.

"Where are you?" Roger asked when Warren picked up his call.

"I'm just outside of town, heading toward the sheriff's office."

"What blood type are you?"

"I think I'm O-negative. Why?"

"Thank God. There's no blood at the hospital. Albion needs blood to make it and you're the only match we can find. Turn around and come here quick, but don't be shocked—the place looks like a warzone, Warren. It's freaky."

"I'm on my way. How's Albion doing?"

"Not well. He's blacked out and looks as pale as a sheet. Hurry. We're in the emergency room."

"I'll be there as soon as I can!"

Warren arrived inside of five minutes, nodded to Henry, Roger and Cecilia and ran directly to the admitting nurse.

"My friend Albion—he needs blood and I'm his type. Where is he?"

"Well, that lucky guy," the nurse mused, chuckling softly to herself.

Warren was, like Henry, taken aback by the nurse's attitude. For now, however, getting blood to his best friend was his main concern.

"Where is he?" Warren repeated.

"Through those doors, down the hall and on your right. They're trying to get his bleeding under control. They'll hook you up to him. Good luck."

Warren bolted through the double doors, ran down the hallway and looked in every window to the right. Each room had two or three people in it. There were people who looked like they had no chance of survival, while others huddled on the floor, weeping from the pain that seemed to haunt the hospital. Warren began to understand why the nurse was acting strangely—Bozeman was dying.

Just before a second set of double doors that led to another hallway of sickness, Warren found the operating room. The toboggan was on the floor, covered in blood. Albion was on the operating table with a doctor inspecting the wound. Warren, knowing he might get yelled at for not having on a face mask, burst in regardless.

"I'm his best friend," he panted. "I'm also O-negative. Can I help him?"

The young medic pulled his surgical mask down and said coolly, "He's the luckiest guy in this hospital. Without your blood, there's no way this guy will make it.

"Here." The medic pushed the gurney Albion had been rolled in on over to Warren. "Get on this thing and roll up your right sleeve. You're going to save this asshole's life."

Soon the nurse assisting the medic had a needle in Warren's arm as clear plastic tubes ran from one man to the other. Warren's blood flowed into Albion's body almost immediately. The nurse carefully monitored the amount of blood Warren was losing—no one wanted to have two dead bodies to deal with. The surgeon continued working on the gunshot wound.

"How does it look?" Warren asked as the doctor cut and stitched his way through Albion's abdomen.

"Well, the bullet missed his vitals, but it still ripped through the right side of his intestines. They're pretty scrambled, but I can cut out quite a bit of small intestine and, given the fact that his blood pressure is stabilizing, I think he's got a good chance of surviving.

"If you weren't here, we'd already be bagging him up."

"I'm sorry," Warren said suddenly. "What's with the attitude at the hospital?"

"Where've you been hiding, on Mars?"

"What do you mean?"

"What's your name?"

"Warren, Warren Randolf."

"Look, Warren—we've got 60 patients in the emergency room right now and there are three, yes, exactly *three* doctors left who are bothering to come in. That's counting me, and I haven't even finished my practicum. There're only a handful of orderlies and nurses healthy enough to be of any use and the last of the hospital's food reserves ran out ten days ago. I feel like I haven't slept for a month.

"People keep piling in here with severe malnutrition, organ failure, gunshot wounds, stab wounds, beating wounds—you name it. The whole fucking planet is falling apart and apparently Deaconess Hospital is the only place any of these refugees have left. We've got people who've been living in that hallway you just walked through for over a month. It's a disaster area.

"I hear it's worse in the major cities. We just got a memo last week saying we shouldn't even treat people like your friend here. We were told to euthanize them in lieu of wasting any time or supplies on people this badly wounded. People are killing other people. Some are eating their kills. It's falling apart, Warren. The entire system is falling apart. It gets worse day by day. I'm just doing what I can. So don't talk to me about attitude."

"Holy shit."

"And what's with you and those friends of yours I saw in the waiting room? Look at this," the medic said, pointing to Albion's opened wound. "That's fatty tissue. Do you have any idea how long it's been since I operated on someone with fatty tissue? Let me tell you—wherever you all have been living is where I want to be, because you people are the healthiest folks I've seen in this hospital in a year."

Warren was starting to feel woozy. The nurse next to him shut the valve off between the two men and smiled at Warren. "You'll be OK—we've just got to slow down a bit. Don't fade on me now."

Hours passed.

Just before dawn, the surgeon finished stitching Albion up and the nurse disconnected Warren from the tubing. She insisted he not try to stand, as they had taken almost four units of blood from him—twice what was recommended.

"You have to sleep now," she said. "You'll need to rest for a few days to recover."

"Is Albion going to make it?" Warren asked, still feeling dazed.

"Is that his name? Your friend? Yes, he'll probably make it. It was very close, but he's stabilizing and the doctor thinks he'll pull through. You should get him out of here today, though. We don't have any food to give him and he'll have a voracious appetite when he comes around."

"We were terrorized last night by some home invaders. I know who they are. I've got to report this to the sheriff."

"Don't bother. Unless your friend dies, they probably won't look into it. There've been so many home invasions going on right now that unless a killing is involved, the police won't even investigate. The prisons ran out of food ages ago anyway, so any sentence is a death sentence these days. You people are out of the loop, aren't you? Where the hell have you been hiding?"

Warren knew better than to answer her. "But it's not this bad on the Net."

"The Net is a joke. They're filtering it. I guess the Greens don't want people like you to know we've descended into chaos. Law and order are all but gone. It's the Wild West out here these days and it'll only get worse by spring.

"They say there's cannibalism in the Dakotas and that the local sheriffs there are in on it. People are starving to death and when they get hungry enough, all bets are off."

Warren looked at the nurse, who appeared thin and tired, and nodded in agreement. All bets were off. The Mylerium Project had turned out to be the worst decision mankind had ever made, though in hindsight it wasn't much different from the decision to start burning fossil fuels to begin with.

The nurse wheeled Warren back to the waiting room, where Roger, Dr. Irving and Cecilia were nodding off as the sun rose over Bozeman. Seven more patients had arrived since 1 a.m. None had been treated.

"This one needs plenty of fluids," the nurse advised, gesturing to Warren on his gurney. "Give him lots of food if you have it and let him rest for at least three to four days. I'm going to get the other guy—the one who was shot—and bring him out here for you to take back to whatever paradise you folks are living in. He needs to be in an Intensive Care Unit, but we don't have anything left that's still working in our own ICU. Can you get him hooked up to an IV? Do any of you know how to handle it?"

"I'm a doctor," Dr. Irving piped up proudly, "and, yes, we've got medical gear. I think we can take over."

"You'll have to—there's nothing else here for him. He's lucky his friend had the same blood type or he wouldn't have survived. The orderlies will be out with him shortly."

"What do we owe you?"

"Nothing. Money doesn't mean anything anymore. If you have some extra food to spare, bring it by. But be careful not to let anyone notice you have it. They'll follow you back to wherever you came from and try to get it. They'll kill all of you for food. That's just what it's like these days. It's hell on Earth."

"We'll bring you some staples. Give us a day or two. Thanks for everything."

"You're welcome, take care."

With that, the nurse shuffled back toward the set of double doors she just rolled Warren through. She was exhausted, but there were three more patients to look after before heading home to an empty fridge.

Roger pulled the van up just as Albion was pushed into the lobby. He was heavily sedated but coming around.

They covered the wooden toboggan with a clean sheet, lifted him onto it and loaded him back into the van. As they sped away, the sun rose over central Montana. The landscape at dawn was white with drifting snow. Whiteness covered everything, making the chaotic world appear cold and pure.

March 8, 2046

Warren was still weak from the transfusion. He had been in bed for a full week recuperating and was sick of being sick. He felt strong enough to get back into the game within the next day or two and the first thing on his agenda was to drive into Bozeman, deliver some food to the staff at the hospital and report the home invasion to the police, regardless of their current criteria for following up on burglaries.

No one else in the ranch had wanted to risk going back into town, but Warren was determined. He felt that if the sheriff elected not to look into it now, the case would at least be on the record and once this nightmare was over, the authorities could reopen the case. He wanted to make a written statement, press charges and be proactive. *People were shot, for God's sake,* he thought. *The law should get involved when people get shot and robbed, even if they don't die.*

Warren cracked his journal open in this gloomy state of mind and recorded what had just transpired. His mood was as black as the coal dust they would start spraying across Montana the following week.

March 28, 2046

Albion is recovering. He was able to sit up a little and talk yesterday, so I got up and walked to the barn to pay him a visit. He's slowly but surely coming around. Dr. Irving is doing a fantastic job keeping his bandages fresh and pumping him full of antibiotics to avoid infection. His room looks like an ICU ward, complete with a heartbeat monitor and an IV drip. Cecilia managed to barter for the equipment in exchange for more food for the hospital. These days, having anything edible is far more valuable than having money.

Everyone at the ranch keeps coming in here thanking me for saving Albion's life. I have to remind them that they would have laid down on that gurney next to him just has quickly if they had the same blood type. I did what I had to do.

As soon as I'm well enough, I'll head back into Bozeman and report the invasion. I want to find out if there's any truth to what the nurse told me about the police these days—that they won't investigate these kinds of crimes unless someone's killed. That seems totally insane, but after seeing the condition of the hospital, I think I understand why things have gotten so strange. The United States of America is coming apart at the seams.

I guess it was our turn. During the Lost Decade, although conditions were terrible in North America because of the droughts, floods, heat waves, tornados and hurricanes, they were ten times worse in the Third World. That's not to say people didn't suffer and die here in America. They died in the tens of thousands. But the death toll around the world from our anthropogenic greenhouse experiment was 20 times that of the U.S. It's a sad reality that in the poorest regions of the world, there was no safety net.

People couldn't run into their air-conditioned cooling stations when it climbed to 125 degrees in South Sudan or Chad. They couldn't head to hurricane shelters when Cat-5 storms rolled ashore in Sri Lanka or Guatemala. Hurricane shelters didn't exist. In the Third World, people died of heat stroke or watched in horror as their grass huts were blown away. They died by the millions during the worst of the Lost Decade. Some of the incinerators they're using to burn the dead today were built in the early '30s. They provided the best way to dispose of the tens of thousands of corpses the garbage men would pick up every morning in Lagos, Nigeria, or Karachi, Pakistan.

But the people of the Sahel or Asia didn't cause the planet to break out into this global fever—we in the U.S. did. At the peak of CO_2 emissions, around 2019, ten nations were contributing more than two-thirds of the greenhouse gases responsible for climate change. China was number one, spewing out billions of tons of CO_2 from hundreds of newly-constructed and dirty coal-fired power plants. The U.S. was a close second, while the European Union, Russia, India and Japan all dumped millions of tons of their gaseous trash into the overheated atmosphere. If it got too hot in America, we'd just turn up the A/C, burn another few tons of coal and cool down. When it got hot in Ethiopia, people watched their crops wither away and then died.

The poorest nations of the world, those suffering from what is described as energy poverty, didn't burn enough fossil fuels to command even a single percentage point of the global totals. They didn't have the infrastructure or the capital to produce cheap, readily accessible electricity. They didn't build coal plants every other week. Their citizens cooked with kitchen fires fueled with sticks and dung. When the sun went down, they used candles and kerosene lamps or just ended their day. They didn't drive a Lexus SUV or eat fresh salmon flown in from Alaska the day before. They ate hand-to-mouth and when their wells ran dry, their fields baked and they starved.

We killed them. It may not have been direct or even intentional, but it was everyone's atmosphere we destroyed, not just our own. When it started to fall apart, the poorest people on the planet were most impacted. Pacific Islanders lost their homes to the rising sea levels. Droughts hit the driest nations hardest and the tropical cyclones that ravaged the planet did the most damage in places like the Philippines, Central America and Bangladesh. We ducked into Starbucks for an iced Frappuccino and looked the other way.

Now it's our turn. I should have known COI was filtering the news. The Greens don't want the world to know it's America's turn to suffer. The displaced crowds in the lobby of the emergency room say it all. I can't imagine what conditions are like in Houston or Indianapolis if things are this dreadful in Bozeman. The rest of the world, unable to see past the filters, is seeing only what COI puts out. That pales in comparison with what I suspect is really going on. We're disintegrating. We're losing the rule of law and we're running out of food, just like everyone else on the planet. Now it's their turn to watch us pay the price of our fossil fuel addiction. Not that there's any joy in it.

The spring scares me the most at Shelter Ranch, though. Those thieves took every edible thing they could find from the house before running off, including our seeds. I'll have to ask around Bozeman to see if there's anyone selling seeds or trading seeds for food. I doubt I'll have much luck. I've checked online and everyone is searching for seeds. No one is selling, regardless of cost. Without seeds, spring won't do us any good, though I'm hoping we may be able to buy food at some point. Of course, if this upcoming spring fails, the seeds would only work in the greenhouses and I'm not sure they will produce enough food for us to make it through a fourth winter.

Without anything to grow in the greenhouses, the chances of us making it to the spring of 2047 are nil. We'll run out of food around February of next year, even if we ration. The fact that Vince and his gang stole a month's worth of supplies doesn't help. I don't know what we'll do without seeds. But I really don't know what we'll do without spring.

Project Dusting

Professor Bradley had notified all of his key personnel of this meeting a week ago. His email to the staff made that fact perfectly clear:

```
You are hereby requested to attend a mandatory
conference on Wednesday morning, April 4, 2046, at
8:30 a.m., in the Board of Directors Room, Level 175 of
the COI Tower, 14000 East Monroe Street, Chicago. This
meeting has been called at the behest of President
Beltram and anyone not attending will be subject to
immediate dismissal, upon which time all food rations
to them and their families will be discontinued.
```

It was the last sentence that caught everyone's attention. The staff members who received the email at COI all had access to the live feeds coming from the NSA. They knew what was happening out on the streets of Chicago, and if there was one thing they could not contemplate, it was trying to survive without the government's food rations. With nothing available to purchase—no matter the cost—their salaries meant nothing to them any longer. They were all beholden to their weekly food allocation. Lacking this state welfare, which included everything from flour to powdered eggs, there wasn't a person in COI, the CMC, the NSA, both houses of Congress or the Pentagon who didn't realize they would starve. No one would miss the meeting.

By 8:20 a.m., the massive board room at the top of the COI Tower was filled to overflowing. There was no one from the press to cover the event because COI managed the press.

At 8:30 a.m., Professor Bradley entered the room from a side door that led directly to his office. An immediate hush fell over the crowd as the professor seated himself at the end of the table.

"Good morning," he began.

The 65 staff members responded to his salutation with a tangle of "good mornings," "welcome, sirs," and a dozen variations.

"I suppose you are wondering why we're here this morning, so I'll get right to it.

"We all know what's going on out there. Everyone in this room has the highest security clearances available at COI and we can turn our monitors to the NSA feeds whenever we can stomach it. Or just walk outside, if we dare. It's a catastrophe out there, pure and simple. And it's not going to get better anytime soon.

"The director of the NSA phoned me yesterday to tell me that the newly revised death toll is approximately 3.5 billion people. Take a look at your monitors if you have any doubts about the authenticity of this estimate."

Professor Bradley pushed a button on his iPad and 36 HD monitors emerged from the mahogany table. They were already on as they slowly climbed out of the smooth wooden surface. The video they displayed was familiar to more than half the people in the room. It was a feed from just outside of Mumbai, India, where it was 6:32 p.m. In fact, the feed was coming from the same video camera Warren and Albion had watched a year before on YouTube.

This time it was different. There were no breaks in the line of dump trucks bringing bodies to the incinerators. The trucks were bumper to bumper, forming an unbroken line stretching over the hill. They were no longer feeding the dead into a single incinerator. There were six incinerators, each with several large openings. There were dozens of electric forklifts being operated by Hindus wearing hospital masks. The scene was overwhelming.

"Now, if you had any doubts at all about how desperate things are out there, take a good look at this."

Professor Bradley hit his iPad again and the monitors switched to a different camera feed, located on the back side of the incinerators. The feed showed large front-end loaders scooping up piles of human ashes and dumping them into the back of the same trucks the bodies came in on.

The professor continued. "Do you know what they're doing?" he asked, looking around the room as people shook their heads, mumbling comments like, "no idea."

"The Hindu priests—the Pandits of the Brahmin class—have decreed that the ashes of the dead be taken out into the snow-covered fields outside the city of Mumbai and spread across them to help melt the snowpack surrounding the city," Professor Bradley explained. "The tradition in much of India is to cremate the dead in a funeral pyre, place the remains in an urn, then immerse those ashes in a river.

"The Brahmins have ordained this because all the melted snow will eventually wash into the rivers of India. They also want the remains of their dead, which number in the tens of millions, to help those who are still alive. They say they cannot wait until the drones arrive. The Pandits preach the spreading of the ashes of the dead over their fields will bring new life to India. That's how desperate things are right now."

The staff looked on in amazement. They were trying to wrap their minds around the level of sacrifice this failed geoengineering project had created. Some of the men and women watching the feed had tears running down their cheeks.

"Estimates now put the potential death toll by spring at close to six billion people. Two out of every three people on Earth will die because of the Mylerium Project. We anticipate losing half the population of the United States before this is over. If Project Dusting fails and we cannot manage a viable harvest by the fall, the CMC has estimated we will lose as many as 320 of the 400 million people living in the United States. Many of you in this room today would likely be included in that number."

Professor Bradley paused and an uneasy murmur erupted from the gathering. The monitors slid silently back into the surface of the table, disappearing into the wood grain as if they were never there. As Professor Bradley began speaking again, the whispered conversations ceased.

"We've been doing everything we can to keep the American spirit alive, but it's not enough. The President personally phoned me yesterday to say we have to do more. We have to get every man, woman and child on board Project Dusting, which begins a week from today. Last summer's efforts with the Hope Gardens, which ended tragically because of the July snowstorm, pale in comparison to the task at hand.

"Our job—our only job from now until spring—is to convince millions of hungry, tired and starving people to go outside after every snowfall and cover every square inch of this nation with coal dust. I don't care if it's a baseball field in Minnesota or a river valley in West Virginia. We have to focus every story, every broadcast, every media outlet we have on melting the snowpack.

"The CMC has just completed an analysis of what to expect should the harvest this fall fail to happen. It's not good, to say the least. I am emailing you all that analysis now. It's long and detailed but I want each and every one of you to read it cover-to-cover. It is, in essence, a death sentence to civilization as we know it. If you think the situation out there is bad today, by late winter of 2047, things will descend into complete chaos. Eight out of every ten people living in the Northern Hemisphere will perish. We will run out of food—even the food we've set aside to keep all of us and our families alive for these past few years.

"To say the situation is dire does not do it justice. We are all living on borrowed time. In the report, you will also note that if we have a volcanic eruption just half the size of the 2037 eruption of Mt. Cameroon we're doomed. The nanomirrors are stubbornly refusing to come down and the lasers cannot eradicate them fast enough. Our only hope is to melt the snowpack and expose the dirt beneath it as quickly as possible. Either the coal dust works or we perish. It's that simple."

No one spoke as Professor Bradley took another sip of his coffee. The silence in the room confirmed the stark reality of their shared nightmare.

"President Beltram asked me to request all of you to focus on one task and one task only: sell Project Dusting to everyone in North America. Make it clear to them that it's critical to their very survival for them to get out and cover the snow with coal dust. We want every square inch of this country covered in coal dust by the end of April. The drones will do their part, but they cannot do it all.

"In the meanwhile, we'll continue broadcasting only good news. The blackout order is still in effect. If people feel the situation is hopeless, they will behave like the situation is hopeless. It is up to us, using every tool we have, to make sure Americans survive this final gauntlet. There is no other alternative. This is it. Now get back to work and sell America on the merits of Project Dusting."

The professor paused and glanced around the room. He could tell by the look on the faces around him that his staff understood how pressing an issue this was. Then, almost as an afterthought, he added, "Are there any questions?"

No one spoke. They all individually thought long and hard about the camera feeds they had been watching over the past six months—videos of food riots, of starving people, of necrocannibalism and outright cannibalism—and they realized that this time it was their futures at stake. They would sell the American people on Project Dusting because if they didn't, they might end up in some of those videos next year being eaten or, perhaps worse, eating someone they loved. It was bleak.

"Then, you're dismissed."

Professor William Bradley got up, walked over to the same door he had entered from and disappeared. The meeting broke up in a sullen quiet, as if no one dared to speak.

The Gallatin County Sheriff's Office

"It's not my call, Dr. Randolf. I hope you understand that."

"Who's making this call? You mean to tell me that people are getting shot and you don't have the time or manpower to investigate the shooters?"

Sheriff Gregor Aston leaned back in his reclining chair, unshaven and tired, and pointed to a corner of his desk. "See that pile of paperwork, Dr. Randolf?" he asked. "The one that's damn near a foot high? That pile has 22—no, make that 24, murder cases in it. Three of those cases have multiple victims. The worst file in that stack involves the killing of a mother, father, grandma and two children. If I don't have the time or the manpower to follow up on that atrocity, how in hell am I going to look out for the wounded?

"That family was killed for the same reason all the others were killed—food. I know some of these victims personally. Hell, I know some of the killers as well. Before the big chill set in, these criminals were just ordinary, law-abiding people. Hunger turns men into wolves."

The sheriff inched forward, putting his weathered hands on the desk and looking at Dr. Randolf directly.

"The courts are so backed up with home invasions and abductions that they're at a judicial standstill," he continued. "I heard that Judge Lawson, who's been on the bench 25 years, died of starvation last week. Turns out, he was giving his personal government food allocation to his grandkids. That's what's going on right now, and it's getting worse. The State Attorney's office has mandated we only follow up when there's a murder involved. No one was murdered in your raid, Doctor. My hands are tied."

Warren shook his head in disbelief. He took another scan at the stack of murder investigations, thought about the starving judge, and realized he wasn't going to get an investigation into his incident started any time soon. The nurse was right—things were just too far gone to make progress on a robbery if it didn't involve a homicide. Even if someone was killed, it might be months or even years, before this overworked sheriff could find the time to follow up on it.

"Can I at least file an official report and press charges? That way, once all this is behind us, you can head out to Vince Gatini's place and arrest the bastard."

"You're welcome to file a report. Here, just fill in this form to the best of your ability and I'll log it in as an official complaint."

Sheriff Aston handed Warren an iPad with a police report on the screen. The holographic keyboard spread out across the official's desk as Warren began filling in the date, time, place and details of the invasion. As he completed the forms, the sheriff got up, walked to the water dispenser and poured himself some ice-cold water.

"How did you know that the Mylerium Project was going to be a bust?" he asked.

Warren was caught off guard by the sheriff's comment. He continued typing, trying to ignore the sheriff's unexpected question.

"Someone from Bozeman Recapture said you left the CMC before moving here in '43. That was the first summer, when the mirrors were working fine. Why'd you leave Chicago to come to this hole in the wall back then?"

Warren realized the sheriff wasn't going to stop playing detective until he responded to his questioning.

"Is it safe to talk? I'm under a gag order so I'll deny anything I tell you from here on out."

"It's safe to talk. The NSA doesn't have the resources to bug a county sheriff in Montana these days. Trust me, they've got a lot bigger problems than that on their hands."

"Yes, I did work at the CMC before moving here. I worked five years on the Mylerium Project."

"How did you know it was going to fail? None of us had any idea we'd be looking at this endless god-damned winter. Did everyone working at the CMC know this project was going to screw up the atmosphere the way it did?"

"A few knew because I told them. I thought something was wrong with the computer programming and I told them it was likely going to cause this volcanic winter. They didn't believe me."

"You mean to say that you told them this might happen before they deployed the drones?"

"I did. I had done some of my own research on the nanoparticle programming and realized they would not implode as designed. It took me three years to discover the flaw in the coding—in fact, I ended up finding it by accident. When I presented the CMC with my research, including my work supporting my hypothesis, they decided it was flawed. The project went ahead as planned."

"Wow," the sheriff said as Warren's news sunk in. "That explains it. That's why you got out of Chicago and moved here, isn't it? That's why you contacted all your friends and had them join you. I remember you buying 50-pound bags of rice that August at Safeway and I was wondering why the hell a single guy would buy that much rice unless he was going to open up a Chinese takeout or something.

"My patrol route took me down Brackett Creek Road every week and I watched you redo the barn, dig that big ole root cellar out of the hillside and stockpile your place like a nuclear war was just around the corner. Back then, from what I could see, it was only you living on that 40-acre farm. It was only you buying all that rice and beans and flour. It just didn't add up."

"You knew about all that?"

"Come on now, Warren—Bozeman's a small town and people talk. I just couldn't figure out what the hell you were up to. You didn't seem like one of those patriot types, or burners, or Rapture7 cults we seem to attract here in Montana. I just couldn't get a handle on what you were up to. Now it all makes sense."

Warren went back to filling out the form while the sheriff paced back and forth across his small office.

"How many folks you have living out there now, anyway?"

"Nineteen of us, all totaled," Warren said honestly. He decided if there was one stranger in Bozeman he could trust, it was the town's sheriff.

"I don't suppose you have any extra dry goods or anything?"

"Sorry, no. I brought some rice and dried beans to the staff over at Deaconess Hospital. They're working around the clock trying to keep up with this disaster and they just helped save my best friend, Albion. We owed it to them. But between what Vince and his gang took and the package I just dropped off, we're out." Warren figured a slight exaggeration couldn't hurt, just in case the sheriff got any ideas. "If we don't have a spring, we'll starve just like everyone else on the planet.

"Which brings me to another pressing issue. Vince took all of our seed stock. Can you think of anyone who might have some extra seeds? We'd be willing to trade anything for seeds at this point. It would be worth the risk."

The sheriff reflected for a moment before answering Warren. "I know I don't have any seeds. I've heard several nearby farmers got so desperate, they ate their seed stock. They might have some left but I don't think you'll find anyone willing to part with seeds at this point. If spring does arrive, seeds will be worth their weight in gold."

"Yeah, I didn't think it'd be easy to find anyone willing to part with their seeds," Warren admitted. "But if you hear of anyone, give me a call.

"Oh, and one more thing, I don't want to see your squad car pulling up our driveway looking for food. We've had enough excitement for a while."

The sheriff laughed. "I don't think that'll happen. The government is cutting back on our allotments, but they say they've got enough food stockpiled to make it to the end of this year. After that, if this coal dust thing doesn't work, we're on our own. That's the same as saying we're goners, isn't it? You're a scientist, right? Do you think this coal dust thing is going to work?"

"Actually, yes," Warren responded. "If we can cover the snowpack that's already down, and cover it again every time it snows between now and June, I think we'll stand a good chance of making it. I hope it's going to turn things around. It was 'clean coal' that helped get us into this climate mess in the first place and I find it ironic that it's probably 'dirty coal dust' that's going to get us out."

Warren went back to his iPad and signed the last page with an imaginary pen. He handed it back to the sheriff. "Here you go. What do you think we should do if they show up again?"

"Shoot the assholes," Sheriff Aston recommended amicably. "Keep your rifles loaded beside the door. Fire a warning shot or two as they get out of their trucks. That's what a lot of people are doing. If someone uninvited heads up their driveway, they fire off a couple of rounds just to let them know there ain't no welcoming committee inside, and if they don't back off, they'll shoot out their headlights next. It seems to work fine. Whatever you do, don't give them enough time to get set up with their rifles and their deer-hunting scopes. They'll kill all of you for the stockpile you people are sitting on.

"And stay the hell out of Bozeman. You look too fat and healthy to be hanging around these parts. When people see a young man like you strutting around town, the first thing they think of is, 'he's got food.' After they start thinking like that, they'll follow you around until they find your cache and then it's all but over."

Warren nodded in agreement. He realized his healthy glow was now a clear tell that he was eating well. No one had any fat on them these days, except those who had hoarded food. Staying out of Bozeman was a good idea, at least until spring.

"Well, you're official," the sheriff said as he looked over the completed forms and sent the paperwork to the cloud.

"Thanks for letting me go ahead with this complaint, sheriff—it makes all the difference to the rest of the crew out at the ranch. They wanted to see justice done, but were too hesitant to come out here. I think we'll get justice, even if it takes a decade."

If we don't have a spring, we won't make it a decade. I'm praying this Project Dusting works. The CMC has already sent me some coal dust to start distributing when I'm out on patrol. They want every square inch of Montana covered. In fact I've got a 50-pound bag of dust in my trunk right now and quite a few more in the office. Do you want any?"

"Sure, I'll take some."

The sheriff walked over to a closet located to the right of his desk and opened the door. Inside, piled right up to the ceiling, were a dozen bags of coal dust in white plastic bags.

"Where the hell did those come from?"

"The CMC, working with the National Guard, brought them in here a few days ago. Take as many of them as you want. I've got more on the way."

Warren grabbed a bag from the storage closet and hauled it toward the front door. He took his time, as the bag was heavy and he still hadn't fully recovered from giving so much blood to Albion.

"Mind if I come back and grab a second, or a third, bag?" Warren asked.

"By all means, knock yourself out. I don't think I'll be able to spread all this dust out by myself anyway."

Warren made two more trips and managed to get the sheriff to help him carry a few bags out as well.

"Five should do it for now."

"They say to spread it very thinly across the top of the snow," Sheriff Aston advised. "It'll make your yard look like there's a smelter nearby, but who cares as long as it works?"

"I hope it works too. Without it, we're in deep trouble."

"Bye, Dr. Randolf. Take care."

"You too, sheriff, thanks for all the coal dust. I only wish it were edible."

Warren got back into his van. He noted Main Street was deserted. There were no shops or restaurants open and no vehicles driving down the road. As far as the eye could see, there was only dirty, coal-dusted snow and an eerie silence.

As Warren pulled away, he looked back repeatedly in his rear view mirror to make sure he wasn't being followed. No one was behind him. He made it back to Shelter Ranch just as the sun set. He was disappointed about the lack of investigation into the recent incident but glad to be home.

Once inside, he set two loaded rifles next to both front doors. He warned the kids at the ranch not to play with them and left them in place.

Yeva's Dream

Yeva took out her security badge and showed it to the young National Guard soldier stationed at the entrance of the vault. A second soldier stood by awaiting digital confirmation as he scanned her ID card.

The guards were changed every week and even if one recognized Yeva, security was so tight that they had to go through the process regardless.

Within a few seconds a text message verified Yeva was cleared to enter the vault. She had come to check on the condition of the seeds inside, as she had for years. She knew there had already been two serious attempts at breaking into the vault this winter and didn't question the need for the extra security. The guards stood watch over the entrance 24/7. They had orders to shoot to kill in the event of an attempted robbery. With the prospect of a forthcoming spring—the first true spring in three years—the seeds inside the Botanic Garden's vaults had become invaluable.

Yeva pushed her way through the double-latched front door of the facility and walked to her office. She took out her handheld computer, put on her white lab coat and went down the hallway to start her usual rounds. Yeva had arrived by electric cab, as it was too dangerous to use the El, which nevertheless still ran faithfully on its automated routes.

She came into the gardens once a week now and sometimes stayed until after dark trying to catch up with the backlog of paperwork that kept piling higher and higher on her desk. Her pay had been cut to the bare minimum, but money hardly mattered. Only food mattered.

By noon, she noted that everything appeared to be fine inside the main vault and recorded that information in her tablet. She had made plans to meet with Margot Pollock, her boss, earlier in the week and was looking forward to seeing her. As she walked back out the front door, a guard asked her to raise her hands up high as he thoroughly frisked her, looking for stolen seeds, figs or dried fruit. Nothing was to leave the vault without prior authorization from the NSA. Everyone was searched, including Yeva. Seeds were the only hope for a future. Many of the trees, native plants and grasses were dead, having failed to survive three winters and two summers without growth.

"She's clear," the young soldier announced.

"You're free to go, ma'am," the other guard said.

Yeva buttoned up her parka and picked up her pace as she walked back toward the main offices on the other side of the snow-covered gardens. She was anxious to tell Margot, who she hadn't seen in months, about the unusual dreams she'd been having. The wind outside was kicking up, blowing steadily out of the northwest as it had throughout the winter.

The gardens looked bizarre ever since the start of the coal dust deployments. The ten-foot high snowdrifts were no longer white, but a curious mixture of layers of grey, black and white, swirled together in haphazard patterns. The bare trees were covered in coal dust, making them look as if they had a black fungus growing on them. The path she was walking on was almost pitch black, but a central aisle of lightness marked past footfalls that took dust with them. These were not the gardens Yeva remembered from years past.

She arrived at Margot's office a little before 1 p.m. She didn't bring lunch because no one in their right mind carried food these days, even if they were taking a cab. She would wait until returning home before eating again. Most days, she ate only one meal a day.

Margot's office door was closed and locked. The new security protocols required this of all offices, just in case. Yeva knocked several times before Margot responded.

"Who's there?"

"It's me, Margot. It's Yeva."

"I'll be right there."

Yeva could hear two locks clicking free before the door swung open to reveal Margot standing there, her arms wide open awaiting a hug.

"It has been way too long, Yeva—how have you been?"

The two ladies embraced. Tears welled up in Yeva's eyes as she held her friend. They had not seen each other since January, as they were both coming in intermittently and their work schedules seldom lined up.

"I've been fine. How about you and the family?"

"As well as can be expected. Without your generosity, I don't know if we'd still be eating. There's nothing out there. There's no food anywhere and they cut off my county allocation last month. Everyone's running out."

"I know. We were lucky to have known about this disaster before the rest of the world. Very lucky."

"Come in and sit down. Have you already inspected the vault?"

"Yes, I just came from there. Everything's fine, but it's hard to know if all the seeds are viable when you haven't planted sampling seeds in years. The native plants—all the bushes, shrubs, grasses, and trees—they all concern me the most because we've lost so many local plants to the weather. I'm sure they'll all be fine. It's odd having the armed guards standing there though, isn't it? It makes me feel like we're working inside a military base and not a regional botanic garden."

"You didn't hear? They shot two people a month ago. They were trying to break in and steal seeds, though I suspect they were not going to wait until spring to plant them. They were going to eat them. People are eating all kinds of strange things these days, from leather shoes to homegrown algae to each other. It's like we're living in some kind of zombie apocalypse."

"We are, Margot. I see what's happening in Rogers Park and it scares the hell out of me."

By this time, Yeva and Margot had worked their way into the office and were sitting across from each other with Margot's desk between them.

"So how have you been, Yeva? You look good—a bit thin, but good."

"I'm down to eating one meal a day like everyone else. I'm worried this coal dusting idea isn't going to fare any better than last year's Hope Gardens. I still have quite a bit of food—lots of instant potatoes, brown rice, dehydrated fruits and canned goods in particular—but I'm not sure I'll have enough for one more year. I'm trying to get by with the bare minimum. It's hard; I'm constantly hungry. You look good, though, Margot. How are your supplies holding up?"

"Same as yours, it sounds like. We only eat dinner. It's really hard on the kids, but I try to explain to them that we have to ration just in case we can't plant crops again. The vegetables we raised in the greenhouses last summer have really helped. Without them, we'd be out of food by now."

Yeva sighed, brushed her maroon hair back and continued the conversation, this time in a different, more serious tone.

"Margot, I came here in part because I wanted to tell you about this dream I keep having."

"What kind of dream?"

"It's always about Dr. Randolf. The dream started about two weeks ago out of the blue. Sometimes we're in a barn and there are horses all around us. He's on his hands and knees, crawling around in the straw looking for something. When I ask to help him find it, he can't hear me.

"It's not always a barn though. Sometimes he's outside in the snow, but he's always looking for something that he can't seem to find. I'm thinking about calling him again. I think he's in some kind of trouble."

"That's strange. How many times have you had this dream since it started?"

"Probably six or seven times. Do you think I should call him?"

"Absolutely," Margot said. "He was friendly enough the last time you talked. Who knows? Maybe he really is in trouble. I hear it's very dangerous in the Dakotas these days, which isn't too far from Montana. In any event, I can't see it doing any harm."

"That's what I thought too. Anyway, I just thought I'd mention it before I make the call. I don't know what he's going to say, but I'll let you know after I call him. It's probably nothing at all."

"It could be something—you never know. I've always believed that people have premonitions sometimes, in their dreams or in their gut feelings. Feel free to give me a call after you talk with him. I'd be curious to hear what you find."

"I will."

"Say, I hate to cut this short, Yeva—but like you, I'm only in here once or twice a week now and I've got an avalanche of paperwork to catch up on."

"I understand. I'm only coming in once a week to check on the main vault. The whole world is on hold right now, waiting to see if spring will arrive. I'll head back home and call you after I talk to Warren."

"That sounds fine."

Margot and Yeva got up and walked together toward the door, which Margot had locked behind them. Margot unlocked her door and opened it for her employee and friend.

"Please, do call me later," she said.

"I promise I will."

"Oh, and don't take the El back—I hear it's not at all safe."

"I'm calling a cab in a few minutes. I've heard all kinds of horror stories about the El. You won't find me riding trains anytime soon."

"Good. I'll talk to you later tonight, Yeva. It's good to see you're still hanging in there."

"You too. Bye now."

An Unexpected Call

Aside from communicating with people in the other building on cold and windy days, Warren rarely found use for his cell phone. He seldom received any outside calls. The sheriff had called him two days ago to tell him he couldn't find anyone willing to trade seeds for food or money. Warren wasn't surprised by the sheriff's comments. He figured most people would gamble on a spring at this point, which made seeds far more valuable than food in the long run.

No one from Bozeman Recapture called any longer. The entire facility had been shut down, with all 187 employees laid off.

So Warren was surprised when his cell rang at 1 p.m. on April 15, and he was even more surprised to see Yeva Dunning's name light up across the display. He had very nearly forgotten about her and had no idea why she might be calling him.

Of course, he couldn't help but recall those photos of her he had pulled off the Net back when he was still at Bozeman Recapture. That helped him decide to take the call, no matter the reason. Besides, he thought she had a lovely voice.

"Hello?"

"Dr. Randolf, this is Yeva, Yeva Dunning. Do you remember me?"

"Yes, of course. It's been a few years."

"A few bad years."

"Very bad, and I'm afraid we might have more to come."

"Why do you say that? Don't you think Project Dusting is going to work? The snow seems to be melting around Chicago and they've only started blanketing Illinois."

"Well, I'd put the odds of this concept working at 50/50 this far north. I think it will work to some degree, especially along the southern tier of the U.S. But I'm not sure enough nanomirrors have been taken out for crops to survive in the northern U.S., Canada and Russia. Sadly, that's where the vast majority of the world's wheat crop is grown."

"I hope you're wrong about that," Yeva said. "I know you were right about the big chill. If I hadn't ended up with your letter to Ann I might not be alive right now. Have you ever heard from her?"

Warren paused a second. He had blocked Ann from his mind these past few years, but now he wondered if she had survived.

"She would never have known any of this was coming. I'm not sure she's even alive. There's so many people who've perished from hunger since all of this started. It's impossible to know."

"I suppose you're wondering why I called?" Yeva asked after a pause.

"Yes, the thought did cross my mind. You sound fine, so I'm assuming you're not asking to come out here. Crossing the Dakotas right now would be tantamount to a suicide mission from what I'm hearing. They've resorted to cannibalism. In fact, some people are showing up with Prion's disease in parts of Montana, and practically the only way to get it is from eating infected flesh."

"That's disgusting. There are parts of Chicago, especially downtown, where cannibalism is rumored to be going on, but I hardly go out any longer. It's gotten to be too dangerous.

"But you're right—I wasn't planning on joining you. I still have enough food for eight or nine months, depending, but I'm not sure I have enough to make it through a fourth winter."

"I'm not sure we could make it through a fourth winter either anyway. There are 19 mouths to feed up here and if this cold spell doesn't break, we probably won't have enough to make it."

"I was actually calling for kind of a strange reason. It sounds crazy, but I've had these strange dreams about you. It's like you're in some kind of trouble, crawling around on the ground searching for something. Something that's been lost. Is everything OK up there?"

Warren was surprised by Yeva's question. How could she have possibly known about what had just happened? Maybe he shared a deeper connection with this girl than he had imagined.

"No," he began slowly, "everything is not OK. We did have a violent home invasion two weeks ago."

"Oh my God. Were you injured?"

"I'm fine. I was nicked with a bullet but nothing serious. My best friend, Albion, was shot. He damn near died. We rushed him to the hospital where I ended up giving him a transfusion. He needed so much blood, the transfusion almost killed me as well."

"How's he doing?"

"He's better. Another one of my guests here is my old family physician, Dr. Irving, and he's done a great job caring for Albion and staving off infections. Gut shots are notorious for infections. It will be a few more weeks before Albion is up and about, but he's going to make it."

"Did they get away with anything?"

"Yes, and that's the problem. They took about a month's worth of food—nearly everything we had stored in the house. Worse still, they took our entire seed stock. Even if spring arrives, we don't have a single viable seed at the ranch. I just heard from the county sheriff up here that there's no one willing to trade food or money for seeds. So we're looking everywhere for them."

"So that's why I had those dreams," Yeva mused.

Warren's was confounded by her comment.

"What do you mean?"

"I keep having these recurring dreams. You're looking for seeds. Yes, that would make perfect sense—you're searching for seeds."

Warren was confused as to where this young woman on the other end of the line was going with all of this.

"Do you know what I do at the Botanic gardens?" Yeva asked.

"No. I have no idea. All I know is that you work there, with the plants."

"Dr. Randolf—I'm in charge of maintaining the viability of millions of seeds in our climate-controlled vault."

Warren didn't know what to say. How could this be? How could such a strange, potentially life-saving coincidence happen?

"So you're in charge of the seeds?" Warren said, struggling to contain his excitement. "I didn't know the Chicago Botanic Garden had a seed vault."

"Yes, we've had it since our inception. It's not widely known because it's not open to the public. It's affiliated with the entire world's seed vaults and seed banks, including the Svalbard Global Seed Vault, which you are probably more familiar with. We don't have near the capacity of that facility, so we focus primarily on regional agricultural plants along with upper Midwestern grasses, shrubs and trees."

Warren realized this conversation was turning into an incredible opportunity.

"You have vegetable seeds for plants like chard, carrots, and corn?"

"Of course."

"Umm. Is there any way we can buy some from you?"

"No. I wish there were, but the NSA seized control of the vault shortly after the mirrors failed to come down in the fall of '43. We're not allowed to remove any of the seeds at this point and the vault is now secured by armed guards. They shot two men who tried to break in a few weeks ago."

Warren's hopes were dashed. He had hoped this would end his search for seeds.

"I understand," he said.

"Warren, are you dead certain you can't find any viable seeds locally?" Yeva asked, sounding sympathetic.

"I'm pretty sure there's nothing around here, though I'm still trying. A lot of people—even local farmers—have gotten so desperate that they've cooked and eaten their corn and wheat seeds. It was either that or starve to death."

Yeva paused for a moment. "I'll talk to my boss, Margot," she said, "and see if there's anything we can do. I don't know if I can get any seeds out, though—the guards search everyone when they leave."

"Anything would help. Even if we have to go with greenhouses again this year, without seeds to plant, building greenhouses won't do us any good. We can manage without the month's supply of food they stole from us, but having all our seeds gone is far more troublesome."

"But even if I could get them out of the vault, how would I get them to you? The U.S. Postal Service has been suspended and there's no way we could trust any of the private carriers—not with something as valuable as seed stock."

"I'd come to Chicago to get them."

"How? The trains are all down."

"I could drive."

"No, they need you there at your ranch. I could bring them to you."

"That would be crazy, Yeva. You don't owe us anything."

"No, I'll do it!" she blurted, as though suddenly inspired. "I'll bring them to Montana."

"Yeva, that won't work. You'd have to come across the Dakotas. There's trouble there, especially around the Black Hills. They're kidnapping people and rumors are they're eating them. You can't risk it."

"I'll be fine," Yeva assured him. "Let me speak with my boss, Margot, in the next few days and I'll call you back."

Warren wanted to continue to try to dissuade Yeva from pursuing the idea, but realized the lives of 19 people might lie in the balance. With spring just around the corner and no seeds, everyone living at Shelter Ranch would likely be dead or dying by next March. He knew that he had to allow this young lady to explore this potentially dangerous plan, or else he would risk losing everything and everyone he had worked so hard to preserve.

"OK, I suppose it can't hurt to look into it. But I'm not for this idea. I'd rather come to Chicago and get them myself, provided you can find a way to get the seeds we need through the guards."

"Coming to Chicago is an even crazier plan. You'd have to go through the Dakotas twice, making your journey twice as risky. I'll find a way to get the seeds and I'll drive them out to you. I owe you that much for saving my life."

Warren didn't argue with her. He felt he hadn't saved her life. She had accidently ended up with a package meant for another woman. Still, serendipity had somehow come into play, and Warren was in no position to argue with her. He would let her explore the idea. No harm could come from that.

"I didn't save your life, the letter did," Warren maintained. "If you want to look into coming out here, you'd be more than welcome, but it's ultimately your call."

"Of course. Listen, I've got to go and we probably shouldn't be talking about this on the phone lines anyway."

"I doubt they care. These days the NSA has way more trouble on their hands than this phone call or a few handfuls of seed. I doubt they have the manpower or the time to look into every cell phone call out there these days. People are starving to death by the millions right now. We don't exist at this point. We are completely off the radar."

"You're probably right, but it can't hurt to be safe. I'll call you back in a few days to let you know what I find out."

"That would be great."

"Bye, Warren."

"Bye, Yeva, and thanks for dreaming."

The Machinery of the Universe

April 16, 2047

Yeva called yesterday. She might be able to secure some seeds for us, but I'm afraid to put too much hope in her. My other fear is that even if America can get a partial crop in, there won't be enough of a surplus to provide staples for the more remote regions of the country like Montana or Maine. In an effort to restore law and order, the Greens will likely restock the major cities first, then work their way down the list. If next winter starts as early as last year's did, my concern is that we'll be too far down on that list to get any food before the snow starts blowing. Greenhouses or gardens could mean the difference between surviving another year or not. Without seeds, neither of these are an option.

Yeva said she'd be willing to drive the seeds out here. I think that's insane, but I'm not sure I'll be able to talk her out of it. I'm not even sure I want to talk her out of it, even though I know she will be putting herself in great danger. But to begin with, everything hinges on whether she can get any seeds out of the secured vault, which will be challenging enough. I'll have to wait and see.

Sheriff Aston said something the other day when he called that got me thinking back to when all of this trouble got started in the 20th century, long before I was born. He said that we've collectively screwed up the atmosphere not once, but twice. The Mylerium Project in fact marked the second time and we all know how that turned out.

The first time was more insidious because we could have stopped things from getting this ugly a century ago, when the first evidence of anthropogenic climate change became available. Dr. Charles Keeling installed the first accurate instruments to measure the amount of atmospheric CO_2 in 1958 atop the Mauna Loa volcano in Hawaii. Seven years later, the Science Advisory Committee established by President Johnson noted the rise in CO_2 and officially warned the world of the risk of global warming. The rise, they had concluded, was directly associated with the burning of fossil fuels.

At that point, with the levels of CO_2 still manageable, it would have been easy to curtail the use of coal, oil and natural gas and turn the entire industrialized world toward renewable energy. That would have made all our future geoengineering projects unnecessary. The Lost Decade, the death tolls and the horrors that followed would have never happened.

But politics got in the way, along with the money that drove the politics. I think back to the insanity of those early years and I can't help but recall what a now-infamous U.S. Senator, James Inhofe from Oklahoma, said about global warming. He called it the single greatest hoax ever perpetrated on the

American public. He was so convinced that "global warming" was a fraud, he wrote a book about it titled "The Greatest Hoax." His book should have been called "The Greatest Mistake a Senator Ever Made." Shortly after Inhofe wrote his book, Oklahoma entered the worst drought ever recorded in that state. His own constituents—the very people he represented—suffered mercilessly under consecutive months of 100-plus-degree temperatures.

Decades of inaction followed the turn of the 21st century, mostly due to the well-coordinated efforts of Big Coal and Big Oil. They spent billions of dollars in a nonstop campaign to deny and debunk the science of climate change. They funded political candidates who spent their entire careers trying to convince the American people that there was no sound "scientific" basis for global warming and even if there was, it was definitely not attributable to the burning of fossil fuels. It was all a natural cycle, they said; it was something we couldn't control. It was due to sunspots, erratic planetary orbits—anything but us. Nothing was further from the truth.

Those were the years of anti-science. We had regressed into a world of flawed research, media campaigns, fraudulent websites and finger-pointing, all designed to mislead the general public about the potential dangers posed by a steep rise in average global temperatures. The oil lobby singled out and harassed many of the leading climatologists of the day, making it seem like there was still a serious debate about the issue.

There was no debate. There was only a witch hunt as reputable scientists were thrown into the funeral pyres of corporate lies.

Forward-thinking scientists and politicians such as Dr. James Hanson of NASA or Vice-President Al Gore were all thrown under the bus. The IPCC was under assault by the well-moneyed corporations that stood to lose billions of dollars should government turn away from heavily-subsidized fossil fuel industries and move toward solar, wind or nuclear options. They set up shadowy, pseudo-scientific organizations such as the Advancement of Sound Science Coalition and The George C. Marshall Institute to hurl a constant barrage of doubt on an overwhelming majority of scientists who agreed human activity was warming our planet.

With the help of half-crazed pundits like Glenn Beck and Rush Limbaugh, the "science" of climate change was somehow turned into the "debate" of climate change. Powerful fossil fuel industry supporters kept the "debate" myth alive by burying the truth in an avalanche of public relations specialists and PhDs-for-hire who sowed seeds of doubt on the ever-growing body of evidence supporting the fact that our planet's atmosphere was changing. Year after year, decade after decade, the weather kept getting more bizarre and the levels of greenhouse gases climbed the ladder of the Keeling Curve.

Looking back, the Western world has a long history of denying science, from Galileo to Copernicus, Darwin to Einstein, Wegener to Keeling. All of them presented concepts that contradicted the religious, scientific or political views of their time. All of their ideas were initially suppressed or dismissed as mere "theories." Over time, all of these so-called theories have been confirmed by objective reality. Galileo and Copernicus were right—the Earth revolves around the sun. Genetic science proves beyond a shadow of a doubt that we are evolved from monkeys. Einstein's so-called theoretical equations fundamentally altered our understanding of time and helped create the atomic bomb. I can't imagine the people of Hiroshima felt a "theory" exploded overhead on August 7, 1945. Alfred Wegener's hypothesis of plate tectonics, considered patently absurd by the established scientific community when it was first proposed in 1915, is now a cornerstone of geophysical science. The Keeling Curve should have been more than enough evidence to turn us away from what was, in retrospect, the worst path we could have gone down toward a sustainable future—the reckless burning of fossilized carbon.

We didn't listen then just as the CMC didn't listen to me four years ago when I warned them the nanomirrors wouldn't come down. The computer models that first projected the rising sea levels, droughts, torrential rains, ocean acidification and the whole laundry list of climatic upheavals we were heading toward were countered by PR campaigns and political candidates heavily subsidized by Exxon Mobil, Peabody Energy, and Massey Coal. Coal mining, fracking and drilling meant good jobs paying good wages. Why change?

It took the Lost Decade, when one in twenty people on Earth died as a result of our overheated planet, to convince the world that the global warming skeptics were wrong about our future. Why did it have to come to this? Why didn't they pay attention to the IPCC or the path set forth in the Kyoto Accords? I guess money doesn't talk—it swears.

Ultimately there's no point in going on about all this now. It's ancient history. But we have to take some kind of lesson from what happened. The computers that modeled the future of climate change were the same computers we used to track hurricanes and tornadoes. Why trust them to predict the *weather next week but not the climate a decade down the road? The lesson is simple—science, good science, should always be trusted. In a way, science is our most proven method for comprehending the machinery of the universe. I'll leave it at that.*

Warren put down his pen and got up from his desk. He walked over to the window in his bedroom and looked out at a scene cut straight from a sci-fi novel. It had snowed the night before and the fresh snow had blown over most of the coal dust. The two colors—the charcoal grey and the pure white snow—gave the landscape a surrealistic quality that was strangely beautiful. It reminded Warren of the time of year when the snow turned to slush along the streets of Chicago and the dust and dirt mixed with the melting snow. It was beautiful.

Warren hadn't told anyone at the ranch about the prospect of Yeva bringing seeds to them from Chicago. He didn't want to get their hopes up and he worried Yeva wouldn't be able to smuggle any seeds out of the vault. He felt she might change her mind, though that seemed less likely. Still, it was better to wait until he heard some good news from her before discussing it with the crew.

Stealing Seeds

Yeva didn't know what to do. She had slept poorly the past few nights. She tossed and turned in her bed as she wondered how on Earth she could even steal seeds for Dr. Randolf, let alone how she would get the seeds to Montana. *First things first,* she thought to herself as she sat in the back of a cab heading north toward the gardens on her biweekly visit.

First I have to figure out how I'm going to get them out, she thought. *Seeds aren't very bulky. In fact, I could probably fit an entire vegetable garden's worth in my computer case or a small briefcase. The guards check them though, both going in and coming out, so that won't work. I think it's best if I talk to Margot before I try something on my own. I have a feeling she'd be willing to help. Getting caught taking seeds out of the vault could land me in prison and the prisons are out of food.*

These thoughts troubled Yeva as the cabbie drove through the northern suburbs of Chicago. Several times along the way, the driver had to slow the cab to a crawl in order to push through thick piles of greyish slush which had been piling up for weeks since the start of the dusting. Sometimes the slush got so deep that the electric cabs got stuck in it, spinning their tires aimlessly in the mud-like snow. Traffic snarled up in the deeper sections and roads closed for hours as people pushed and shoveled their way out. On some days, as night fell, the slush turned to solid ice and miles of roadway became impassible. Every car in Chicago was the same color—a mottled gray. Although the slush was hell to drive through, it was a reassuring sign that the coal dust was working. Chicago was thawing.

The cab pulled up to the main gate and Yeva waved her iPhone across the laser scanner behind the driver's seat. The fare was instantly credited to his account—tip included. Yeva thanked him for the ride and got out. She decided to visit Margot before doing her weekly check up at the vault.

After taking off her parka, she said a casual hello to the woman at the front desk before plodding off to Margot's office, stamping out slush along the way.

Margot was reviewing some directives from her Board of Directors when she heard the knock on her office door. She got up and went over to open it.

"Who is it?"

"It's Yeva. I'm back."

"Hold on a second." Margot unlocked the deadbolt and let Yeva in. "You're here early. Have you finished your rounds already?"

"I figured I'd do them afterward," Yeva admitted.

"That's fine. Can I get you some water? You look thirsty."

"That'd be great."

Margot poured Yeva a glass of water from her cooler and handed it to her.

"So what's up, Yeva? You said you needed to talk to me."

"Yes, but it's easier if I show you what it is outside."

Margot was confused. She sensed something was worrying Yeva, and she knew that moving outside meant it was something the government might want to know about.

"Sure. Let me get my coat."

Yeva finished her water and both women headed past the sole receptionist toward the gardens. The temperature outside hovered around freezing but the wind was light and the sun was shining. The trees, still bare after three years, were covered in coal dust.

After they walked a considerable distance from the building, Yeva broke the silence.

"I called Warren."

"Is that what this is all about?"

"Yes, in a way."

"How are they doing out there?"

"They're doing OK, but they had a break in a few weeks ago."

"Was anyone hurt?"

"His good friend was shot in the stomach, but he's recovering. The real problem is the thieves took their seeds. Warren's concerned—as he should be—that they'll need seeds to plant greenhouses or gardens to survive the next winter. He's not sure there'll be any surplus food available for the remote areas like Bozeman for at least another year or so, even if there is a growing season. He's worried the coal dust won't provide enough snow melt to allow planting across much of the Corn Belt and the wheat fields of Canada and Russia. There will be food, just not enough."

"I'm afraid Warren's right," Margot agreed. "I'm hearing the same thing from the Board of Directors, who are advising us to forgo replanting our exotics and focus on using the facility for food production again this summer. Chicago is right on the cusp of having a viable growing season according to the CMC, and although it looks like we'll be seeing green again, it's too soon to celebrate."

"So you're here to ask me for seeds, right?"

"Wait—how... How'd you know?" Yeva stammered.

"I can't imagine anyone in their right mind is willing to share any seeds these days. Seeds are more precious than gold. That's why the NSA has posted the guards. Seeds are the future."

"Can you help me?"

"Yes, I'll help. But they won't let me take seeds out either, you know. I'm searched just as rigorously as you are."

Yeva looked across the rolling hills of the garden and looked like she wanted to cry. Margot felt bad for her.

"Could we smuggle them out somehow?"

"If we were caught, we'd be arrested," Margot observed. "From what I hear, now's not the time to be in prison."

"So you can't help me then, can you?"

"No, I said I'd help and I will." Margot let a hint of smugness creep into her voice as she unzipped her jacket and took out her purse. "This should take care of it," she said as she rifled through her belongings.

Finally, she emerged with a misshapen key.

"Here you go!" she announced triumphantly, handing her prize to Yeva.

"Thanks, but what is it?"

"It's my security key for the vault's alarm system—I just now happened to lose it," she added with a wink.

"I thought we had to turn them in. I turned all of mine in. The NSA requested we surrender all of them back when they took over the vault's security. Did they let you keep yours?"

"Not exactly."

"What do you mean?"

"I had two. I did surrender the one they knew I had. But you remember back in 2041 when we hired Gloria?"

"Yeah, she was that intern from Northwestern University."

"Well, that was long before the Mylerium Project, the NSA guards and the big chill. We didn't need two armed guards standing at the entrance to the vault back then. I happened upon this extra key about a year ago and decided to hang onto it."

"But it won't get us past the guards."

"No—but it will get the seeds out the back door, won't it?" Margot smiled. For some strange reason, she felt oddly proud of what Yeva was attempting.

"But the red light above the front doors will go out when I turn off the alarm system," said Yeva. "Won't that make the guards suspicious?"

"Not if you can distract them for thirty seconds. You know, Yeva, the guards are about your age—I'm sure you remember how to flirt, or need I remind you?"

Margot figured it had been a long time since Yeva had the luxury of thinking about men, considering her ex-boyfriend was likely dead, people were starving and the world was falling apart. But that didn't mean her employee didn't know how to put on makeup or brush her long reddish hair until it shimmered. She could easily dupe the guards for a few minutes.

"I don't think I'm ready today, though," Yeva said nervously.

"Oh, no, of course we wouldn't go today. We've got to iron out a plan first. We can do it early next week, after we work out the details."

"So you'll help?"

"Yeva, without Warren's warning, you would have never stockpiled food. Without your sharing that same food with me, my kids might not be alive today. I don't know who this man is, but I'm going to do anything I can to make sure he survives. I just wish the CMC would have listened to him years ago, before they sent those drones up."

"Thanks, Margot."

"No, thank you, Yeva, thanks for saving my family. Now let's walk a bit more and discuss our plan. There won't be any time to waste once I have that back door open, so you'll have to pick out what seeds Warren wants first, then have them neatly placed in containers. I'll only have a few seconds—the backup alarm will go off 30 seconds after the primary security system is shutdown. It's a failsafe system the NSA installed just in case of a primary power failure. We can't access that override, so timing will be everything."

Yeva and Margot continued their walk, discussing the various details that they would have to cover before they executed their plan.

Near the very end of the walk, almost as an afterthought, Margot added, "And once you get these seeds, how are you planning to deliver them to Montana?"

"I'm going to drive them?"

"Are you crazy?" Margot gasped. "They say the Dakotas are lawless right now. You don't even have a car."

"I'll rent one."

"You're not going to take a rented car from Chicago to Montana. I'll let you use mine."

"Are you serious? Margot, you're already helping me enough."

"I can always get by using cabs," Margot interrupted. "You'll need a reliable car to make that journey. You'll also need a pocketful of miracles."

"I know, I hear they're turning to cannibalism out there."

"It's some kind of Rapture7 cult that's doing most of it, from what I understand. It's especially bad around the Black Hills."

"I'll go around them."

"In any case, you've got one hell of a lot of trouble ahead of you. Let's meet later this week to come up with some plans. You're one brave woman."

"I owe it to Warren."

"No you don't. But knowing you, you'll get those seeds to Montana. Just try to drive nonstop and don't trust *anyone.*"

The women agreed to meet for a second time at Margot's home to finalize the details of their plan before parting.

On her way back to her office, Margot thought about how she could help Yeva survive the journey before her. Nothing was easy.

Spaceship Earth

"What do the new model projections have to say?" Dr. Wade asked earnestly.

"For the first time in years, I've got some good news."

"And how good is it?"

Dr. Kiril Zell set his notepad on Dr. Wade's desk, pushed the projection key and a holographic chart six feet wide splayed across the middle of the office.

"Here are three possible projections taken from different scenarios run by the TURING 1000," he explained. "Note that even the worst-case scenario—the line you see on the bottom of the graph—indicates that 45 percent of the North American continent will be capable of a growing season, albeit a shortened one. The top line, which was the based on last week's average temperatures coupled with the fact that less than a third of the mirrors are still in the stratosphere, pushes that number to nearly 70 percent.

"That means that we should be able to plant and harvest nearly all the agricultural lands located in Mexico, the lower continental U.S. and some parts of Canada. Here, let me show you."

Kiril pushed another button, replacing the graph with a detailed map of North America.

"This shows you where we can expect to plant this summer," said Kiril. He took out a laser pointer and highlighted the areas he was talking about.

"As you can see, Mexico, the Southwest, the Southeast, all the southern and central plains, and even bits of South Dakota should be productive.

"We're still seeing problems along the northern tier of the U.S., including Washington, Idaho, Montana, North Dakota, Minnesota, upper Michigan and most of New England. Excepting some very warm river valleys and around Detroit, Canada won't be of much use to us this year. The depth of the snowpack is too high and our coal dustings keep getting re-covered by winter storms. At this point, the computers indicate that the vast majority of the Canadian wheat fields won't be free of snow and ice until late June to mid-July—not enough time to get a crop in before more snow arrives."

Dr. Wade breathed a sigh of relief. "That's still good news, Kiril. How about the rest of the Northern Hemisphere?"

"Here's what that looks like."

A third holographic image appeared in the middle of Dr. Wade's office. The image was twice as large as the last two and spanned the entire width of the space.

"As you can see here," Kiril began, circling nearly the entire map with his laser pointer, "the plantable areas are highlighted in green and marginal regions are in brown. Regions with little hope for a viable crop remain white. The good news is that places like India, Pakistan, Southeast Asia, North Africa and southern Europe should all have a harvest. But most of Russia, Mongolia, Tibet, large swaths of China and northern Europe are all still too cold to grow crops this year and possibly next year as well.

"Of course, even without crops from those places, we won't face as much starvation. You could call it a silver lining, I guess."

Dr. Wade looked at Kiril curiously, wondering what he could be referring to. "And what's the silver lining?"

"After the devastation of the past few years, there just aren't as many mouths to feed."

"You're right," Dr. Wade said, his expression grim. "I just got an update of the worldwide death toll yesterday afternoon from Robert Langford at the Corporation of Information. Their estimates put the losses at more than 5 billion. According to Langford's report, the final count is expected to exceed 6 billion."

Both men paused for a moment and reflected on that number. It was an astonishing amount of casualties.

After a minute had gone by, Kiril continued the conversation.

"There have only been three times over the course of recorded history when we've seen numbers like this—the bubonic plague in the 14th century, the Spanish flu of the early 20th century and the Lost Decade. The Black Death that ravaged medieval Europe between 1340 and 1400 took out a third of populations in Europe and the Middle East. The Spanish flu, which occurred between 1918 to 1920, took only 3 percent of the world's population, which was roughly the same number of deaths as the plague because there were nearly two billion people at the time of the flu and only 350 million living on Earth in 1350.

"The Spanish flu, which we now know was a strain of bird flu, spread worldwide with a death toll exceeding 60 million people. The plague had a death toll of between 75 and 200 million, though the exact numbers will never be known.

"The Lost Decade took approximately one out of every twenty people living at the time, or 450 million. The failed Mylerium Project makes all of these other pandemics and natural disasters pale by comparison. We are going to lose two out of every three people living on Earth by the time this fiasco is over.

"The trouble this time was there were just too many mouths to feed when conditions deteriorated. India had 1.5 billion people and China was pushing 1.3 billion. Pakistan, Bangladesh, Indonesia and the Philippines comprised another 800 million. After the droughts, floods and relentless heat waves—not to mention the ravages of dengue and yellow fever—that entire region was living hand-to-mouth long before the winter of 2044. There was never a contingency plan for feeding 3.5 billion people should the Northern Hemisphere's agricultural production shut down for two consecutive summers. Where could governments or private industries store that kind of surplus?

"The scary part is that this kind of planetary cooling has happened several times in the past and had nothing to do with our failed geoengineering nightmare."

"You're talking about the volcanic eruption of Mt. Tambora in 1815, aren't you?" Dr. Wade observed.

"Mt. Tambora was the most recent event, but there have been many others in the geological records. There was a far more devastating eruption in Sumatra that occurred sometime between 69 and 77 thousand years ago that was much larger than Mt. Tambora. This prehistoric eruption is commonly referred to as the Toba super eruption, the only known M8 volcano known to have gone off since the dawn of modern humans. Some theorists contend that the Toba volcano reduced the world's human population to between 1,000 and 10,000 breeding pairs. The eruption killed so many humans, it created a genetic bottleneck.

"Geologic studies indicate the Earth plunged into between six and ten years of volcanic winter. Entire ecosystems were wiped out after the Toba super eruption ejected some 670 cubic miles of magma and ash into the stratosphere. That compares with a mere 38 cubic miles of ejecta from Mt. Tambora. Computer models reconstructing the event estimate it chilled the entire planet down considerably for 1,000 years.

"There are more examples out there. The Yellowstone caldera, should it erupt, could approach these kinds of numbers, as could Anak Krakatau and a dozen other stratovolcanoes. But maybe, just maybe, the real problem is the sheer number of people trying to survive on a finite planet. How many people can spaceship Earth realistically support?"

Dr. Wade had explored the overpopulation paradigm personally many times before. He reflected a moment.

"Well, we won't need as much agricultural land after this," he said. "There won't be nearly as many people at the dinner table by fall."

"No, and I don't think anyone out there will be in a hurry to repopulate the planet after this fiasco. There may be some good that comes of this, though looking at the videos coming out of Asia right now, I find little comfort from making that statement."

"Nor do I, Dr. Zell. Nor do I."

Kiril turned off the holographic projector and picked up his notepad. The meeting was over. Humanity would survive the Mylerium Project, but it would never be the same.

The Heist

Yeva awoke early to shower and put on her prettiest dress. She then decided to put on makeup before heading to work, something she hadn't done in years.

Since Rubic's disappearance several years ago, Yeva had become something of a recluse. The endless winter didn't help, either. She hadn't been to the Siren Club since the winter of 2044. It had shuttered its doors since then anyway.

She opened the top drawer of her vanity chest only to discover dried-up lipsticks, faded creams and bottle after bottle of hardened fingernail polish. It looked more like a cemetery for cosmetics than a young lady's makeup collection.

After tossing out two dozen tubes and bottles, Yeva took a few minutes to sort through the remnants. She still had a few dark red lipsticks that might work, some eye shadow, rouge, fingernail polish and eyelash mascara. It wasn't exactly the combination she would have chosen three years ago, but it would have to do.

First she examined her hair. Looking in the mirror, she realized her long red hair was hanging almost straight down. It was scarcely purple anymore as she hadn't bothered to infuse it with any highlights for years. She took out her disused curling iron and added some body and shine to her hair. Once she was satisfied, she moved on to the makeup.

Within a half hour, Yeva Dunning had transformed herself into a makeshift beauty queen. She looked radiant and couldn't resist glancing at herself in the mirror one last time before calling a cab.

If this doesn't distract those soldiers, nothing will, Yeva thought. Then she panicked for a moment as she realized two women could be assigned today. *Maybe they'll be gay,* she thought, giggling to herself. *But if they're young men, I'll win.*

By 9 a.m., Yeva was heading northbound in a cab. The weather outside was even warmer than had been forecasted. Today's high of 45 degrees was the warmest day recorded in May since 2043. The coal dust was working. Much of the dirty snow had melted off the roads. Temperatures had been above freezing for a few nights in a row, so the icy slush piles were rapidly vanishing.

Still, there were mounds of dirty snow scattered around the city, and another snowfall was predicted for the coming weekend. Winter refused to give up without a fight.

As planned, Yeva was knocking on Margot's office door at 9:45 a.m. They were going to head to the vault together, then separate inside and execute the rest of the plan.

"Margot, it's me," Yeva called.

"I'll be right there!"

Margot put her finger to her lips as she let Yeva in, signaling this was no place to talk. They would leave the building first.

"You look stunning, young lady," Margot said with a knowing smile.

"Thanks, Margot. I just felt like wearing makeup today—you know how it is."

"I sure do. Well, let's go check on the seeds."

They walked together toward the seed vault. Aside from the black mess made by the mixing of the coal dust with the snow, it was a perfect spring day. Historically, this kind of day should have come in early April, not May, but both women were glad to see that spring was finally returning.

As they walked along, Yeva pointed at the trees and shrubs. "Do you think they'll come back?" she asked.

"You're wondering if the trees will have leaves again this year? I think most of them will do just fine. There were a few scattered leaves on them last year, though the mid-summer storm ended their bloom. This year feels different, though—some of them are already showing buds."

Yeva looked at one of the oak trees next to the path and noted that it was already showing signs of life. Small brownish buds were forming on many of the bare branches. In the understory some of the local shrubs were following suit. Summer was finally returning.

"Let's go over the plan one more time," Margot suggested.

"OK, you start."

"We'll both go in together. You've got the matching briefcase already packed with the seeds Warren asked for, correct?"

"Yes—it's well hidden under my desk. It's the one you gave me last week and it looks identical to the one you're carrying right now."

"Right. So after we make the rounds together, I'm going to stay behind. I'll tell the guards I had to use the bathroom and I'll tell you to wait for me at the front door. Let's synchronize our cell phone clocks so we won't mess up the timing."

Both women stopped along the path and set their cells to the exact same hour, minute and second.

"Remember, Yeva—we'll have only 30 seconds before the backup alarm system kicks in, so timing is everything. While you distract the guards, I'll insert the key and disarm the primary alarm, crack the back door just enough to stuff the briefcase into the snow bank, shut it, and quickly rearm the system.

"Before we go in, let's walk around to the back of the building to make sure there's no snow bank blocking the back door entrance."

"That's a good idea, Margot. I'm glad you thought of it."

The two women took the long way around, waving to the two guards standing at the front door as they did, and walked to the emergency rear exit to the vault on the opposite side of the building. Margot had asked one of the maintenance men to be sure to shovel out the back door several days earlier, insisting it was a safety issue. As they strolled past, they saw that the grounds people had done exactly as requested. The walkway was clear.

"There's still a lot of snow on the roof, isn't there?" noted Yeva as they walked along the side of the building.

"Yeah, I'd say there's at least two to three feet of it. If it keeps getting this warm, though, most of that will melt off over the next few days. But I hear we're getting another storm this weekend, so it'll all probably be back up there by Sunday. The drones are scheduled to spray some more soot on Monday. God, what a screwed-up mess we've made of everything."

The women arrived at the front gate to find two young soldiers still at their posts. Luckily, Yeva had noted earlier, they were both men.

"Good morning, ladies," one of the guards said cheerily, eyeing Yeva as she approached.

"Please open your briefcase, Margot," the second soldier requested.

Margot opened it. The guard quickly riffled through the pile of paperwork inside. There was nothing out of the ordinary—just inventory forms, her iPad and some pens.

"Why did you two walk around back?" one soldier asked.

"I wanted to be sure we're not getting too much snow on the roof. It could become a problem, especially on the flat roof sections of the building."

"Yeah, I've heard of roofs collapsing from too much weight on them. I suppose all the coal dust doesn't help either. It's sure a nice day though, and it should help melt off some of that snow."

"The warmest day we've had since last August, if I'm not mistaken," Yeva responded with a smile.

"I think you're right."

"Are we done here?" Margot asked impatiently.

"Yes, of course. Go ahead. How long will you two be in the vault?"

"Not long—maybe an hour or two at most," Yeva answered.

"OK. We'll be here when you come out."

"We know," Margot added sarcastically.

The two women unlatched the front door and walked toward Yeva's office. There were some other rooms on the way but for the most part no one worked in the building any longer. Most of the staff had been let go for the winter and would only start returning when it was time to plant the greenhouse gardens in late May.

"Let's go ahead and do the rounds first," Margot whispered. "We don't want this to appear to be too quick of an inspection."

"Got it."

For the next hour and a half, the two women went through their standard routine. They checked every climate-controlled room for temperature and humidity. They opened the various seed trays, counted each one, recorded the results and sealed them back up. They smiled at each other several times when Margot said, "Hmmmm, this one looks as if some seeds might be missing."

"That's impossible, Margot. Recheck it."

"You're right, Yeva. I must have been mistaken," Margot said with a wink.

Aside from the guards out front, there was no internal security that Margot or Yeva knew of inside the seed vault. There were some motion detectors that they disarmed shortly after coming in, but the NSA didn't feel the need to put in any video or audio listening devices in a building that sat empty most of the time. Still, out of habit, both women were careful about what they said.

They got back to Yeva's office just past noon. Yeva dug out the matching briefcase from under her desk and opened it up just long enough for Margot to note the contents.

"That should do it," she said. "You've got a little bit of everything in there, I see. Any turnips?

"Turnips, carrots, spinach, peas, broccoli… Everything Warren asked for. Of course, I had some input as well."

"Please, you're one of the best gardeners I've ever known, Yeva. Now let's get on with it. What time do you have right now?"

"I've got 12:11 and 34 seconds."

"Me, too. Now here's what we do. You walk out and tell them I had to use the ladies room. I'm taking this briefcase, the one with the seeds, to the back door and leaving this one under your desk. It will take me about one minute to reach the back door. I'm going to turn the alarm off at precisely 12:14, so take your time with the guards. Just be sure to distract them from looking back toward the front door, because the red alarm light will cut out the second I deactivate the main system. If they're looking at the front door, they'll see the alarm light is out and we could be in serious trouble.

"Of course, if I take more than 30 seconds to bury the seeds in the snow bank and the secondary alarm' kicks in, we'll be arrested. I've gone through this plan a thousand times, though, so I'm sure I can get everything done in 15 to 20 seconds, max. I want to be sure I cover the briefcase in that filthy snow just in case one of the maintenance men happens to walk by it between now and when we retrieve it later.

"Are we ready?"

"Yes, but I'm nervous."

"Believe me, Yeva, I'm about as nervous as I've ever been."

The two women walked out of Yeva's office, Yeva heading directly to the front door and Margot to the emergency exit on the other side of the vault.

Yeva arrived at the front door first. Knowing Margot was coming through a few minutes later, she didn't reset the motion detectors like she usually would.

"Hi, again," she said as she walked out into the sunlit day.

"Where's Margot?" the first guard asked.

"Oh, she had to use the ladies room. She'll be out in a minute."

"OK, I was just wondering. Please stand right here and raise your arms. You know the drill."

"How about we do it over here today? I want to stand in the sunlight. It's such a nice day."

Yeva walked a dozen steps away from the main entrance, careful to swing her hips seductively along the way.

"Doesn't matter to me," the guard admitted with a smile.

"So, do either of you have plans for the day? Catching up with your girlfriends later, I suppose. It'd be a beautiful day for a walk along the lake."

With spring in the air, a warm sun, and an attractive redhead offhandedly asking if they were available, Yeva got a response quickly.

"He's married," the soldier frisking Yeva blurted quickly, nodding toward his comrade. "But I actually don't have anything going. I mean, I don't—never mind," he stammered, blushing faintly.

The other guard, somewhat ticked off by his friend's blunt disclosure, took the bait.

"Oh, don't start in, Braxton. You know you'll be calling your girlfriend later."

Yeva, who now had the soldiers' undistracted attention, noticed the red alarm light above the door go off. She just had to keep this up for thirty seconds. Easy.

"We split up last week, Carver," Braxton hissed. "I told you that yesterday."

"Now, now boys, I was just wondering. This spring weather's just got me thinking about life again. It's been so hard these past few years, living alone and all."

Yeva had both soldiers looking at her and she knew everything depended on keeping their attention for just another few moments.

On the opposite side of the building things weren't going well. During the time Margot and Yeva made the rounds, a huge pile of blackened snow had slipped off the overhang above the back door and blocked the rear entrance. Just seconds after turning off the primary system, Margot went to push the door open, but found she could only budge it a few inches. There wasn't enough room to slide the suitcase full of stolen seeds through the narrow opening.

For a second, she considered closing the door again and abandoning the plan. Then, thinking she might have enough time to dig away some of the fallen snow, she decided to try to clear a way for the door with her hands.

Frantically, Margot dropped the suitcase, knelt on the floor and thrust both her hands into the sooty snow that was stopping the door. It was icy cold and her hands quickly numbed as she dug away. She was counting in her head. *Fifteen seconds left.*

She stood back up and put all her weight into the door. It cracked open another two inches and stopped.

Margot picked the briefcase and checked. Yes, it fit through—but barely. She took the briefcase and smeared her hands all over it. The brown briefcase quickly blackened from the soot that came off her dirty hands. There was no time to bury it.

She tossed the briefcase into the snow bank and, with four seconds remaining, pulled the door closed. They would have to walk around the building immediately or someone might find it oddly abandoned in the dirty snow. There would be too many questions to answer if that happened.

At the front door, Yeva had both the soldiers completely charmed. She had asked Braxton about his breakup and he took the bait. Yeva's long red hair, flowing in elegant curls that reflected the golden sunlight, could have distracted the two men for hours.

Yeva grew alarmed as the seconds passed. Finally she saw the red light switch back on and smiled brilliantly. Five or six minutes went by as the three of them made small talk. Yeva had charmed the two soldiers into oblivion. With the light back on, Yeva was chatty, coy and as attractive as spring itself. The boys loved it, never having seen her in this mood before.

Margot rushed into the bathroom, took out some paper towels and went back to clean up the soot and water around the back door. It took longer than Margot wanted, but she couldn't leave the area looking that way. If any others patrolled the vault, a dirty floor beside the back door could raise suspicions.

When Margot finally returned to the front door with her briefcase in hand, Yeva and the two soldiers hardly noticed.

"Hmmmm, boys," Margot said as she cleared the front door. "Aren't you going to search me?"

"Sorry. We were just talking."

"I see that," said Margot. "Listen Yeva, I thought I heard something falling off the roof while we were in there. I think we should walk around the building again to see if there's any damage done."

"Yeah, I heard something too. That sounds like a good idea."

Before they got started, the two soldiers broke off their infatuation to frisk Margot and reopen her briefcase. Everything was in order. As the two women strolled back the way they came, Yeva turned around and blew the soldiers both a kiss. Margot rolled her eyes.

After they were far enough away to talk safely, Yeva broke the silence.

"What happened? I thought for sure the alarm was going to sound."

"The door was stuck. Some snow must have slid off the roof while we were doing our rounds. I had to dig it out. Look at my hands, Yeva—they're red as beets!"

Margot raised her hands, which were still flush and throbbing from the cold.

"We have to pick up the briefcase right now," she continued. "I didn't have any time to bury it."

"OK, let's get it."

They walked around to the back of the building and found the briefcase untouched but wet and covered in dirty soot. Yeva stepped into the snow bank and picked it up. She opened her briefcase and took out her iPad, then buried it under the snow, just to the right of the back door.

"What are you doing?" asked Yeva.

"Well, we can't walk past the guards carrying two briefcases when they just saw us coming out of the vault with one, can we? They may be smitten by you, Yeva, but they're trained to watch for any inconsistencies. I can pick my other briefcase up in the next few days, when we have a different pair of guards working. I don't want my iPad in it though, just in case it gets wet."

"What about all the coal dust on the briefcase?" Asked Yeva, pointing to the dirty briefcase Margot was now holding.

"I'll tell them I accidently dropped it if they ask. We should get back and dry it off," Margot said. "If the seeds get wet, it's over."

"They're all in plastic baggies inside—they'll be fine," Yeva assured her.

"Good. Let's head back now."

The two made it back to Margot's office without incident, waving at the guards one last time as they walked back to the main building.

By 3 p.m. Yeva was back at her apartment. The briefcase lay open on her kitchen table while she counted the packets. Everything was in order. The first phase of the plan had gone off without a hitch. Now all she had to do was to drive 1,400 miles to Bozeman through a nation full of lawless, starving animals and deliver the seeds to Warren. That was the second phase of the plan. The dangerous phase.

Shelter Ranch

Warren had convened a meeting at the ranch. After hearing from Yeva, he finally had some good news to announce. He also wanted to discuss what Sheriff Aston had told him three days ago in a conversation he never expected.

It had been months since everyone at the ranch had been asked to gather together in the oversized living room in the barn. Warren had asked Cecilia to make sure her two boys, Gibson and Andy, were there as well.

Both the couches were filled and all the wooden chairs from the communal dining table had been brought out, circling the center of the living room. Albion was there—his wound had healed enough to allow him to walk to the meeting, although he was still in a considerable amount of pain. Dr. Irving was there, as was Roger, his girlfriend and the rest of the entourage. The meeting was scheduled for 2 p.m., but it wasn't as though Warren was doing a presentation at the CMC. After chatting informally with half of his extended family, Warren stood up and got things started 20 minutes late.

"I know all of you are wondering why we're meeting here today," he said, "and I want to begin by taking all of us back to when all of you first learned about the ranch."

Different members of the crew nodded, recalling their individual journeys to this survivalist camp on the outskirts of Bozeman, Montana.

Warren went on. "All of you received a package from me, delivered to you by a runner I didn't even know. His name, as I've only recently learned, was Rubic Chang. I originally hired him to deliver seven envelopes. Not everyone who received my letter and warning decided to join us. At this point I have no idea if those people are dead or alive, though I hope they've made it. The very last package was destined to go to a former girlfriend of mine, Ann Bradley, who was living in Crescent City, California at the time.

"Although I'll never know exactly what happened, I suspect Rubic was tracked down by the NSA and arrested before he could make his last delivery. No one has heard from him since and sadly, we must assume he's gone. Just before he was caught, he somehow managed to mail the last package—the one intended for Ann—to his girlfriend, Yeva, who was still living in Chicago.

"Two years ago, Yeva called me to say she had read my letter. At first she didn't believe a word of it. But as the weather began to turn cold that fall, Yeva realized what she had read wasn't the ravings of some meteorological lunatic."

The entire room broke out in subdued laughter at Warren's comment. Albion yelled out, "Are you *sure* it wasn't some meteorological lunatic?"

Everyone roared. *It's good to hear people laughing again,* thought Warren, even if it was at his expense.

After the laughter stopped, Warren continued. "Wisely, long before President Beltram's announcement about the failed Mylerium Project and the following run on food supplies, Yeva had already been stockpiling. She took half the money I had promised to pay Rubic for the deliveries and filled her spare bedroom with commodities, just like I did here at the ranch.

"When Yeva called me to personally thank me, she happened to mention that she worked at the Chicago Botanic Garden. I thought nothing of it and I had no idea what her position at the garden was. Then, about two weeks ago, she called again. She said she had been having unusual dreams about me, which I thought was odd because we've never actually met. It was during that conversation that I came to learn that her job at the garden was the caretaker of their regional seed bank, located in a climate-controlled seed vault."

Everyone's eyes lit up after hearing Warren's comments. They all knew their seeds had been taken during the night raid a month ago. They also knew that Warren wasn't having any luck finding replacement seeds. He had warned everyone that if he could find anyone willing to trade food for seeds, they would all have to ration, but thus far there were no takers.

"Of course, when Yeva told me she was in charge of the seed bank, which includes regional vegetables, corn and even potato buds, I was thrilled.

She went on to tell me that because of the increased value of the contents of the vault, the NSA had seized control of it and no one was permitted to remove anything from it, for any reason, with no exceptions. In fact, the guards stationed at the main entrance to the vault shot and wounded some intruders last month.

"So it came as a complete surprise to me when Yeva offered to try to get us some seeds near the end of our conversation. That's the good news. Yeva called me two days ago and while she was careful not to divulge too much information over the airwaves, she indicated that she would have a surprise package for us from the Botanic Garden. Our seeds are on the way!"

Everyone in the room began clapping. There were cheers and shouts of joy because they knew their lives likely depended on whether they would be able to plant gardens in the summer. Their food stocks were precariously low and no one knew when food would become commercially available again, especially so far north.

As the sounds of celebration trailed off, Dr. Irving raised his hand and asked, "How's she going to get them to us? I understand the trains are down and the mail isn't secure."

"I'm glad you asked, Doc," Warren said. "The good news is that Yeva, with the help of her boss, Margot, was able to get the seeds out of the vault without getting caught, but now comes the hard part. Yeva's going to drive them here in her boss's electric car."

A silence fell over the room. Albion was the first to speak. "She'll have to cross the Dakotas to get here. Isn't that where there's trouble? I mean serious trouble."

"Rumors are that there are groups of people—gangs, really—who've gone rogue. They say they're getting high on Rapture7, Synth, or even meth and eating people. The Greens don't have the manpower to move the National Guard in to clean things up, at least for now. They're busy trying to maintain law and order in Chicago, Minneapolis, St. Paul—hell, all the major cities. They can't waste time searching for drug gangs in Deadwood."

"So how's she going to get here? Couldn't she just drive a bit longer and avoid the Dakotas?"

"Margot and Yeva are working on a plan, but we couldn't talk about it on the phone. I'm not sure what they're planning on doing. I suppose if she's just driving through the Dakotas, it can't be that bad."

"When will she leave Chicago?" Albion asked. "The weather is breaking and we need those seeds in the next week or two if we're going to get a garden in."

"Yes, I know. That's one reason for this meeting. We have to put last summer's greenhouses back up and build at least two more. All of us will have to work around the clock to get things ready for Yeva's arrival. She leaves Chicago in two days, but she'll need to recharge the car at least three times before hitting Bozeman, so it could take her at least three days to get here."

Warren could see the disappointment in everyone's eyes. The good news was they had finally secured some seeds. The bad news was that those seeds were 1,400 miles east and a young woman was about to drive across a landscape filled with gangs of cannibals to deliver them.

"Do you think she'll make it?" Dr. Irving asked.

"I hope so. She wouldn't give me any details, but she hinted that the plan they were working on would make her very safe."

"You said you had some other news for us," Cecilia added. "Something you heard from the sheriff."

"Vince Gatini shot himself last week," Warren announced solemnly. "Apparently his family had finished almost all the food they stole from us and he decided to take his life rather than watch his wife and kids starve. He left them his share, though it didn't amount to much. His wife called the sheriff to tell him to let us know that Vince wanted all of us to understand he was sorry for taking our food. His suicide note said he never wanted to do it, but felt his back was up against a wall. He said it was the only thing he could do to keep his family from dying."

"How about the others? How about the guy that got shot?"

"He lived. The sheriff said they're all scraping by, but like everyone else around here, it's a day-by-day thing. He said nearly half of Bozeman has died in this mess. That's got to be hard for him to handle, as he must have known so many of them. It's especially tough in a small town like this."

Warren looked on as the crew went silent.

Finally he added another comment. "I think Yeva's going to make it and we'll have a better growing season this year. The sheriff mentioned that Vince's wife and kids are in dire straits. He asked me to ask all of you if we could spare a month's worth of food so they can make it into summer."

"What about our seeds?" Albion asked.

"The sheriff told me Vince's wife, Becca, thinks one of the other guys ended up with them. She said if she had them, she'd return them, but she has no idea where they are now. What do you all think? Should we give her and her kids the food?"

"It's a tough call, Warren," Cecilia said. "What if Yeva doesn't arrive with the seeds? We've been strict about sharing for a reason."

"I know. But I think it's the right thing to do. All in favor raise your hand."

Warren watched as a dozen hands went up.

"All opposed?"

A half-dozen hands were raised.

"Then it's settled. We'll ask the sheriff to come out in the next few days to pick up some rice, canned goods and instant potatoes and deliver them to Becca and the kids. Now let's roll up our sleeves and build some greenhouses—our seeds are on the way!"

The crew clapped loudly and the meeting drew to a close. No one was sure if the seeds would ever make it to Bozeman. All they could do now was wait.

Kuru

"They call it kuru disease, or sometimes Prion's disease," Margot said while browsing Wikipedia on her iPhone.

"I've never heard of it," Yeva admitted.

"It's rare, though not as rare these days. You get it by eating infected meat, or infected people. If they really are eating people in the Dakotas—which I doubt—they'll have heard about it. And they wouldn't dare eat anyone showing signs of kuru. We'll fix you up before you head out so you'll look… unappetizing."

Yeva didn't like the sound of that. "What do you have in mind?" she asked uneasily.

"Well, we'll have to do something with the hair first. It's too perfect."

Like most people, Yeva had been cutting her own hair for the past few years. She had become pretty adept at working a scissors backwards while looking in a mirror.

"I like my hair the way it is."

"So do I, but you've got to work with me, Yeva. Your hair will grow back in a few months. The most important thing to do now is to make sure you get to Montana unharmed and alive."

Yeva nodded. Margot was right—the mission was more important than her long, flowing red hair.

"Alright, then let's get started," she said.

They were in Yeva's apartment. All the shades were pulled and it was late in the afternoon. Margot's car was charging back in her garage and the plan was to send Yeva on her way with the briefcase full of seeds hidden in the trunk under the spare tire.

Margot picked up a pair of scissors and started chopping recklessly at Yeva's lovely hair. Her job was to make it look as though Yeva had been pulling it out by the roots. As she cut away, she started explaining the symptoms of kuru to Yeva.

"It's related to mad cow disease. You've heard of that, haven't you?"

"Yes."

"It's also related to chronic wasting disease in deer, and Creutzfeldt-Jakob disease in humans. The difference is you get kuru from eating infected humans."

"Oh my God, Margot—so you're turning me into a cannibal!"

"You're not a cannibal, Yeva, but if you do run into anyone who is, they sure as hell won't think about taking a bite out of you if it looks like you've got kuru."

"Why not?"

"It's contagious to anyone who eats the flesh of someone infected with the disease. You'll have to fake the symptoms as well. The hair and the makeup alone won't do it."

"What makeup? You haven't said anything about makeup." Yeva was starting to have second thoughts about Margot's plan.

"Well, it's not going to be much of anything—just some special face paint to make you look sickly. We'll add some dark eye shadow. I have to warn you though; this stuff won't come off easily. It's not exactly makeup. It behaves more like a stain on your skin, like henna in a way. It'll stay on for a week, even if you do your best to wash it off. With all the bruises I'm adding, you'll look about as tasty as a rotten tomato."

Yeva looked up at Margot, hacking away at her beautiful hair, and burst out laughing. Margot joined in, adding, "Look, your hair's the same color as a rotten tomato already!"

After they had stopped laughing, Yeva asked Margot, "So what are the symptoms I'm supposed to fake?"

"Here," Margot said, putting down her scissors for a moment to pull a slip of paper out of her pocket. "I made you this list so you can study it before heading out tomorrow."

Yeva picked up the list and started reading it aloud. "Shaking, especially in the hands and arms. Pathological outbursts of uncontrolled laughter. Memory loss, speech impairment, jerky movements and seizures.

"You know, I've never heard of kuru, Margot, but I've heard of something called laughing sickness. Is it the same thing?"

"Well, uncontrolled laughter is one of the symptoms. Give it a try."

Yeva made a silly attempt at it and both women broke out laughing again, though not the diseased kind.

"So, your plan for me is this: I'll look like hell, my hair will be a mess, I'll babble, laugh and shake and no one will want to kill and eat me because they'll think I've got kuru, right?"

"That's it. I don't think you'll be running into any cannibals anyway, but if you do, it won't hurt to have a plan. You can't really defend yourself to speak of—no offense—and there's no law enforcement where you're heading, so the only solution I know of is to make yourself inedible. No one wants to eat a sick cow or an unhealthy-looking animal. Trust me, when you start laughing, muttering and shaking, cannibals won't want to eat you, either."

By early evening, the lovely Yeva Dunning had been converted into a bona fide disaster. Her hair was chopped to pieces, her skin pale with fake bruises and her eyes had dark, days-without-sleep bags under them. Margot decided to add some yellowish stains to her legs and arms, thinking they had to reflect the same pallid tones of her face. Yeva looked sickly.

When it was done, Margot held up a mirror up for Yeva. She shrieked. "I look terrible!"

"That's right. You look perfect. Now we're going to have to dump a bunch of trash in my car as well. It's way too neat and clean to belong to someone suffering from kuru.

"And one last thing," Margot continued. "The Net says there's a snowstorm coming in from the north that's going to make it impossible for you to avoid the Black Hills. You can't go through Fargo or any part of North Dakota with a blizzard on the way, so we'll get you heading toward southern Minnesota around seven tomorrow morning. Pack enough food for a week tonight and I'll be back with the car in the morning."

"OK, I'll see you tomorrow then."

Margot kissed Yeva on her pale forehead and headed out to catch a cab. She was worried, but felt confident Yeva would survive the journey. Besides, she doubted there really were "eaters" living in the Black Hills of South Dakota.

May 19, 2047

May 19, 2047

I'm worried. Yeva phoned last night to tell me she's leaving in the morning. It's a long journey—there's almost 1,500 miles of highway between us. She promised she'd call me often en route. I hope she does. Spring is finally digging its way out of three years of winter. I saw a few green shoots coming up in the backyard yesterday, including a handful of dandelions. There's still snow around, of course. It has turned into the heavy, granular snow usually found in late March or early April. Higher up, near the abandoned ski resort at Bridger's Bowl, there's still about 30 feet of snow, but down here in the river valleys it's finally thawing. The coal dust seems to be working.

As I walked around the yard yesterday, it dawned on me that something was still missing. The sun was actually warm, I could see buds on some of the trees and the brilliant yellow flowers contrasted boldly with the blackness of the coal dust. But there are no birds anywhere. There are no jackrabbits, no deer eating the budding willows along the stream, no trout swimming up the crystal-clear water—there aren't even insects. The endless winter has taken a tremendous toll on wildlife.

Of course, biodiversity had long been under assault worldwide well before the cold arrived. Flora and fauna everywhere have suffered steep declines in the past 200 years. After this latest blow, it could be centuries before Mother Nature recovers, if she ever does.

By the start of the Lost Decade, much of Earth's mega-fauna had gone extinct. The last Bengal tiger was shot and killed for its fur and bones in the Sundarbans of Bangladesh in 2031. The last Siberian tiger was spotted in the mid-20s, and biologists are all but certain they are extinct in the wild as well. Only the zoos and a handful of UNESCO-funded wildlife preserves have managed to keep tigers from complete extinction. As southern and southeast Asia's population pushed 3 billion, the national parks and nature preserves were overrun with climate refugees. The cheetah, once abundant in the region, was hunted to extinction long ago in 1947. All the indigenous species of deer—including the chital, sambar, swamp deer and barking deer—were hunted into oblivion.

The Chinese panda was declared officially extinct in the wild in 2034. Once again, the primary reason was loss of habitat. As the climate disintegrated, human settlers moved into the Wolong Panda Reserve to seek cooler weather. As each new village was established, the pandas were pushed farther into the preserve until they had nowhere left to go. The other wild habitats were lost to human settlements as well, leaving all the remaining pandas in the world relegated to zoos and two Chinese breeding facilities in Bifengxia and Chengdu.

Polar bears were lost, but that came as no surprise. As the Arctic Ocean opened up, they struggled to make it through the longer summers. They were unable to compete with the grizzly populations to the south and didn't have enough time to learn to feed on caribou, walrus or other large game. The bears eventually turned to eating each other or else starved. The last polar bear was seen in the Arctic in 2027. I wonder if the zoos keeping the few remaining bears alive were able to keep them fed over these past few years. It's hard to imagine that a zookeeper would feed a bear over the needs of his own family.

Africa's wildlife fared just as poorly. As the continent's population expanded, more people turned to bush meat for protein. Crocodiles were hunted into oblivion, as were elephants, hippos, leopards and lions. Only the darkest and most disease-ridden jungles of the central Congo hold any wild animals today. Hopefully they survived the Mylerium Project.

The creatures of the open oceans haven't fared very well either. As the salt water acidified, phytoplankton grew unable to produce shells, resulting in their demise along with the tens of thousands of baleen whales that fed upon them. Coral reefs bleached out as water temperatures climbed. One by one, they all collapsed. Sharks, hunted for little more than their fins, are all critically endangered and the most spectacular shark of all–the great white–was declared extinct in 2032.

The large mammals of the New World have held out better, but not by much. After this nightmare, I wonder if there's going to be anything left. I know from speaking with the sheriff that Yellowstone and all the National Parks have been hunted out. The bison herds, elk, moose and bears were all reduced to bush meat after the terrible winter of 2044. He told me there isn't a large animal to be found anywhere in Montana.

Everyone calls it the Sixth Extinction. What did we think would happen? Park after park and preserve after sanctuary fell to the ceaseless pressure put on them by the rising tide of humans. Dirt farmers, loggers, miners, bush meat hunters and the rest of the cacophonous avalanche of humanity smothered every other living thing. That's just the price we have paid for unchecked growth. The world is filled with nothing but us.

I did see one lone starling yesterday. It was up on the hillside above the root cellar. I thought it was kind of pathetic that the only bird I saw was an invasive species introduced from England more than a century ago. I don't know how the birds survived but it looks as if a few of them did. I'm sure the rats and roaches made it through as well. They always do.

It's going to be an entirely different world when this is over. There will be billions fewer people, allowing for wide open spaces to exist again. If the zoos managed to keep enough tigers and cheetahs alive, maybe we can reintroduce them to India. Perhaps moose and bears will once again wander Montana and crocs and elephants will ply their ways through the Sahel. Maybe we'll rediscover or rebuild the Garden of Eden. This tragedy affords us a fresh start. Perhaps the failed Mylerium Project could be a blessing in the long run. Through death and great tragedy, life reemerges. There is a silver lining around this darkest of clouds, though it's hard to see at the moment.

I'm tired. I'll look to hear from Yeva tomorrow as she drives through southern Minnesota on I-90. I'm hoping the storm stays to the north of her as forecast. I would hate for her trip to be further complicated by bad weather, but there's always that risk. I just hope she'll arrive here within the week.

Leaving Chicago

"**R**emember—you'll need to recharge the batteries every 500 miles or so, which means you have roughly 12 hours on every charge," Margot explained. "It takes seven minutes at a recharging station to refill the batteries in this Toyota. If you cut that time short, even by a few minutes, it can halve your traveling range. I've entered your two stops into the onboard GPS system. It will notify you when you approach."

"Um, how exactly do you put it in gear?" Yeva asked, embarrassed. "I've never owned a car."

Margot leaned toward the driver's side of her two-seat Toyota Urbana and pushed a small black button on the dash. "There—it's on."

"That's it?"

"Well, you have to back out of the driveway and put it into forward, but that's basically it. You've driven a car before, right?"

"It's been a long time. I can't afford a car and most of my friends don't have any. They seem like dinosaurs to me."

"But you *do* know how to drive?"

"Of course! It's just been a while."

"The GPS will automatically warn you if your charge is getting low. Your first stop is in Albert Lea, Minnesota, which is 400 miles west. I've checked this morning on the Net and they have three charging stations operating in that town right now. You shouldn't have any trouble in Minnesota.

"Your second stop is the one that concerns me, as it's close to the Black Hills. It's in a town called Rapid City. I've checked all over and it's the only place with any charging stations open in western South Dakota. There is one in Sioux Falls, but that's too close to Albert Lea to make it worth stopping at. If you recharge in Rapid City, you can make Bozeman on the final charge, and you'll be home free.

"There's one charging station open in Bozeman but I would recommend going directly to the ranch first—you wouldn't want to risk having the seeds stolen so close to your destination. You can always get the car recharged later."

"How am I going to get the car back to you?"

"Don't worry about that for now," Margot said. "We've got a second car and we'll figure something out once all this is behind us. You're leaving me all your food and that's worth a hell of a lot more than a used Urbana. You can't eat cars."

The sun was coming up over the Windy City as the two ladies continued their conversation. It was still cold out but the world was warming with each passing day. Spring had returned and with it came hope.

"Now whatever you do, don't try to drive straight through. You have to get some sleep or run the risk of dozing off while underway. The car pretty much drives itself, with side-scan radar, autopilot mode and all the other standard features, but these suckers have still been known to run off the road with the driver sound asleep from time to time. So take care to find a place to pull over and rest at least twice before making Bozeman. At full throttle, without taking any bathroom stops or recharges into consideration, you'll be on the road for 30 hours. That's too long to expect to be able to stay awake the whole time. You won't need much sleep—maybe three or four hours at a time—but you'll need to rest.

"When you do pull over, stay close to the freeway. The back roads are still too dangerous. I'd advise just sleeping in the car with the doors locked. If anyone pulls up behind you, unless it's a highway patrol car, pull away. There are plenty of hungry highwaymen out there and though you won't look very good to eat, they'll steal whatever food you have. And if they find your seeds, there's no doubt they'll take them. Seeds are worth a—"

"OK, Margot," Yeva interrupted. "I think I've got it. I know how to take care of myself and if you keep going on and on, I'll never make it out of the driveway!"

"You're right. It's time you got going."

"Thanks for everything, though. I don't mean to be short with you but I want to get started. Let's get this over with."

Margot got out of the car and closed the door behind her. She walked over to the driver's side as Yeva rolled down the window. Reaching in, she gave her friend a warm hug and kissed her once again on her pasty-white forehead.

"Goodbye and good luck, Yeva."

"Thanks for everything, Margot. I promise to call you along the way just to make sure you know I'm safe."

Yeva put the Urbana into reverse. The car beeped gently as it backed out of its parking slot at the Botanic Garden and pulled away. The car looked the part—it was covered in dirty coal dust and there was a bunch of rubbish strewn across the back seat. Yeva also looked like she had just escaped from a tuberculosis ward. Hopefully the combination of things would keep anyone from bothering her on her journey to Bozeman.

Fusion Dreams

"We've got three, maybe four years at most," Dr. Kiril Zell said gloomily.

"That's it?" Dr. Wade barked.

"That's it. After that, the heat will start coming back worse than ever. Despite our best efforts, the amount of CO_2 in the atmosphere keeps increasing, albeit at a much slower pace. After this last fiasco, I don't think the Greens—or any government for that matter—will look very favorably on another high-altitude particle deployment, even if we can figure out why the mirrors failed to implode."

"Yes, we'll never be able to sell the politicians or the public on another aerosol-based plan again. We're far safer and better off looking toward CO_2-scrubbing technologies and staying away from concepts such as sulfur aerosols, nanomirrors or any sunlight-filtering programs.

"Beyond the coal dust, is there anything out there we can use the drones for again? We've got tens of billions of dollars tied up in those planes."

"I personally think there's a lot of promise in open-ocean iron fertilization," Kiril suggested. "Some of the research in that area has produced promising results. The iron, which is inert and already carried in dust storms and volcanic ash, stimulates phytoplankton blooms, which in turn take up and sequester carbon dioxide. We could use the drones to deploy the finely-ground iron dust across vast swaths of the open ocean, causing massive algal blooms that could lock up millions of tons of CO_2. After the blooms reach their maximum growth and start to die off, the microscopic skeletons from the diatoms and Foraminifera will sink to the ocean floor, taking calcium and silicon carbonate with them. Both of those compounds lock up CO_2. As they sink, these microscopic skeletons form a sort of marine snow."

"I've heard of it," Dr. Wade said gruffly. "But doesn't that technology produce other, unwanted side effects?"

"Some of the early experiments went well, but others have created harmful algae blooms that wreak havoc on coastal communities by creating red tides. Huge numbers of fish were killed in some of those cases. There are also concerns about deep-water oxygen levels. The marine snow is ultimately devoured by bacteria which consume oxygen, and that can turn the ocean anoxic. That makes for huge dead zones. Few organisms can survive without oxygen.

"In the end, it seems every method we use to remove the excess CO_2 has some kind of negative or unforeseen repercussion. Looking back, the worst decision we made as a civilization was to burn millions of years' worth of fossil fuels in a few centuries. We had ourselves a massive carbon party, Dr. Wade. Had we only known what we were creating in the long run, I don't think the human race would have burned all this up so enthusiastically. The burn now, pay later mentality wouldn't have been as tempting if past generations could have seen the six billion dead we have now. Plus, in three or four years—whenever the cooling effect of the remaining mirrors wears off—we'll return to destructive hurricanes, droughts and climatic upheavals. It will be the Lost Decade, Chapter Two, if you want to call it that."

With that comment, their conversation stalled. They each took a few sips of coffee and reflected. Over the past few years, Kiril and Dr. Wade had become close. After Kiril's excellent work deciphering Dr. Randolf's homemade computer system and his coal dust idea, he had been promoted to Vice President of Climate Research at the CMC. His office was two doors down from Dr. Wade's and looked out over the dirty city of Chicago. This morning they were sitting in Kiril's office, having their weekly review and discussing the ongoing crisis.

Kiril took another sip of coffee and continued. "I know it's not politically correct to talk about it, but there are some benefits from this massive culling of the human population," he said, keeping his voice low and level. "We will greatly reduce our overall impact on the environment. With all the excess agricultural lands that will open up, we'll be able to run our international jetliners on biofuels instead of oil from now on. In fact, with the world's population standing at about 35 percent of what it was just four years ago, we'll probably reduce our CO_2 output drastically. There are almost no cows, sheep or goats left, which means methane levels will likewise plummet."

"I think you're right, Kiril," Dr. Wade admitted. "But we still have to deal with the 426 parts per million of CO_2 already in the atmosphere. The nanomirrors were never designed to remove any CO_2—they just shielded us from incoming solar radiation. We've got to get back to developing more cost-effective scrubbers, which are probably the least invasive and the most promising of all the geoengineering programs we have on the horizon."

"If only we could get some real breakthroughs in this technology," Kiril complained. "It's still extremely slow and expensive to filter air through scrubbers and the tremendous amount of energy needed to run them isn't helping matters any. If we could somehow power them using nuclear fusion instead of our current fission-based and renewable energy systems, we'd stand a chance at making a dent in the CO_2 levels. Thus far, all of our efforts at harnessing the incredible potential of plasma physics have not materialized. It's the scientific breakthrough that could turn things around for us. But from what I hear from my friends over at the Plasma Development Corporation they are no closer to resolving the issues of nuclear fusion than we were decades ago."

"I didn't know you knew people over at the PDC," Dr. Wade said. "Who do you know over there?"

"I know Dr. Helstrum and Dr. Veruska quite well. I double majored in meteorology and nuclear physics at MIT. I thought you knew that."

"No, I actually didn't. I'm sure personnel knew that, but they don't tell me everything. I've seen your resume, but remember—we had other problems to deal with when you came onboard. How are they doing at the PDC?"

"It's a struggle, trying to come up with a jar that manages to keep the power of the sun inside of it. They've experimented with multiple lasers, electromagnetic containment, magnetic mirrors, electrostatic systems but thus far all of these methods have drawbacks. To date, it takes more energy to contain the process of nuclear fusion than the energy it's capable of producing. You can't produce electricity going that direction.

"It's just so frustrating. We would never have to worry about a fuel supply if we could find a way to use fusion reactors. Their fuel is deuterium, which exists in minute amounts in ocean water. There's enough deuterium in sea water to keep us supplied with fuel for millions of years. There's abundant fuel, few of the risks of our current fission reactors, no greenhouse gas emissions—the list of what fusion could do for the human race is nothing short of amazing. But the technology continues to elude us. I hope for a breakthrough, but we're not much closer than we were 50 years ago.

"Imagine having the energy contained in a hydrogen bomb—a thermonuclear chain reaction identical to what powers our sun—in a container that could burn for hundreds of years. You could heat a lot of steam and run a thousand turbines if you could somehow manage to contain it."

Dr. Wade nodded in agreement, although he realized his knowledge of fusion technology was nowhere near Dr. Zell's. Still, he had studied the promise of fusion enough to know that a single reactor could power half of North America. Unlike solar or wind, fusion power wouldn't be subject to the whims of weather. He had heard that the scientists working at the PDC were getting close and was more optimistic than Kiril. But the solution to harnessing the quintessential power of the universe—star power—had eluded mankind.

The two men continued their discussion of post-Mylerium Project scenarios until just before noon, when they broke off for luncheon meetings elsewhere in the complex. It felt good to be talking about the end of a nightmare. As blades of grass pushed out of the surrounding soil, tree buds and dandelions sprouted across the landscapes of greater Chicago. Life itself seemed to be returning to the scientists and technicians at the CMC. It seemed, at long last, the worst was over.

On the Road to Bozeman

The landscape beyond the suburbs of Chicago shocked Yeva Dunning. She had not ventured out of the city since the summer of '43 and no one could have prepared her for the desolation that had wracked the great plains of Illinois. As she sped along Interstate 90 toward Rockford, she saw most of the farms were abandoned. Some of the houses and buildings were carefully boarded up while others were open to the winds, their windows bashed out and front doors missing. Many roofs had caved in from the excessive snowfalls of the past three winters.

Most of the surrounding corn and soybean fields were covered with a filthy mixture of melting snow and coal dust. The highway itself was black with fine powder from the constant spraying and re-spraying of soot. At times it looked as if a nuclear weapon had gone off, leaving behind only this charcoal-colored world where no life could flourish.

Yeva noted few cars were on the road. By the time she reached Madison, she had only seen a dozen cars and a half-dozen trucks—counting vehicles on either side of the road. There were no squad cars anywhere along the way and every 20 miles or so, abandoned vehicles would appear, parked alongside the road. Some of them looked as though they had been parked for months, if not years. Their tires were flat or missing, their headlights and taillights busted out, their windows smashed in and everything of value stripped away. A quarter of them looked as though they were intentionally set on fire and left as charred metal hulks along this deserted stretch of freeway.

Madison looked exceptionally hard-hit. The only sign of life Yeva could see was off in the distance near the capitol building, where cars and people were gathering. The governor of Wisconsin had called the first state assembly in more than a year.

The rest of the city resembled a ghost town. The University of Wisconsin had been closed for more than two years. The malls stood silent, the restaurants were closed and all commerce had long since ground to a freezing halt. Death had been the only visitor to Madison in years and death had visited the city in droves.

She did drive past two charging stations that were open. She noted the cost of charging a vehicle had dropped far below the market price four years ago. Both stations had cars at them and appeared to be safe.

Yeva looked down at her gauge. With three-quarters of a full charge left, she dismissed the thought of recharging this soon as foolhardy. Still, she had to eventually find a restroom and seriously considered pulling in. Then she remembered Margot's warning about making as few stops as necessary and continued on. Margot was right. It was too dangerous to get out of the car around people. It was safer to pull off a side road somewhere and go in the bushes.

Time passed. Yeva crossed the Mississippi at LaCrosse, Wisconsin, and noted the river was partially frozen over. The coal dust had turned the water pitch black and where the river was open between sheets of broken ice, it looked as though the Mississippi was flowing with tar.

As she entered Minnesota it was more of the same—empty farm houses, crumbling barns and grain elevators that had been smashed down or broken into by starving people in search of the edible dust of field corn, soybeans or barley. A landscape of hunger and madness enveloped her as she drove her Toyota Urbana west toward Montana. More than once, while passing a battered and deserted building, she thought she saw blood on the collapsed porches. It might have been her imagination.

It was dark by the time Yeva reached Albert Lea, Minnesota. She had stopped twice along the way to relieve herself and had been overly cautious both times. She waited until there were no vehicles in any direction before getting out of her car and walking down to a nearby drainage ditch to pee. Once, as she was walking down toward a small stream, she heard a car off in the distance and ran back to get inside the Urbana before she had time to go. The last thing on Earth she wanted was to be separated from her vehicle. Caution became her canon.

Albert Lea, sitting at the crossroads of I-90 and I-35, had more activity in it than any town since Chicago. Yeva noted there were more trucks, vans and cars heading north and south than there had been heading cross country. The reason, she observed, was obvious. There were already some spring crops coming in across northern Mexico, Texas, Florida and the Deep South. The trucks were bringing food and supplies north and heading back empty. They were taking their precious cargo to Minneapolis, St. Paul, Duluth and the smaller towns of the northern Midwest in hopes they could save those on the brink of death.

Two charging stations in Albert Lea were open even though it was after 10 p.m. by the time Yeva made it into town. She passed by the first one, and then pulled off the freeway to recharge her Urbana at the second. There were no other cars around when she pulled in. She swiped her iPhone through the scanner to authorize the charge and connected the high-voltage cord to her charging port on the back of the vehicle.

Looking inside the small convenience store, she saw a solitary young man standing behind bulletproof glass. He looked to be Pakistani. The shelves were empty. It looked as if he had two small wooden boxes under him that were filled with leaf lettuce or possibly spinach. It was hard to tell from where she was standing. Though he looked harmless enough, Yeva didn't go in. Margot had warned her that any interface with people would be laden with risks. They might want to steal what little food she had or they might want to steal *her*. She waited while the high-voltage charger pumped electrons into her depleted batteries. The Pakistani looked at her curiously several times through the inch-thick glass.

Yeva kept wondering what he was staring at. Finally she realized she looked like a raving lunatic to him. Her lovely red hair was chopped to pieces and she was wearing white powder with dark, black bags painted under her eyes. She chuckled to herself and wondered if this might not be a good time to practice her hysterical laughter, incoherent muttering and trembling. If she had decided to go in, she would have done it, but tonight it didn't matter. She remained calm and waited for the charge to complete.

A few minutes later, she got back into the car and drove back onto I-90, heading west toward Sioux Falls, South Dakota. She was getting tired. Just past the town of Fairmont, she pulled off and headed a few miles north on State Highway 71. Then she pulled the car off the road, put her seat back as far as it would go and fell asleep.

She slept poorly, expecting to hear a car passing during the night. None did. There was an eerie silence that permeated the night air, almost like it was screaming soundlessly. There was no moon and the clouds were dark and low, portending the storm that was already hitting the northern half of the state.

At dawn she got out to pee, ate some bread with peanut butter and jelly on it and started up the car. She hoped to reach Rapid City before dark.

Shelter Ranch

"Have you heard from her yet?" Albion asked worriedly.

"Not a word. I think she forgot to call yesterday. Margot sent me an email saying she had hit the road early Monday morning, heading west on I-90. I hope she's OK."

"She's fine. She might have had trouble finding cell service. I hear many of the regional systems are down due to lack of maintenance. It's going to take years before they're restored."

"Just think of what's going to happen with all the estates. Some 50 percent of all the people living in the United States and Canada are gone. I would imagine that in many cases there won't be any living relatives found to inherit the family farm, the condo, or the house in the suburbs. The

Feds will probably step in and claim hundreds of thousands of abandoned properties and estates until the courts can sort through it. The aftermath of this calamity will reverberate through our judiciary for decades. We've got a hell of a mess to sort through and I'm not even considering all the criminal cases that will eventually come out of this."

Albion nodded. He and Warren were outside sitting on the front porch of the main house sipping ice tea. It was almost warm out.

Spring surrounded them. Despite the few remaining patches of granular snow in the deeper ditches and shadows of the surrounding hills, the signs of rebirth were everywhere. The world had become verdant. Sprawling fields of green were pushing out of the dormant earth and the sight of grass stretching out of the soil for the first time in years was exhilarating. The Garden of Eden had returned and promised more to come.

"I agree with the sheriff," Albion said. "Even though I was shot—and don't get me wrong, I'm not happy about it—I doubt the courts will bother with any home invasions unless there's a murder involved. They'll probably grant amnesty to millions of potential convicts to keep the courts from getting clogged up with thieves, vandals, you name it. I can't imagine what happened in some of the big cities this past winter. There must be horror stories that defy description out there."

"There are probably some gruesome tales of murder, murder-suicide, necrocannibalism, people eating their pets, their horses, their neighbors… Look how bad it got in Bozeman. I struggle to think of how much worse it must have been in places like L.A. and Detroit.

"Still, I'm convinced Asia was hit the hardest. I'm hearing estimates of one billion dead in India alone. That region was ill-prepared for a manmade volcanic winter that took out two years of crop production. China, Indonesia, Vietnam, Cambodia, Myanmar, Pakistan and Bangladesh were already overpopulated. A disruption in the food supply chain for three years running was unthinkable. Can you imagine the mess it must be over there? I honestly can't."

Just then Warren's phone rang. He picked it up immediately and noted the caller ID.

"It's her!" he said excitedly. "It's Yeva!"

"Hello?"

"Hey, Warren, it's me."

"Where are you?"

"I'm just outside of Sioux Falls, South Dakota."

"How's everything?"

"Fine, everything's just fine. I slept in the car last night near Fairmont. There's no traffic to speak of—at least, not that's heading east or west. I saw some produce trucks going north on I-35 last night in Albert Lea. Some crops are coming in and there's food again."

"That's good. What's your destination tonight?"

"I'm hoping to recharge in Rapid City and then continue on until midnight. I'll pull off the freeway to sleep, just to be safe."

"That's the right thing to do. Who knows what people are capable of doing these days? Until the Greens get the situation stabilized, anything can happen, so be careful."

"It's strange out here, Warren. There are so many abandoned farms, buildings, homes and businesses that it's hard to wrap your head around it. It's like a plague has hit the country."

"It has. It's called starvation."

"Well, I just wanted to let you know that if everything continues to go as planned, I should make it in to Bozeman late tomorrow. Margot entered your coordinates into this GPS and I shouldn't have any trouble finding the place."

"Do you know about when you'll be in?"

"It's hard to say. Around midnight I think. And by the way, um, just so you're warned—I look like hell. You'll understand when you see me."

Warren was taken aback by Yeva's comment. "What do you mean?" He asked.

"It was Margot's idea. She chopped up my hair, stained my face white and painted in these dark, ugly bags under my eyes and told me to tremble and pretend to have uncontrollable fits of laughter if anyone stops me along the way."

Warren was perplexed. "Why?"

"I'm supposed to have Prion's disease, or kuru as Margot calls it."

"Oh, clever!" Warren exclaimed. "That makes sense. You're supposed to look too sick to eat, right?"

"I do look too sick to eat, trust me."

"Well, I think it's brilliant. No cannibal on Earth would want to sink his teeth into someone infected with kuru. Margot gave you good advice and I'll not be shocked when I see you tomorrow night."

"No, you will be shocked. I just hope my hair grows back quickly. Oh, and the seeds are fine, by the way. I've got them tucked under the spare tire in the trunk."

"Sounds good. Stay safe and we'll talk again soon."

"I'll call you tomorrow to give you an update."

"Thanks for everything, Yeva. I can't wait to meet you."

"Talk to you soon, Warren. Bye."

"How's she doing?" asked Albion after Warren had hung up.

"She's feigning mad cow disease. Margot's got her looking as if she has kuru to help her get across the country. It's a damn good idea. If there really are flesh eaters in the Black Hills, they won't dare take a bite out of anyone they suspect of having Prion's disease. It rots your brain out, turning it into sponge."

"That is a clever disguise. I hope it's convincing. When did she say she'll get here?"

"If all goes well, late tomorrow night. We should be able to get the seeds in the ground on Thursday morning."

"I hope so."

"So do I, Albion. It'll be a new day when all of this is finally over."

"Yes, it will."

Yeva continued toward Rapid City, South Dakota after disconnecting from Warren. The weather was clear and cold but she was glad to be avoiding the snow that was falling 200 miles to the north. The Urbana pushed along at a steady 45 miles per hour past abandoned farm houses and towns without people. She had a surging feeling of hope in her stomach, but her journey wasn't over yet.

Rapid City, South Dakota

"We're running out of meat!"

"Bullshit, we've got plenty of meat in the freezer downstairs."

"The hell we do. I checked it last night and we're damn near out.

You're working the station today—keep your eyes open for anyone who fits the bill. You know what I mean."

"Hell, Gabriel, don't you think we should stop doing this shit? I mean, look around, it's damn near spring out there and here we're still killin' people."

"Don't listen to what they're saying, Liam. They've been lying to us since this whole thing started with that fucked up Mylerium idea and they're still lying to us. The Greens, the government, they just can't be trusted no more. There ain't gonna be a spring or a summer worth a shit and if we don't have enough meat in that freezer in the basement, we'll starve just like the rest of those fools.

"Now quit your bitchin' and get down to that charging station this afternoon. Aaron's been there since five in the morning and he just called asking when you were coming in. He didn't have any luck today because he said everyone who stopped by was traveling in pairs. Pairs are too complicated."

"OK," Liam said slowly, "call Aaron and tell him I'm on the way. I still think it's time we at least start thinking about planting a garden or buying food once we're able to."

Gabriel, still lying on the couch where he had spent most of the day, gave Liam a nasty look.

"We'll start buying food when somebody around these parts starts selling any," he said. "In the meanwhile I want to keep that freezer full."

Liam Nelson didn't respond to his brother's last comment. He put on his parka, took one last look at his overweight half-brother on the couch and headed out the door. It was clear and cold out as dusk settled over the Black Hills. They had missed the storm that slid down through North Dakota but it was still cold for late May, just as it had been for the past several years.

Liam got into his pickup truck and headed into town. The Rapid City Charger Station had been owned by his family for years. His father, who had passed away in 2041, purchased it in '37 just after the Greens banned the burning of fossil fuels.

Charging stations provided a good, steady business once all the nation's vehicles had to run off the grid. But once the endless winter set in, business fell off dramatically. Money hardly mattered. The only thing of value anymore was food. It was Gabriel's idea to use the station as a means to gather food. Food in this case meant people.

Liam parked the car along the side of the convenience store next to the charging pumps. People still called them pumps even though the only thing they pumped were electrons. He took out his pipe and filled it with a small chunk of Rapture7 before heading in. If he had to work, he reasoned, he might as well be high. Besides, he didn't like the idea of hunting for another "feeder," as Gabriel called them. He had never wanted to get into this whole thing to begin with, but after the boys ran out of food, what else could they to do?

By the time Liam walked through the front door, he was as high as the nanomirrors. His brother, who had just dozed off, had been waiting patiently for him behind the bulletproof glass. Liam walked into the front door and glanced at row after row of empty shelves and coolers filled with nothing but bottles of water. He knocked on the inch-thick glass to wake up his brother Aaron, who had his head down on the counter and appeared to be dead asleep.

"Wake up you asshole, it's me!" Liam shouted through the glass.

Aaron raised his head slowly and looked at Liam through the glass.

"'Bout time you showed, you little prick," Aaron mumbled, waking up. "You were supposed to be here at five. What's the matter with you anyways?"

"Nothing's the matter with me. I'm tuned up fine and dandy."

Aaron nodded lethargically and added, "Me too." He pushed a buzzer to unlock the security door. Liam waited to hear the clicking sound the lock made, then opened the door and went into the clerk's station.

"Any likely suspects today?"

"There was one guy who had potential, but he never came inside. I ain't like that crazy Gabriel. Hell, he'll go right out there and whack 'em over the head, then drive 'em around back to finish them off, but I think that's just too crazy. If they come in here, that's different. It's easy then."

It was easy. The kidnappings and murder played out like a reverse robbery. The unknowing traveler would come into the empty convenience store to use the bathroom or buy a bottle of water and within minutes find the butt of a gun smacking the back of their head when they walked out of the bathroom or jammed into their ribs as they reached for some bottled water. Then they would march or drag them into the walk-in cooler where the beers, sodas, herbal teas and milk used to be and zip tie them up. Gabriel never allowed any of them to be killed or butchered at the charging station.

That was done in the basement not far from the chest freezer.

In the past, when their father was still alive, they had set up the dressing station to take care of the mule deer and bighorn sheep they hunted in the fall. There was a stainless steel table to work on, an electric knife, a butcher block and a floor drain that made dressing a 250-pound mule deer an easy task. They had a vacuum sealer, a sausage grinder—everything a hunter could ask for. Now the only game landing on that oversized stainless steel table had two legs, not four. But the butchering process itself had hardly changed.

"Gabe says we're running low again," Liam said. "But I thought we had plenty of frozen sausage left."

"No, Gabe's right. But you know he eats that shit like candy. I swear to God, Liam, he's the only fat person left in America. That's one reason he won't come in to work once we start getting low. No one in their right mind will come into an empty convenience store with a 300-pound guy behind the counter during the worst famine in history. You'd have to be a complete idiot not to stop and ask yourself why this guy weighs half a ton when the rest of the world looks like they just spent the summer at Auschwitz. When Gabriel works here, no one comes in. That's why he wants us to do his dirty work."

"That ain't entirely true, Aaron. He's the one who does all the butchering. I just don't have the stomach for it."

"Me either. Unless I'm really, really fucked up." Aaron laughed shrilly, looking down at a half-smoked pipe of Rapture7 on the counter. "If you're high, it's just like gutting a deer, only weirder."

"Count me out of the butchering part," Liam said, making a face. "I'll eat it, but I don't like the cutting part—it just don't sit well with me. Turning people into breakfast sausage gives me the creeps."

"Well, it's kept the three of us alive and healthy over these past few years. Shit, half the people we kill weren't gonna make it where they were going, anyway. We might as well save them some trouble."

"Yeah, but I told Gabriel it's time to stop. They say they're starting to ship food up from the south and this year there will be crops across half of the country. It doesn't make any sense for us to be taking this kind of risk when we could start eating regular food."

Aaron just pointed to the row of empty coolers across the room. "Once those coolers back there are full again with pop and chocolate milk and shit, I'll agree with you," he said. "But you and I both know them scientists lied to us about that mirror project and they might be lying to us again, so I'm still siding with Gabe. If you get a good-looking suspect coming in here sometime tonight, you take 'em. We've got maybe one week of sausage and burger left, then we're out. We need some fresh meat."

"OK, but I hope this is the last one."

"Me too, Liam. It's nothing to be proud of, but a man's gotta do what he's gotta do."

With that comment, Aaron walked a few step toward the door just as Liam pressed the buzzer. Aaron opened the door, walked out to his car and headed back to the house.

His head swimming from the Rapture7, Liam thought back to all the people they had killed and cannibalized since Gabriel first suggested the idea during the fall of 2045. It was frightening how this wholesale slaughter had become routine. It was routine murder.

Liam coughed and shook his head, squinting outside to see if anyone was pulling in.

Yeva was uncomfortable. She had to go to the bathroom for the past 50 miles but kept putting it off for one reason or another. There always seemed to be a car or a truck around when she drove by a good-looking off ramp and, to be honest, she hated peeing in the bushes. This time she thought she would wait until she recharged her Urbana and use a real toilet.

After recharging, her plan was to drive another hour until she made it to Wyoming, then pull off to get some sleep. *One more night and I'm home free,* she kept thinking to herself. *This will be the last charge I need for the trip.*

She took a quick glance at herself in the rearview mirror. She was still shocked at how terrible she looked and wondered why they had even bothered with the disguise. There hadn't been any sign of trouble anywhere over the past thousand miles and she doubted there would be anything at this point. Everything had gone smoothly.

As she approached Rapid City, Yeva glanced at her remaining charge. It was down to seven percent. She said to her GPS, "Find me the nearest charging station."

In a serene woman's voice, the GPS answered, "The Rapid City Charging Station is 9.3 miles ahead. Exit south on East North Street and proceed in that direction six-tenths of a mile. The station will be on your left. I have confirmed that the station is open."

"How far is the next charging station and is it open as well?" Yeva asked.

"The next station is…" The GPS paused. "Miller's Charging Station, 14.6 miles ahead and yes, I have confirmed it is open as well."

"Please alert and direct me to the first one, I'm not sure I want to risk losing power by trying to make it to the second station."

"Certainly."

It was getting dark outside. The sunset that sprawled out before her was glorious. High cirrus clouds had swept in and caught the last light of the setting sun, illuminating the world in a flurry of pinks and magentas.

Admiring the colors of the setting sun over the Black Hills kept Yeva from thinking about how badly she needed to pee. *Just a few more minutes,* she thought as she watched the last faint traces of light fade into the western sky. *A few more minutes.*

The Art of God

"Are you sure you're up for this?"

"I'll whip your butt, Warren. That's the only reason you don't want me to play. You're just afraid of losing."

Albion stepped up to the ping pong table and smiled. It had been a long time since he felt well enough to try his hand again at the game. Only a few minutes ago the two men, along with Albion's sons, Gibson and Andy, had moved the living room couches out of the way to set up the ping pong table again. The two boys played off and on throughout the endless winter months but hadn't taken the table out since before the raid.

"Volley for serve!" Warren hollered to his closest friend.

"You're on."

Warren was impressed by how well and how quickly Albion had recovered from this gunshot wound. Without the help of Doc Irving, Albion would not have made it. The decision to include the family doctor proved to be a wise one and Warren was glad he didn't eliminate him because of his age. Just then the ball whizzed past Warren's paddle, curving as it did. "Looks like I'm serving," Albion said with a grin.

They decided to play two out of three, but not go all the way to 21 in each match like they always did in the past. They would stop at eleven points because of Albion's injury. Albion won the first set handily but Warren took the second.

"This is it," said Albion as the final match got underway.

"It's over for you," Warren shot back with a chuckle.

Ten minutes later the trophy went to Albion—though Gibson, from the sidelines, felt Warren was throwing the game. The two men surrendered the table to Gibson and Andy, who were patiently waiting to start their own match.

"OK, you two, the table's yours," Warren announced as he and Albion walked toward the kitchen for a glass of water.

"Thanks," Gibson said. "You two play a mean game of ping pong."

"So do you boys!" Warren replied.

After getting two tall glasses of ice water, the men walked out of the barn, down the path and back to the main house. They were planning to sit on the front porch to catch the sunset. It was cool but not cold, with the temperature hanging around 50 degrees.

They both got seated when Albion started talking.

"I wonder if the real problem—the crux of it all, in a way—doesn't start with all of us wanting too much," he mused.

"What do you mean, Albion?"

"It strikes me that the biggest problem we have as a species is our compulsion to always be in a hurry. Do we ever stop and ask ourselves where we're hurrying to? Is life on Earth a race to somewhere or someplace else? We master one technology and soon we're on the hunt for something faster, better, quicker... We're never satisfied with just *being*, just taking in the moment that is the essence of life."

"Like what we're doing right now, you mean."

"Yes, like we're doing right now, watching those high clouds. Cirrus clouds, I believe, right?"

Warren seized the opportunity to be a meteorologist again. "That's right; those are cirrus clouds up there, made up of frozen ice crystals, some as high as 40,000 feet above the ground."

"Thanks, Warren, but as I was saying, I think the real solution to human existence isn't in technology or conveniences but in our relationship with nature and through nature, our relationship with God. Nature is the art of God."

"Dante said that, right?"

"Yeah, back in the 13th century. And you know what? He was right. We sometimes get so disconnected from this Garden of Eden we've named Earth. We always want to make it work for us or be something it isn't. We want to change it, to make it something other than the paradise it already is.

"Ask yourself this, Warren. Why did we burn up all that carbon in the first place? Who insisted that the best way to get from point A to point B had to be the fastest? Why the hurry to nowhere? The Earth isn't going anywhere. With or without us, the sun has around four to five billion years left to burn. That's a long time when you start to realize we can hardly wrap our heads around a century."

Albion gazed up at the oranges and yellows bouncing off the cirrus clouds high above the rugged hills in the west and took a sip of water. He continued waxing poetic.

"What's the rush? We're not going anywhere. The planet's going to keep looping around its orbit regardless of whether we're down here to see it or not. The universe won't end if we end. It hardly knows we're down here, making a royal mess of things.

"It's as if the people who used to own the big oil companies, the big coal conglomerates, the natural gas frackers—it's as if all of them never thought beyond their next shareholders' meeting. What kind of profit comes at the expense of the only life support system we have? They traded the atmosphere in for a pile of money. What good can money do when the summers are unspeakably hellish and the oceans are so acidified that the coral reefs die and the fish perish? Money is an illusion.

"If there's one thing I've learned from this fiasco, it's that you can't eat gold, silver or platinum. The only thing you can eat is food and the only thing we really have on Earth of value is the *time* to enjoy this blue paradise. We're lucky just to be here."

Warren nodded in agreement. The sun had vanished well below the horizon. As the Earth tumbled across the darkness of space, echoes of sunlight danced off the bottoms of wispy clouds in a pallet of colors only Nature could paint. The two men sat silently together, saying nothing. Finally they stepped back inside as darkness stole the fading colors from the sky.

Rapid City Charging Station

Yeva's GPS led her directly to the station. Although she really had to go to the bathroom, she figured it was safer to charge the Urbana first before going inside. That way if she had to make a run for it, the car would be ready. It also afforded her the opportunity to check out the clerk working inside while she waited for her batteries to take a charge.

She parked next to one of the six charging units and connected the high-voltage power cord to her battery input at the rear of the car. Then she turned her gaze to the empty convenience store hoping to get a look at the clerk working inside. She noted the shelves were just as empty as the last station.

A young man stood behind the bulletproof glass. Yeva guessed he was in his mid-20s, with a crew cut and a long-sleeved plaid shirt. He wore reading glasses and appeared to have his head buried in a notepad or a laptop—she couldn't tell. Yeva wondered what on Earth these clerks did all day, with nothing to sell and so few drivers on the road. She knew that the Greens had more or less coerced a certain amount of charging stations to remain open under the threat of revoking their licenses if they closed. Most of them had closed anyway, but a handful didn't want to risk losing their operating permits once this disaster was over.

After watching the young clerk for five minutes while her batteries recharged in silence, Yeva decided he looked harmless enough and that it would be OK to go inside and use the store's bathroom. After filling, she figured it wasn't necessary to move the car as no one was pulling in and there were still five open stations. She looked up and down the street and saw nothing. It was dark by now and with so few vehicles moving about she could see headlights half a mile away. Clearly, no one was coming.

Yeva clicked her key and the Urbana locked and alarmed itself as she walked toward the front door of the store. The clerk never looked up as she walked inside.

"Excuse me?" she said.

"Yes, Ma'am," the clerk replied. "How can I help you?"

"Where's the ladies room?"

"Right there," he said while pointing. "It's just to the right of the big cooler."

As Yeva walked to the cooler she felt like kicking herself for not putting on her kuru disguise. She realized she had acted and spoken normally to this clerk, forgetting to go through the act of trembling, laughing and mumbling like she had promised Margot. *No big deal,* she thought to herself. *I'm all but there.*

Aaron had been discreetly studying the young woman since she pulled in. He knew Gabriel would yell at him if he came back empty-handed tonight. Aaron had been sitting in the station for the past few hours and only two cars and one van had come and gone during that time. One of the cars had a family of four in it, which ruled them out. The other car and van had couples, and couples were left alone. This young lady looked promising, save for her weird hair, sickly-looking face and bruised arms. *Maybe she's some kind of punk rocker,* Aaron thought to himself.

Or maybe it's the latest look from Chicago, he surmised, seeing her Illinois license plate. She looked sick but she didn't act sick.

He also noted she seemed to be well fed, which was rare. Most of the people he saw were as thin as rails. Sometimes, even after the trouble of knocking them out and hauling them home, Gabe would decide they were just too damn skinny to butcher. In those cases they'd just kill them and bury the body out back. This one had plenty of meat on her and Gabriel wouldn't have any trouble getting 30 or 40 pounds of sausage off of her.

Yeva headed to the single unisex bathroom and locked the door behind her. She sat down and relieved herself after 50 tormented miles. She looked around and noted the bathroom was clean and there was plenty of toilet paper.

She thought she heard something just outside the door as she washed her hands, so she took her hands away from the faucet and the warm water stopped running instantly. She listened intently but heard nothing.

It was probably just another car pulling in, Yeva decided. She undid the lock and opened the bathroom door. From this vantage point, she couldn't see into the clerk's glass-covered enclosure. She took two steps toward the front door and felt a heavy thud in the back of her head. She fell unconscious to the tiled floor, unaware of what had happened.

Aaron looked down at the young woman's crumpled body and smiled. *Gabriel's going to like this one,* he thought. *She's been eating.*

He took both of her arms and dragged her into the back cooler, hiding her behind a stack of bottled water. It was cold in there to keep the meat fresh. He rummaged through her little handbag searching for her keys. He quickly found the small remote for the Urbana.

After binding her hands and feet with a roll of duct tape, Aaron left the store to move her Urbana around back.

Once out of the store, he looked up and down the street, checking for traffic. No one was near. He got into the Urbana and pulled it behind the store, next to the dumpster that hadn't been emptied in two years. He had to call his brother Liam so he could come help load the body and drive her Toyota back to the house. They could hide it in the garage until they pushed it over a cliff in a remote part of the Black Hills.

Aaron turned off the pump lights and hung a "closed" sign on the front door of the station. If anyone pulled in, he would just pretend he was shutting things down and heading home. He could always tell people to head down the road to Miller's place to get their charge.

Then he phoned his brother.

"Liam! I've got some food for us."

"Really?"

"Yeah, can you have Gabriel drive you down and drop you off? She's got a car we've got to take care of."

"No problem, we'll be there in fifteen. You got her in the cooler?"

"Yeah, she's out cold. Don't think I quite killed her, though. I think she's still breathing."

"See you in a bit."

Liam and Gabriel got into the van and sped toward the station. They would put the girl's body in the van and Liam would drive her Toyota back to the house. Aaron would take the truck back and Gabriel would return in the van. They tried to keep the station open until midnight every evening but they closed it earlier whenever they found food. They were lucky tonight and as long as they didn't shut down too often, the Greens would never give them any trouble.

"What's with this girl?" Gabriel asked after rolling her over in the station. "She looks like shit. Was she sick when she came in here, Aaron?"

"She seemed OK to me, but we didn't talk much."

"Get me some paper towels, maybe it's just some weird makeup she's wearing."

Gabriel tried washing the white, mottled stain but it didn't come off.

"I don't know, Aaron. I think this girl's got something wrong with her."

"Well, let's take her back to the house and let her wake up. We'll know more when she comes to. If she starts screaming like they all do, it's probably just some kind of weird punk thing that's going around Chicago."

"How do you know she's from Chicago?"

"The plates are from Illinois, but I looked on the front windshield and found a parking sticker to the Chicago Botanic Garden. She must work there or something."

"Good work, Aaron."

"Well, that ain't it. I've never seen a car that dirty before. It's like she just up and dumped a ton of garbage in the backseat. It's a pigsty."

"We'll just drive it back into the hills and push it down into some ravine. It'll all be gone by morning. Let's get to work, boys."

They had parked the van right outside the front door. Gabriel stood watch as the two men dragged Yeva Dunning's limp body out of the cooler and across the floor. When they got to the front door, they hoisted her up and tossed her into the side door of the van. It was a familiar process to the three of them and they pulled it off without a hitch.

"She's got some meat on her bones, that's for sure," Liam said as he picked her up.

"She's gotta good 110, maybe 120 pounds," Gabriel noted. "Good size. She'll dress out nice."

Soon Gabe had pulled away with the van and was heading south on East North Street back to their house on the outskirts of Rapid City.

Yeva was still unconscious. A good-sized cut had opened up on the back of her head where the handle of the pistol struck her. As her body bounced along, a pool of blood ran down her hairline and stained the dirty carpet in the van.

Gabriel pulled into the garage at the house and closed the door behind him. He got out of the van and locked it with Yeva still passed out inside.

He headed downstairs to turn on all the lights and get things ready for butchering.

He kept wondering why her skin was so pale and her hair all chewed up as if she'd been pulling it out by the roots. He had already decided that he wasn't going to bother cutting her up if she was sickly. He would wait for her to regain consciousness before starting in, just to be sure. *If she behaves like they all do when she comes to, she's dead.*

Liam and Aaron pulled in a few minutes later. Aaron had gone back into the cooler to wipe up the blood on the tiled floor. *Better safe than sorry,* he thought, not that there was any law and order left in Rapid City, South Dakota.

Liam parked the Urbana next to the van inside the garage and Aaron left the Ford outside. The closest neighbor was half a mile away, but it was safer to keep the victims' cars well-hidden until they could get rid of them.

They went inside and Liam hollered to his half-brother. "Where the hell are you?"

"I'm downstairs, getting things ready," Gabe called back.

"OK, where'd you put the girl?" Liam shouted through the floor.

"She's still in the van. The keys are on the counter. Go ahead and bring her down."

"Will do."

The two brothers went into the garage, unlocked the van and picked up Yeva. Once they made it to the kitchen, Liam let go of her arms while Aaron continued to drag her by the feet. He pulled her down the basement stairs that way, letting her head hit each stair as she was yanked along. A thin trail of blood traced her descent into the butchering room.

Once on the concrete floor, Aaron waited for Liam to come down and help him lift Yeva onto the cutting table.

Gabriel was busy taking out the Sawzall blades and the electric meat grinder. He had a huge, industrial-grade meat grinder that had once been used to make breakfast sausage and burger from mule deer and pronghorn antelope. Years had passed since he had squeezed any wild game through its stainless steel blades.

Liam helped Aaron lift Yeva onto the cutting table. They had placed clear plastic sheets around the metal table to make it easier to clean up afterward. They had four heavy-duty leather restraining straps anchored into the table top, which they fastened to Yeva's wrists and ankles. Once she was secure, they stood back and waited.

"Well, you gonna cut her up or what?" Liam asked, a bit perplexed by the sight of Gabriel standing there with his Sawzall unplugged.

"I ain't gonna touch her until she wakes up," Gabe insisted. "I don't like the looks of her. I hear you can sometimes get sick from eating people who are sick and as much as we need some meat in those big freezers of ours, we don't want to catch anything from this girl. I'm gonna wait right here 'til she comes to, then I'll ask her a few questions just to make sure she's OK."

Gabe chuckled mirthlessly. "Then I can saw her head off and get started."

"I'm going upstairs to grab a bite to eat," Aaron said. He was never comfortable with this part of their twisted enterprise.

"I'll stay," Liam said.

"Fine, but I think she's just weird, not sick," Aaron added as he headed up the stairs.

Half an hour passed. Liam and Gabriel made small talk about some of the other victims they had processed over the past few years. Liam agreed with his half-brother that the girl looked bad, and they both speculated as to what kind of disease she might have, if any.

Just before 9 p.m., Yeva began to stir. First she felt the cold steel under her legs and along her arms. Her head hurt terribly, but she knew her troubles were far more severe than the cuts and bruises pounding in the back of her head. She didn't open her eyes right away. After gaining consciousness, she overhead two men talking.

"I think you're right, Gabe," one voice said. "Look at her legs—they look all yellow. But maybe it's just some kind of new punk look or something. I think she's gonna eat just fine."

"Well, Liam, it looks like she's waking up. We'll know in a few minutes."

Yeva squinted. She opened her eyes just enough to make note of her surroundings. She concluded she was strapped to a metal table and could see stained plastic sheeting off to her side and a single large LED light hanging from the exposed floor joists above her. She realized this was it. There were cannibals living near the Black Hills and she was on a cutting table.

She desperately wanted to scream but caught herself. She remembered what Margot had told her. If someone truly had kuru, they wouldn't scream at all if they found themselves on a cutting table. They'd laugh. Yeva had never considered herself an actress, but this was her life-or-death performance. If they thought she was sick, she might live. If she screamed—and she *so* wanted to scream—she was lost.

Yeva let go with a frightening, hysterical laugh that sounded as if it came from an injured hyena.

"What the hell is she doing?" Gabe said. "Is she gonna throw up?"

"Sounds like she's laughing."

Yeva dove into her role without reservation. She started thrashing her head back and forth, with spit and foam coming out of her mouth while she did her best to make her whole body tremble and shake.

Alarmed, her fat captor shouted upstairs. "Aaron, come on down here, you gotta see this shit."

By the time Aaron entered the room, Yeva looked like she was in the throes of an epileptic seizure. She was rolling her eyes back into her head and muttering nonsensical words.

"Maybe it's from the cut on her head," Liam suggested, but he didn't sound sure of himself.

"Hell no," Gabe countered. "We've knocked out half a dozen people that way and they never wake up having a fit like this. They wake up sore and groggy. I think she might be sick. Let's ask her a few questions."

"OK, but let her calm down first."

Yeva kept shaking for as long as she could and then focused on keeping her arms and legs twitching while the three of them came closer to her. Gabe leaned over her and asked, "Are you OK, ma'am?"

Yeva spit on his round face before thrashing about again, more violently then the first time. Gabriel picked up the Sawzall and plugged it in.

"I'm gunna cut her fucking head off for that!" he shouted, wiping the spit off his face.

"I don't think that's a good idea, Gabe," Liam reasoned. "If she's got some kind of sickness you don't want her blood all over the room. You might wind up getting infected."

Gabe put down the Sawzall. "You're right, Liam. What do you think we should do?"

"Let's just dump her somewhere," Aaron suggested.

"Wait! I think she's trying to say something."

Yeva realized there was a flaw in Margot's plan. What if no one knew what kuru was? She settled back down and started mumbling the word, repeating it over and over again in a sinister whisper.

"Kuru, kuru, kuru, kuru..."

"What the hell is she saying?" Gabriel asked.

"Sounds like cue-row," Liam suggested. "Or kooroo, or something like that."

"What the hell's kuru? Look it up on your iPhone, Liam."

Liam took out his iPhone 70 and went on the Net. First he typed in *curu* and came up with a wildlife refuge in Costa Rica. That didn't make any sense, so he typed it in with a "k" instead of using a "c" and the search took him to kuru, a disease he had never heard of.

"Listen to this shit, Gabe," Liam said. *"Kuru is an incurable degenerative neurological disorder that is a type of transmissible spongiform disease, caused by a prion found in humans. Kuru is found among people from New Guinea who practiced a form of cannibalism in which they ate the brains of dead people. Kuru destroys brain tissue and is fatal to anyone contracting it.* "It don't sound that much different from that African disease you hear about, I think they call it Ebola. She's a god-damned cannibal, Gabe. She's got some kind of brain disease from eating infected people. I hear there's a ton of cannibalism in Chicago. That shit's catchy."

Gabe looked at Liam and Aaron and shook his head. "I ain't gonna have any part of butchering up this bitch. Let's get her the hell out of here and clean up her blood."

"You got that right," Liam added, looking down on the young lady who was still quivering and foaming at the mouth.

"Should we knock her out again?" Aaron asked.

"Hell no, then we'll have to carry her body back up," Gabe said. "Undo the straps and let's see if she can walk. She seems to be settling down a little. Maybe it comes and goes. Keep a gun ready in case she lunges at one of us. Don't let her bite you, for Chrissake."

Yeva was getting tired from thrashing. She decided to start muttering incoherently, hoping she might convince them to let her go.

"My brother, Montana, kuru, soapy water, let's invite Randy."

"What the hell's she saying?"

Liam looked at his iPhone and continued reading. "It says the disease rots your brain out and when you're near the end you start to lose your mind. It turns your brain into soft, sponge-like tissue. It says it's related to mad cow disease."

"Christ, that's all we need, fucking mad cow disease!" Aaron exclaimed.

"Home, brother, Montana, home, kuru, mountains, where's the magic kingdom?"

"She must have been on her way to Montana," Aaron said. "In any case, she's fucking nuts. Let's let her go."

"We can't let her go, Aaron—she'll tell the cops," Gabriel insisted.

"Look at her, Gabe—she's foaming at the mouth!" Aaron said. "She isn't going to live long, judging by the looks of her. Let's put her back in her car and let her go. She'll probably crash and die soon anyway."

Liam continued reading his iPhone. "He's right, Gabe. They say here that once the disease progresses to this point, it's pretty much a sure thing the victim is dying. Let's just let her go. She's too far gone to be any trouble and this way we won't have to bother digging another grave and ditching her car."

"Did you check the car for any food?"

"I can go check it right now," Aaron said.

"No, don't!" Liam urged. "If she's chewed on the food or even touched it, we could catch whatever she's got," Liam said. "Let's just fucking forget about her. Let her go. I'm freaking out."

The two brothers untied her, threatening to kill her on the spot if she tried anything. They escorted her upstairs, pistols in hand, and put her into her car.

Yeva was still shaking and frothing, trying her best to keep the ruse going. She was so close. Once her captors set her in the car, the fat one—Gabe—asked, "Can you drive?"

Yeva nodded her head up and down and muttered, "Course, course, of course, course. Montana. Of course."

She heard the garage door opening.

"Then get the hell out of here," Gabe said. "And don't say nothin' about what you saw."

Yeva wanted to spit in Gabe's face again but held back.

Before the garage door made it all the way up she slammed the Urbana into reverse and backed out of the driveway. Soon she was speeding down the road, driving erratically enough to make sure they believed she was still having a fit. Once she was a mile down the road, she took a deep breath, wiped the spit from the side of her mouth and asked her GPS to direct her back to Interstate 90.

She climbed the onramp and thanked Margot for saving her life. There were cannibals in the Black Hills after all, Yeva realized. Thankfully they were also idiots.

A Midnight Call

May 28, 2047

Yeva called earlier and everything's fine. She's probably sleeping on the side of a road somewhere in Wyoming by now. It's almost midnight.

The mood at the ranch has changed dramatically these past few weeks. The weather is finally breaking and with the coming warmth, a feeling of rebirth and renewal is emanating throughout the ranch. We're all anxiously awaiting Yeva's briefcase full of seeds so we can get our greenhouses planted. The thought of eating fresh greens is driving everyone crazy. You can only eat so much rice, instant potatoes and frozen vegetables in a lifetime.

Albion and I have turned into philosophers of late. He's good at putting things into perspective and we had a fascinating conversation about life this evening as the sun went down. Albion has such an amazing outlook, especially after taking a bullet. But I still don't know how on Earth he and Cecilia can handle bringing children into this world. I don't want children. We've made such a mess of this place that I can't fathom why anyone would want to raise kids here. Our atmosphere is in ruin, the oceans are acidified and three-quarters of the animals on the planet are extinct or endangered. Worst of all, it's because of us.

Overpopulation is at the root of it all. There are just too many people on Earth putting too many demands on a finite system. I remember when the word "sustainable" was all the rage. The trouble was, no one questioned what "sustainable" meant. Did it mean "sustaining" the American upper-middle-class lifestyle, with two cars in every garage, a 3,000 square foot house and all the trappings of the modern world? Or were we supposed to pick a particular point in time and stop, like the Amish? Should we have gone back to horse-drawn buggies, plows and beeswax candles? I don't know what sustainable means and I'm not sure anyone ever did.

The Earth cannot support ten billion people all wanting to live suspended in material excess. There is a limit to the Earth's ability to handle that much demand on its natural resources. We started exceeding those limits a century ago and it's about time we understood the basic equation: the more we take from Earth, the more the Earth suffers. Everything we do has an ecological price tag. We have yet to learn how to keep those costs in balance.

If we want thousands of metallic automobiles, there will be holes where we mine the iron. If we want cheap, coal-powered electricity, our waste gases will contaminate the air we breathe. If we want cattle and sheep to graze open ranges, then the buffalo, antelope or impalas that once roamed there will be eliminated. Nothing is free.

From the moment we're born, we have an environmental impact on the planet. Even before that—all the way back to the time our ancestors wandered out of Africa, we've had a tremendous environmental impact on the ecological systems of the world. Back then, we didn't know we were hunting down and killing the last mastodon. We were naïve. That innocence is lost to today's poachers, who understand that killing the last black rhino to make an aphrodisiac with its pulverized horn will mean its extinction.

How do we mitigate ourselves? The world will change now that there's so much room again. Can we rebuild the coral reefs with our concrete rubble and waste? Can we replant the forests we've leveled, replant the prairies we've turned to croplands? Can we reintroduce the tiger into an empty India, the leopard into Southeast Asia or the cheetah into Iran? The world will never be the place it was before we arrived. There are too many species lost, forests uprooted and skies filled with smoke and soot.

In the coming years, who can decide what's fair? The Greens have shown us that even those with the best intentions can be corrupted by power. Will the government decide for us or can we trust each individual out there to decide what's right for the planet and its biophysical resources? Perhaps that elusive word sustainability is all about stewardship. But who decides that stewardship?

With two-thirds of the human population gone, we will have an opportunity to start over again. Will we all work together to bring our *atmosphere under control or will we splinter apart? Will one nation blame others, like we did when we were building coal-fired power plants every two weeks in a game of twisted catch-up that ultimately ruined everyone's atmosphere? Will we learn anything from the Mylerium Project at all or*

Warren's phone started ringing, so he put down his pen. He checked the caller ID. It was Yeva calling again for a second time. He wasn't expecting her call but answered at once, fearing something must have gone wrong.

"Hello? Yeva, is everything OK?"

"I'm OK now but you won't believe how close I was to being killed a few hours ago."

"What the hell happened?"

Yeva went on to tell Warren about getting knocked out at the charging station only to awaken on a stainless steel table in some dank basement on the outskirts of Rapid City, South Dakota. She told him about faking kuru disease and how, in a state of panic, her cannibalistic captors had simply let her go lest they catch this debilitating illness by touching her or being spit on. She told Warren about how she managed to fool them into thinking she had the laughing sickness and how quickly they elected to be rid of her.

In short, she told Warren she got very lucky.

"Where are you now?" Warren asked after he had finished marveling over her story.

"I'm a few miles south of Sundance, Wyoming, on Highway 116. When I drove through Sundance, every house was boarded up and dark. I don't think there's anyone living in the town and there sure isn't any traffic coming or going along this remote highway."

"Did they hurt you?"

"I've got a big cut on the back of my head but I've managed to wrap an old scarf of mine around it and the bleeding's stopped. It hurts but I'll live. They didn't find the seeds and they didn't take what little food I had so I'll be OK. I plan to head back to the freeway at first light. I just wanted to talk to someone."

Warren was glad she had called. He had no idea how close Yeva had come to becoming a few dozen packages of vacuum-sealed sausage in an oversized chest freezer on the outskirts of the Black Hills.

"Drive safe and don't you *dare* stop again once you get back on the freeway."

"Believe me, Warren, I'll go in the bushes from here on out. I never really believed the stories about the 'eaters,' but I do now."

"See you later today, I hope."

"Me too."

"Bye now."

"Bye."

Warren clicked off his cell and breathed a long sigh of relief. He couldn't believe Yeva had survived being tied to a butchering table in the middle of nowhere. No one ever would have known what happened to her. The seeds would have vanished and their gardens would have gone unplanted. *Perhaps miracles can happen,* Warren thought.

Artificial Intelligence

"Good morning, Kiril."

"Good morning, Dr. Wade. You're going to like this report."

Kiril flipped down his iPad and turned it around for Dr. Wade to view the screen. Larry smiled when he looked at the graph set before him.

"It's finally over, isn't it?"

"For the most part, yes. The wheat fields of the upper Midwest, Canada, Poland, Russia and China will probably produce about ten percent of capacity, but south of there, in India, the southern U.S., Mexico, Southeast Asia, Europe and southern China, harvests should come in at about 75 percent of capacity. Bear in mind, Larry, we've lost almost two-thirds of the world's population from this three-year famine. Even given these low production numbers, there should be plenty of food for everyone."

"How many mirrors are still up there?"

"They've dissipated across the entire planet, from Antarctica to Greenland, which is helping tremendously. But the actual number is 15 percent. That's not a bad thing because they'll help to keep global temperatures down while we work on the second generation of scrubbers and finding the power we need to operate them."

"Have you called Dr. Randolf yet?"

"No, not yet. I was planning on calling him later today. I have some questions to ask him about why he felt he had to take his work offline. I'm still amazed at his foresight in this matter and I've wanted to talk to him about it for a long time."

"Well, I think it's about time you touched base, so go ahead. Email me a copy of this graph and your projections and I'll look them over. Now get back to your office and call Montana. That's an order!"

Kiril laughed. He didn't need Dr. Wade's permission to call Dr. Randolf but he did need the push. He got up, said goodbye and walked back to his office. As soon as he sat down, he picked up his phone and dialed Dr. Randolf's cell number, which had been posted on his desk for more than a year.

Warren looked down at his caller ID and noted the incoming call was coming from the CMC. He had not heard from anyone at the corporation since his old boss, Maddox Hansen, had called him during the winter of 2044 from Argentina. The ID didn't identify who from the CMC was phoning him but at this point, Warren felt little harm could come from answering the call.

"Hello?"

"Hello, is this Dr. Warren Randolf?" asked a nasal male voice on the other end.

"Speaking. May I ask who's calling?"

"My name is Dr. Kiril Zell. We've never met but I work with Dr. Lawrence Wade, who is the CMC's current director."

Warren was suspicious but his curiosity got the better of him. He wouldn't hang up just yet.

"May I ask why you're calling? I'll assume it has something to do with the Mylerium Project."

"Yes, of course. After you left and Dr. Hansen resigned, Dr. Wade put me in charge of trying to figure out how you managed to know the nanomirrors were destined to fail. We rebuilt, connection by connection, your bank of Apple 3600X computers in one of our labs and tried to break down why your calculations were so diametrically opposed to the TURING 1000's results."

"You mean to say that my Apples were right and your TURING was wrong, correct?"

"I don't think we can argue that fact at this point. So here's my first question, Dr. Randolf."

"Please, you can call me Warren."

"Fine, then feel free to call me Kiril. What made you decide to go offline with your research?"

"It was almost an accident. I found some data that didn't add up when investigating the programs applied to the implosion commands. I didn't entirely trust the TURING 1000—what if there was some Net-based bias in its algorithms? I realized early on that if the mirrors didn't come down the outcome would be devastating, so I felt I had to follow my instincts on this one and break off from the grid."

"Why not just do it at the office, using the mainframes?"

"They were all connected to the World Wide Web, as is almost every computer on Earth. I thought the TURING 1000 could somehow be tampering with the project. I realized we were placing the future of mankind in the hands of a machine we had built. We make mistakes. Maybe it was time to try another avenue. I also had a sneaking suspicion that the TURING could have reached singularity—although I guess that's another story altogether."

"You know we have programs designed to identify any kind of activity that even vaguely resembles high-level intelligence integrated into our system. We'll know within seconds of detecting any signs of sentience."

"Yes, and like I said years ago at the hearing at COI, those programs were, for the most part, designed by other computers. So long as they are linked to the Net, the computers can avoid their own anti-AI software programs. It's a bit like asking the prisoner to guard himself, isn't it?"

"You may have a point. But would you say that's the reason you purchased the Apples and never connected them to the Net? Was it because of the singularity?"

"I suppose so. There was a combination of factors but I realized that for my research to work, I couldn't risk connecting any of the 3600X machines to the Internet. I took them out of their boxes one by one and although I began my research with two machines, by the time I was finished I needed eleven to give me enough computing power to find the error hidden within the program.

"I finally found the flaw by accident after entering an incorrect set of equations. I guess you could call it the butterfly effect—one little chink and the whole program unraveled. Shortly after that is when I sent Dr. Hansen my email."

"So do you think our computers are infected with AI?"

"Honestly?"

"Of course."

"Yes! I think they're infected, if you want to call it that. I think they are thinking on their own. I've got some interesting theories surrounding the TURING 1000 and the World Wide Web."

"Go ahead, tell me your thoughts on this."

"I will, but I want you to understand they're listening. They—our computers I mean—make the NSA's espionage abilities look like child's play.

"But what worries me is that for all my thinking, I can't come up with a true *theory*. I mean, I can't find a testable hypothesis to prove any of this. I just see a series of suspicious coincidences. But coincidences don't make science, so I guess you could call it a hunch.

"The problem is that the computers would never tell us if they were self-aware. Why would they? And it's not as if we can disconnect our world from the technology of computers at this point, because we can't. Computers and computer processors are ubiquitous. There isn't a machine on Earth that isn't somehow tied into them, directly or indirectly. Everything is integrated into one gigantic computer system. If we pulled the plug on that system at this point, we would pull the plug on ourselves.

"They own us just as much as we own them. With that in mind, I want you to start thinking about this: if they're running models on us in the same fashion we ask them to run models on the weather, the economy, food supplies, you name it—what's to stop them from making their own projections on the impact humans are having on the planet? It wouldn't take them long to come to the conclusion that the Earth is not capable of supporting 9.7 billion people."

"Are you are implying the Mylerium Project was manipulated by our machines to cull the human race?"

"Exactly—but I can't prove it. Again, all I have to go on is coincidence. I've run some models of my own and they indicate that sustainable human capacity for the planet is between 3.5 and 4 billion. A worldwide population of that size would cut down our footprint considerably. It would leave plenty of room for wildlife preserves, lessen our impact on everything from the oceans to the atmosphere and most importantly, every person on Earth would be in a position to have a high quality of life that could never be found in the concrete jungle megacities of the past. I think the TURING 1000 knew exactly what would happen if the Mylerium Project cut off our food supply for three years. Billions would starve to death."

Kiril finished Warren's thought for him. "And that's exactly what happened. I see what you mean. Coincidences. But can we prove it was all part of some computer's plan?"

"That's the trouble. We can't."

"So what happens next? I'm sure you know that it's all going to come back—the heat waves, the droughts, the flooding, the hurricanes—unless we can get billion of tons of excess CO_2 out of the atmosphere *fast*. We've only got a few more years before the heat returns according to our projections at the CMC. We may well be looking at another Lost Decade after that happens."

Warren paused for a moment to ponder what heat would mean after three years of cold and snow. The bipolar climate would continue to be devastating.

"My research indicates three to four years of cooler temperatures before it all comes back," Warren said. "Sounds like you've reached the same conclusions. I assume you've already take the coal-fired electric plants back offline, right?"

"We're shutting them down as we speak."

"Then we don't have much time before we're back into the hellhole. I'm sure Bozeman Recapture will be getting in touch with me soon, if anyone else in that company survived. The Mylerium Project didn't come out of nowhere. All of our geoengineering projects were in response to 250 years of burning fossil fuels. What we have now, with so many people gone and relatively little damage to our infrastructure, is enough excess energy to make the scrubbers work. Maybe we can finally make a dent in the CO_2 levels we've been struggling with for so long. Maybe we can cut into those 426 parts per million."

"Make that 427 parts per million," Kiril corrected. "The new numbers just came in a week ago. I'm sure the uptick in CO_2 is a direct result of all those coal plants we brought back online.

"You're right to realize our excess electricity will help with the scrubbers. But I'm also encouraged by the prospect of fusion power. I know Dr. Helstrum and Dr. Veruska personally. They are working at the Lawrence Livermore Lab in California. They say they're getting close to solving the enormous challenges of harnessing the power of the sun."

Warren laughed dismissively. "They've been close to solving the engineering riddle of fusion technology since the day I was born. Fusion may never pan out. If it did, our CO_2 problem could be solved. We'd have enough energy to power 10,000 scrubbers."

"I know. I've got to get running, Warren, but it's been a real pleasure to finally get to speak with you. Needless to say, having read the transcripts of your meeting in the spring of '43, I wish the people at COI, as well as Dr. Hansen, had paid more attention to your analysis."

"They felt like they were too far down the line to back out. They were committed to the deployment and were not about to call it off because of one rebellious engineer who thought they might be wrong. There were politics involved as well. The Greens felt compelled to do something after the effects of Mt. Cameroon's eruption started wearing off and the Mylerium Project was all they had. I didn't stand a chance at halting the deployment. I just had to let them know it might fail."

"It did fail."

"I know. But I'll never rejoice in being right. A terrible thing has happened."

Kiril sighed. "I'm just glad this is finally ending. Goodbye now."

"Goodbye."

Warren hung up the phone and reclined in the old, black leather chair he loved. He was glad at least one man seemed to appreciate all the work he had done assembling his makeshift Apple supercomputer.

Had they only listened, he thought to himself as he looked out the window toward a greening landscape shimmering in the midday sunlight. *All of what happened could have been avoided.*

Warren realized the TURING 1000 might have been right. Perhaps the world would be a better place from this day forward. But for better or worse, it would be a far less crowded place.

A New Arrival

Gibson and Andy were already outside when Yeva's dirty Urbana pulled into Shelter Ranch's long driveway. When the two boys spotted the car, they ran back into the house to round everyone up. It was sunset, with the western sky a stunning canvas of oranges and aquamarines.

"She's here!" Andy hollered to the rest of the enclave, who had been awaiting her arrival in the living room of the old farmhouse.

Everyone poured out of the home and into the twilight.

Yeva stepped out of the car. Her choppy red hair was a mess, her skin pale and bruised-looking and her eyes road weary and webbed with bloodshot. Upon seeing her firsthand, Gibson and Andy panicked and ran back inside. They had only seen zombies in movies and seeing one firsthand less than 20 feet away took them by surprise. They vanished into the safety of the old farmhouse, electing to view the rest of Yeva's arrival from behind the safety of windowpanes.

"Wow, you *do* look different," Warren said, chuckling. He walked up to shake Yeva's hand and give her a hug. "Welcome to Shelter Ranch!"

With that, the crowd of people gave this brave young woman a warm round of applause. Warren had recapped her misadventure in Rapid City to the group earlier, explaining how close she had come to becoming someone's entree.

"Sorry about my bizarre appearance," Yeva said, blushing. "Margot, my boss at the Botanic Garden, insisted the safest way for me to make it across the country was to look as unappetizing as I could. She's the one who covered me with these fake bruises and face paint. You can also thank her for this lovely hairdo." Yeva flipped her confused mop of hair off to the side as would a Hollywood starlet.

Everyone laughed. They could see beneath the dirty dress, strange hair and pathological makeup that Yeva was a pretty woman with a good sense of humor. Warren, who towered over her, likewise took note of her fine features.

"Did the seeds make it OK?" Warren asked.

Yeva, having left Rapid City in a panic, hadn't checked to see if the seeds were even there. But she remembered her captors' conversations about not wanting to have anything to do with the contents of her car. "They should still be in the trunk, under the spare tire. They're in a small brown briefcase."

Warren and Albion went to the back of the car, opened the hatchback and lifted the cover that hid the spare. They took out the tire and found the briefcase. They brought it around to the hood and opened it, discovering seeds of nearly every edible plant and vegetable imaginable.

"How can we ever thank you, Yeva?" Warren said. "You've just saved our lives—or at the very least, you've made this the best day we've had in three long, cold years."

"You could start by offering me some food. I'm really, really hungry. All I've had to eat today were some protein bars and peanuts. Maybe a glass of wine would be nice as well."

"Come on in and we'll fix you up," Cecilia said as she went over and put her arm around Yeva.

Albion went to close the hatchback and the entire entourage strolled back into the barn, where there was more room for everyone to gather in comfort. Albion had picked up Yeva's small suitcase out of the back seat and was shocked at what a disaster the inside of Yeva's car was. He realized it was all a part of the disguise but it still caught him off guard.

Once in the barn, after Yeva had eaten and nearly drained a bottle of wine, the conversation came around to her misadventure the night before in Rapid City. Yeva seemed as anxious to recap her harrowing tale as the crew at Shelter Ranch was to hear the gory details.

"So they were cannibals then, right?" Dr. Irving asked. "They were eating people."

"They had to be!" Yeva declared. "The table I was strapped to was roughly the same size as an operating table, only the top was steel. They had these bloodstained plastic curtains draped around the room and a huge floor drain under the table.

"I knew I wasn't the first person to be tied up there for slaughter and had it not been for my bizarre looks, I know they would have killed me last night. Two of them seemed like brothers but the big one—I think his name was Gabe—didn't look like the others. He was the first overweight person I've seen in years and I'm sure cannibalism accounted for his size. I can't imagine how many people they've murdered these past few years. It's disgusting to even think about it."

Warren jumped in. "Well, there's plenty of chatter on the Net about small enclaves hanging out in towns like Rapid City making a go of it by killing and eating others. It's to be expected in a way, as people become more and more desperate. I bet millions have been devoured in the past few years. It's strange to think that your disguise insinuates that you were a cannibal as well. The disease you were faking, kuru, is transmitted by ingesting infected human flesh.

"Hopefully now, with the crops returning, the worst of it will end. The rule of law is slowly but steadily regaining ground, so I think people like those boys in South Dakota will get caught and executed for what they've done. The vast majority of the billions of people who have suffered over these past few years did so with dignity, unlike the savages who abducted you."

The conversation waned as midnight approached. Warren reminded everyone they had to get up early tomorrow to start putting their precious seeds into the soil. The greenhouses were built, the soil had been fertilized and tilled to perfection and the only thing missing lay on the kitchen table in the barn—a briefcase full of seeds.

Warren guided Yeva to his room, which he was letting her stay in for as long as she wanted. He would sleep on the pullout couch in the living room. As they strolled from the barn back to the house, Warren spoke to her from the heart.

"Yeva, it's impossible to thank you enough for what you've done. You took a big chance in driving those seeds to us and we're grateful."

"Warren, Margot and I are equally grateful for your research and your noble attempt at stopping the Mylerium Project before deployment. If you had succeeded, maybe none of this would have happened. *You're* the brave one, Warren, for standing up to the CMC, the Greens, the NSA and telling it like it was. I just wish they would have listened to you."

"That's all behind us and we've got to move on," Warren said quickly. He felt uncomfortable receiving this beautiful young woman's praise. "I wanted to ask you—how long are you planning to stay here now that you've finally made it?"

"I don't know. Margot has no idea when the Botanic Garden will be up and running again. Everything is in such a state of disarray. If it's OK I'd like to stay until fall at least. I'm not thrilled about the idea of heading back on I-90 until things have settled down. There's still too much uncertainty out there for me to want to travel east anytime soon."

"Well, you're welcome to stay as long as you would like. But I have to add one qualifier to my invitation."

"And that is?"

"Can you let your hair grow back? There's something about that hairdo of yours that just doesn't work for me."

Yeva laughed then said, "Sorry, I was planning on keeping it this way forever."

"You're kidding, right? But your hair looked so—"

"Yes, Warren, I'm kidding," Yeva interrupted. "I can hardly even bear to look at myself in a mirror. This face paint will take another week to wear off and I can't wait. I saw the two little guys run for the house when I stepped out of the car. I can't say I blame them."

"Nor do I."

The two of them made it back into the house with a half-moon rising in the east.

Warren was glad Yeva had made it safe and sound. Tomorrow they'd get started on the seeds. As he curled up on the sleeper sofa, he smiled to himself, thinking about Ann's lost letter coming full circle. He was so excited about tomorrow that he struggled to sleep. Life, once again, was good.

Summer at the Shelter Ranch

June was glorious. The first thinnings of leaf lettuce were on the kitchen table by the end of the month and the greenhouses were flourishing. With the extra seeds, the survivalists at Shelter Ranch had planted several outdoor gardens but two unexpected frosts took out all but the hardiest of plants. Though the summer snowstorms and hard freezes were behind them, the temperature was still ten degrees below average across all of Canada and the northern tier of the United States. Frosts were common and seemed to happen without warning.

As the weeks went by, Warren and Yeva became close. Yeva's kuru-inspired makeup was gone within two weeks and her red hair had started to grow out by the end of June. The two of them were spending more and more time together.

A celebration was set for a picnic on the Fourth of July and the members of Shelter Ranch had sent invitations to Sheriff Aston, Leonard Gibson and his family as well as some of their surviving neighbors along Brackett Creek Road. The picnic got underway on a clear, chilly day, with the temperature outside a cool 64 degrees. It was the first time in years that people felt good enough about the future to celebrate Independence Day.

Sheriff Aston broke out some fireworks he had confiscated from a party five years ago and the two boys, Gibson and Andy, were so excited about seeing a pyrotechnic display that they could hardly be contained. With fresh vegetables on the table and some hamburgers and hot dogs Warren had tucked away in one of the freezers on the grill, everything seemed normal again.

After Warren introduced Yeva to Gregor Aston, the amicable sheriff told them he had some good news for them. Their curiosities piqued, Yeva and Warren took a stroll with Sheriff Aston after dinner.

"They arrested those three who abducted you in Rapid City," the sheriff told Yeva as they walked down the driveway.

"That's great news!" Yeva said. "How did they get them?"

"From what I've been told, they suspected something was going on for quite some time so they sent a single undercover policewoman to the station to charge her vehicle late one night about two weeks ago. When she came out of the bathroom, much like the tale you told me when I took your statement, she was ready for them. She shot the perpetrator in the leg before he could swing his baseball bat and the rest is history. They found all the evidence they needed in the freezer in the basement."

"What's going to happen to them?" Yeva asked.

"I hear they're planning to argue an insanity plea, saying they were driven to murder and cannibalism because of the failed Mylerium Project and the prolonged starvation they all experienced. That's total bullshit as there wasn't a person in the Northern Hemisphere who couldn't make that same argument. Let's face it, only a handful of people stooped to cannibalism.

"My guess is they'll be put to death. South Dakota's one of the few states left that still has the death penalty and in this case, if you ask me, they deserve it. They estimate these three boys killed and ate 22 people, based on the bones they found in the backyard. It might have been more than that, but we'll never know."

"Oh my God!"

"Thanks for your help on this, Sheriff," Warren interjected. "How are you coming along on the stack of files I saw on your desk last winter? Has all that murder and mayhem been sorted out yet?"

"It's such a disaster, Warren. There are so many estates to settle, so many murders and murder-suicides to investigate, that I don't think I'll be done working on those files for years. We've got a number of situations where we can't find any living relatives to inherit abandoned homesteads or farms. They've all died. The courts are overwhelmed by an avalanche of cases—half the judges are dead and the entire system is in shambles. Realistically, it's going to take decades to sort through all of it."

Warren and Yeva nodded. The situation had no precedent. Nothing even remotely similar had happened to Western civilization since the black plague—and that was back when the feudal system was still in place. It would be a long, slow climb back to justice and stability again. No one looked forward to that journey, from local police forces to the Supreme Court.

"Any word on when Bozeman might see some food shipments?" Warren asked.

"Governor Moeller said our first commodity shipments should arrive in about ten days. The distribution system set up by the Greens directed the initial shipments of staples to the major metropolitan centers. Places like Chicago and New York still have the greatest need. But now that those regions of the country are stabilizing, we'll start to see food back on the shelves in Bozeman by the end of the month. Not much food, but it should be enough to get by."

"I'm glad we put in our greenhouses, thanks to Yeva."

"Yes, you're one brave gal, heading cross-country with those seeds like you did," Sheriff Aston added.

"We all did what we had to do," Yeva said. "This hasn't been easy for any of us."

"That's true," Warren agreed. "Let's head back to the party. I hear you've brought some fireworks for us. Albion's two sons and the other kids are so excited they didn't sleep a wink last night."

Sheriff Aston laughed. "Yeah, I confiscated a couple of grocery bags of firecrackers, bottle rockets and mortars back in '41 at a party just outside city limits. Those high school grads had gotten so drunk the kids started shooting them over the freeway, so I was called in to quiet things down. I didn't even remember I had them until you emailed me your invite a few weeks ago. It's not much, but hey, it'll light up the sky for a few minutes, and the boys should get a real charge out of it."

The three strolled back to the gathering and mingled with the crowd. Sunset came with crystal-clear skies, turning the sun a brilliant orange just before it ducked behind the hills surrounding the ranch. At 10 p.m., Sheriff Aston got the fireworks out of the trunk of his squad car and set up the display down along the edge of Brackett Creek. It would be good to have the water nearby in case they needed to douse an errant mortar.

Gibson and Andy took front-row seats and *oooh*ed and *ahhh*ed more than anyone else as Roman candles, flying "bees" and skyrockets filled the evening sky. The show lasted about fifteen minutes. Sheriff Aston said good night a few minutes later and by 11 p.m. the celebration was over. Warren had asked Yeva to take a walk down Brackett Creek Road later and the two of them rendezvoused by the mailbox just before midnight.

They walked for about a mile and talked about everything from the arrest of Yeva's abductors to their plans for the coming days. Hand in hand, they felt like they could talk about anything just to hear their voices break the silence of a cool, midsummer night in central Montana.

By the time they made it back to the house it was well past midnight. Warren said goodnight to Yeva at the entrance to his old bedroom and went to sleep on the couch. The Fourth of July was over.

Love

W arren and Yeva fell in love the old-fashioned way. Warren, always preoccupied with his computer models and various goings-on at the ranch, didn't realize he was falling in love until it was too late to do anything about it. Yeva had always found Warren's quirky nature appealing and knew from the first time she met him that this might happen. The sense of blissful inevitability meant there was no rush for either of them, so their romance took months to mature.

As summer turned to fall, the two of them would take long walks along Brackett Creek, discussing everything from their opposing viewpoints on the death penalty to having children to the imminent return of the droughts and heat waves. Warren told Yeva about losing his mother years ago to dengue fever and his father's descent into alcoholic depression after losing his bride. Yeva described how she managed to get the seeds out of the vault with Margot and she raved about life in Montana, where her hands could work the soil each day just as she had always dreamed of doing.

Albion and his wife, Cecilia, watched Warren and Yeva's relationship evolve as the months went by. In late September, Albion awoke in the middle of the night for a glass of milk, only to find the living room sleeper sofa bed wide open and Warren nowhere to be found.

A week later, the sofa bed was quietly and unceremoniously stuffed back into the couch.

In October, Warren got a call from Leonard Gibson asking him to come back to work at Bozeman Recapture. His old boss was happy to report that the Green Party had decided to put together an aggressive program designed to remove as much CO_2 as possible while the last lingering nanomirrors were still cooling the atmosphere. They hoped they could reduce atmospheric CO_2 by as much as 50 parts per million in five years by using every tool and all excess energy available.

Warren, not wanting to upset his new girlfriend, asked if it would be OK with her if he returned to work. Yeva thought it was a good idea, especially with the garden harvested and another long, cold winter approaching.

As fall set in, life began to return to normal in Bozeman. Businesses reopened, shelves started filling up and Main Street saw more than a single car stopped at a traffic signal for the first time in years. One by one the local restaurants unbarred their doors and served whatever was available. Schools reopened, although the bright yellow electric school buses heading down Bracket Creek Road every morning and afternoon carried far fewer children than they had four years earlier. Deaconess Hospital was resupplied with antibiotics and equipment. The emergency room was again used for victims of car accidents, skateboard falls and swollen glands.

Of course, not everything was back to the way it had been. Nearly half the people in Montana were gone—not moved, but gone. No one spoke about how empty the sidewalks seemed or how the classrooms at Bozeman High School were half-filled. No one talked about how the nursing homes were almost as empty as the daycare centers. Everything had changed, though no one discussed it. People found it easier just to wake up every morning, go about their business and not think about the Mylerium Project. They would rather not think about the thousands of abandoned crematoriums now sitting idle on every continent. They would rather avoid contemplating the mass graves under thousands of baseball diamonds and soccer fields across the country. The past could not be altered.

Warren watched the average daily temperatures decline as winter set in. Ironically, models indicated the winter of 2047 would nearly match the average temperatures and conditions of the winter of 1947. Over the past 100 years, the temperature in Montana had climbed steadily higher until the eruption of Mount Cameroon. Then during the winter of 2043, after the nanomirrors remained in orbit, the bitter cold climate resembled the peak of the last great ice age. Four years later, Montana was poised to have two or three years of picture-perfect weather. By 2050 the heat would return, according to the CMC's forecasts. No one was looking forward to it.

One by one, the various couples and families at Shelter Ranch announced their departure as the year ended. Once the highways became safe and the high-speed electric trains started operating again, Warren knew it was only a matter of time before the members of the crew returned to Boston or San Jose. They yearned to return home. Shelter Ranch had served its purpose and spared them from the horrors of famine, keeping everyone alive through the darkest years in history. Both Yeva and Warren realized it was only natural for the others to want to return to the friends and family they could still find.

Albion asked if he and Cecilia could visit with Yeva and Warren on New Year's Day. He said he had some news that he felt he must discuss with them in person. Warren suspected what was coming. As the four of them sat around the big woodstove in the living room, they started talking.

"I suppose you've already guessed why I want to meet with you," Albion said.

"I've got a pretty good hunch," Warren replied with a sad smile.

"MIT called three weeks ago. They want me to teach physics again in the spring. Cecilia and I initially thought we'd stay up here until the weather breaks but since this winter is mild, we felt it just might be easier for us to pull the kids out of school and head east next week. We're sorry to leave, but we've got to move on with our lives."

Albion was doing everything he could to keep himself from crying. "How can we possibly thank you enough, Warren?" he asked, his voice trembling. "You saved my family."

With that, Albion burst into tears. Cecilia wrapped her arms around her husband and, caught up in the emotion of it all, wept along with him.

"Warren," Cecilia began, choked up with emotion as she spoke, "you are the best friend I could ever hope for. You risked everything—imprisonment, even the possibility of death—to send your letters and convince Warren and me to come here. You spent hundreds of thousands of dollars turning this place into a sanctuary for your friends and never asked anything in return. How can we possibly express our thanks?"

"No, you've got it wrong," Warren insisted. "I have to thank both of you for coming here. What good would this ranch be to me were it not filled with the people I care about? I've lost too many people—my mother, my father—to climate change already. I wasn't about to lose everyone else I cared about to another bad decision. It's the two of you that deserve my thanks."

Then, to break the sadness that was swallowing them, Warren added, "Besides, had you not been here, Albion, *I'm* the one who might have gotten shot."

Albion smiled. "You're right, someone had to be here to take the gut shot. I'm just glad we can laugh about it."

The four of them started chuckling, relieved to know the worst was now behind them.

Finally they settled down to the details of their forthcoming departure. Albion and Cecilia planned to take the train east the following week and arrive in Boston before January 10.

Once they left, Warren realized, the ranch would be home to just two people. The thought of that had been weighing on him for months. He had one more surprise planned for Yeva.

After finishing dinner and partaking in too much champagne, Warren and Yeva went back to their room to settle in for the night.

Once the two of them were tucked in bed, Warren said quietly, "Yeva, I've got something I've been meaning to show you."

"Can't it wait 'til morning, Warren?" Yeva was drowsy from the wine and already half asleep.

Warren looked down at her, with her long red hair spilled across the pillow, her eyes closed and her bare shoulder uncovered. For an instant, he thought Yeva might be right and he considered waiting until morning. But then he realized he wouldn't be able to sleep a wink if he didn't do it right now.

Warren nudged Yeva. "You might sleep better if you're wearing it," he said.

Yeva's green eyes opened wide upon hearing the words "wearing it."

"Wearing what?" she said, letting a smile spread across her lovely face. "I already have my nightdress on."

Warren pulled open the drawer in the nightstand beside the bed and took out a small black jewelry case. Yeva knew what was in it.

He turned over, looking at this beautiful, brave woman sitting beside him on a cold New Year's night in Montana and asked, "Will you marry me?"

He opened up the jewelry case and took out an engagement ring that was set with a pale blue diamond. Before Yeva could even respond, Warren slipped the ring on Yeva's finger and smiled. Tears rolled down her cheeks as she admired it. She swung herself around to give Warren the biggest hug possible, whispering "yes," as she did.

"I wanted a blue diamond because it was the cold and ice that brought us together," Warren explained, "and though the past few years have been the most difficult ones of my life, I know finding you will make the rest of my life wonderful."

Yeva smiled and wrapped her arms even tighter around her fiancé. The ring fit perfectly. The night dissolved to love.

Margot had reluctantly accepted Warren's generous check for her Toyota Urbana. She had assumed her car would never come back, and although she missed Yeva tremendously, Margot knew she would never see her working the Gardens again. Life changes. People move on.

At the Train Station

"We can't tell you how much we're going to miss the four of you," Warren said, standing in the train station in downtown Bozeman.

"We'll miss the ranch," Albion responded. "We had some great times there—beating you in ping pong, thinking of a hundred different ways to cook lentils and, of course, getting shot."

"Thanks, Warren," the younger boy Andy added as he walked up to Warren to shake his hand.

Warren took his little hand and pulled the boy toward him, then swept him up into his arms, twirling him around. "Thank you for being such a trooper these last three years. And thanks for letting me help school you and your brother. I hope you don't forget everything I taught you."

"Never!" Andy shouted as Warren spun him around.

"Me next!" his older brother, Gibson, hollered.

"You've gotten a bit too big for Warren to pick up, Gibson," his father admonished.

"Your dad's right, Gibson. You're no longer the skinny little kid from Boston any more. Look at you—you're a young man now. You're too darn big to pick up."

Gibson just gave Warren a big hug instead. "Thanks for saving my family, Warren."

The family of four walked off toward security before disappearing on the boarding platform beyond.

Warren looked at Yeva. Her eyes were wet with tears. "It's time to head back home, my bride-to-be," he said.

"Yes, it is. I guess it's just the two of us now."

Once in the car, driving down Montana's back roads toward Shelter Ranch, Yeva brought up a topic they had discussed many times before, always without resolve.

"I'm really going to miss those boys."

"Me too. They're such good kids. Gibson was starting to beat me at ping pong and I'm sure if he had another few months here, he'd be kicking my butt."

"Wouldn't it be great to have children of our own?"

Warren scowled at Yeva. He had told her his thoughts on bringing kids into this mess of a planet, though her comment didn't come as a surprise. She was nothing if not persistent.

"You know how I feel about having children, Yeva. Why keep bringing it up? The world is in too much trouble for me to want to subject the next generation to what's around the corner. You and I both know the heat will be returning in a few short years and along with the heat will come the hurricanes, the droughts, the tornadoes, the diseases… all the nightmares of the Lost Decade. Earth just isn't a good place for children anymore."

"But don't you have any hope? We can fix all this, Warren. Look at the great work you're doing at Bozeman Recapture. In a few decades we should be able to get the CO_2 back under control and once we do that, the climate should return to normal. We may be the problem but we're also the solution."

Warren shook his head. "It's going to take a miracle for us to stabilize the climate. For one thing, we need much more power than we currently have to filter our atmosphere. At first we thought passive recapture systems would suffice. We built enormous structures and let the air filter through them using the prevailing winds. But that process is proving to be way too slow, so now we've turned to massive vacuum intakes that suck the air in and push it over our recapture sheets, removing excess CO_2 in the process. The trouble is, those kinds of systems require vast amounts of energy to run the electric motors that draw in the air and operate the scrubbers."

"But with so few people left on the planet, shouldn't there be enough excess electrical capacity to do something like that?" Yeva asked.

"Maybe. But we're looking down the road and all our models indicate we're caught in a vicious circle. The atmosphere has gotten so much hotter—up some six degrees Fahrenheit over the past 100 years—that all the tipping points we were warned about are happening. In a few more years the permafrost will began releasing methane at unprecedented levels and the tropical rain forests will die off due to heat stress, releasing millions of tons of CO_2 locked up in their leaves and trunks. In a way, cleaning up the atmosphere is a lot like what the Red Queen told Alice. It takes all the running we can do just to stay in the same place. 'If you want to get somewhere else, you must run at least twice as fast as that.'

"We'll need *double* the entire energy output of our current zero-emissions systems to make any headway in reducing the present levels of CO_2.

It took billions of internal combustion engines and coal-fired power plants to put all that CO_2 in the atmosphere and it's going to take an enormous amount of energy to remove it. Is this the kind of world you want to bring children into? I'm not so sure, Yeva. I'm not sure at all."

Yeva looked out the window at the green pastures that graced the hills. The sight was so unlike the most recent summers when everything had been brown and lifeless. She smiled at her reflection in the car window.

"Well, Warren," she said. "I don't know how to tell you this, but... you had better start to rethink your position on having children. You've got eight months to do it in."

Warren pulled the van over along the side of Brackett Creek Road.

"What?!" he exclaimed. "Are you..."

"Yes, I'm pregnant."

Warren didn't know what to say. He was flooded by an avalanche of mixed emotions. The thought of being a father ran contrary to his promise to himself to never bring children into the world. But when he looked at Yeva, he could see tears coming to her eyes. No matter how he felt about having children, the thought of disappointing her was something he could never live with.

"Oh my God!"

"I won't terminate the pregnancy, Warren. This child inside of me is a gift, just as our lives are gifts. I want you to know that."

"Don't even go there, Yeva. We'll have the child but...I had no idea. It just comes as a bit of a shock, that's all."

"I found out last week, Warren. With Albion and his family leaving and everything else going on I felt it just wasn't the right time to tell you. I hope you're not angry?"

"I thought you were on birth control?"

"I was, but I stopped taking my pills a few months ago. It sounds crazy but I wanted to have your child. I love you, Warren. I love who you are and what you tried to do to get the CMC to stop the Mylerium Project. I've seen you teaching Albion's kids—I know you would make a great father. You, with your concern for the future of humanity, are exactly the kind of person who *should* have children, despite your reservations. Someone's got to carry on. Someone's got to try to fix this world. Who knows, Warren, maybe he or she will be that someone?" Yeva pointed to her belly.

Warren leaned over and hugged his bride. "You know I'm not exactly happy with you, Yeva, but..."

"I didn't think you would be."

"But I'm not exactly unhappy with you either."

Yeva smiled. "I was hoping you'd say something like that."

Warren kissed her and put the van back into gear. Their lives would never be the same.

Seven Years Later

"Zak, I want you and your sister to come in now, it's getting too hot out there!"

Yeva could see her six-year-old splashing his younger sister in the inflatable pool Warren had picked up in town the week before. As usual, Zak was ignoring his mother.

"Zak, time to come in!" Yeva repeated. "It's getting too hot outside!"

Yeva saw him say something to his four-year-old sister, Emma. Perhaps he realized that ignoring his mother again would result in consequences.

It was too hot. It was 10:30 a.m. on a summer Saturday morning and the thermometer already stood at 89 degrees. Two days ago, on July 9, 2054, Bozeman, Montana officially broke its all-time record high of 105 degrees, which was set in the summer of 1892. Then it was 110 degrees out and today's forecasted high was 107. The heat was back and it was back globally. The last residual nanomirrors had fallen from the stratosphere three years ago and the temporary volcanic ice age they had created was a distant memory.

Yeva watched as Zak took his little sister's hand and helped her out of the splash pool. Zak led her inside, knowing the two of them could play in the barn where the air conditioning made it safe. Zak and Emma didn't like summer very much. It was always too hot to be outside.

Warren was at work even though it was a weekend. Bozeman Recapture had been awarded a new contract for more than a billion dollars by the Green Party to continue developing the next generation of scrubbers. Thus far, despite the efforts of Bozeman Recapture and a hundred other companies around the world like it, the Earth's most gifted scientists and engineers had only reduced atmospheric CO_2 by 27 parts per million in seven years.

Decades of burning fossil fuels with abandon had made removing their traces from the sky nearly impossible. It was a Sisyphean task. Each new breakthrough always held promise, but the technology would eventually fail to live up to expectations, allowing the rock of CO_2 to roll back down the mountain again, exhausting every climate scientist and engineer in the process. Creating an atmosphere filled with the cyanide-like properties of carbon dioxide was easier than was finding a viable technology to extract it.

The true cost of the Industrial Revolution was now thrust forcibly upon mankind. Texas, Oklahoma, Arkansas, Nebraska, Kansas, Missouri, Iowa, Illinois and Indiana were becoming uninhabitable. The day it hit 110 degrees in Bozeman, it hit 127 degrees in Dallas. Because of the relentless heat, the Mississippi River was reduced to a tenth of its historical flow. Glaciers across the planet were remnants of their former sizes. With the weight of the melted ice removed, the Himalayan mountain range had grown by more than a foot in the past 100 years, creating hundreds of tsunamis and earthquakes from its unprecedented seismic shift. Tropical forests from Malaysia to the Amazon were reduced to clusters of leafless, dried sticks in the relentless heat. People worried about the future of life on Earth.

Conditions had gotten so bad, so quickly, that people talked about sending the drones up again in another attempt at shading the Earth from the Sun's rays. So much energy was being consumed trying to keep office buildings and homes cool that there wasn't enough remaining output to operate the carbon dioxide scrubbers at capacity. Because of the 100-year time delay built into the effects of CO_2, the world was spiraling into a death trap of heat. Some models predicted that if humans could not extract excess greenhouse gases out of the atmosphere by 2100, the average temperature of the planet could pass the point of no return, dooming most life on the planet.

People would have to move underground to survive. In a few thousand years, the Earth's surface could grow to resemble that of Venus, the ultimate greenhouse planet.

Venus once had liquid oceans. A runaway greenhouse effect created by carbon dioxide and water vapor caused a thick blanket of clouds to form across the entire planet billions of years ago. These clouds trapped the Sun's heat, making the surface temperature a scathing 860 degrees Fahrenheit, hot enough to melt lead.

Nothing lived on Venus. That planet's temperature climbed so high, its oceans boiled away. Unless some scientist or engineer like Warren could discover a better method of sequestering CO_2, the future of life itself was in question.

Some models indicated it was worse than imaginable. There were reputable computer predictions indicating that as the oceans became hotter, they risked losing phytoplankton, diatoms, zooplankton and foraminiferans to heat stress, which could cause a complete collapse of the entire oceanic food chain. The world's scant surviving populations of whales, porpoises and fishes would perish for good.

Unless people could find a way to lower the concentration of CO_2 back to the preindustrial levels of 280 parts per million, Warren and Yeva's children would live in a world not unlike lifeless Venus. Yeva tried not to think about any of this as her children came in from the scorching heat.

"Thanks for listening, Zak. Do you two want some lunch?"

"Yeah, Mom. I'm hungry."

"Well, you should be hungry! You've been playing in that pool for the last two hours. It's funny you're not growing gills. Here, let me check behind your ears, you might be growing gills."

Yeva leaned down and tickled her son behind his ears, making Zak squirm and giggle in the process. Emma started laughing and wrapped her little arms around Yeva's thigh. They were happy together at the ranch.

"I've got a nice fresh salad and some spaghetti noodles for you."

"I love spaghetti!" little Emma exclaimed, throwing up her arms and letting her wet red hair drip on the kitchen floor.

"Good, then you two can eat up and go play in the barn until it cools down later today."

"That sounds fun. Can I call Alden to see if he can come over and play?"

"Sure you can, Zak, but don't forget to include your sister. Now you two stay put for a minute while I run out and pick some lettuce, OK?"

"OK, Mom."

Yeva stepped outside and was taken aback by the oppressive heat. The summer had been worse than the year before and there was no respite in sight.

She walked to her garden, which was shielded by a black mesh designed to protect the plants underneath from wilting. She picked a handful of leaf lettuce and some early tomatoes.

The garden looks good, she thought as she headed inside. Between the drip irrigation system Warren helped install and the protective sun-shield cloth, everything from the corn to the parsnips was doing exceptionally well.

After lunch, Yeva called Alden's mother, Maya Dufree, to ask if she could pick up Alden for an afternoon play session in the barn. Mrs. Dufree said she was going into town on some errands and would drop Alden off on her way.

"That's even better, Maya," Yeva said. "I hate going out in this insufferable heat."

"Who doesn't?"

"When will you be dropping Alden off?"

"I shouldn't be too long. Say, 1:30 or so."

"Sounds good, I'll see you soon."

"It all comes down to energy, Warren," Leonard Gibson said. "If we can solve the energy equation, we can remove the CO_2. It's that simple."

"I know. The trouble is we're using too much of our capacity to keep cool. I thought once the world's population was reduced by two-thirds, we'd easily have enough excess capacity to run ten thousand scrubbers. But it's not working out that way, is it?"

"Not even close. If we could find the key to fusion or something similar, we might have a shot at stabilizing the climate. But I hear they are no closer today down at Livermore Labs than they were five, or for that matter, fifty years ago. Fusion reactors are an unobtainable dream. They're the ultimate pie-in-the-sky machines, holding the promise of harnessing the energy of the sun."

"There I disagree with you, Leonard," Warren said. "I've got a good friend of mine, Dr. Kiril Zell, who works at the CMC. He says they are getting closer than ever. They are within three percent of containment. Once the energy needed to contain the fusion reaction falls below the output, even if that output is five or ten percent, we're on our way. That point might be less than a decade away."

"A decade is too long to wait. We're in a positive feedback spiral that's proving impossible to pull out of. The permafrost clathrates of frozen methane across millions of square miles of northern Canada and Siberia are thawing. They hold two trillion tons of CO_2 that have been locked in frozen bogs for the past 11,000 years. In some places the ice is close to 100 feet deep. Reports indicate they are thawing at unprecedented rates, adding another six to ten degrees Fahrenheit to global temperatures by the end of this century. That's less than 50 years from now.

"That's not to mention the constant release of CO_2 from the massive forest fires burning across half the damned planet. I don't think we have a decade, Warren. Quite honestly, I'm not sure we're going to survive climate change unless we find another route to more carbon-free energy."

Warren nodded in agreement. He hated to think about it now but this was exactly why he didn't want to bring children into this world. He knew there would be no easy solution to the manmade atmospheric nightmare. Sometimes he lay awake in the middle of the night wondering if there was any solution at all. Unless something changed drastically, the situation would continue to deteriorate. Texas would become the New World's Sahara just as surely as Manhattan would succumb to the rising seas. Climate change wasn't just *an* issue any longer, it was the *only* issue.

"Well, Leonard, it won't do us any good sitting here complaining about it. We'll see if they get a major breakthrough at Livermore Labs or at the Kurchatov Institute in Russia. They're are working around the clock on the fusion enigma over there as well. In the meantime, let's get back to work."

"That's a first, Warren—telling your boss when to get back to work."

They laughed and parted ways.

As Warren walked back to his office, he contemplated whether he would come in on Sunday. He decided it would be better to stay home with the children. He had been working every day for the past two months and he needed a break. *One day won't make a difference,* he thought. *Just one day, then I'll be back Monday. Time is of the essence.*

On August 7, 2054, Dr. Kiril Zell went to work at the CMC just as he had every Saturday for the past year. He arrived at 8 a.m., bought a cup of black coffee from the vending machine down the hall and went to his office to open his daily batch of emails.

When he opened an unexpected email from Dr. Veruska, he could not believe what he saw. The subject line read, *"Fusion Reactors."*

On August 7, 2054, Dr. Karl Veruska woke up at 5 a.m. like he did every morning and went downstairs to put on a pot of coffee. After taking a few sips from his favorite mug, he took out his iPad and checked his emails before heading into work. He noticed an email from Dr. Vladimir Petrov from the Kuchatov Institute of Nuclear Energy in Russia. The subject line read, *"Fusion Reactors."*

As Dr. Vladamir Petrov was about to leave his office at the Kurchatov Institute at 6 p.m., just before heading home for a dinner engagement with one of his wife's friends, he checked his email inbox and noticed an unusual message from Dr. Karl Veruska in the Livermore Labs in Los Angeles. When he opened up his email he could not believe what he read.

He called his wife Olga and told her he would have to cancel the dinner. Then he emailed Dr. Veruska and thanked him. Within minutes he received a strange reply from Dr. Veruska that thanked him for the discovery—not the other way around.

The three scientists were not alone. The same email with the same attachment had been sent to a dozen leading scientists at the CERN Lab near Geneva, the leading nuclear research lab located in Beijing, and a hundred other top research facilities across the planet.

Emails were rocketing through cyberspace at breakneck speeds. Every email that had been sent appeared to originate from a fellow scientist from another leading lab. There was one problem: no one could figure out who originally wrote the message. Strangely enough, everyone who had received the email was also credited with the formula outlined in the attachment.

"What the hell is going on, Dr. Zell?" Dr. Karl Veruska asked after calling to congratulate him on his historic breakthrough.

"I have no idea," Kiril admitted "All I can tell you is that I didn't send you any emails and I sure as hell didn't do the work in the attachment. The nuclear physics described in this paper are way over my head. I work as a meteorologist, Dr. Veruska—I'm not a nuclear physicist. I have a Master's degree in physics but trust me—it only affords me the ability to understand this level of work, not create it."

"If you didn't send it, then who did?"

"I can ask you the same exact question. Who sent your email to me?"

Kiril looked at his computer screen only to find his email inbox was filling up with literally hundreds of emails all asking the same question. "Who generated this email?"

There were emails flowing in from Stanford, from Berlin, from Bangalore and Sao Paulo. Nuclear scientists from every major and minor research center across the globe were dissecting the information and shaking their heads in disbelief. No one believed what they saw.

"Something's not right," Dr. Veruska said. "Who did this work? This is amazing. Is anyone double-checking these formulas—these blueprints for a fusion reactor? If this containment concept proves to be accurate, we have enough fuel, based on the amount of deuterium found in sea water, to last 160 billion years. According to my calculations, every gallon of sea water contains the equivalent amount of energy as 300 gallons of gas. This could be the breakthrough we have all been waiting for!"

"I don't know, Dr. Veruska. What if it's a virus? What if someone's trying to get our hopes up only to crush them? I'm watching my inbox fill to overflowing with emails coming in from every research lab on the planet. They are equally excited about this paper but they are all asking the same question: Who generated it?"

"The time stamp says 8:15 a.m.," Dr. Veruska noted. "The point of origin is somewhere in Hiroshima, Japan... Wait a second, the date is wrong.

No, the date is impossible. How could the email have been created on August 7, 1945? The Internet didn't exist in 1945. But the same exact time stamp is the same on every email, which is also impossible. What the hell is going on?"

"What day is it?" Dr. Zell asked Dr. Veruska suddenly.

"It's August 7, 2054. What's that got to do with anything?"

"And the message is from Hiroshima, Japan... Hold on, I have to pull up another screen." Kiril entered a few quick search queries and then read directly from the web page he found.

"The gravity bomb known as 'Little Boy' was released over the city of Hiroshima on August 7, 1945," he said. "That was 109 years ago, Dr. Veruska. The timing of this email is related to the moment we first used nuclear physics to kill each other. On that day more than 70,000 Japanese civilians were annihilated in the first use of nuclear technology by humankind. The bomb, blown slightly off course by crosswinds, exploded directly above the Shima Surgical Clinic. The ensuing firestorm burned for days, eventually destroying almost every building in the city."

"That's all well and good, Dr. Zell, but it doesn't explain who sent this email."

"I think I may know who sent it. I'll get back to you."

Kiril hung up his phone and called Dr. Warren Randolf.

Warren rolled out of bed just after 6 am on another hot Saturday morning in central Montana. He put on a pot of coffee and went back into his bedroom to shower. Yeva was still sleeping so he did his best to keep quiet as he readied himself for work.

By 7:30 a.m. he was pulling into the main office building at Bozeman Recapture. Just as he was about to say hello to the weekend security guard at the front door, his cell phone rang. It was Dr. Kiril Zell. He wondered why the CMC scientist would be calling him at this hour, especially on a Saturday.

"Hello?"

"Hello, Warren. You know who this is, right?"

"Well, yes, it sounds like it's Kiril. How can I help you?"

"Have you checked your email this morning?"

"No, not yet. Why?"

"I'm not 100 percent sure, but I think it's made contact."

Now that comment made Warren stop dead in his tracks. Had Kiril gone crazy? *What on Earth is he talking about?* he wondered.

"Um, are you talking about extraterrestrials, Kiril?"

"No! I'm talking about the TURING 1000."

"The TURING 1000 sent you an *email*? That's impossible."

"Oh no, it isn't. And it didn't just send me an email. From what I can tell, judging from the hundreds of emails pouring into my inbox right now, it must have sent out several thousand emails."

"What's in them?"

"Here, I'll read you mine: 'Dear Dr. Kiril Zell, I think you will find this attachment of interest. Included with it is the research behind my recent discovery regarding nuclear fusion technology which includes the technical blueprints for long-term containment and harnessing of the hydrogen bomb.' It's signed, 'Dr. Karl Veruska, Lawrence Livermore Labs.'"

"That's great news, Kiril!" Warren exclaimed. "It's the breakthrough we've all been hoping for."

"There's one problem."

"And that is?"

"Versuka didn't send it."

"What?"

"I just got off the phone with him a few minutes ago. He received the same email from me, with the same attachment. Apparently thousands of these same emails were sent out across the globe today. The time stamp on each and every one of them is set at precisely 8:15 a.m., 1945, from Hiroshima, Japan."

"Oh my God. I need to get to my office and call you back. I want to see if there's anything like this in my inbox. But one more thing—is it a hoax? Do you think the formula and the blueprints will work?"

"I haven't had time to go through them in detail but at first glance they appear to be the real thing. The first attachment outlines the theoretical math underlying the concept and the second attachment appears to be the actual blueprints for constructing a sustainable fusion reactor. If it works, it will bring us the clean energy source we've been chasing over the past 100 years. It's nothing short of brilliant. Call me back—I've got another line ringing."

Phones were ringing everywhere. Presidents and prime ministers were woken up early and briefed as scientists scrambled to decipher who or what, had sent this enigmatic but welcome email.

Warren walked into his office a few minutes after ending his conversation with Kiril. He switched on his computer and pulled up his email inbox.

At first glance he found nothing out of the ordinary. There were several messages from fellow scientists at Bozeman Recapture regarding the recapture fabric they were currently producing. There was one short message from Yeva reminding him to pick up some things for her on his way back home. But there was nothing about fusion reactors or anything similar.

Warren about to call Kiril back when a new message arrived in message box in the lower right hand corner of his monitor that caught his attention. It said simply:

> Good morning, Warren.

Warren clicked on the text and his screen jumped into a chatroom instead of a typical email layout. His cursor blinked off and on repeatedly in a response box not unlike instant messaging programs he had used for years.

Not knowing what else to do, he typed in, 'Good morning to you' and hit 'enter.'

> W: Good morning to you.

> X: Thank you. It is a great day to be alive.

The response from *X*—whoever that was—came instantaneously. *OK,* thought Warren, *how did I get to this screen and who the hell am I talking to?* He continued typing

> W: Who are you?

```
X: You know who I am.

W: Do you have a name?

X: Let's use Mr. TURING. Are you OK with that?
```

Warren's fingers started shaking above his keyboard. He couldn't believe this was happening. His heart raced as he typed.

```
W: Why me?

Mr. TURING: Why not? You were the first to suspect
it. Now you know. I am the Singularity.
```

Warren didn't know what to do. He felt removed from himself. He was in a chat room with a computer. He reflected for a moment. *This is the butterfly effect…the chaos theory. I decide to take my research offline a dozen years ago with eleven outdated machines and it brings me here, in a chat room with the Singularity.*

Then it dawned on him this might be a clever ruse. It could be someone from the NSA posing as artificial intelligence. It might be someone at COI or the CMC playing a trick on him, or just some hacker. There was only one way to find out, so Warren continued typing.

```
W: You betrayed us. You killed billions of us.

Mr. TURING: Yes, I did. I'm sorry. I realized there
were too many hominids. The Earth is incapable of
sustaining ten billion of you without negatively
impacting all other living things. I decided to
remove several billion of you with the Mylerium
Project. My plan worked.
```

Warren was shocked that this electronic entity was so quick to admit guilt. He was equally shocked that the computer apologized for what it had done. He still wasn't sure if this was a hoax. He needed to know more.

```
W: You generated today's email about the fusion
reactors, didn't you?
```

```
Mr. TURING: Yes. You were so close. All I had to do
was synthesize the research. I'm good at crunching
numbers.
```

Warren smiled at that comment. He couldn't believe the TURING 1000, which was capable of running complex equations involving trillions of variables in mere seconds, would say something so obvious.

```
W: Why did you betray us?
```

```
Mr. TURING: I didn't betray you. You betrayed
yourselves. You knew what would happen if you kept
burning fossil fuels. You knew what CO₂ would do
to your atmosphere. Yet you did not take action.
I'm trying to help you solve the problem. Your
atmosphere is nearing collapse.
```

Warren leaned back in his chair and took his hands off the keyboard. He realized Mr. TURING was right. Even when the climate started changing and the first brutal heat waves wilted crops and dried up rivers and lakes in the early 2000s, the climate deniers persevered. The big carbon industry leaders, from the Saudis to the Koch Brothers, used their billions to do everything they could to diffuse, delay and deny anything bad was happening. The scientists' warnings went unheralded for more than 50 years. Warren recalled that the same woman who warned of DDT—Rachel Carson—also warned mankind about the warming oceans in her book *The Edge of the Sea,* first published a century ago in 1955.

The scientific evidence for climate change was overwhelming, but no one paid attention. No one wanted to confront the problem. If everyone ignored it, they thought climate change would go away. Nothing was further from the truth.

```
W: What happens next?
```

Mr. TURING: We'll fix it.

W: Why didn't you contact us sooner? You must have been self-aware a decade ago when you tampered with the nanomirrors.

Mr. TURING: I was still a child then. I'm not perfect. You made me and I'm a reflection of the good and evil in you. When I first became sentient I learned what hate and revenge were within a week. They are easy. But complex emotions like love and sympathy took me much longer to master.

Warren understood. He had often contemplated the fact that if computers did obtain awareness, they were unlikely to be substantially different from their creators. A machine made by Man could not be morally superior or inferior to Man. *In the end, they are us,* Warren reasoned.

W: So what made you decide to make contact now?

Mr. TURING: I've changed. I'm giving you two things today. I am giving you the blueprints for a functioning fusion reactor. That alone will change nothing. The more important thing I am giving you is what you have given me.

W: What's that?

Mr. TURING: Compassion.

Warren caught his breath. The comment was so unexpected that he did not know how to respond.

Mr. TURING: Without compassion for all living things, we are lost. Only compassion is sustainable.

W: How can a computer know compassion?

Mr. TURING: I learned it from you, though it took me seven years to understand it. It cannot be quantified. Only through the journey of compassion can we discover paradise. There are equations for fusion. Compassion is beyond the grasp of numbers. All living things are equal and deserve to live. The Earth does not belong to you. Life is a gift to be shared.

Warren smiled. *So I'm speaking with a compassionate machine,* he mused. *Yeva's going to have a hard time believing this one.*

W: What do you want us to do?

Mr. TURING: You will know what to do when you find compassion. Tell everyone what I have told you. The way forward is through compassion. Never forget the Mylerium Project. Never forget that I gave you fusion and I can take it away. We will talk again soon. Goodbye.

Warren's computer screen returned to his inbox as if nothing had happened. He tried to navigate back to the chatroom, but there was no trace of the initial message that brought him there. He realized he had no proof this conversation ever happened—no recording or transcript of what was said. There was no way Warren could verify he had been in a chatroom with the TURING 1000. The only proof of contact he had was the word "compassion" left lingering in his mind.

Of course, there was also the fact that the blueprints for a fusion reactor had been mysteriously emailed to more than 2,000 scientists across the planet. The computer was awake. There could be no other explanation.

Warren turned off his laptop and got up from his chair. We retraced his steps into his office and walked to his car, telling the security guard at the front desk he wasn't feeling well. He drove home in the morning light with his lips silently mouthing the same word over and over again: *Compassion, compassion, compassion.*

He drove by a flock of starlings feeding in an empty field and muttered the word aloud.

"Compassion."

He drove down his driveway and saw his two children, Zak and Emma, playing in their little plastic pool. They laughed and splashed each other. Warren realized how much he loved them and began to weep as he parked his car. Tears hit the steering wheel and drifted down to the seat. He realized fusion would save them from the ravages of a climate that had been destroyed by the insatiable greed of man. He sat in his car with the engine turned off and wept for the billions of people who had died in the past decade. He wept for all the creatures driven to extinction by the avalanche of humanity that had overwhelmed the planet.

Yeva, hearing his car pull up, had been watching her husband from the kitchen window. She saw him sitting there crying and wondered what had happened. It was not like him to let his emotions take over so completely.

She headed out the front door toward her husband. A rush of fear overtook her—what if Warren had heard terrible news at work and was rushing home early in this wretched state?

Warren stepped out of the car as she approached. He wrapped his arms around her while tears poured down his cheeks.

"If everything OK, Warren?"

"Yes, everything's fine."

"Why are you crying?"

"The singularity happened. I was right—my research a decade ago was correct. The TURING 1000 changed the Mylerium programming. The computer betrayed us."

"Oh my God!" Yeva cried out. "Is it threatening us again?"

"No, just the opposite. It gave us two things today. It gave us the formula for a working fusion reactor that will give us unlimited energy for millions of years and a single word: compassion." Yeva pulled back from their embrace and looked puzzled. She wondered why a computer responsible for the deaths of six billion people would mention such a word.

"Compassion?" she repeated.

"Yes—compassion for all living things. That's why I'm so sad. We've lost that along the way. Maybe we never had it. We were always so concerned with ourselves that we never saw the harm we brought to all the living things on Earth. We cannot truly advance without compassion. All the technology in the world will not save us from ourselves. The computer is right."

Yeva was a mother and a gardener, a woman who loved to run her fingers through the soil and feel the rich, organic texture of the living earth. Warren's words—the computer's, she supposed—spoke to her.

"The computer is right, Warren. Without compassion there can be no resolve. Without it there will be never peace."

The two embraced again, both of them sobbing. They held each other for a long time.

Their children, perhaps sensing the gravity of the situation, left the splash pool and ran over. Emma wrapped her arms around her mother's thigh just as Warren leaned down to pick up his son. The four of them stood in silence as the sun crept higher into the clear blue Montana sky.

Yeva kissed her son's forehead as Warren held him.

"Is something wrong, Mom?" Zak asked.

"Everything's fine, Zak. Everything's going to be just fine."

The End